Gabrielle Festing

John Hookham Frere

and his friends

Gabrielle Festing

John Hookham Frere
and his friends

ISBN/EAN: 9783337400163

Printed in Europe, USA, Canada, Australia, Japan

Cover: Foto ©Andreas Hilbeck / pixelio.de

More available books at **www.hansebooks.com**

JOHN HOOKHAM FRERE

AND HIS FRIENDS. By GABRIELLE FESTING.

LONDON: JAMES NISBET & CO., LTD.
21, BERNERS STREET. 1899.

PRINTED BY
HAZELL, WATSON, AND VINEY, LD.,
LONDON AND AYLESBURY.

IT is impossible to let this book go forth without trying to express my gratitude for the help and advice afforded by those whom I consulted while writing it.

Mr. William Rossetti generously placed at my disposal the whole of the correspondence between his father and J. H. Frere, and his own valuable notes in explanation of it. He also revised the MS. of Chapter XV.

Some of Lady Erroll's letters have already appeared in *Longman's Magazine* under the title of "Love-Letters of a Lady of Quality." They are here reproduced by permission of Messrs. Longman. *Temple Bar* published selections from some other letters addressed to J. H. Frere as "An Ambassador's Letter-Bag." Mr. Murray has kindly allowed me to reprint any of Canning's letters that appeared in my article in the *Quarterly Review* for July 1897.

My thanks are also due to Mrs. Merivale for many suggestions and corrections; to Mr. Frere for the loan of all the MSS. at Roydon; to Miss A. Frere and Miss S. Frere for allowing me to look through their collection of letters; to Mr. W. E. Frere for the loan of papers, and for permission to quote from the " Life of J. H. Frere," of which his father was part-author ; to the representatives of Sir Bartle Frere for a similar permission, and for leave to print some of the letters in Chapter XVI. ; to Mr. A. H. Frere, and to all other members of the family who have shown a kindly interest in my labours.

The extracts from Lady Erroll's letters are due to Mrs. Frere, who deciphered and copied several hundred sheets, Lady Erroll's writing being almost illegible to the ordinary reader. Mr. E. H. Coleridge has kindly permitted me to use the letters from his grandfather in Chapter XI.

GABRIELLE FESTING.

August, 1899.

CONTENTS.

CONTENTS.

CHAPTER VIII.

CHAPTER IX.

CHAPTER X.

CHAPTER XI.

CHAPTER XII.

CHAPTER XIII.

CHAPTER XIV.

CHAPTER XV.

CHAPTER XVI.

INTRODUCTORY.

MOST of the letters given in this volume were found in an old chest in a library. Their existence had almost been forgotten, and from their appearance it seemed as if they had been flung there, after a perfunctory sorting, to wait for a time when some one should be at leisure to examine them. The three letters from Nelson fell out of a packet labelled " Miscellaneous, of no importance," and the most interesting of those from Canning lay with papers of no value, strewn in utter confusion about the chest.

After arranging and reading them, it was discovered that many of the letters were interesting either from the personality of the writers, or from the circumstance that they reflected the manners and customs of a bygone day. Such records now seem better appreciated by the general public than was the case a few years ago; and it is therefore hoped that a selection from the Frere MSS. may prove attractive to others besides members of the family.

These letters having for the most part been addressed to one man, the Right Honourable John Hookham Frere, it has been thought advisable to follow the story of his life. At the same time this is in no sense of the word a biography ; the memoir by his nephews, Sir Bartle and W. E. Frere, has done everything that was necessary to show the world what manner of man he was. But at the time this memoir was written, it would have been impossible to publish many of the letters given in these pages, and it is doubtful whether the greater number of them were then known to be in existence.

All letters are reproduced as the writers penned them, with some necessary omissions, but no alterations. The punctuation has been occasionally supplemented (especially in the case of Lady Erroll, who once performs the feat of writing a letter almost without stops), to make the sense clearer. The original spelling has been faithfully reproduced, even in the letters from India, in which each correspondent has his own fashion of rendering the names of persons and places.

CHAPTER I.

FAMILY LETTERS.

1774—1801

" The Flanches on our field of gules
Denote, by known heraldic rules,
A race contented and obscure,
In mediocrity secure,
By sober parsimony thriving,
For their retired existence striving ;
By well-judged purchases and matches
Far from ambition and debauches :
Such was the life our fathers led ;
Their homely leaven, deep inbred,
In our whole moral composition
Confines us to the like condition."

SO wrote John Hookham Frere when requested by his brother to furnish a motto for a Frere Parentalia. The " known heraldic rules " were of his own invention, but the lines are an excellent description of his ancestors for many generations. Although the family of Frere can be traced from a certain Richard le Frere who fought under the banner of the Conqueror, no member of it seems to have attained to eminence before the time of John Hookham Frere himself. They were quiet country squires, with a happy faculty for marrying heiresses.

Frere's father, also John Frere, Fellow of Caius College, Cambridge, was celebrated as having contested the Senior Wranglership with Paley in 1763. His fluency and dexterity had created a favourable impression, which was overcome by the "general disgust" excited by his self-confidence and overbearing manner, "till he very happily apologised for it in the thesis to his second act." Some of the Fellows of Caius College accused the Moderators of partiality when the lists were published, but Frere came forward and at once acknowledged that Paley was the better man. From various sources we gather that Frere was tall and handsome, with bright blue eyes, which his eldest son inherited. His temper was quick, but his disposition was affectionate, and his manners were singularly charming, even in an age that prided itself upon its courtesy.

In 1768 he married Jane, only child of John Hookham. Through her mother she was descended from Mary Dee, the great-niece of Queen Elizabeth's John Dee, and among the wealth that she brought to her husband was the astrologer's silver cup. It was shown at the Tudor Exhibition a few years ago, and legends were told of its use by the doctor in his experiments; but nothing of this would have been believed by practical Mrs. Frere, who employed it for domestic purposes. In a letter to her son Bartle, she says, " My great thrice Great Uncle (was) John Dee, who, because he was a wise man, was taken for a Conjurer. I have his Silver Cup now here with me and you may drink of it; but I know no Story in the Family that he ever divined by it. It serves me here for a Sugar bason."

The young heiress, although Ladies' Colleges were unknown in her day, had read and studied as profoundly, if not perhaps as widely, as any of her great-grand-daughters. History and Divinity were the principal subjects of her reading, both in French and English. She composed ponderous verse, both in her waking and sleeping hours,* but she had none of the ways of the typical literary or intellectual lady, and ruled her household and brought up her children with unfailing vigour. She also dabbled in medicine, and in her letters to her sons occasionally prescribes some gruesome compound, which one hopes they did not think it necessary to take. She had lost her mother at the age of five, and the step-mother who entered the house seven years later had no children to act as companions or rivals. Perhaps it was not wonderful that she grew up strong-willed and masterful, although sensible and clever. Some letters from her step-mother are still in existence. They deal chiefly with matters of dress, advice as to which gowns the young lady shall bring up to London with her, etc., etc., and are such as a mother might write to a daughter with whom she was on perfectly good terms, save for the fact that they begin " My dear *Miss Hookham.*"

Tradition says that Jane Hookham was beautiful; and a portrait now at Roydon, representing a young lady in white, with a basket of flowers in her hand, and a little dog at her feet, has a sufficiency of good looks for an heiress. There must have been many suitors for her hand, and she has left a curious paper in which she gives at length her reasons for declining a match that her friends deemed advantageous. The disparity of years, assigned amongst them, does not seem great between a girl of eighteen and a man of thirty, especially when we know that her own daughter at twenty married a man of forty-two. But Miss Hookham's rejected lover was a Roman Catholic, which, in itself, was a sufficient obstacle to such a sound Tory and Churchwoman, and although he could have given her a title, she protested that the thought of being styled " My Lady " had no charms for her. John

* A paper is headed " Verses composed by me in my Sleep."

Frere's blue eyes may have influenced her resolution, for she became his wife at the age of nineteen.

John Hookham Frere was their eldest son, but there were six other sons and two daughters, who were brought up at Bedington in Surrey, their mother's property, and at Roydon Hall in Norfolk, which had been purchased by their grandfather, Sheppard Frere.

Mrs. Frere was a rigid moralist, but possessed some sense of the ridiculous. There is a letter to her husband (undated, but evidently written before June 1774, when Lord Stanley married Lady Elizabeth Hamilton), describing a *Fête Champêtre* given by Lord Stanley, which contrasts amusingly with the garden-parties given in these days in honour of a *fiancée*.

" My Dear Love,

    . . . The entertainment last Night was extremely Magnificent and Elegant, and everything conducted with utmost regularity without Noise or Confusion. The Company assembled at 7, Ld. Stanley receiving them at yᵉ Entrance of yᵉ Garden (the Duke of Argyle and Family were his Guests). They were all presented with Nosegays by Boys habited as Cupids, and when they were introduced into the Gardens, Messrs. Vernon, Bartlemen, etc., welcomed them to these rural abodes, and thanked them for Honouring them by there (*sic*) presence ; they then proceed'd to all kind of Rustic Sports, Running, Leaping, Skittles, Shooting with Bows and Arrows, and some foreign Games of the same kind.

The gardens, Pavillion, etc., were Illuminated in a very Splendid Stile about 10 o'clock, and then Dancing in the Principal Tent succeed'd ; they enter'd it by a Vestibule which open'd into the Marquée (I think is the Military name for it), which was of a Circular Form, and as Briliant as Lamps and the most expensive decorations could make it. Round this was yᵉ Supper Room separated from it by Curtains between the Pillars which when yᵉ Entertainment was ready were drawn up in an instant and united the two Apartments; they were however let down again when the Company were seated to prepare for the Opera, and when they were drawn up, one Composed for and suited to the occasion, was perform'd; after which a Mr. Pigot in the character of an old Druid recited a Copy of Verses in Compliment to Ld. Stanley and Lady Betty Hamilton * (who sat at the upper End of yᵉ Room in a Vandyke dress, his Ldship attending behind her chair), and towards the close of it display'd a Banner with yᵉ Arms of Stanley and Hamilton (was not this too much for any Woman breathing to bear? she did set it out, but fled as soon as it was ended), asserting that before yᵉ Oak was reverenced in this Isle by Druidical rites it had received its utmost degree of Dignity and Pre-eminence over all the other productions of yᵉ Earth by being chosen for yᵉ distinguishing Badge (is a bad word, but Mr. Orde used it so I suppose there is no better to be found, because of its vulgar application to Parish Boys) of the Illustrious House of Hamilton. N.B. 'Tis their Crest. Ld. Stanley having recover'd his fugitive fair prevail'd on her to dance a Minuet with him, and their Example renew'd the Dancing which continu'd when my Visitors left the Oaks, and with which this famous *Fête Champêtre* was to conclude. . . . "

In the spring of 1788, the eldest daughter, Jane, was taken by her parents to the trial of Warren Hastings, of which she wrote a long account to her little brothers :—

* Lady Elizabeth Hamilton, only daughter of James sixth Duke of Hamilton and Brandon and the beautiful Elizabeth Gunning.

"*March 7th*, 1788.

"I went on the 26 of last month to the Hall at Westminster. My mamma had been before she went with me, on the 18th, which was a more entertaining day, as Mr. Burke then spoke the whole time, which was 5 hours, stating in brief the history of India from the time we first had any possessions in it till the time of the return of Mr. Hastings, which was in the year '85. He was very violent in his accusations, accusing Mr. Hastings of everything that was bad, of which nobody believed one third part. . . .

"The first day (which was one of the 4 on which your Papa went) they read the indictment; when I went they read the evidence, consisting of letters from him to the East India Company and from them to him, tending to prove that he once had a great esteem for Chite Sing [Cheyte Sing], whom in the next day's evidence they meant to prove he used ill. You may imagine that hearing letters for 4 hours to the right honourable Sir and Sirs, etc., of the East India Company was not very entertaining to me. . . .

"Mr. Hastings looked very ill. He is a little man, grey-headed; he is very grave. . . . The Princes sit among the Lords; the younger sons of Peers stand round the throne, the Lords are all in their robes. The King does not go. There is likewise a box for the Queen; but as it is never the custom for either the King or Queen to go to State Trials for fear of influencing the Lords, and the Queen and Princesses had a mind to go, they went once like private gentlewomen in the box of the Duke of Newcastle. The boxes are like those at the playhouse, covered with matting or baize; the throne is raised a few steps from the ground, with a canopy over it. We sat in the Board of Works' box; the Peers, throne, Prisoner, Judges, Bishops, are in the pit, from whence the boxes rise gradually."

Jane enclosed a plan, which she explains in a postscript :—

"The large square in the middle is a table of State
covered with a Turkey carpet, in the front of which, facing
the prisoner, with his back to the King, is the Lord
Chancellor on a Stool of State, when he sits as a Peer of
Parliament. All the Peers bow as they come in or go out
in procession to the throne. . . . When the Chancellor sits
as Judge he sits on a Woolsack behind the Judges, who
have likewise two woolsacks covered with red cloth. The
Heralds' coats are made of red cloth embroidered with coats
of arms. When Mr. Hastings comes in, he throws himself
on his knees before the Bar which separates his box from
the Peers ; but upon the Chancellor saying 'You may
rise' he seats himself in a chair in the box. He is not in
Prison, but gives very considerable bail for his appearance."

Jane was also taken to see the illuminations on the
King's recovery from a fit of insanity in March 1789, and
caught a most violent cold in St. James's Street :—

"The press of carriages was so great as to oblige us to
go all the way with the coach windows down to prevent
their being smashed. The squares were very brilliant ;
we saw them all, and returned home at about 12 o'clock
very safe. There were several transparent paintings and
colored lamps ; there was hardly an alley without lights.
I saw two or three cobblers' stalls with candles in the
windows. Colonel Brittle, our opposite neighbour (in
Bedford Row), was the only dark face ; all the opposition
lighted. The Queen sent in the morning to Lord Bathurst
to say she should be with him at tea and supper, but that
he was not to mention it. At six she came with the 5
eldest princesses ; she dismissed the royal carriages, and

after staying for some time they set off in private carriages
to see the illuminations, after which they returned to Kew.
The King, who had rode to Windsor in the morning,
found Kew and the green before it lighted with great
taste by the Queen's order, and at two o'clock the
family returned."

On leaving Eton, Frere graduated at Caius College, Cambridge, where he took his M.A. degree in 1795. He then
found a post in the Foreign Office under Lord Grenville,
and in 1796 was returned member for the close borough
of West Looe in Cornwall. He and his father spent much
of their time together, but family cares generally kept
Mrs. Frere at Roydon. Her husband was a constant and
delightful correspondent, blending great events and triviali-
ties on the same page. In a letter dated November 6th,
1797, he gives his wife instructions about the beds to be
prepared for visitors, and advises her, as a precaution
against the epidemic sore throats then prevalent, "to have
oven coals set in the brazier in the hall, whenever you
have them, and sprinkle frankincense upon them, etc."
He goes on to say that "the King does not go to St. Paul's
on Friday, and it is so little certain when, that the
Bishop is going to Buckden, though he must come back
again when it happens. It is said that he holds his
resolution of going, but people in general wish he would
not.* The King told Bennet Langton 'something which,'
he said, 'they two should like'—viz. that immediately
after the victory [of Camperdown] Duncan ordered all his
men upon deck and had a general thanksgiving, and that
it affected Winter much."

* On December 19th the King went in state to St. Paul's to return
thanks for the naval victories of Lord Howe, Lord St. Vincent, and
Lord Duncan.

On November 11th, 1797, he writes: "John came in in high spirits from the House of Commons last night, where a spirited motion for an address was supported by a most spirited speech of Pitt's; but, what was most delightful, all the House sung in chorus to 'Britons, strike home.' Such members as Martin said that war was inevitable, and that we must make up our minds to it, and submit to every privation with cheerfulness, to enable ourselves to carry it on, etc., etc. If this spirit should spread and prevail without doors, it will either bring us peace or, with the blessing of God, successful war."

These early years in London must have been among the happiest of Frere's life. He was on intimate terms with most of the chief personages in the social, political, and literary world. Canning, the dearest of all his friends, was now an M.P. and an Under-Secretary of State, and the two were continually together, whether at work at the Foreign Office, dining with Lord Malmesbury, or writing the *Anti-Jacobin* at the table in Wright's room.

The first great change in his home circle was caused by the marriage of his eldest sister. The next break was the appointment of his brother Bartle as Lord Minto's private secretary in a diplomatic mission to Vienna. Bartle had the family talent for correspondence, and his letters, even when they are of no public interest, are always amusing reading. One of the first sent from Vienna gives some curious stories from Paris :—

"*16th Oct.*, 1799.

"There is a Lady who arrived here the other day from Paris. She says the people are enraged to such a degree with the directory as to abuse them openly and to rejoice at the defeat of their armies. A Centry has been established in the place where the King was beheaded to disperse the people who assembled there in great numbers and said that they heard him groan.   She travelled as a Prussian, and when stopp'd on the Frontiers by the Guard to whom she spoke German and said she was a Prussian, they laughed at her and said 'No, no, you are an Emigrant, but you may pass on.'"

A little later, Bartle was introduced to a celebrated man, and recorded his impressions for his brother's benefit :—

"VIENNA, 28 *January*, 1800.

"What a strange-looking Animal Suwarrow is, to have made such a noise in the world.   When first Ld. Minto went to him, he was kept waiting for half an hour in an Antichamber whilst Suwarrow was said to be making his ablutions; at last the door opened, and out scuttled a little old figure scarce 5 feet and ½ high, in a pair of red breeches and coarse shirt, without any neckcloth, Coat or waistcoat ; after having kissed him first on one cheek and then on the other, and paying him a great many Compliments, he began to talk about business in just the same wild style in which he dictates his notes, some of which you have seen.   When I saw him, he was at Mass before a little crucifix at one corner of the Altar, where he continued for the hour that we were there, praying and crossing himself except when he ran out a step or two towards the middle of the Altar and touched the ground with his hands and forehead, looked wildly around him, and ran back again. After Mass we went to dinner, and I am sorry to contradict Mr. Gillray, who, I think, under the print predicates of him that he 'is now in the prime of life and drinks neither wine nor spirits,' for he began dinner by drinking a half pint tumbler full of liqueur, and ended it with two or three such of Champaign which rather overcame him ; for before dinner he had jumped very nimbly on to a chair to embrace Casamajor, and passing by him after dinner, he attempted it again, but could not manage to get up. He was very much amused with Casamajor's height, and told him he was the first of the Giants he had ever seen. He asked for the name of some Giant ; but as nobody told him one, he went on talking about something else (for he was not silent a minute in the three hours that we were there) and every now and then stopped in the middle of his story to ask for this Giant's name. At last somebody told him Typhous, which he made them spell to him, and called Casamajor by it, then he would run on with some story of his Campaigns, and stop short to call out Typhous. In short, his conversation, countenance, and manner gave me the most complete idea of crazyness I ever conceived. Lord Minto says that he talked to him one evening in a very sensible but rather romantick manner about his ideas of religion, Justice, policy, etc. ; but from all that I saw of him he seemed much crazier than it is necessary even for a great man to be. He was very decently dressed in his Uniform, with his face washed from the snuff which generally covers the lower part of it. . . . When we got to Prague we heard that Suwarrow had been very gay and given a ball and handsome supper a few days before, where he had danced himself. The way in which he gave it was this. He desired one morning to speak with the Lady of the house where he lived, Baroness somebody, and telling her that he wished to give a Ball and supper, gave her a 50 florin note (value about five pounds), for which she was to furnish an entertainment for all the Nobility of Prague, Russian officers, etc."

Society in Vienna cannot have been agreeable to an Englishman. In a letter to his brother, Bartle gives an account of his going to an evening party and overhearing the conversation of a German lady to two of her own countrymen.   The topic she chose was one that cannot be mentioned in these pages.   After a while she noticed that the Englishman was listening, and broke off her story, to tell another which she considered more fit for his ears, and of which it is impossible to give even a hint.   The cold of the winter was very trying, especially when the roads were blocked with snow, cutting off the communication with Constantinople, whence news of Sir Ralph Abercrombie's army was eagerly expected.   Bartle must have been thankful to leave Vienna in the summer of 1801. As early as the January of that year, Mrs. Frere had written to her eldest son :—

"Bartle and Lord Minto's family had packed up for departing from Vienna before the signing the Armistice, and he said he thought his moveables as well collected in a Trunk ; he is indignant at the Apathy manifested by the generallity of People there.   As Moreau approached nearer Vienna, the Ladies became inquisitive to know what sort of a Gentleman he was, and as he advanced every day's report made him more amiable.   When the Archduke Charles returned to Vienna and assembled the Officers on the Parade, to give them marks of his Praise or disapprobation, though he took the swords of seven General Officers and broke them at the moment, dismissing them the service in terms of strong reproach for their cowardice, no murmur of indignation against them was heard among the Spectators, though it was a circumstance unprecedented in the Austrian army."

Soon after Bartle's arrival in England he was appointed Secretary of Legation to John Hookham Frere, who had gone to Madrid at the end of 1800 as Envoy Extraordinary and Minister Plenipotentiary.

CHAPTER II.

LIFE IN THE PENINSULA.

1800—1804.

FROM one of Canning's letters we gather that Frere, always dilatory, spent so much time over his preparations for departure to Lisbon as seriously to displease his chiefs. Frere was a by-word amongst his acquaintance for never doing to-day what could possibly be deferred until to-morrow; but it must have taken him some time to collect and pack his outfit. Lisbon, the scene of his first mission, was better furnished with some of the necessaries of life than Madrid, whither he was transferred in September 1802. A correspondent writes to him from Lisbon: "By this time Donaldson will have arrived in Madrid, and you will be able to dine in comfort. I shall occasionally send you another supply of *Toothpics* as opportunity may offer." In a letter from his brother George are some particulars of the outfit required for an Ambassador. Poor George, the one business man of a talented but erratic family, pleads that the instructions received from his brother had been of the shortest, which may account for the vagueness of the last item. The charge for carpets cannot be termed excessive; but it is difficult to imagine what Frere could want with six hundred pounds' worth of "Callico."

" Callico .	£600
Carpets	£200
Lustres	£350
Plate .	£400
Ormolu dogs, 3 sets to be used as one, 2, or 3, handsome and cheap, made by Auguste at Paris for the King of Sardinia, and never used	£100
Other articles	£400
Perhaps about	£2000 "

There are several sheets of paper signed " Robt Walpole," with a schedule of the expenses incurred by Frere's predecessor at Lisbon, who sent many useful hints. House-rent had risen considerably, but Frere must have two houses, one in Lisbon, and another in the village of Cintra as a summer retreat. Frere must have six mules to drag his coach to court at Quelus, a carriage and a special set of liveries for " Court days and formal occasions," and others for ordinary use—an expensive establishment, as the keep of each mule was computed at fifty-two guineas a year, and the bad pavements soon wore out the carriages. Twelve men servants (besides, presumably, personal attendants) formed Walpole's establishment ; their wages, which included board in the case of seven out of the twelve, came to £315 16s. per annum. But he hastens to inform Frere that " Every article of Consumption has increased in Portugal 100 per cent. since my first going into that country," and adjures him to remember " the Defalcation which attends the discount upon the Portuguese paper money."

At least, Frere was more fortunate than his friend Lord Elgin, who wrote to him from Constantinople, Dec. 29th, 1799 :—

" As to my Extraordinary Mission, it appears to have a good Effect here. It gives a Superiority in a much greater degree than that Difference of Rank would do in any Court in Europe. And the pomp attending it is by no means immaterial in these Climates. But the Expence of it is to me incredible. In preparations at London, and in necessary outlay since my arrival, I have already spent more than £8000 str., besides what I had to advance for my plate (above £2000) till the Government allowance shall become due. I have had an immense house to put in order, after above a hundred French prisoners had been long and successfully employed in destroying every part of it. And the private presents expected of me on all occasions is absolute ruin. As for what I have received in return, they consist in two old fur cloaks, such as are not unfrequently exhibited to view in Monmouth St., a great profusion of fruits and sweetmeats, and a horse which proved to be lame and stone blind." *

Then, as now, it was impossible for any public servant to obtain the money for his just expenses without a prolonged correspondence over every item ; and the difficulty was then increased by the fact that the Civil List was continually in arrears. Mr. Broughton, of the Foreign Office, wrote many letters to Frere on the subject of allowances, and suffered much from the inroads of Frere's tradesmen with bills which he was unable to pay. A

---

* Lord Elgin was not always so unfortunate in his missions. Lady Glasgow (Lady Augusta Hay) writes to her sister-in-law, Lady Erroll, some years later, when his lordship, whose first marriage had been dissolved by Act of Parliament in 1808, was about to take another wife: "I suppose he has bribed her with all the valuable Jewels and Trinkets which were presented to his former Wife by the Grand Signior, and which she for the sake of security had placed in her banker's care. His Lordship has most shabbily taken possession of them, saying that as they were given to the *Countess of Elgin*, they are of course his property. He is finely abused for this mean trick."

coachmaker is mentioned as being particularly trouble-some. On March 9th, 1802, Broughton wrote : " It is expected that in consequence of the measures which have been adopted by Mr. Addington, the arrears of the Civil List will be liquidated, and that the Foreign Ministers will be paid up to the 5th of January, 1802. But before that desirable circumstance takes place, another Quarter's Arrears will accumulate, there not being the smallest probability of anything being issued from the Exchequer till after the 2nd Installment of the Loan."

If Court ceremonials were few in number, they were interminably long. " My Brother was at Church six whole hours the other day," writes Bartle, " hearing Mass and Te Deum." At this point the elder brother came in, and has scrawled over the line " Te *D—n* 'em, say I, J. H. F." As the thanksgiving was for the peace which Addington was negotiating with France, neither of the brothers was likely to join in it with much heartiness.

Lisbon was not then such a place of exile as it would seem to a modern diplomatist. It was a favourite resort for invalids before the Riviera became fashionable. Lord and Lady Holland spent some months there, and collected round them all the choice spirits in the neighbourhood. Another visitor was Elizabeth Jemima, Countess of Erroll, the childless and beautiful widow, whose many sorrows had not quenched her gay spirit or prevented her from making merry over the discomforts of the Peninsula. " So Bartle is going to Batalha too," she wrote afterwards to J. H. Frere, " where I was once so gay and so happy, in fact enjoyed it all, and above all the horrible incon-veniences we found in our journey, the swearing of General Wemyss, all the Portuguese Women Sleeping upon the floor without night Caps in one Room, Mrs. Douglas with my Monkey and her own, all the Men going to her Carriage for Brandy, she scolding and cursing all the Portuguese. I assure you it was very amusing altogether, and Bartle's having mentioned his intended jaunt has brought the scene so exactly before me that I am convinced I shall sleep at Marinha this night instead of old Mr. Keppel's bed. Besides, I know Bartle will sleep in my bed, which is within the Drawing-room, and where Single men in general sleep on the other side, was a large Room with three beds where I even now see all the Portugueses and the maids on the floor, in short I see it all."

The Inquisition was not yet extinct, although it retained but a shadow of its former power. While at Madrid, Bartle had an opportunity of attending an Autillo, or little Auto dà Fé, and was impressed chiefly with the ugliness of the culprit, a woman between thirty and forty years of age. She was condemned to do penance in the church, wearing a sugar-loaf cap and holding a green candle, and then to undergo several years' imprisonment —a light punishment for one who had pretended to be a saint and to work miracles.

The manners of the ladies who formed the society of Lisbon must have seemed strange to English prejudices, although previous experiences at Berlin may have taught Bartle something of foreign customs. "Mme Lannes has a son," he writes to Lady Erroll, with whom he kept up a correspondence after her return to England, "and Rehaussen, who tells a story better than I can, amused us with the account of his introduction to it. He called in the evening, knowing nothing of the matter, and was shown upstairs, where he found no one but an old woman, who, upon his asking for Madame, shewed him into a room, where he saw she was in bed, and was retiring, but was desired to come in. On raising his head from his bow, he spied the young gentleman, and Madame told him that he was about an hour old, and seemed to wonder that he had not heard of it. A short time after, all the dinner-party came up into the room, and you would have thought that nothing had happened."

From another of Bartle's letters comes a story which he thought worthy of being included in a second edition of Miss Edgeworth's "Essay on Irish Bulls." "Capt. Yescombe, who is veracity itself, is one of what they call the Sick and Hurt Office at Falmouth; when a seaman is to be relieved by them, the bill must be signed by five members. Now one of these members was, and is, an Irishman, and would not agree to relieve a person who all the rest thought deserved it; however the Clerk drew up the bill, and having taken it round to be signed by the other four, brought it to my Irishman; he was furious, and taking his pen, wrote, '*I won't sign this. Patrick Macmurdock.*' (I must make a name, for I have forgot the true one.) So the bill was paid by the Treasurer, and the sailor relieved according to the law in that case made and provided, the bill being signed by five members."

When it was proposed that J. H. Frere should be transferred from Lisbon to Madrid, one of his first and most characteristic objections was that Lisbon suited him admirably because he had little or nothing to do. After looking through the mass of papers left at Roydon, one is obliged to conclude that there was plenty of work, but that Frere must have left it to his secretaries, or paid no attention to it whatever. It was not until Ainslie[*] had returned to England that Frere evolved the idea

---

[*] Mr. (afterwards Sir R.) Ainslie had been acting as Frere's secretary before Bartle Frere's arrival.

that he wished his first forty-three despatches from Lisbon to be copied into a book for future reference. As this would mean spending many long hours in Mr. Broughton's room at the Foreign Office, Ainslie, then fully occupied with his own private affairs, was aghast at the thought, and wrote a long letter of remonstrance, half plaintive, half indignant, in which he styles Frere " the laziest of God's creatures." Old John Frere mentions with much distress a report that the Envoy keeps important papers lying on the table, and important persons waiting in the ante-room, while he amuses himself with the news-papers.

The official despatches, written on the stiffest of paper, and tied up in neat bundles with red tape, are not inter-esting, and may well be left at the bottom of the old chest, where they have reposed for so many years. Some have long communications between the lines in sym-pathetic ink. Some are written in cipher, with figures instead of the important words. Occasionally, more elaborate precautions have been taken to ensure secrecy. An English official at Madrid tells Frere that before writing again to head-quarters, he must have some more gilt-edged paper, which Frere can send him, and encloses a sheet to give the exact size ; the sheet originally looked blank, but now faint traces of writing are to be seen among the blisters, which show where the fire scorched the paper.

One of the most distressing of Frere's tasks must have been the business of the French *émigrés* who were then scattered all over Europe, living as best they might, seeing that the funds raised by the sale of the jewels which some of the more fortunate had been able to secure, had long melted away. The Government made some allowance to these unfortunates, and Frere, always open-handed, often supplemented the dole from his own means; but only the inexhaustible purse of the fairy legends could have been of real service. Pitiful are some of the stories written on the dusty sheets. Take, for instance, the following memorandum: "The Marquis and Marquise d'E—— came to Lisbon upwards of four years ago, with their five Sons. They had lost a good Estate in France, and they brought strong letters of Recommendation to me as a most Respectable family. The Marquise has lately had a paralytick stroke, and is become quite helpless. The Marquis had 3 Shillings a day, and each of his sons 1/3 besides Rations —all which they lost by the departure of the Troops."

The Chevalier de J——, a native of Corsica, solicits help, "n'ayant pas de quoi subvenir aux frais qu'occasionne la naissance d'un enfant. . . . La cherté des comestibles m'écrase," he adds, despairingly.

Sometimes there is a comic side to the applicant's distress, when vanity, or the hope of pleasing the Envoy, led him to express himself in English. It does not appear whether the modest individual whose letter is given below succeeded in impressing any one else with a sense of the justice of his claims :—

"Illustruss Sir,

"My having been confined to my room with a violent cold and fever has pervented my personnaly reminding Your Excellency of my dispatch, and informing that a few days ago Mr. Luis Pinto dispatched Some Gentlemen of the Law and that as yet I have not been so Fortunate as to be contemplated in any one of them when it was genneraly thought and hoped, that I should be the first on the list in attention to the very powerful protection of Your Excellency Whom I have the Honor to interest in consequence of the Services performed to His Britannick

Majesty for Whom I have so much risked my life with a view to Save the Stole money intended to supply necessarys of His Royal Fleet." . . . " This . . . is what Mr. Luis Pinto ought to do, if He wish to do me justice through means of the great and respectful authority of Your Excellency attending to 9 years that I have served my Prince, to dispatch me Corregidor de Lagos in Algarre, granting me the honor of the Habit of Christ in reward of the services which at the peril of my Life I did His Britannick Majesty. All is in Mr. Luis Pinto hands, I know very well, and if Your Excellency will take my honest word, all is only in His power, if he is desiderous to attend, respect, and contemplate the high representation of Your Excellency of Whom I have the distinctive honor to be," etc., etc.

At least Frere had no reason to complain of want of variety in his correspondence. Dainty billets from ladies of the Court, offering him a seat in a coach, lie side by side with long complaints from the captains of British vessels who thought themselves aggrieved by the action of the authorities in some Spanish port. Then follow smooth and irrelevant replies from these authorities, in one case committing the captain of an English frigate detained in quarantine " to the Divine protection," which pious aspiration must have added fuel to the flames. An indignant remonstrance from " Martin Slack Smallpiece, Liveryman of the Vintners' Company," who has been ordered to furnish a man to mount guard at six o'clock in the morning under pain of imprisonment, comes to the hand that searches for the piteous entreaty of the crew of the *Lapwing* to be delivered from the " sickly prison" to which the French had consigned them. From a bundle labelled " Miscellaneous of no importance" fall several letters written in the firm left-handed characters that we know so well :—

' *Victory*,' *July 24th*, off TOULON.

"Sir,

"Not having received any letters from Gibraltar since my sailing on June 4th, I have not had the honor of Your Excellency's answer to mine and Mr. Elliot's letters of that date. I am sending some of our Ships to Barcelona for refreshments, and I will not allow myself to suppose that they can be refused to us; if they should be, Your Excellency knows what course to pursue to obtain from Spain an exact neutrality, or she must take the consequences of a breach of it. French Privateers go in and out of her Ports, and look out from them on Merchant Vessels passing, and put to Sea from the Port after a Vessel, capture her and return to the Spanish Port. As an instance I relate a Bombard french privateer lay under the fort of the island of Caprera near Majorca. She saw the *Ant*, an English Brig belonging to North Yarmouth, went to Sea, captured her and returnd with her. A French Convoy put into Malaga, I am sure the French Troops and vessel of War were supplied with everything they wanted. I only mention these instances of the conduct of Spain in case she should act differently by us. I send Your Excellency an account of the only thing worth Your Excellency's knowing from him who has the Honor to Remain with the Greatest respect, Your Most Obedient Humble Servant,

"NELSON AND BRONTE."

Again he writes :—

' *Victory*,' *Sept.* 13th, 1803.

"Dear Sir,

"I should feel very much obliged if you could procure me the best edition of the Bible publish'd in Spain. I have been told that with the notes it is finer than any hitherto publish'd. I trust to Your Excellency's forgiveness of this trouble and I am, With Great Respect, Your Excellency's Most Obedient Servant,

" NELSON AND BRONTE."

And again·:—

' *Victory*,' *May 3rd,* 1804.

"Sir,

"I take for granted that I have to thank Your Excellency for forwarding a letter to me from Sir Edwd Pellew for which I feel very much obliged and have to request that you will have the goodness to send to him my answer, and I wish that my communication with England was kept up thro' that channel or Lisbon, when such an accident as all my letters falling into the hands of the Enemy would have been avoided. I only hope that dispatches of any consequence would not have been sent in such a Vessel. The french fleet at Toulon are daily moving out of the harbour for Exercise, and it is clear that either they are preparing for a Run, or keeping in perfect readiness to form a junction with some other fleet, therefore Your Excellency will see the importance of my knowing whenever the french squadron at Ferrol may put to Sea, and particularly if they are joined by any and what number of ships from either Rochford or Brest. We have reports that some few Russian Troops are arrived at Corfou and Zante, and that the Russian fleet from the Black Sea may be in the archipelago by this time.

"I have the honor to Remain with

"Great Respect Your Excellency's

"Most Obedient Servant

"NELSON AND BRONTE."

As we know, in the following year Villeneuve failed to

relieve the blockade of Ferrol, and was out-manœuvred by Nelson.   But by that time Frere was no longer Envoy at the Court of Spain.

From the hour of his arrival in Madrid it had been plain that there could be no good understanding between him and Godoy, the "Prince of the Peace," who was all-important at the Spanish Court.   Godoy is said to have done his best to obtain Frere's recall, but it was at his own request that Frere returned to England in the September of 1804.   He had long been desirous to be among his old friends, and only Canning's strong representations had kept him at his post.   He was well received on his return by the King "with an appearance of real kindness and interest."   Bartle, as usual, stayed behind, like the wife of a celebrated traveller recently deceased, to "pay, pack, and follow."

CHAPTER III.

THE YOUTH OF CANNING.

1800—1801.

ONE of Frere's favourite stories was that of a peer, "a fine specimen of a thorough-going old country Tory," who came to call on his father with the news that Pitt was out of office and that Addington had taken his place. He ran over the names of all the members of the new Cabinet, and, rubbing his hands with satisfaction, sighed in conclusion: "Well, thank God, we have at last got a ministry without one of those confounded men of genius in it."

This story well illustrates the ordinary Briton's attitude of mind to all men of genius. He has an inborn conviction that there is something not quite respectable, something unsafe and deplorable, connected with the possession of brilliant talents of any kind. His ideal minister is a steady, elderly man of methodical habits, who goes to church with unfailing regularity, and leads a quiet and rather dull life in the bosom of a large and virtuous family.

In no case has this inherent distrust of extraordinary genius been more strongly exemplified than in that of Pitt's pupil, the "warmest, most intimate and most congenial friend " * whom Frere ever possessed—George Canning.

The friendship began at Eton, where the two boys founded the *Microcosm*, a magazine in which appeared Canning's celebrated "Criticism on the Story of the Queen of Hearts," and Frere's "Ode on Athelstane's Victory at Brunanburh." Mrs. Frere, writing a description of the Montem of 1787 to her son George, mentions Canning in terms which show him to have been already well known to Frere's younger brothers. A temporary separation came when the friends left Eton. Canning went to Christ Church, where his portrait now hangs in the Hall; Frere graduated at Caius College, Cambridge. But their correspondence continued, although it has not been preserved at Roydon; and there were probably occasional meetings before Canning took his B.A. degree in 1793 and prepared to enter public life.

Young, brilliant, strikingly handsome, with a strange power alike of winning and of repelling the hearts of others, Canning was a promising recruit for either Whigs or Tories. By family connection and association he was a Whig, as Frere was a Tory. But he early decided to choose for himself and make his own way. The celebrated Mrs. Crewe, whose name the Whig refrain coupled with " buff and blue," was anxious to patronise him, and before he left Oxford he had received through her a letter from the Duke of Portland, offering to bring him into Parliament. But Canning refused, and gave as his reason to Frere the probability that the Duke would change sides— as he soon afterwards did. " I will go over in no man's train," he said. " If I join Pitt, I will go by myself."

Shortly afterwards, Frere arranged that Canning should be introduced to Pitt, with whom he became a great

* " Memoir," by Sir B. Frere.

favourite. "Dundas used often to have Pitt to sup with him after the House rose," Frere told his nephew during one of those long talks at Malta, "and one night he took Canning with him. There was no one else, and Canning came to me next morning before I was out of bed, told me where he had been supping the night before, and added, 'I am quite sure I have them both,' and I did not wonder at it, for with his humour and fancy it was impossible to resist him. He had much more in common with Pitt than any one else about him, and his love for Pitt was quite filial, and Pitt's feeling for him was more that of a father than of a mere political leader. I am sure that from the first Pitt marked Canning out as his political heir, and had in addition the warmest personal regard for him."

Frere by this time was in the Foreign Office under Lord Grenville, and it must have seemed to the two friends as if the days of their boyhood had returned when they found themselves once more together, and busy over a weekly paper. This was the *Anti-Jacobin, or Weekly Examiner*, of which Gifford was the working editor, assisted by Canning, Frere, George Ellis, and other contributors.

The *Anti-Jacobin* ran for some eight months, shocking and offending many respectable people, but exceeding the fondest hopes of its authors by the sensation it caused. Some of its pleasantries are too ponderous and heavy for modern taste. It has been said that Erasmus Darwin's "Loves of the Plants" is only remembered for the sake of the "Loves of the Triangles"; but who, in our days, knows the "Loves of the Triangles"? The attack upon Charles Lamb is indefensible, and must have been sincerely regretted by Canning and Frere when they knew more of the personality of their victim. "The Needy Knife-Grinder" still survives, thanks to its having

found its way into several volumes of Elegant Extracts ;
and perhaps the performance at Eton in 1898 of a scene
from *The Rovers* may have induced some persons to
revive their acquaintance with that exquisite travesty of
the old-fashioned German play. It was this last *jeu
d'esprit* that drew down upon Canning the heavy and
implacable wrath of Niebuhr, who persisted in regarding
it as a malicious libel upon German universities in general,
and on the " U-niversity of Gottingen " in particular, and
roundly abused Canning as "a sort of political Cossack."

In 1799 Canning was succeeded by Frere as Under-
Secretary of State in the Foreign Office, and was removed
to the Board of Trade. The next event of his life was
his marriage with Joan, daughter of Major-General John
Scott of Balcomie, which took place in July 1800.
Although Canning and his friends had long recognised
the necessity for his marrying an heiress, and although
his wife brought a dowry of £100,000, the marriage was
one of genuine affection on both sides. Mrs. Canning
never became a prominent figure in the political world,
like Mrs. Crewe, Lady Malmesbury, and other women
of her time, but she devoted herself to her husband
from the hour of their marriage with a constancy that
never failed. She copied his letters, listened to his
schemes, sympathised with his grievances, and frequently,
as we shall see, attempted to make peace between him
and Pitt when the impatient temper of the one and the
calm inflexibility of the other had caused a serious
rupture. Canning had evidently a high opinion of her
judgment : " Joan and I think that," " Joan and I are
doing this," are phrases often to be found in his letters.
When Charles Ellis lost his wife, the highest praise that
Canning could bestow on the dead woman was that Joan
loved her. A little while before, Ellis had written to

Frere: "Canning has been here with his Wife, whom I and Eliza like extremely, and appears as happy as I could wish him." Joan received Frere as Canning's old friend, and often sent familiar messages to him at the end of her husband's letters.

Two years before his own death, Frere thus described Canning's wedding to his nephew :—

"I was to be best man, and Pitt, Canning, and Mr. Leigh,* who was to read the service, dined with me before the marriage, which was to take place in Brook Street. We had a coach to drive there, and as we went through that narrow part, near what was then Swallow Street, a fellow drew up against the wall, to avoid being run over, and peering into the coach, recognised Pitt, and saw Mr. Leigh who was in full canonicals sitting opposite to him. The fellow exclaimed, 'What, Billy Pitt! and with a parson, too!' I said, 'He thinks you are going to Tyburn, to be hanged privately,' which was rather impudent of me ; but Pitt was too much absorbed, I believe in thinking of the marriage, to be angry. After the ceremony, he was so nervous that he could not sign as witness, and Canning whispered to me to sign without waiting for him. He regarded the marriage as the one thing needed to give Canning the position necessary to lead a party, and this was the cause of his anxiety about it, which I would not have believed had I not witnessed it, though I knew how warm was the regard he had for Canning. Had Canning been Pitt's own son, I do not think he could have been more interested in all that related to this marriage." †

* Mr. Leigh had married Canning's aunt.

† From a letter to Frere's brother Bartle, it appears that the marriage took place at the uncomfortable hour of half-past seven in the evening.

The first of Canning's letters to Frere is dated from Brighton, a little before his marriage, June 20th, 1800. The prospects of Europe were then gloomy. The Tsar, after coquetting with the idea of an Austrian alliance, seemed disposed to side with France, and the First Consul, darting across the Alps,· had completely defeated the Austrian army under General Melas, on the plains of Marengo. Most of Canning's letter is taken up with the affairs of a third person, of whom he speaks by a nickname, and has no interest for the general reader; but the postscript is curious :—

"What do you think of the Italian News? And what consolation does Pitt point out, after looking over the map in the corner of his room, by the door? Does he make out that Bonaparte is in a scrape? that old Melas has not lost his head—or will recover It? and that Moreau is advancing no faster than Kray chuses to let him?"

Was it this same map which the dying Pitt bade his attendants "roll up" after the battle of Austerlitz?

The armistice with Austria was now drawing to a close, and the French refused to renew it unless England would consent to a general truce with full powers of communication by sea and land. This, of course, would have given them an opportunity of sending provisions and reinforcements to their army in Egypt and their garrison at Malta. Lord Grenville proposed that Malta and the maritime towns of Egypt should be placed on the same footing as the places in Germany held by Austrian garrisons, everything that could give additional means of defence being excluded, and provisions for only fourteen days admitted. The French declined this compromise. Canning's indignation vented itself in the following letter, marked "*Private.*" It is curious as being the only one among the scores of letters and notes addressed by him to Frere that does not begin "My Dear Frere," but plunges at once into the subject. As a rule, his letters to Pitt begin thus abruptly, Canning seeming to think "My Dear Sir" too formal, and "My Dear Pitt" too familiar. There is no superscription, and the cover has disappeared, but it is impossible to imagine that such a letter can have been addressed to Pitt, and have found its way to Frere, as was the case with some of the papers at Roydon :—

"PUTNEY HILL, *Tuesday, Sept.* 16, 1800.
Private.

"There must be a great taste for being laughed at amongst us, if we go on discussing, after this answer. I give Talleyrand great credit for having discovered the fright in which we were, and having seen it in so ridiculous a point of view. Is it possible now, do you think, that we can so far overlook the insolence of this proposal as to begin treating gravely about a modification of it? and that we can really take the trouble to explain to the French Gentlemen 'that they must have misunderstood us, to be sure (for to suppose that they would make such a misrepresentation on purpose is wholly out of the question) that we never meant to propose, in good sooth not we, an Armistice for separate negociation—no—that it was only for the sake of Austria that we consented to It at all, and that we rely upon their good nature, and good intentions, not to press us to agree to an armistice for a separate peace, because in that case ——we *shall* agree to it.' Gracious God! as Mr. Fox exclaims: it makes one sick to see ourselves become

3

the object of such broad, undisguised contempt. But pray do not *ask* beforehand, whether or no *if* pressed to a separate armistice for a separate negociation we shall agree to it—pray do not. The idea will of course be rejected with apparent scorn. But in the end it will come to that.

"It is incredible—but so it will be. So it *must* be, if we return any other answer to this impertinence, this outrageous, indecent contumely (as saucy, as if a man in private company were to pretend not to hear distinctly what you have said, and make you repeat it, and then answer you, laughing in your face all the time, as if you had said something else)—if to this we return any other answer than shortly this—that 'our offer not having been accepted, we have nothing more to say, and will have no Armistice or any condition at all.' If we argue, and remonstrate, and distinguish, and set right what has been mis-stated—in short, if we do not show that we feel the contempt and ridicule with which they have treated us, and are heartily ashamed of having given so much room for it—there is an end. Do people hold up their heads? And does the Cabinet meet by daylight? Who kicks them individually, as they go into the Cabinet-Room?"

Before the disputes over terms had ended in the rupture of the negociations, Malta surrendered to the English squadron in September. In October Frere was appointed Envoy Extraordinary to the Court of Lisbon. Before his departure Canning addressed various letters to him. The first, dated from Spring Gardens, December 2nd, 1800, gives an account of a House of Commons debate, in which Canning, much to his disappointment, had had no opportunity of speaking. He confesses: "I am not fond of following Sheridan, Speech for Speech, on a motion of his own, though I do not mind jostling with him in Debate." He continues :—

" I believe it is since you went that I have seen the Pamphlet printed at the Thuilleries (supposed with Bonaparte's connivance) and said to have been sent under Lucien Bonaparte's cover to the Prefects of the Departments. It is entitled 'A Comparison between Cesar, Cromwell, Monck, and Bonaparte' or something to that effect—'a Fragment from the English.' The purpose of it is to rescue Bonaparte from the guilt belonging to the excesses of the Revolution, to represent him as the Restorer of Order, etc, and as one who ought to be not only Sovereign himself, but the founder of a new Dynasty. It is very curious. I have little doubt that some blow will be struck in this sense, if he returns triumphant from the opening of the New Campaign. Does not such a project, so announced, prove more and more clearly, how prudent it would have been to enter into some discussions with him *personally* in the course of last Spring? We might have moulded him."

A letter, written on December 10th, to catch Frere at Falmouth, dwells with complacency on the thought that the armistice was really at an end, and that Pitt and England were presenting a bold front to the war. " Never was there a game put so completely into the hands of those who are to play it, and in which (contrary to Lady Malmesbury's proverbial admonitions) the standers-by appeared to have so confidently abandoned all Opinion." There is an affectionate allusion to "the Lion"—a sobriquet for Lord Malmesbury among the younger Tories—and a word of good advice to Frere. "Bestir yourself at Lisbon when you get there—and find, or make business to raise a dust that may blind Lord Grenville's eyes to the length of time that you have been in going. Adieu. Joan would send her love, only that she thinks that too good for you—but she does send it, nevertheless."

From this time Canning's letters to Frere went with great regularity, although, thanks to the eccentricities of the postal service, some of them never reached their destination. The first of the year 1801 was written at 10 p.m. on January 17th from the Pay Office, and opens with a long criticism of Frere's first dispatches. The anxiety that the new Envoy should please the authorities at home, and the pride in his cleverness, are worthy of an elder brother :—

"First—for your dispatches. I have read them with very great satisfaction—that I suppose will please you ; but I do not know that you will be equally well pleased to hear, that they were much better than I *had expected.* Much better, I assure you—so much so, as to diminish (perhaps you will not like that, either) the regret which I felt at your going a-foreign-ministring, and to lead me to hope that you may do great things in that way. Your French Note is so good as to have a full claim to the qualification of Excellence which Hammond insists upon my refusing to you. It is very good indeed—somewhat too long, but that is no matter—and perhaps a little above its work, considering that it is only about Portugal, and addressed to nothing better than a Portuguee, and that the worst that it portends is a small degree of ruin and revolution to a Govt. that does not seem very desirous of making exertions to avoid them—but that is all the better, and the generalities, if too good for Lisbon, tell very well here. I am persuaded the K[ing] will like it. I understand from Hammond that Lord G[renville] expresses himself perfectly satisfied. And the cheerfulness with which he appears to have approved of what you have done, and the promptness of his answer, are likely to efface from his mind the remembrance of your want of promptness in setting out, and of the displeasure which he certainly felt at it.

"One or two things only I have to find fault with in your dispatches. 1st. You ought not to date them *"Monday"* Jany. 5th, but *"Lisbon"* Jany. 5th—or if you insist upon the supererogatory date of the day of the week, you must not *omit* the place. I added it in a hand as like the original as I could make it, before your dispatches went to the King. 2ndly. Your conclusion ought not to run thus 'I have the honour to be, *my Lord, with great truth* etc.,' but 'I have the honour to be, with great *truth* (or whatever it may be), my Lord, Your Lordship's.' If you ask me *why* one of these is wrong and the other right, I cannot tell you. But so it is. Johnson said to somebody one day who asked him a question about some proposition apparently equally indifferent in its nature, 'Sir, my name *might* originally have been Nicholson, instead of Johnson, but it *is* Johnson, and if you call me Nicholson now, you call me wrong.' 3rdly. You ought not to mix many distinct subjects in one dispatch. It is the habit of Office, (you know), and besides it gives an air of business and detail, to send Nos. 1 to 10 by the same conveyance if you have points ten in number to state, or discuss, especially if they are such as may be separately answered. For instance—you cram into your long dispatch what you have to say about the preparations for receiving Prince Augustus.

This at all events ought to have been the subject of a separate Dispatch. It need not have been longer than the Paragraph as it now stands, with a 'my Lord' at the beginning, and 'My Lord, Your Lordship's' at the end. And depend upon it, the K. would have liked it better."

Canning then discusses the character of the British Consul at Lisbon, concluding with the remark : " People grow wonderfully more tolerable when they have something to do—and above all when they have 'had losses' and so forth, and the like of that. By the way, do the Portugueezes or Portingals intercept our Letters and read and decypher them ? or will the Enemy get hold of them and publish them with preface and notes ? If so the world will be some nonsense in pocket—which it has long wanted, having had nothing but stupidity of late, which is a very different thing—and much less edifying to the world, tho' much more gainful to the Professor.

"From your consul, I come to your Secretary—of whom I like the character that you give me very well, all except his not liking nonsense—or not *understanding* it—which last, however, is not so bad—he may have an excuse for such a fault in his education, and may mend of it. Is he respectful to you ? if so he has great merit for discrimination. If not—there is no joke at all—and I have therefore been amused without reason at his want of respect to Boringdon. B., you must know, told me that he did not much approve of him. ' Why not ?' says I. ' Frere tells me he is clever, and agreeable, and modest.' ' Modest !' says B., ' the rudest young gentleman I ever saw.' ' Why, what did he do ?' ' Do—I don't exactly know—but he was quite at his ease, and put his legs up on the sofa.' This was all the fact, but it was clear to me that the K. and his palace had not *imposed* sufficiently —and I was prepared to give your young man some credit for his want of awe and astonishment. But if he does not come to understand nonsense, there is no hope of him."

He reverts to the state of foreign politic^s, and speaks of the spirit shown " by the Country and the City," which had put him into such good humour that " I have no occasion for the forbearance which in other events I had determined to exercise."

Little did he know how soon his resolutions were to be tested. Never was a more disastrous day for him than that which saw Pitt retire from office. The story of his resignation has been often told, but it may be as well to give a brief summary of the events that led to it.

After passing the Act of Union with Ireland, Pitt felt himself in honour bound to take some measures for the relief of the Roman Catholics, who had given their support to the Act in the hope that their claims to justice would receive favourable consideration. It has been said that no definite pledge was given to them : this may be true, but it is certain that there was a general belief that, when the Union was completed, some of the harsh distinctions between the Irish Catholics and the rest of His Majesty's subjects were to be abolished. It is also certain that, without the support, or, at all events, the neutrality of the Irish Roman Catholics, the Act of Union would never have become law at that time.

In the autumn of 1800, Pitt and Lord Grenville had drawn up a scheme by which a political test was to be substituted for the sacramental test hitherto imposed upon all persons holding office under the Crown. The Lord Chancellor Loughborough was consulted privately on the matter, but nothing was said to the King. In the September of 1800, Loughborough was staying with His Majesty at Weymouth, and while there received a confidential letter from Pitt, with various letters drawn up by Lord Castlereagh, which were to be laid before the next meeting of the Cabinet. Knowing the King's strong prejudice against a large class of his subjects, and his obstinate belief that the barest measure of justice to that class would be a violation of his Coronation Oath, the Lord Chancellor thought he perceived an opportunity of supplanting the Minister and gaining the King's confidence. He showed Pitt's letter to George III., whose religious bigotry instantly took alarm. At the levee on Wednesday, January 28th, 1801, "he intimated to Wyndham that he should consider any person who voted for the measure as personally indisposed towards him." Such a public declaration of the King's feeling obliged Pitt to tender his resignation on January 31st, and although the King, at first hesitated to accept it, they could not arrange a compromise. Pitt's friend, Henry Addington, the Speaker of the House of Commons, was invited by the King, and encouraged by Pitt, to form a cabinet. While this was in process of arrangement, the King was seized with one of the attacks of mental derangement from which he had been free for the last twelve years. Pitt and Addington, the one Minister *de facto*, the other *de jure*, were obliged to transact business in concert, and to confer on the necessity of a Regency Bill. But in the beginning of March the King recovered his senses.

Pitt gave up the Exchequer Seal on March 14th. The general impression has always been that the Roman Catholic claims were the sole cause of his retirement from office. But several of his contemporaries were of opinion that this question had been used as a cover for Pitt's real motive. It was impossible that England, single-handed, could carry on the war against France, with wheat at the famine price of 120s. a quarter. It was impossible that Pitt, whose health was breaking, could continue much longer in the place he had held triumphantly for more than seventeen years. A breathing space was necessary alike for the country and the Minister. Pitt would resign to another the unpopular task of making peace, and return refreshed to his labours when the new ministry were at the end of their resources. Lord Mahon * and Lord Ashbourne † strenuously deny that Pitt had any such motive in resigning office, but it was the opinion of such men as Lord Malmesbury and Frere, who had every opportunity of knowing what passed behind the scenes. " It looks at times to me," says Lord Malmesbury, in his diary of February 7th, 1801, " as if Pitt was playing a very selfish, and, in the present state of affairs, a very criminal part ; that he goes out to show his own strength, and under the certain expectation of being soon called upon again to govern the country, with uncontrolled power."

Lord Grenville, and the other members of the Cabinet who had given their support to the Roman Catholic claims, could only follow Pitt into retirement. But there were some young and promising men, such as Canning, holding the lesser posts under Government, whom it seemed unnecessary to displace, and·there were others who might be willing to join the new administration if they were assured that their support of Addington did not involve hostility to Pitt. Pitt made it a special request that his retirement should not affect his friends; and several (his brother, Lord Chatham, for instance), found that their attachment to Pitt obliged them to remain.

---

* " Life of Pitt."
† " Some Chapters on Pitt."

Canning's dismay and disappointment were severe. The change came upon him, as on Pitt's other friends, like an earthquake shock, but it hardly can have affected any one else so deeply. With brilliant talents and a large fortune, treated by Pitt as his son, the world seemed at his feet. Now, at one of the most important crises through which England had ever passed in her struggle with France, Pitt was deserting his post, and Canning was left to his own devices. Addington made several efforts to secure him, probably not so much from a real desire for his services, as from a terror that his gifts of satire would be employed against the new administration ; but no offers could tempt Canning to remain. The fiery soul that had chafed at Pitt's cautious measures was not likely to take service with the good dull conscientious man whom the good dull conscientious King fitly described as " his *own* Chancellor of the Exchequer."

The state of feeling among the younger members of Pitt's party is shown by the following letter from Charles Ellis :—

" LONDON,
" *Tuesday, Feby.* 10, 1801.

" MY DEAR FRERE,—

" You will have received from Canning the History and Particulars of the Change of Administration, but he probably will not have told you that his own Conduct has been that of the truest and sincerest Friend to Pitt, and, I am sorry to add (with only a few exceptions) his Conduct alone deserves that Character. Pitt certainly has requested his Friends to remain in office, and he has pressed his request strongly—and those who remain, all of them, say it is from Motives of Friendship to him ; and some, feel their Friendship for him, and their Duty to their Country, *particularly* and *more* strongly to call upon them to take office in support of their Country at the Crisis, when he deserts it.*

"... You will probably receive a dispatch from Jawk [Lord Hawkesbury] as your new Lord and Master, by next Mail. I wish in the mean time you would finish (and return with your first answer) the Song of the little Ploughboy 'so simple as may be' from a scrap of that song by Canning (Ralph *loquitur*):

> "'So great a man! so great a man! so great a man I'll be,
> You'll forget the stupid Speaker who sat behin' the Lee.'

"You will hear with pleasure that people very generally do Justice to Canning's conduct and feelings towards Pitt. (I am not quite satisfied that Pitt himself feels the obligations as he ought.) However fine the Motives of disinterestedness may be, of those who have taken the opposite method of expressing their Friendship, his plain simple reason 'that when Pitt, the only man in his opinion fit to be Minister, goes out, he follows his Example—and that in the choice between following that Example or serving under the Person who has the foolish Vanity to think he can replace him, there cannot be a moment's Doubt'—so perfectly sound in theory, and so manly in practice, that it cannot fail of being felt by all men of common understanding and common notions of Morality,—and so God help us all, for our Ministry cannot."

Pitt cannot be blamed if he did not regard Canning's behaviour in the light in which Canning's friends regarded it. There are times when the minister at the head of affairs cannot take his subordinates into his confidence. He requires them to trust him, to follow his lead without

---

* This is a hit at Lord Eldon, who took the Great Seal " only in obedience to the King's command and at the advice and earnest recommendation of Mr. Pitt."

question, and this was just what Canning was not prepared to do. Frere would often speak of an occasion when Canning had been moving heaven and earth to abolish slavery in the conquered colonies by a simple order in council. Pitt would not issue the order. and " Canning was as angry as he could be with Pitt." In speaking of the events which followed Pitt's retirement, Frere said : " I have no doubt Pitt foresaw what would happen. He did not wish to have to make the peace which was inevitable, and knew he must come in again soon after it was made ; and he wished, on his return, to find Canning in office, where he might have retained him without difficulty from his aristocratic supporters ; but Canning would not let him. I was obliged to remind Canning of it afterwards, when he was crusty with Lord Dudley for much the same thing. I told him, ' Dudley is now doing to you what you did to Pitt—refusing to follow a lead the necessity of which you see, and he does not.' It is the hardest of a minister's trials not always to be able to acknowledge his own weakness, and give his reasons in such a case."

The first of Canning's letters after the change of ministry is dated from the Pay Office, on March 24th. It dryly announces that the old ministers are out, that the new ministers are setting about making peace as fast as they can, and that he is moving to a house in Hereford Street. He is in the middle of a long letter that will explain everything, to Frere. " For the rest, I do not like things at all. But Joan is pretty well, and bears all like a little heroine."

Mrs. Canning was then so near her confinement that it would have been dangerous for her to move, and in the end Canning remained in his old quarters, at the earnest request of his successor, until after the birth of her son. She was dangerously ill ; but the child, born on April 25th, was " a fine large handsome Boy, in the highest possible health and spirits—whereof wish me joy"—as his father proudly wrote. The long letter to Frere was first sent to Pitt, who returned it with a letter that may be found in Stanhope's "Life." It is calm, dignified, and not unkindly in tone, but its very temperateness must have irritated Canning's restless temper. A few sharp words, followed by an affectionate reproach, would have had more effect on the impetuous Irishman than the lofty assurance that "I do not acquiesce in the idea that there has been anything unkind, much less unfair in any part of my conduct, or anything either for me to excuse or for you to complain of or to forgive." . . . "Under the circumstances," he concludes, " I most deeply regret your having misunderstood me as you now appear to have done, and still more the effect which that misunderstanding has produced ; but I really cannot ascribe this to any fault of mine."

Whether a copy of this letter was sent to Lisbon, is uncertain, but it mattered little to Frere, as Canning's letter with all its inclosures was lost in the *Earl Gower* packet. By the time that he heard of its fate, Canning was settled at South Hill, the country house which he had recently purchased, whither he took his wife as soon as she was able to travel. From thence he wrote to Frere, on Tuesday, July 7th :—

"I could not write to you on Sunday, in pursuance of my plan, adopted since I came here, to take you immediately after morning service. I had only just received the confirmation of the loss of my long letter and all its enclosures in the *Gower* packet. And it is really so disheartening that I know not how to set about repairing it. That Letter contained answers not only to all the questions that you do put to me, but to every possible

question that you could put to me respecting the present
state of things, as far as I am concerned with it.   And its
Inclosures were papers which I would not have lost for any
consideration, or risqued for any short of that of giving you
the most perfect and correct notion of all that had passed
here—some of them copies, of which I have no duplicate,
others originals of which I have no copy, and which it
is vain to think of recovering by memory, or by any
other means.   God send that they are safe at the bottom
of the sea—that is my only anxiety now—for I should
be loth to see them published with Notes and a Preface
such as the Prince of the Peace's Secretary would write
to them. . . .

" Perhaps you do not know where I am now, for this
information, if I am not mistaken, was contained in my
long Letter.   I have bought a Place—and a very pretty
one—not very large, but large enough, in Windsor Forest
—28 miles from Town, 9 from Windsor—a good house,
and a farm of 200 acres—with Cows, and pigs, and sheep
(which I have just shorn and got 15 todd of wool—no,
not 15—I forget exactly how many todd, but I shall get
£15 for it), and sundry other appurtenances, of which it
is impossible to convey an accurate idea by writing, but
which this Portuguese Peace may perhaps send you home
to survey with your own eyes. . . .

" See the Despatches !   Lord help you, not I !   I have
seen nothing since—March I think—since, in short, the
Change of Govt. was completed—and seeing absolutely
nothing, I learn nearly as little in any other way.   I
foresaw that Hammond would soon be ordered not to
tell anything.   And I thought it kindest to him therefore,
as well as pleasantest for myself, to desire him beforehand
to make no scruple of treating me like an Alien to the
Foreign Office at once—and so I have of course been

treated. Not that I have any coolness with Jawk*—not at all. He has behaved perfectly well in the only point in which he had to behave at all, that is in talking to me kindly about you, and expressing a great desire to gratify your wishes in all respects. . . .

"Adieu. This is all for the present—except to tell you that my loss of office does not imply the loss of rank as a Privy Councillor, which you seem to imagine."

Mr. George Hammond, whose name frequently occurs in these letters, was the first British Minister ever accredited to the United States. On his return to England, in 1795, he became Under Secretary at the Foreign Office, and was on intimate terms with both Canning and Frere. He contributed to the *Anti-Jacobin*, and the *Quarterly Review* is said to have owed its birth to a dinner-party at his house in Spring Gardens. He was a most convenient friend, as parcels of all kinds could be sent from Lisbon to his care, at a great saving of expense and trouble. The orange-trees for "Joan's" conservatory, which Canning demands of Frere in every letter at this time were to be addressed to Hammond at the Foreign Office.

On Sunday, July 12th, Canning was still lamenting his "poor long letter," which seems to have played the same part in his correspondence that "the great fire at Wolf's Craig" fulfilled in Caleb Balderstone's domestic economy. After dwelling on all that Frere must suffer by its loss, he pours out his grievances against Pitt in an almost incoherent burst of feeling. The dashes and the underlined words show how excitedly he wrote:—

"My dear Frere,

". . . Was it in that, or in any previous or subsequent letter, for instance, that I told you that I considered my

* Lord Hawkesbury. .

intercourse with P. as closed for ever? I did so consider it for some time. His conduct towards me was neither what *I* had a right to expect from *him* nor what any one man would have had a right to expect from another under similar circumstances. Confidence, just enough to mislead, and not enough to guide; enough, and more than enough, to make one feel one's self a party to all that he did, and bound therefore in common honour to share in all the consequence of it, but stopping short of the point at which one might have begun to see that he had an intention of separating himself from those who ought naturally to be his followers; complete and unreserved sacrifice of me to A.—not (I am willing to believe) because he loved me less, but yet on what other principle [am I] to account for it?—a want of determination (I firmly believe) when he *began* to act, how far he should go, or what line he should take, but a hesitation to own that he was so undetermined; and *then* a zeal, not originally felt by him, but which kindled as he went on, for the real, as well as ostensible, support of his new creation, which, never having in the outset *attempted* to inspire me with it, he yet pretended to think it strange I did not catch—like others (who, God knows, caught it readily enough, and inflamed by it, devoted themselves to continuance in office); a want of candour, which I have never met with in him before, in discussing retrospectively the motives upon which he acted, or might allow it to be possible for others to act, and a stubborn self-satisfaction in the consciousness that, whatever I might think or feel, I could never easily make my case good to others, but should be obliged to acquiesce ultimately in the broad, general, and in respect to me utterly *false* description of having acted, singly, against his known wishes,—the rest—the how and why—being, as he knew, between ourselves only; if I could forget and forgive, *well*;—but it must be upon the condition of his not being called upon to own that there was any thing to be forgiven;—if I resented lastingly, *well* too; for then—— In short I filled up this conclusion for him in the way most calculated to justify me in the belief, and in the resolution, that our intercourse was closed for ever.

"Such are the rough features of his conduct towards me; and such the motives, or the excuses, or the aggravating circumstances which I attributed, and in great part do still attribute to it. But yet my heart is a little softened towards him. I have long been acting, as if it was so; long before I felt any compunctious visitings of kindness.

"I acted then because I had a pride and a pleasure in exhausting all the sacrifices that I could make for him, in adding to those of office, of ambition, of hopes and prospects, which he did not chuse to take to himself, the more acceptable offerings of all the prejudices, and dislikes, proud, resentful, or jealous feelings as he would call them—all the natural and justifiable manly and consistent judgment of others, and estimation of one's self, as I think them, which, indulged to their full extent, would have made a cordial reconciliation between A. and me impossible. This sacrifice I did make; *how*, you would have known in detail, if my long letter and its enclosures had reached you. You would have known too in equal detail how this sacrifice had been met on the part of him who was the subject of it. All this it is not now worth while to describe minutely, but it is but just to A. to say that his behaviour throughout was fair, mild, and conciliating—much beyond what *I* could have adopted towards any person in such circumstances

—but then such is his behaviour to every body, friend or foe, and I therefore take it as no particular merit to myself, and ascribe it to him only in justice, not in praise. So it is, however; what after the correspondence which you have seen, you would not readily believe, we are excellent good friends, A. and I—so much so, in *his* estimation, that I happen to know that the other day it was used as a topic of persuasion to a friend of mine—(I do not like to mention names in a letter which is so very likely to fall into other hands than your's)—whom a common friend of *his* and A['s] wished to induce to take office, that there could be no objection on my account, for that A. considered me as perfectly kind and cordial towards him.

"The utmost feeling of good-nature towards P. with which I agreed to do my part towards producing and evincing these amicable dispositions, was a sort of sullen gratification that I had in doing everything that he could desire in return for his having done by me so little that was either for my comfort or my interest. This arrangement made, however, took away something from the awkwardness and embarrassment of our meeting, and I would not meet him without having brought to my remembrance so much of former kindness, and undoubted good disposition, as, without in the least degree altering my opinion of his recent conduct, to incline me very much to think that I ought not to be extreme in judging it, that I ought to make allowance for the hurry and agitation in which he acted at that time—(and yet this hurry and agitation did not prevent his doing scrupulously and magnanimously *right* by everybody *but* me)—and that I should forgive in fact—not in words; (to forget would be foolish, if it were possible).

"We, therefore, parted perfectly on our old footing, and I expect him here.

"If you could have known how sick I am of this whole subject, if you knew the pains which I bestowed upon the full and circumstantial history of it, in all its parts and progress, which I sent to you eight weeks ago, and could appreciate the degree of nausea I feel in skimming it over a second time, you really would feel obliged to me for having so far complied with your injunctions.

"Here I must rest for the present.

"J. sends her love, and begs you not to forget the Orange Trees.

"Adieu."

It is evident from this letter that Canning's heart was yearning after his old chief, and that, although he would not himself find excuses for Pitt, he was anxious that Frere should find them. In the mean time, Portugal had succumbed to France, and signed a treaty by which she renounced her alliance with England, and closed her ports against English ships. This was good news for Canning for two reasons : it opened a prospect of Frere's speedy return, and it gave him a triumph over Pitt. In a letter of July 24th he speaks in quite charitable terms of "Poor P.," who "has been dreaming away about Peace and had really convinced himself that we were to have it before midsummer." "It is very extraordinary that all his own experience should have taught him no better, but he certainly did believe that a determined disposition to peace on *one* side only would bring it about in spite of Bonaparte. I apprehend he is undeceived by this time," writes Canning complacently.

Before he dispatched his next letter, intelligence was received of the loss of another Lisbon packet with one, if not two, of his letters on board. This, and the certainty that the Portuguese peace had done nothing to hasten Frere's return, reduced Canning to the depths of despair. He has no heart to write another long letter; if Frere wishes for information on any point he must ask questions and repeat them till they are answered. "I have scarcely any pleasure in writing, and know not how to trust to so precarious a conveyance anything that it would be at all interesting for you to read. . . . If you have received none of my Letters, I cannot help it. I write and send them—and can do no more. I scold here as if it were *your* fault—which I know it is not. But it is surely strange that the correspondence with our Minister at such a place as Lisbon should be suffered to remain on a footing more uncertain than the penny post."

The next letter contains little but a reiterated demand for the orange trees, some of which were designed as a present for Lady Jane Dundas, the best being reserved for Mrs. Canning. It took many letters to stir Frere to the point of getting them, but they did arrive at last, and gave satisfaction. Canning was settling down to the life of a country gentleman, and trying to persuade himself that he liked it. A man that reached maturity without knowing that tadpoles turned into frogs until he was enlightened by Frere (who instructed his nephew "not to tell *that* story of Canning to the first fool he met") was not likely to be successful with agricultural pursuits. On August 17th he gives a humorous account of his difficulties. Mr. Borrowes was the man of business who transacted affairs for the various members of the Canning family. "Boo" is nowhere else mentioned in the letters to Frere:—

"I am in the midst of my harvest, and of sundry calculations connected with It, by which I have the satisfaction of proving to myself that I shall lose about £100 a year annually by my farm (supposing It to prosper as It is now doing with every help of fine weather and high prices) in addition to the interest of the purchase money. This is a cheering result. But as Boo's Mama said of *his* loss by his two political Pamphlets, it is better than throwing away one's money, as other idle young men do, in worse pursuits. And as I have never yet made by anything (except by two old diamond snuff-boxes which I sold—or got my friend Borrowes to sell for me to a Jew the week before I left Town for £300—Guineas I should say, I beg the Jew's pardon) I am the less at a loss how to bear my present prospect of success in farming. I hope you find Foreign Ministering a more profitable trade. If not otherwise you can get the government here to accede to the French and Spanish Treaty, and then you will get a snuff-box, and Borrowes shall recommend you a Jew. Or, if you chuse to retire after the war, (which however and without joking I hope you will never think of doing) you might come and take a tight little Farm House that I have to let here with 20 acres of ground about it, and so lose your proportion of my £100 loss yearly.

"Then we might go together to moralize over Sir W. Trumball's * monument, who, you know, retired to this Parish from the Secretaryship of State—and after many foreign missions—and 'enjoyed the liberty he loved,' as Pope very foolishly sings of him. But do not retire. I

---

* Sir W. Trumball, Secretary of State to William III., and the friend of Pope, who dedicated his First Pastoral to him, and alludes to him in his " Windsor Forest." The quotation is from the epitaph by Pope.

am very serious. Retirement is well enough at 64 (which I think was Trumball's age) but at your's and mine, it is rather to be *borne*, if it *must* come, than sought or continued if you can avoid it. *I own* this to you—and yet I know nobody who has more to make them happy, or who *is* more happy and more thankful for the means of happiness within their power than I ought to be, and than I *am*. But the thought will obtrude itself now and then, that I am not where I should be—*non hoc pollicitus*. I dismiss this and such-like reflections as well as I can."

Although every-day happiness in a quiet country home was not of itself enough for Canning, he was passionately devoted to wife and child. He received a long string of questions from Frere, some of which had reference to the political situation ; but when next he wrote from " South Hill *Park*—not *Farm*, nor *Grove*, still less *Place* to which It has no analogy," he only cared to answer those relating to his little boy :—

" My little boy's name is George Charles, but he drops his Charles as you do your Hookham, never signing it but to dispatches, nor allowing it to be printed except in the red book. He came by it, by having the Prss. for his Godmother. By rights he ought to have been Charles— and Charles alone—that being the male name answering to Caroline. But the Prss. knew that Joan was very desirous that he should bear my name, and she therefore very good-naturedly commanded that he should be called George—and Charles I added for her sake. If my second lost Letter had reached you, it would have told you all about the Christening—how Leigh officiated with Mrs. Leigh and Aunt Fanny to support him, not as Godmothers, for a boy has but one, but as being my nearest She-Relations, commanded by the Prss. to their no small contentment to be present at the ceremony. Dundas and Lord Titchfield were the God-fathers. Dundas was present, Ld. T. was not, but Sneyd was there to represent him, and Pitt was allowed to come to answer to Aunt Fanny. If you had been to be had, you would have filled up my number. And I cannot tell you how much I should have liked your being there. You would have found Pitt and Leigh as capable of being brought into collision at dinner that day as they were, some ten months before, at your grand dinner on the day of my marriage ; but the Prss. being by, and understanding P. as well as she does, and Sneyd helping her to a just understanding of Leigh, the effect was much more happy. It is very extraordinary—but P. with all that he has done, and thought, and seen, is such pure nature, that Leigh is himself scarcely more an *ingénue* than he. (You see I feel kindly enough about him still—but notwithstanding all your magnanimous forgiveness I must feel that he used me most unfairly.—I have really forgiven him too, but as to putting myself in his power again—I shall be not a little cautious.)

"But to return to my Boy. You ask me the Nurse's opinion of him. I should be sorry to mislead you, and I therefore hold it a point of conscience not to detail to you the excessive and perhaps exaggerated expressions of admiration which I hear every day from both his nurses. . . . I should not think I was dealing fairly with you if I did so. His mother too is naturally partial to him in a degree which may perhaps inflame her good opinion of him. But to give you a cool and candid and considered opinion of him myself, I do honestly think that he is one of the finest boys, if not the very finest, that ever was seen : plump, goodhumoured, lively, full of health and vigour and spirits—having blue eyes, which I am assured are to turn to the exact colour of mine and Joan's—having been inoculated with the Cow Pox, when he was but three weeks old, and having had the disease very favourably, and being now busy in teething as fast as he can ; a surprising child, in short ; and promising, for his years— or weeks rather, beyond what it would be prudent for me to announce to a world naturally bent upon depreciating extraordinary merit.

" To conclude his history—the Fairy his Godmother is coming to South Hill this week to see him.   Joan is at this moment bustling about the new Chintz Bed which is put up in the Bow Bedroom for her, and which Mr. Smith, the Windsor upholsterer, has sent home all wrong-done-up —never was anything like the blunders which that Up-holsterer has fallen into on this occasion.   It would be tedious to particularise them, all—suffice it to say the Bed does not at all answer the expectations formed of it, and if the Prss. condescends to sleep soundly in it, it must be more from her own goodness than the bed's desert."

The Princess was, of course, Caroline of Brunswick, Princess of Wales.   It was probably Canning's intimacy with Lord Malmesbury—one of the few reliable friends that she possessed—that brought him into the little circle that visited the Princess at Blackheath, were invited to her informal dinner parties, and took part in the merry games of romps which generally concluded the evening. As we shall see, his life was clouded by the tragedy of her's.

Mrs. Canning must have succeeded in making her guests forget the shortcomings of the Windsor upholsterer, for there is a letter from Sneyd in which he assures Frere that " South Hill is in every respect the most comfortable house you can imagine, resembling *—in this one particular, I fancy, only, that it is a place where 'a Man may stay some time at.'" The *ménage* must have been expensive if one may trust the report of that delightful gossip, old John Frere, who writes thus to his son on November 25th, 1801 :—"When I was dining at Leigh's the other day, a very fine gentleman called for commands to Mr. Canning's. I learned afterwards that he was going down as Cook, at £100 salary. I am afraid our friend will forget his diminution of income by the loss of his place, and mis-calculate his expenses, for he has no more notion of the value of money than when he was an Eton school-boy." Of economizing and saving for himself, Canning had certainly no idea. The small pension to which he was entitled on his retirement from office was at once secured by him to his mother, and at the time of his death his effects, sworn under £20,000, amounted to about £5,000 or £6,000.

In the autumn of 1801, strenuous efforts were made to bring Canning into the ministry. For a time he seemed to yield, wrought upon by the desire to be once more in the midst of the strife. But, spoiled by too much success in early youth, he could not bide his leader's time, and he could not obey a man whom he rightly esteemed in every way his inferior. The scheme was defeated, as he wrote to Frere in a letter that exhibits at once his best and his worst characteristics—his steadfast loyalty to his friends, and his obstinate perversity and domineering temper :—

"SOUTH HILL,
"*Sept.* 30, 1801.

". . . I remember writing to you once, while I was endeavouring to make up my mind to comply with P.'s

---

* Word illegible.

wishes, and had actually got so far as to bring myself to believe that I could not bear being out of office much longer. This was a false fictitious feeling, which P.'s representations, and my own interest and anxious meditations upon them had generated—but which upon sober reflection, passed away again, and left me in a condition to determine, as the enclosed letter will show you. . . . I would rather be let alone—for a time at least—than have any offer made me. I could not now take any office with comfort—nor I think with credit—anything but responsible office neither now nor ever.

"You will easily conceive how much I must have wanted you, during the struggle that I have had with myself and with others upon this occasion. Your letter came, not opportunely—with its recommendation of poor P. to forgiveness and reconcilement. I do love him, and reverence him as I should a Father—but a father should not sacrifice me, with my good will. Most heartily I forgive him. But he has to answer to himself, and to the country for much mischief that he has done, and much that is still to do. I cannot help this—but I can help bearing a hand in it, and I will. I have an answer from him to the enclosed—the most kind, and in every respect, the most satisfactory imaginable. . . .

"Leveson is the person with whom I have consulted most upon this business. He is strenuous in approving my determination. Next to him I have talked with Scroggs, who is entitled to be consulted with by me on such points, by having refused to take the Under Secry. in the Home Office, when it was offered him at the time of the change, against my remonstrance—but almost solely, I believe, on my account. He too approves. And both approve very disinterestedly—for I had stipulated that if the discussion should end otherwise, offer should be made to *both of them* .at the same time with me and P. had undertaken for the performance of this stipulation—L. perhaps would not have accepted—S. probably would—and he *ought* still, and I *hope* will, and if I can make him, *shall* accept any offer (A. is very likely to make him one) that is creditable and advantageous to himself."

The negotiations for peace continued, and at last the preliminaries were settled, and signed on October 1st. We restored to France, Spain and Holland all the colonies or islands occupied or conquered by us in the course of the war, with the exception of Trinidad and Ceylon. Malta was restored to the Knights of St. John, and Egypt to the Sublime Porte. The prisoners made on each were to be restored without ransom, after the plenipotentiaries had concluded the definitive treaty at Amiens.

Lord Stanhope quotes a saying which he attributes to " the author of Junius," which exactly describes the situation. " It is a peace which every body is glad of, though nobody is proud of." The relief to all classes in England was considerable. When General Lauriston, the First Consul's A.D.C., arrived at St. James's with the ratification of the Preliminary Articles, he was dragged in triumph through the streets with loud cheers, by the mob. London and some other towns were illuminated, as a sign of the universal rejoicing.

Canning, Lord Grenville, and a few others, did not share the general satisfaction. They could only see shame and humiliation in a treaty by which we made such concessions.

" Upon this subject of the Preliminaries, I will not enter till I can write more at large. GOD forgive P. for the hand he has has had in them ! You will read in the Newspapers (in Porcupine* I hope) of the drawing of Bonaparte's Aide-de-camp through the streets of London. I envy you your absence from the scene of such disgrace to the Country. For my own part, I am sick of all that has happened, or is likely to happen, as far as I can foresee—and if I can have my own way, I will not stir from South Hill this winter. But more of this, when I write next. To-day I am going to see Ld. Grenville. It is a comfort to talk with any person—who is not absolutely infatuated—what a comfort it would be, if I were in a situation to act with such. But I am not—at least till a new Parliament . . .

" The Prss. was here for two days, very quietly and comfortably—nobody with her but Mrs. Vernon—and we had nobody to meet her—for I had relied on P. and he did not come. There was nobody else I liked to ask—or who would have been natural in her society.

" My little boy grows and improves wonderfully. He is really much the nicest little boy that ever was seen.

" Shall you not come and see him, do you think, this winter? Between her two peaces, one that she made for herself, and one that Hawkesbury has made for her, I should think that Portugal might let you away for a month or two, and yet have you back by the time that she is called upon to purchase a third."

Before Canning wrote again, the aspect of affairs had changed a little. In spite of its humiliating concessions, the peace had been received throughout the whole of the United Kingdom with the most unbounded joy and gratitude; and in spite of the contempt with which Addington (according to Canning) was regarded in the City and the House of Commons, his administration seemed to be gaining strength. Members of the old Opposition were

* Cobbet's organ, so styled from his pseudonym of "Peter Porcupine."

gradually joining his party, and there was a talk of such influential men as Tierney and Grey being bribed into supporting him. Under these circumstances, Canning intended to resign his seat in Parliament which he owed to Pitt, to stand for an independent constituency, and to take his own line in the new Parliament. He wrote a letter of four sheets to Frere on November 7th, describing his intentions. It would be amusing to read the assurances of steadiness and temperate conduct, were it not for the thought that in breaking them, Canning ruined his whole career.

"I need not say to you that the idea of the possibility of being entirely separated from P.—of taking part on a different side from him in the H. of C. is very painful to me. But surely the situation in which he places me is cruelly unfair. Determined, he assures me, never again to take a leading part in public life himself, and devoting himself to the support of a man, of whom I know he must, and does think as I do, that he is utterly unfit to fill the station in which he is placed—has he a right (indeed he does not pretend to it) or am I, in the most refined construction of what I owe to him, bound,—to consider my allegiance as bound up in his, and necessarily transferable with it ?—to consider myself as obliged to give my support to measures, not *his*, not in all cases which he approves, but which, even disapproving, he thinks it right to support the man who proposes them,—because he has said he would—because the Man relied on his promise,—and because he is magnanimously resolved to keep his word, cost him what it may in character and consistency. Am I bound to this though he may chuse to continue to think himself so,—even after the pretext on which A.'s government, feeble and foolish though it is, was represented originally as entitled to the support of all right-thinkers and well-disposed —the keeping out Opposition—is not only done away—but done away by A.'s own act—and those very men whom he was put in to exclude, and whose exclusion was the ground on which support was claimed for him, are taken to his bosom—when peace has been already made in their spirit—and when they (as may probably be soon the case) and not *he*, are the most efficient and ostensible Members of Govt. in the House of Commons? . . .

" I will not become factious if I can help it—I really have no inclination to it—and I do believe I shall be able to guard myself against any seductions, either of ill company, or of tempting opportunity : but I believe too, at least I very much hope that a temperate and mitigated Opposition in Parliament, in which one should judge and act fairly upon *measures* as they arose, contending, however, uniformly all the while and upon every occasion that the *Man* was utterly the fool he is, and that it is mischief and madness to trust the Country in his hands—might do a great deal of good, and presents a highly respectable line of Conduct, not to say a very amusing one—for the opposition to a fool, *quætenus* fool, would be a new, and hitherto unexhausted ground."

So, in mere gaiety of heart, and thinking that it would be " very amusing "—as he had thought, no doubt, of school-boy pranks at Eton, of boyish escapades at Christchurch, and of the wildest vagaries of the *Anti-Jacobin*, did Canning prepare to sow the crop that he was to reap throughout his life in the estrangement of old friends, the undying rancour of enemies, and the surly distrust of the general public. "The character for honesty and well-meaningness and so forth," which by Canning's own admission no one denied to Addington, was, after all, a more valuable possession than all his own brilliant talents. It appealed to the mass of dull respectability which constitutes the majority of Englishmen, as Canning's impassioned eloquence and dazzling wit could never succeed in doing.

Pitt might still regard the young man as his political heir, but Canning had practically disinherited himself for life when he entered upon the campaign against Addington.

CHAPTER IV.

CANNING, PITT, AND ADDINGTON.

1801·—1806.

AT the end of the year 1801 Pitt must have had enough
to harass him without the fresh sources of irritation
which Canning was about to open. Besides the state of
his health, there were his affairs, which had long been
in much embarrassment, and he was forced in the end
to accept a loan from some personal friends, and to sell
Holwood, where as a boy he had gone birdsnesting. He
was in no condition to restrain Canning, and after an
attempt in September to induce him to support Addington,
he left his irrepressible follower to go his own way, first
sending him a letter, a copy of which in Mrs. Canning's
writing, is at Roydon. " It is a satisfaction to me to think
that in attempting to do good, I have at least not done
any harm," writes the overwearied statesman. "At all
Events be assured that tho' for your sake as well as my
own I regret your determination, It can make no variation
in my Sentiments of Friendship or Affection towards you,
or in my Solicitude for whatever may best unite your
Fame and Happiness with the Public Interest."

In November Canning was called up to town by the
threat of a motion by Sir Francis Burdett for inquiry into
the conduct of the war. There he met Pitt, and flattered

himself that he began to see signs of a coldness between him and Addington.   Tierney was joining the new ministry, and Canning looked forward to quarrels between him and Pitt on questions of finance.

" SOUTH HILL,
" Nov. 21st, 1801.

" . . . A. is endeavouring (as in my last letter I told you he would) to strengthen himself as fast as possible, independently of P. Sheep as he is, he is calling in the Wolves to his assistance. . . . Tierney's business is notorious, and so far P. sanctioned it long ago, as to agree that it would be prudent to buy him off; but I am persuaded he had then no notion of their bringing him in *at home*, but looked to his going to the East Indies— which at first A. looked to, also, and which T. himself very prudently pretended to be ready to accept, until the negotiation had gone too far to be broken off—and then he suddenly bethought himself of—what do you think ? *an aged mother*, whom he should perhaps never see again, if he were now to leave the Country.   And with this plea A. was dolt enough to be satisfied—and so Tierney is to be his bully in the House of C. . . .

" I am to see P. again on Monday or Tuesday—when I go to Town in order to dine at Blackheath—and he has promised to come here as soon as the Session of Parlt. is over.   Bad as the Peace is (and it is worse than my most sanguine confidence in A.'s baseness and Jenksbury's diplomacy anticipated), I am consoled for it by the one consideration that, being once made, it removes the only subject of strong practical difference of opinion between P. and me.   As to all that must follow, of large peace establishment, of active vigilance, of jealous preparation, his opinion is as determined as mine.   He tells me that

A. thinks as he does.   But I do not much believe it—or at least that he will long continue to think so.   If not— *Then* . . . ."

Part of the letter is taken up with Frere's affairs.   Frere had talked of asking leave to come home, and Canning, although longing for his presence and sympathy, was obliged to dissuade him from the idea.   " You could not live much with me without exciting suspicion and giving room for numberless misrepresentations and falsehoods, of which the most impudent and malignant are daily fabricated, and willingly credited by the Addingtonians. You *could* not *conceal* your opinion upon the Peace—and you could not give it, not only without offending your employers, but without separating yourself from P. . . . You will not suppose that I do not wish you here.   But I should act very unfairly by you if I were therefore to conceal from you my firm persuasion how much better you are where you are."

At the end of the year, Frere received the offer of being transferred to Madrid, which at first he was anxious to decline.   He preferred Lisbon as a residence, and had no wish to lay himself under the shadow of an obligation to the new ministry.   Canning discussed the matter on December 20th, in a letter of three sheets, with that mixture of absurdity and seriousness characteristic of himself, and came to the conclusion that " if you go to Madrid, you must make it appear, you must *record* it, (which a private or separate Letter to Mr. Secretary Hammond *on office paper* would do), as a sacrifice of your own comfort (if you feel it so), and at least as a thing that you do not desire—that you had rather had passed from you—but that you will take if it be any accommodation to the King's service."   Frere did accept the appointment, but he was not transferred to Madrid for nearly a year.

There is a gap of a couple of months in the correspondence. From another source—Mrs. Frere's letters to her son—we learn that it was occasioned by the alarming illness of Mrs. Canning. Her husband sat up with her at night, and grew thin with anxiety and watching. When Canning wrote on February 15th, 1802, she was able to leave her room, and he could turn his mind once more to his schemes for annoying " the Doctor," as Addington was now universally nicknamed.

" . . . I am agoing to make a motion. A. proposes to sell the lands in St. Vincent's and Trinidad. I propose that he shall not—at least without limitations and restrictions, such as will prevent the increase of Slave Trade and so make his sale unproductive. Slave Trade, you know, is a subject which has nothing of party politicks in it. It was therefore free to me to take it up. And Pitt *must be with me*. Indeed, he *is* so. I showed him my plan when he was here (he was here for a couple of days the week before last), and he approved it. Not but that he is sorry that I have such a handle to plague A. And not but what A. is just as mad with me as if it were a hostile question, and so considers it. But that I cannot help. I am all meekness and disclaim hostility. . . .

" While I was in London last week, I happened to go into the House on the night of a debate on the Army Extraordinaries. You will have read it in the newspapers. Tierney, you see, abused Pitt without reserve, and praised A. at P.'s expence—for an act which *not* A. but P. had done (the sending a commission to the West Indies—but no matter what). A. said not a word, till little Scroggs got up and in the genteelest manner imaginable set Tierney right. A. then rose and admitted that P. had the merit of the transaction, but it had *slipped his memory*. O ! how I enjoyed this, and how I did write about ·it to Pitt, who is at Walmer, the next morning !—not violently—not a bit —do not imagine it—simply a narrative of what I had heard pass, and almost without comment."

Canning then explains why he had not taken upon himself to defend Pitt—the reasons being, that his enemies would have seized upon the opportunity of persuading Pitt that he had taken the matter up intemperately. "As a spectator they dreaded me more, and hated me quite as much—if I had taken part, they could have misrepresented me. Now they know I have to represent them." He adds, characteristically, "Not but that, with all these wise reasons for holding my tongue, I should have found it utterly impossible to restrain myself, had not William Dundas said quite enough to make the incompatibility of Tierney's and Pitt's continued support to the same administration quite evident."

Where were all the wise resolutions not to be factious, not to be led away into reckless provocation ? They were broken at the outset—as was that promise not to laugh at Addington's ministry, which Pitt exacted at the time of his retirement. When Canning next wrote to Frere, about two hours after dinner, on the evening of Sunday, March 7th, "Joan" was busy at the opposite side of the table by the drawing-room fire, copying out various manuscripts that were to disturb "the Doctor's" peace. One of these was in verse, and had its origin in the following circumstance :—

" In one of the speeches which the Dr. made upon the repeated adjournments at Christmas, he declared that he had long *doubted* whether to adjourn or no—but that with him 'to doubt was to decide.' 'What a d—d decided fellow this is,' says Leveson in a letter to me soon after, 'he is always doubting.' On this hint I wrote—the stanzas are a defence of the Doctor's dictum."

The poem is among the other papers; it is ,not particularly amusing, and the last of the six stanzas will give a sufficient idea of the style :

> " If Pitt would hear his Country's voice,
>   Say, wouldst *thou* point thy Sovereign's choice
>   To worth and talents tried ?
>   Shake not thy empty head at me,
>   Thy modest doubts too plain I see ;—
>   To doubt is to decide."

Pitt, unfortunately for Canning's hopes, was not going to pick a quarrel with Addington :—

" I was not disappointed (though provoked), when I found, upon his coming here last week, that he had 'had an explanation that was perfectly satisfactory,'—in short, that, not choosing to resent the insult and treachery as they deserved, he had agreed to take the best apology that could be trumped up for him, and to think—or say he thinks—no more of it. I did not attempt to combat this magnanimous resolution. I only laughed, and said it *was* magnanimous, and bepraised and befooled it."

Canning then discusses the prospects of peace, which were doubtful. " If the Peace is concluded, it cannot last six months (even supposing three of them to be occupied with the bustle of a general Election), unless Bonaparte changes his system—which is not very likely—or is overthrown, which would be too provoking a piece of good

luck for this wretched, pusillanimous, toadeating administration. . . . I shall for ever thank God that I had no
hand or thought, no privity or concurrence, no share
whatever, art or part, in a transaction of such eternal
disgrace and infamy.

"It cannot last; and but that one must not be too
sanguine, as I said before, I should even now be antici-
pating in my own mind the triumph of no distant day,
when the miserable and insulting experiment of governing
without talents (for such is the history of this last year's
vagary in this country) should be brought to a shameful
end, and the Asses who have been made the subject of
it, turned out to derision and brickbats. But one must
not be too sanguine.

"I have stated these wishes to P. more than once in
language not more picked and guarded.. 'His Honour'
smiles. He will not own it, but he must be weary of the
world as it is.

"We talked last time he was here (Friday sennight) upon
this subject. He prophecyed my opposition, but 'let me
hope' (said he) 'that it will be a *liberal* opposition, not
savage and personal.' 'Why,' said I (which is very true,
I think), 'it is not a case that admits of what I suppose
you mean by a *liberal* opposition. I consider the Dr.'s
occupation of the Govt. as a usurpation of the vilest kind.
When of two men or two parties, who have tolerably equal
pretensions to be Ministers—you and Fox, Walpole and
Pulteney, and so forth—one is opposed to the other, each
must and will respect the talents of his opponent, and may
spare his person while he combats his principles. But
where was it in ancient history that, while two great parties
were contending for the mastery, the slaves rose and possessed themselves of the citadel? Both parties joined (did
they not?), and first put the slaves to death, or scourged

them soundly, and then betook themselves to the discussion of their quarrel. So is the Doctor's elevation and that of his colleagues a conspiracy against all the talents, of all sides, and sorts. The opposition to him must be an opposition of contempt and derision, of the whip rather than the sword.' He was very angry—but not very angry neither.

"But this is all prospective. It belongs to a new Parlt. For the present I have nothing to do but to hold my tongue—like Thady—and smoke my pipe and say nothing.

"Not but even now, though I must not goad and pelt the Dr., as I could wish, I am enabled just to put a thistle under his tail, and P. must aid and abet me. This Slave Trade—Trinidad—Question is delightful. He writhes and kicks under it, every time that it is renewed by a little hint or enquiry, in the most amusing and preposterous manner. . . .

"And, truth to say, though to plague the Dr. is something, it is not that only that instigates me—for *I do* feel (you know I do) a conscientious conviction and duty upon the question of the Slave Trade, which has pushed me sometimes almost to extremities with P. himself (about the cultivation of Demerara, Surinam, etc.).* The Devil himself should not persuade me to be more forbearing with the Dr."

That Canning really took a deep interest in the abolition of slavery has already been shown. In spite of the epithets so freely bestowed on Addington and his party, the spirit in which he set out to torment them is so like that of a mischievous, irresponsible schoolboy, that it is difficult to regard the question seriously. He rushed up to town to obtain documents, and there met the elder Mr. Frere,

* See chapter III.

who gave him advice—of which he stood much in need—
concerning the management of his crops at South Hill.

At the beginning of April Canning and his wife were
at Claremount with the Charles Ellises. Mrs. Ellis was
already sinking into the decline which soon ended her life,
but the whole party were spending the time " very comfortably, and liking each other and our wives and children
respectively very much." The Definitive Treaty had
arrived in England, but the orange trees had not, much to
Canning's disappointment. By this time it was settled that
Frere should go to Madrid, and on the whole Canning
approved of the change.

" Hammond writes to you by this packet, and will tell
you how graciously the King expressed his approbation of
your appointment, and of his own accord suggested that
your brother should go with you. This is very flattering—
and solidly useful, as it gives you an existence independent
of the favour of Ministers. Anti-gallicanism is fortunately
your nature, and it is one of the surest claims upon his
good liking. Cherish, and do not hide it—you can easily
let it shine through your despatches—though I suppose you
must not let it influence your conduct. . . .

" I have been in Town, but have but just *seen* Pitt, this
week. He is lost. I know nothing that can bring back
his importance, and the desideration of him in the country,
except a new war—and that I take for granted we shall
submit to all sorts of injuries and resort to all sorts of
baseness to avoid, and with his full countenance and
encouragement. You will ask what has worked this
change? The Loan and Budget. The Loan the most
fortunate that ever was made—the Budget a [very well
conceived one (as it strikes me), but certainly a very
popular one from the single circumstance of the repeal of

the Income Tax. That the materials of the Budget are in fact Pitt's, no one doubts—and you will not. But A. worked them up himself—or rather Vansittart did—and his (A.'s) friends know this and say it—so that the effect of Pitt's assistance to the degree to which he has availed himself of it, is to pledge P. to the support of everything and to diminish at the same time the notion of the absolute necessity of his constant superintendence of A.'s measures. The præstigia of finance-business are dissolved. What A. has been able to do, no man need despair of doing. Pitt at the head of the Treasury is no longer essential to the salvation of the country. He has been resolutely working his own ruin—and I really believe he has at length effected it. I have some slight notion too that he feels it—A. has used him like a dog. The manner in which he gave up the income tax in the midst of a clamour raised against it and its authors, as if it were the most vicious in its original principle, the most oppressive and so forth of all the taxes ever invented, was so evidently calculated to make Pitt odious (if not intended to have that effect) that it is quite impossible that P. should have not been sorely wounded by it. I am persuaded he was so. But the way to help himself? His situation is indeed truly pitiable and embarrassing. I doubt if he has one friend left, who thinks precisely with him, both upon public subjects, and upon what ought to be his personal conduct—certainly among those with whom he was in the habit of communicating not more than one—if Long be that one—as I rather suspect he is. Those whom he put into office or forced to remain there, I do not count. They of course are for his supporting them—and thinking of nothing and nobody besides. They are jealous of his intercourse with any of his friends out of office, with Ld. Grenville, with Dundas, with me—and I have little doubt show their suspicions

in a way that makes him uncomfortable.   I believe he so
far differs with them, and so far only, as that he will not
give us up entirely.   But I can see by his shirking air (you
know it) when they have been endeavouring to make an
impression on him.   On the other hand, Rose—the Bp.
of Lincoln * and I—perhaps too Ld. Carrington—I know
not whether any others—point out to him occasionally the
scurvy treatment which he meets with from the doctor—
and certainly have no reason to complain of his want of
sensibility to the many instances of it, which have taken
place of late.   But 'as a child when scaring sounds assail,'
he seems resolved to stick to them the closer—and though
he admits our premises, resists all our conclusions.   Lord
Grenville, and I believe Dundas, differ from him about the
peace, which he of course means to support, and pretends
to approve—even Malta !   Long is the only one that I
know, who does not declare a difference of opinion on
one or other point.   And there are who suspect that he
labours hard to counteract all attempts to separate P. from
A. and even that he (Long) is in good time to become
connected with A.'s administration. . . . For my own part,
I begin to grow sick of the struggle, and if it were not
for my Trinidad motion (which I will not abandon, both
because I am engaged to it, and because I sincerely think
I may do good) I should be glad to retire for good and all
till the new Parliament—and sulk at South Hill without
seeing P.'s face, or exchanging a line with him again."

The orange-trees arrived safely and in good condition
on April 25th, as Canning gratefully acknowledges in a
letter to the elder Mr. Frere.   At the conclusion he earnestly
deprecates the idea of J. H. Frere's coming home.   " He is
better—even at Lisbon, in prison with the British Captains

* Pitt's old tutor, George Pretyman [Dr. Tomline].

of men of war, or in Lannes' antichamber than here." The postscript is curious. M. Otto had been originally sent over by the First Consul as agent for the exchange of prisoners. One feels how gladly Canning would have incited the mob to break his windows had there been a fitting opportunity :—

" I understood a few days ago from very good authority, that M. Otto in the Illuminations (for which you are probably at this moment preparing to bring your candle from under your bushel) proposed to exhibit his G.R. *without a Crown* over them—not to spare his lamps, you may be sure. If you happened to have a friend in the Mob to whom you could recommend a particular notice of this circumstance, you might do some service."

On the same day (April 26th) Canning wrote to J. H. Frere, enclosing a copy of verses :—

" You must not read them till you know the occasion for which they are prepared. They are for singing (not by myself, but by Dignam or some of those fellows) at the London Tavern, at a great Dinner on Pitt's Birthday, the origin and purpose of which is as follows. The day after Burdett's motion, it occurred to some Country Gentlemen —namely, to Mildmay and Buxton—that it would be a proper testimony of regard to P. to have a public dinner on his Birthday—why not on his, as Fox's friends do on Fox's? Mildmay mentioned the thing to me, before it had gone any further. It struck me as being capable of being turned to great account, and the better if it were made to *originate* in the City. I accordingly wrote to Borrowes, to set it agoing without naming me as having suggested it. It took ' like wildfire,' as Borrowes tells me ; and presently ten or a dozen of the greatest names in the

City—Thorntons, Raikes, etc.—were down as Stewards—the great Room at the London Tavern bespoken—and every prospect of an immense attendance. In the mean time the best people of the H. of Commons have been spoken to, and almost uniformly come into the plan with great eagerness.

"I think you will instantly see all the advantages of such a celebration. It brings Pitt forward again, in spite of himself, on ground of his own, distinct from A. It reminds people that the Man to whom, after all, they owe everything—their salvation in the war, if they look back to that, the termination of the war by peace, if they like that, public credit, etc., etc., is out of place, and likely to remain so ;—that the juggle, in the confidence and belief of which they so cheerfully gave their support to A. merely as P.'s substitute, just to make the peace, or to see if it could be made, and in either case to retire immediately and make room again for his principal—that this juggle existed only in their own imagination—that there Addington is for life —like him, or like him not—and that the only way to have P. again is to get A. out again, against his will—and against P.'s professed wish, also, for, depend upon [it] no City personage believes sincerely in the reality of P.'s self-sacrifice and foolish magnanimity. . . .

"Thus much for the City. Amongst Members of Parlt. it will afford a sort of test of who are attached to P., who to A. for *his sake* only—and who for the Dr's own. The Stewards may easily be selected out of those who hold to P. only, and if with a mixture of those who are known to hold the Dr. cheap, at the same time without opposing his Govt., so much the better. The Doctorites will be in an unpleasant dilemma—whether to attend and hear nothing of the Dr. nor his peace—at a public dinner given within six weeks after the Treaty, and within four after the illuminations—than if no such person, or things had existed—or to absent themselves, and thereby draw a broad line of distinction between themselves and Pitt's other friends. . . . . *I* must not be a Steward—not I— nor Ld. Grenville—nor Windham.   But we shall all attend, I hope. . . . .

"As for poor P., he will be all astonishment at the fuss made about himself—and, if he knew how, would think himself bound to try to prevent it—not that in his own secret heart he will so much dislike it, either —not he.   But he *ought* to prevent anything that will embarrass A. and divide *his* friends.   He will think—and perhaps say so—and will try a word or two about the bad taste of a public celebration—but there I *have* him in my power—for he has suffered Dundas for these eight or ten years past to give a public dinner on his (P's) Birthday and has dined at it himself, which here we do not wish him to do.   He may dine, if he will, with the Dr. . . . .

"Criticize and correct the song—and if you will, write another, and send it to me.   It will arrive in time—the Day is the 28 of May.

"P. was here last week on his road into Somersetshire. We were talking over A's 'power and place.'   He said he was now fixed beyond the reach of any assault or machination.   I said 'Yes, you have at last cut your own throat—and I suppose I ought to wish you joy of it— but I cannot.   I still hope, however, that there is enough left of you for your friends to make use of against the Dr. without your consent—and please God, we will try.' He would have had me explain how—but I thought it best to leave him bewildered."

The song was " The Pilot that Weathered the Storm "

—the finest production of Canning's pen, and one of the grandest tributes ever paid by a man of letters to a statesman. The copy (in Canning's own hand) sent out to Frere differs slightly from the version usually printed, the most noticeable alteration being in the last lines :—

> " And O ! if again the rude tempest should rise,
>   The dawnings of peace should fresh darkness deform,
>   While we turn to thy hopeless retirement our eyes,
>   We shall long for the Pilot that weather'd the Storm."

The dinner was a brilliant success, notwithstanding the demurs of such old-fashioned Tories as the elder Mr. Frere, who considered it as " a foolish thing, tending to put Pitt on an equality with Fox." Canning sent a full description of it to Frere in a letter of seven sheets, begun on June 1st and finished on June 7th :—

" . . . I am glad you like the Song. I suppose It may be good as you say so. But it has been received and applauded here (meaning in London, at Merchant Taylors' Hall) with an enthusiasm so much beyond its possible merits, that I was becoming rather ashamed of it —especially as I myself, not aware of my being detected as the Writer, took a very fair share in applauding and (if I am not misinformed) in encoring it, at the dinner. But that is no great matter. The Effect and impression of the Dinner altogether was much more than I could have ventured to expect. As your Father and Hammond were both there, and as they were both writing to you the next day, I need not tell you all that passed—Addington not there—Hawkesbury coming—but retiring to dinner into a private room. Ld. Cornwallis—my Lord of Amiens —retiring at a proper time into a corner of the room that his health might be drunk with the more delicacy, and returning never the better—820 people present, the

flower of every rank and description of persons in London
—the Song *taken* in its true intent and meaning—repeated,
with increased acclamations, and the last verse *called for*
over again—these are, I think, the principal features by
which you may judge of the tone and temper of this
Celebration.

"For its effect (beyond exciting ideas and impressions
favourable to Pitt's return into power) I will not answer.
As to P. himself, that the whole thing goes to his heart,
and that he feels with a deep and quick sense, beyond
what I should have believed him capable of feeling, the
testimonies of public and private attachment, I know.
But that he will stir hand or foot to place himself where
he ought to be, I hardly hope. As to the K(ing) it is
not to be disguised that the effect is very probably to
harden his mind against P. But that is *not* doing mischief. It was sufficiently hardened before, to make P's
recall with entire good will utterly hopeless. And now,
if troublesome times should come, while nothing has been
done by P. to justify the K. in resistance to the choice
of the Nation, enough has been shown of the determination of that choice, to make compliance with it on every
account highly advisable."

Canning then tells the story of the celebrated night
of May 7th, when Lord Belgrave's general Vote of Thanks
to the late Ministry was passed by 222 against 52, in
spite of the resistance of Fox, Tierney, Grey, and others,
and followed by a Vote of Thanks to Mr. Pitt by name.
This, of course, was delightful to Canning, but he had
intended a still greater *coup* :—

"The Plan was originally thus—Belgrave had given
notice of a Motion to thank P., which, upon consultation,

he softened into a general Resolution of approbation to all mankind, 'the Army, Navy, Pulpit, Bar, and Stage' —or according to another formula, by which I intend to illustrate it, 'All the Doctors, both the Proctors, and all the Heads and Principals of Colleges and Halls with their respective Societies.' This I determined should not be,—at least should not be the whole. I determined, if nobody else would, *I* would myself move an amendment to Nicholl's Motion against Pitt (which was to precede Belgrave's) converting individual censure into individual thanks—and this determination I communicated to Lennox, Morpeth, Mildmay, Scroggs and others, desiring them to lay their heads together to devise how such a Motion might be best brought forward—being perfectly willing to give it into any other hands provided it *was* brought forward. They thought, and I agreed, that it *would* be better in the hands of a country gentleman than in those of a friend of Pitt's. Mildmay undertook to move, and Cartwright to second it. So far, all was well. The next thing that I endeavoured to inculcate was, that a most cautious silence should be preserved as to our intended operations, lest the Enemy should change their plans in order to defeat them—especially that no confidence should be made to any of Pitt's friends, who have not taken the line of doing what is best for him, without or against his own consent. . . . . This caution you already anticipate was given in vain. Up to the very day before the Motion was to be made all was snug. And on the very day I went up to Town in the highest hopes and spirits, fully persuaded that we should come upon the House by surprise, and upon Belgrave and his movers, or stillers rather, like a thunderclap—that we should get all the debate upon Pitt personally, and in our own hands —while B.'s motion, relegated to the end of the day, would come limping and languid, and be passed without any animated Debate, as a corollary to ours. All this would inevitably have happened, had our counsel been kept— but unluckily, the night before the Debate, Mildmay fell in with old Rose, and to old Rose disclosed his intentions for the next day. Old Rose is the person of all others who would have been most delighted with the thing if it had succeeded, and would in that case have had no objection to have *owned* that he had known it all along— but really to know it beforehand while it was yet possible that it might fail, was too much for his nerves. He flew to Pitt. P. put in possession of so awkward a confidence had but one thing to do—to set about suppressing it as earnestly as if he really wished it had not been thought of. Rose was employed with Mildmay, and, after I came to Town, with me, for this purpose. I positively refused to interfere, except to urge M. to perseverance. And M. atoned for his indiscretion by his firmness. He positively refused to give the motion up. But the grace, the sur- prize, the effect of the proceeding was ‘cruelly mangled’ and, comparatively speaking, ‘without signs of life.’ Belgrave, forewarned, changed his separate motion into an amendment to Nicholls, and rose with Mildmay. The Speaker called upon B. of course—and there was an end of our fine project—or at least of the first part of it. The rest you know from the newspapers. M. made his motion at the end of the night. Addington endeavoured to get rid of it. I supported it (all this, by the way, you do not know in detail from the newspapers, as it passed after the doors were shut; the same cause pre- vented its being much worth knowing, as there was no use in debating for any extent without a Gallery) and it was at length carried triumphantly, all the world seeing how much in the Dr.’s teeth.”

Another cruel disappointment had been Canning's own Trinidad motion. Addington at first was obstinate, and Canning began to indulge hopes of a debate and a division in which Pitt would be obliged to side against Addington. However, at the last moment, whether warned by Pitt, or convinced of the justice of the case, Addington "veered round and pledged himself body and soul" to all that Canning had asked, "and a great deal more," and left Canning obliged "to take Pitt's advice and close at once with Addington's pledges as if I believed them."

Charles Ellis had sorely disappointed his two uncles, Hervey and Hawkesbury, by voting against the Peace, which "is of course referred to me," observes Canning, resignedly. The remaining four sheets of the letter are taken up with trenchant criticisms of various acquaintances concerning whose behaviour Frere had been asking questions. The first of these is " D "—evidently Dundas. According to Canning, Dundas had forced the measures for Catholic Relief in 1801, "not that he cared three brass farthings about the Catholic Question—but he had for a long time been weary of his situation,* and partly from fancying that he should like to try retirement for a little, partly from disgust at the K[ing]'s behaviour, who had thwarted him in a good many projects (jobbs some people called them—but in one instance unfairly . . .) he was desirous of finding a safe and honourable opportunity of giving up his office." Canning was now of opinion that Pitt was at last goaded into resigning by some of his own followers, who never expected him to retire in good earnest. About a fortnight before the change took place, Canning had warned Wyndham that, once out of office, Pitt would not return easily, but his

* Secretary of State for War.

advice was thrown away. Since then, Dundas had been gradually leaning to Addington's side, and was about to accept a peerage. He was now staying at Walmer with Pitt, who had declined the pleasure of a visit from Canning, to the great indignation of the latter. Pitt, out of health and depressed in spirit, probably shrank from discussions, but Canning was persuaded that "there is something in his mind which he wishes to hide from me." Lord Castlereagh was intriguing for office, in case of the promotion of Lord Liverpool or Lord Hawkesbury. "He has taken precisely that line in Parliament which P. laid down for *me*. Whether *he* had any difficulties about the Peace, I do not know. If he had he has overcome them manfully—*I* could not. But I do not disguise from myself that in not doing so, I have preferred character and my own consciousness of doing right, to opportunities of fame and power such as may not easily come within my reach again—and I am afraid to P.'s friendship—or at least to that place in it, which, with such a man, is alone worth holding."

There was a doubt whether Frere's position at Madrid was to be that of Minister or of Ambassador. Canning speaks of the slights and insults heaped on the British Ambassadors at foreign courts, and ends, despairingly: "Our policy is so obvious in all these respects that I am provoked at our compliance. But I have no hope of the same sentiment being generally felt. Pitt, I am pretty sure, would think it idle punctilio. Alas! Alas! It is anything but that. It is as substantial and vital a concern as the Exports and Imports he has taught Castlereagh to quote as the sum of our political existence. Will times, when mind shall have its share again in politicks, ever come round? or is Tare and Trett established for ever?"

Mrs. Canning had again been very ill, which may account for the gloomy tone of this letter. She must have recovered before Canning wrote on July 26th, as they were then entertaining George Ellis and his wife. The lady was the daughter of Nelson's old patron, Sir Peter Parker, and Ellis's marriage to her seems to have surprised all his friends. When the rumours of the engagement first reached him, Canning could hardly believe in it, and wrote of it to Frere more as a *canard* than as a genuine piece of news. The marriage was now an accomplished fact, and the outspoken Lady Malmesbury called it "a very foolish thing" on Ellis's part. Her opinion was evidently shared to some extent by Canning, who, sitting at his writing-table, watched "poor Joan suffering under the duty of entertaining" the Ellises. "Not but I am very glad to see G. E.— and *I* do not mind *She* G. E.—but *Shes* in general do, I think—and Joan is of all Shes the shyest." Under these circumstances he could only spare time to send Frere the following song for September. 29th, "which is (or ought to be) Addington's birthday—and at least may be celebrated as such *at Apothecary's Hall.* N.B. It is supposed to be written bona fide, by an *admiring Fool.* Does it shew so?"

"THE BIRD OF TO-DAY.

"A new Song as sung at the celebration of Mr. A.'s birthday, at Apothecary's Hall, on the 29th Sept. 1802.

"At the feast of St. Michael, when Harvest they house,
And rich in the produce of plenty carouse,
When tenants their rents are assembled to pay,
How cheerful a festival, Michaelmas Day!

"But *we,* for the harvest by Addington sown,
The full Harvest of *Peace,* to maturity grown,
The *Rent* of our *Thanks* to our Addington pay,
And *this* Festival mark as *his* Michaelmas Day.

"'Tis thro' Addington's Peace that fair Plenty is ours;
Peace brighten'd the sunshine, Peace soften'd the showers;
What yellow'd the cornfields? what ripen'd the hay?
But the Peace that was settled *last* Michaelmas Day? *

"The Saviours of States were rewarded of old
With statues of Silver † in porches of Gold—
'Twas thus did old Rome her acknowledgments pay
For her Capitol saved, by the Bird of To-day.

"And shall not such Statues to Addington rise,
For service more timely—for warning more wise—
For a Treaty, which snatch'd us from ruin away,
When signed with a quill from The Bird of To-day.

"Long may Addington live to keep Peace thro' our borders—
May each House still be true to its forms and its orders—
So shall Britain, tho' destined by Gaul for her prey—
Be saved as old Rome by the Bird of To-day!"

Owing to a report of Frere's return to England, Canning
did not write to him for more than another month. His
excuse was that, although the report was soon proved
false, "the habit of not writing is very difficult to be
broken through, and you must rather praise me for
beginning again at all after such an interruption and
disappointment, than wonder at my taking so long to
recover from them." In the meantime Canning had received
fresh overtures from Addington—on this occasion through
Gifford. Canning was inclined to think that the offer
was not genuine, as Pitt knew nothing of it. He broke
off his letter at this point on August 28th, to resume it
on September 7th in a different frame of mind. Pitt
and he had met, and were on easier terms. Dundas,
as he foreboded, had been intriguing: first, to induce
Pitt to take office, and then to creep back into office

* "Note.—Not *signed* till the 1st Octr., but settled finally on the
29th Sept., to coincide with the festival of that day. G. C."
† "Note.—auratis volitans argentens anser
          Porticibus Gallos ad limina adipe canebat. G. C."

without him, and had been met in both cases with a refusal. All this Canning had from Pitt's own mouth.

"For some weeks after I had written to you, I sulked, and would have nothing to say to P., thinking he had treated me scurvily. (I think so still.) But at length, hearing a rumour of his going—I forget when—into Somersetshire, or to some distant part, I did not like the notion of not seeing him for many months again, and therefore wrote to desire to know when he was to be in Town, proposing (as I had other reasons for going to Town for a day or two) to time my journey so as to meet him. This Letter produced a proposal on his part to come here. He came. I found him much better in opinion than I had *ever* seen him—disgusted with the Doctor and his system as much as one could wish, but—but—but—as to *acting*—no hopes of that yet. Then he proposed to me to pay him a visit, which I promised—and performed my promise last month. I found him alone, and passed three days with him in very comfortable, ¦quiet, perhaps useful discussion. I am sure he thinks of A. as I do. He thinks of A.'s system —of the degradation of the country under it—of the contempt which Europe feels, and any Englishman ought to feel for it—*almost* as I do. But what of this, if he is bound to support it?

"One most satisfactory acknowledgment I obtained from him in the course of the conversations at South Hill and Walmer—that *I* was right and *he* was wrong in the discussion about the propriety of my taking office last year—'that unless I could have re-modelled all my notions of what was right, dignified, etc., in Government, or (what was out of the question) could have altered *theirs*, I must infallibly have resigned office three months after I had taken it.' Is it not satisfactory to hear this from him? and at a time too when he is thinking with me—and ought therefore to act as (so thinking) he admits I must have done?

"While I was at Walmer, and when in the intervals of these conversations, I was reviewing the spots where other conversations still more interesting had passed three summers before (for it was at Walmer, you know, three years ago that I first saw my own Joan). When I looked at the cottage where Lady S. E. had lived, during the time that she was negociating for me, and where she afforded me opportunities of negociating for myself, it struck me that Joan and I might pass a few weeks very comfortably in this same cottage; and I had no sooner let P. perceive the thought in my mind, than he seized it, and pressed our coming there. I agreed. Joan liked the plan. It will do George good. And we set off for Walmer to-morrow."

It was not so long before this, that Canning had considered his intercourse with Pitt as closed for ever; but Pitt had only to hold up his little finger for the younger man to hasten to his side. Impulsive, warm-hearted, and undisciplined, he treated Pitt much as he would have treated the father whom he had never known, and whose place Pitt in some degree had taken : he would have shed the last drop of blood in his cause, but nothing would make him obey.

Canning's stay at Walmer was pleasant to both parties. Their differences, though not forgotten, were softened, and the warm personal affection revived as of old. "I cannot say that he has always cordially agreed with me," writes Canning to Frere, on October 5th, "yet he has every day found it more difficult to maintain a difference of opinion

Bonaparte and the Dr. between them really wrest his weapons from his hands. Would to God he could be brought to see, while there is yet time, that with such Champions as Bonaparte and the Dr. on either side, this country has not a chance of being kept on its legs—that a change there *must* inevitably be, and that there is but one man—and that one himself—to whom we can look for safety in any alternative, whether of Peace or War.

" I am persuaded that this is felt more and more in all parts of the Kingdom—in the City most especially—and that the Dr. could not do better for himself, and can in no other way do common justice by the King or the Country, than to negociate for himself, as quick as may be, a retreat with honours and emoluments, and entreat P. to take off his hands a weight that ought never to have been placed there.

" No endeavours of mine are wanting to put this necessity in its true light here. And yet I understand that the Dr.'s friends, so far from being obliged · to me for the services which they suppose me to be desirous of rendering him, are extremely disgusted and angry at my visit to Walmer.

" Whatever be the result as to this great Object, I am on other accounts most happy indeed that I have come here. I have had opportunities of quiet, comfortable, uninterrupted conversations, such as for two years past I have desiderated in vain ; and have had the satisfaction of finding, after that two years' interval, filled as it has been with the most unpleasant events, and with consequent differences of conduct and opinion, no change in P., no diminution of cordiality or confidence, and a gradual, but I think growing approximation of sentiments in regard both to persons and things ; for which I thank Bonaparte, and by which I am almost reconciled to the Dr.'s misconduct and folly.

" It has been an addition to my satisfaction on these accounts, that I think my being here at this time may have been of some use and comfort to P. He was very, very ill when we arrived here, about the middle of last month. The newspapers will probably have told you this —but perhaps not to its fullest extent. For one day, if not longer, his life was certainly in danger. God be thanked, all danger and all serious cause for alarm is quite [at] an end. He is recovering strength daily ; and during his convalescence—which I of course spared all painful and perplexing subjects of discussion, and endeavoured to make him feel at his ease, as if I had no political notions to trouble him with—I have, or rather *We* have (for Joan is a great help to me in this, as in everything else, and loves poor P., and has always taken his part in the worst times) been in the way to pay him little attentions, which, though nothing in themselves, he has appeared not to dislike at our hands."

If Frere had been anywhere within reach, Canning would have rushed to him after leaving Walmer. As it was, he had to find some one in whom to confide ; and kindly old Lord Malmesbury, sitting over his fire in Spring Gardens, was startled by a visit from Canning at eleven o'clock at night. Canning poured out the substance of his long conversations with Pitt, and implored Lord Malmesbury to use his influence with the Duke of York. It was thought that the King might be prepared for recalling Pitt through the medium of His Royal Highness.

There are few things more worthy of respect in Lord Malmesbury's character than his readiness at all times to lend an ear to the schemes, hopes, and grievances of the younger Tories. Cut off by his increasing deafness from any very active part in political life, his time and sympathy seem to have been at the disposal of any one who claimed them, and Canning was a special favourite with him. He waited on the Duke of York, who gave a favourable hearing to his representations. Canning, being fully convinced that the country was as weary as himself of "the *Dumplin* ministry"—to use a contemptuous nickname of Lady Malmesbury's—set to work to collect signatures to a petition requesting Addington to resign in Pitt's favour. Lord Mulgrave betrayed this scheme to Pitt, who had no choice but to command that the petition should at once be dropped. " I am confident—perfectly confident," Canning writes to Frere in the August of 1803, " that had not my plan of last November been betrayed to Pitt (by Mulgrave), and had P. done what he ought to have done—turned a deaf ear to the disclosure, and let it (the thing) go on as if he had known nothing of it, the Government would have fallen before the end of the before Christmas Session." Lord Malmesbury did his best, remonstrating earnestly with Pitt himself, but to no purpose, and further action was postponed until after Christmas. Lord Malmesbury, disposed himself to wait, with the patience of a man who has lived many years, while privately lamenting that " the four young persons who composed the secret committee were not of sufficient *fathom* for so great a purpose." The four were Canning, Lord George Leveson, Lord Morpeth, and the devoted Mr. Sturges Bourne (" little Scroggs "), whose obedience on all occasions was ultimately rewarded by the posts of Secretary of State for the Home Department and Lord Warden of the New Forest, when Canning became Premier in 1827.

Either Canning's time was fully occupied by these intrigues, and in the composition of satirical verses on " The

Doctor," his family and his adherents, or some letters to Frere have been lost. After that written at Walmer in October 1802, there are no more till February 2nd, 1803, when he replied to a long string of questions sent by Frere. The absence of Frere's letter makes it difficult to understand the answer, but the substance of it evidently relates to Pitt's conduct, although no name is mentioned. "'His conscience' (like Lancelot Gobbo's) 'hangs about the neck of his heart'—or rather his heart about that of his conscience, and will not let him do what he knows he ought to do—and so we shall go on in the downward road, —nor will he set about retrieving our affairs till there is nothing left to retrieve.

"He promises great things indeed! He has chalked out a course for himself, which in three or four stages is to lead to vigorous action ; but at each of these stages there are stops and conditions to be interposed, of which those whose interest it is, will easily know how to take advantage : first by smooth words to obtain a remission of his exertions, and then by delay to disappoint their object. He will join in no *retrospective* censure ; because that exposes *them* without producing any immediate public good. He will join in no *prospective* resolution ; because that implies a distrust of them, which it is impossible for *him* to avow without directly countenancing an attempt to turn them out. Then who to succeed them ? If himself, is not that selfish, etc. ? This is the course of miserable apologies for an inaction that he is ashamed of. And he reconciles it to himself by the determination that they shall know from him what he thinks they ought to do, and if after knowing it they act against it, or *not up* to it— *then* indeed. . . . Alas! alas! alas! Even *then*, I am afraid, new excuses—what is now in prospect will then be past—and then there is an end of the public good to be done—and censure for censure's sake he will be as far as ever from agreeing to. I see no hope therefore : Holland will follow Switzerland—Malta, the Cape. And the next Session of Parliament (if we survive as an independent country so long) will begin with the same expectation of a better system, and will end with the same disappointment. Yet Malta and Holland are the two points to which he swore!!! I wish I could yet trust his oath—but I dare not."

Frere had suggested resigning his post at Madrid, or, at all events, coming home for a short holiday, but Canning would not let him think of either proceeding. "I would give anything (except George or William Pitt, my new little boy) to have you here for a few days, if you could be back again at your post, without having been missed there, or known to be here ; but I would not for any consideration that you should run yourself into such difficulties as a week spent in London during the Session would necessarily bring upon you—or should incur to no purpose the regrets and mortifications of a life of idle indignation while there is yet a chance, however remote, of your being made useful where you are, or being useful by your own making."

Canning's desponding view of public affairs was partly occasioned by his private anxieties. The birth of her second son in December had made Mrs. Canning seriously ill, and when her husband wrote to Frere, six weeks afterwards she was only able to move from her dressing-room, and had not yet ventured downstairs. Charles Ellis, one of Canning's most valued and intimate friends, was on the point of losing his wife, who had been sinking into a decline for more than a year. Charles Ellis seems to have been one of those unlucky men who are always getting into difficulties. He is seldom mentioned in Canning's letters otherwise than as " poor Charles," with details of his last misfortune—whether falling from his horse, losing his seat in Parliament, or bringing home his wife's corpse from the Continent. His anxieties for " Joan " had not prevented Canning from getting into mischief. Old Lord Malmesbury, his confidant in all such matters, had endeavoured to soothe his impatience, and represent that he must make allowance for " hitches." About a week after the letter to Frere had been sent off, Canning descended upon Lord Malmesbury with a letter of eight pages addressed to Pitt—" too long," sighed poor Lord Malmesbury, who had to read it, then and there. Pitt, when in town, had been rather reserved, and had not written to Canning since he went away. This led Canning to infer that " he was going on wrong," and occasioned the letter, which Lord Malmesbury pronounced " too admonitory and too fault-finding for even Pitt's very goodhumoured mind to bear." Canning, however, persisted in sending it, and received, as he deserved, a short dry answer from Pitt. Canning was then hurt and sore, and Lord Malmesbury " preached patience," a virtue which the good old gentleman himself must have had opportunities of practising at that time.

The negociations for peace were not proceeding smoothly. Napoleon, deceived by the readiness with which we had agreed to the Preliminary Articles, demanded further concessions. It was evident that war must soon follow, and in the March and April of 1803 an attempt was again made to bring Pitt back to office. Each side declared that the first overtures proceeded from the other. There seems to have been some misunderstanding between the principals, which, no doubt, their followers did their best to increase. Without entering into the details, it is enough to say that Pitt at first showed no unwillingness to take office if the King wished him to do so, and to join forces with Addington. But the same Cabinet could not possibly include Addington and the Grenvilles, who were among the most able of Pitt's supporters, and the negociations were broken off amid angry recriminations, leaving Pitt, in Lord Malmesbury's opinion, farther than ever from office.

Malta, which Canning had prophesied would "follow the Cape," was the final cause of our rupture with France. On May 18th, 1803, war was proclaimed in the King's name. A change of some kind seemed imminent, and all eyes were turned to Pitt, who had resumed his parliamentary attendance. Canning hurried up to his favourite quarters with Leveson at Whitehall, leaving his wife and children at Welbeck, to which place Mrs. Canning had been taken after her confinement, as South Hill was in the hands of workmen. "I am an unnatural husband and father to have been away from them so long, but it was so much better for them than being cooped up in Town," pleaded Canning.

There had been an important division in the House of Commons on the night of Friday, June 3rd. Colonel Patten moved for a Vote of Censure on "the remissness and want of vigilance of the Ministry previous to the Declaration of War." The course of action which Pitt had marked out for himself forbade him to join in the censure ; on the other hand, he could not openly support the Ministers against his own party. He therefore moved "that the question should be put by, and that the House should proceed to the Orders of the Day." Only fifty-six followed him into the lobby, and Canning was not among them. The King and the Ministry openly rejoiced at this signal defeat, and Canning was not altogether sorry for it.

"WHITEHALL, *June 9th*, 1803.

" . . . Now shortly for Politicks.

"Our great project for the Session has failed.   A. is not out.   Nor P. likely to be in.   But the next best object is fully attained.   P. is completely, avowedly, *unmistakeably* and irrecoverably separated from A., and if not in direct hostility to him, restrained from being so only by consideration for the K[ing].

"This consideration prevented him from speaking out on Friday night what he thought of the conduct of the Ministers in the late discussions with F[rance].   He took a middle line, which as middle lines generally do, and generally *ought* to do, led to discomfiture and disgrace. He divided but 56.   We his friends, who had already declared against A., could not in honour or consistency follow him in this Division—(one or two did—but in mass we could not)—we had afterwards a Division of our own when Pitt was gone out of the House.   See here it is—and divided for your information into its Classes " :

Then follows a list of names, divided by Canning into " Grenvilles and Windhams "—" Us or P.'s friends "—and " Ld. Fitzwillms."   Among " Pitt's friends " are of course the faithful three, Leveson, Morpeth, and Sturges Bourne. The last named also voted with Pitt ; one hopes that Canning forgave him for it.

" All P.'s moderate friends went away.

" Fox, and most of his immediate followers did the same.

"Those of *old* Opposition who did stay, voted with Government.

" Bootle shirked, and Boringdon voted with Government in the H. of Lds ! ! ! after joining for the last two months as heartily as heart could desire, in the cry against the Dr.

No matter. I am glad he has been brought to the test.
Others (upon the whole) stood it well. And we could
muster a few more than are here recorded.

"Now one word about yourself, and I have done.

"I hear from Hammond that you have not been very
diligent in writing lately. For God's sake mend this fault.
Make the very best use you can of the time that you have
to remain. For many reasons you ought to take special
care to give no *prise* against you. But even without this
prudential consideration, recollect how kindly, with what
marked kindness and attention the K[ing] has behaved
towards you, and pray do not let him have to think that
he has spoiled you."

As soon as he could possibly do so, Canning left town
for Welbeck, with the intention of not again setting foot
in the House until the autumn session, at all events—
perhaps not then, "unless Pitt should in the interval have
seen fit to take some more decisive line of his own." But
only three weeks had passed in making holiday with wife
and children when Canning was surprised by the sight of
a division in the House on an amendment of Pitt's to the
Property Duty Bill. Forgetting all his grievances, real and
imaginary, he rushed up to town, "in the hopes of being in
Pitt's next minority." He arrived too late to take part
in any division, but his presence at Pitt's side for a week
together, disposed of the rumours of a quarrel between them
which had been spreading ever since the night of Colonel
Patten's motion. It was also a gratification to Canning to
see how completely Pitt was now separated from Addington,
and to watch "his contempt, dislike, and thorough ungovern-
able indignation against the Dr. and his whole system. It
was so much satisfaction to me, whom he and his neutral
friends, the Camdens, Villiers, (Longs perhaps,) had been

accusing of passion and acrimony, to find that P. was in a temper to which mine was mildness, whenever he was personally opposed to A., and that he had in the judgement of impartial people, and still more (as you may suppose) according to the cry of the Ministerialists, infused into the debates a degree of contemptuous asperity not likely (one should imagine) to be generated upon the modifications of a Tax Bill."

This, however, was a matter of personal triumph, and Canning grieved over the thought that Pitt's conduct towards Addington was not likely to be appreciated by the general public. "Whether . . . the plain unrefining down-right fatheaded Public will see nothing in the distinctions which he has taken but bad generalship, clumsy opposition, good opportunities romantically lost, and ill ones sought for to repair them—this I do not pretend to determine." Leveson was of opinion that Pitt had done himself good and the Government harm, so far as the House of Commons was concerned. "And the Lion, with whom I have been in constant communication since November upon these subjects, and whose notions have for the most part been precisely the same with mine, who thought with me before-hand of what P. *ought* to do—writes me to me that he is perfectly satisfied upon reflection that what he *has* done is upon the whole the best ; that the Public *in time* will see it all in a right point of view ; that it goes to the support of P.'s *character* which is all in all ; and that ultimately such a system of conduct steadily pursued, under all difficulties and discouragements, *must* bring him back to the administration, much more surely than any shorter and quicker and bolder course could have done. So be it."

But Canning himself could see "no reason now why A.'s administration should not hobble on, and outlast the Country. And this is the more provoking, as I do really think that there are means and hopes of raising the Country to a pitch of glory and power, such as it has never attained before, if the administration were in able hands. Nay, I am not sure that the tendency to rise is not so strong that it *will* rise, in spite of the overlaying suppressive stupidity of the present people. And then they will have the credit of what they could not help, and a long lease to ruin us at their leisure."

Two enclosures were in this letter, which was dated from Elford, where Canning was staying with Sneyd in August. The first was a pamphlet recently published by Hatchard. Its name is not given, and the pamphlet itself is not to be found, but it must have been the "Cursory Remarks upon the State of Parties, by a Near Observer," which caused a great sensation in the summer of 1803. The author was unknown, but Canning believed him to be a member of the House of Commons "from many minutiæ which would have escaped a person out of doors." Hatchard refused to disclose the author's name, but he brought Canning the proofs of the part relating to himself, offering to refuse to publish it, if Canning objected. The pamphlet professed to give an account of the recent negotiations between Pitt and Addington. It accused Pitt of deceit in pledging himself to support Addington's Government without having the least intention of fulfilling the pledge, and of making no effort to restrain his own party. Canning was singled out for special blame :—

" Mr. Pitt unequivocally approved the peace. Mr. Windham, the Grenvilles and their adherents as decidedly affected to lament and condemn it ; while the personal friends of Mr. Pitt, and the members most attached and devoted to him by the habits of private life, took the liberty of disclaiming him for their leader, and indulged in every species of rancour, malice, and hostility against the person who had the *presumption* to fill his vacant place in the Cabinet. Of this party, Mr. Canning, if not the founder, had the reputation of being the leader."

The " Near Observer" then made merry over Canning's displeasure at Pitt's refusal to join in the vote of censure against the Government :—

" Mr. Canning's indignation has carried him so far that he has scarcely since made his appearance in the House, but I hope he will forgive the *weakness* of his right honourable friend and return."

He taunted Canning with being "a mere partisan and stickler for the house of Grenville," and asked him—

" Whether he had been juster to himself and to his own just pretensions and character than we have seen him to the sensibility of his friend and patron, when he condescended to become a hero of squib and epigrams, a leader of doggrel and lampoon, a power in the war of abuse and invective, an instrument of Mr. Windham, and an auxiliary of Mr. Cobbett ? "

With this pamphlet Canning sent to Frere a copy of Pitt's final letter to Addington at the time of the negotiations in the spring. It was copied by Sneyd, because Mrs. Canning, who generally acted as her husband's secretary, was too unwell for the task.

" P. at the time he gave it to me absolutely forbade its being communicated—except to two or three Persons then in London. But the transaction is now so long past that it is a matter of history, and the representation so impudently given of it in the Pamphlet makes it necessary that the true statement should accompany it. This letter from P. to A. was the conclusion of the negotiation. A., I believe, did reply to it—but his reply was mere *bother* and lame exculpation and profession ; except indeed that he insinuates, or rather asserts pretty roundly, that P. first intimated to him, A., his desire to be brought into office— and that he, A , thought he was coming up exactly to his wishes in proposing to bring him in as he did, *with* the present Govt. and in aid of *it.* This P. says is a lie.

"For the rest you will find the pamphlet entertaining enough, and may rely upon it as their party creed. I think it may be well answered—and have had some thoughts of answering it myself, but I shall probably be too lazy, and I shall at all events wait to see what turn P.'s mind takes towards the Meeting of Parlt. in November, before I make up my mind whether to give myself any more trouble about party politicks in or out of Parliament."

At this time Canning's opinion was similar to that ex- pressed by Lord Lovat on his way to the scaffold—"the mair mischief, the better sport." He believed that he should be asked to make answer to the " Near Observer," and Mrs. Canning, to whom all his speeches and writings were rehearsed, must have been called upon to admire many shrewd sarcasms during the summer's recess—fresh " thistles " to irritate " the Doctor." The semi-official cha- racter given to the attack upon Pitt by the fact that copies of the Pamphlet were sent to several persons by Mr. Vansittart, secretary of the Treasury, and the sensation that it caused in the political world, made an answer of some sort necessary ; but Canning was not requested to supply it. Even had the authorship been kept a secret, his style must have betrayed him. Any reply from his hand could only cause fresh irritation to the other party, and would have no weight with the sober-minded individuals on both sides, who regarded him as a troublesome young man with a lamentable want of control over his tongue and his pen. The disappointment was extreme, and when Canning next wrote to Frere on November 23rd "the Doctor's pamphlet" had become "the most atrocious instance of private ingratitude and personal injustice that ever was published. Such as it is, it gives you a better notion than you could have acquired anyhow else of the views, the language, and the temper of the Addingt. Ministry. They have certainly thrown off P. entirely, and defy him.

"I hoped by this time to have had an answer to this Pamphlet to send you. And it is not my fault that I have not one to send you of my own writing. I should have been very glad to be asked to undertake the answer. Unasked I would not meddle with it. Proffered services are too cheap to be prized. And I am now pretty well used to the difference between open and tacit encouragement; and know what it is to act upon one's own conviction that what one is doing is agreeable to those for whose sake it is done, at the risque of being disavowed in the face of the world for an irregular and an ungoverned zeal if the result should be unsatisfactory, or the policy of the hour changed. Had P. expressed a wish, and *promised to abide* by my answer, I should have been ready to do my best, and I could have done better than I ever did anything. I am sure I could. But I hope it was not from a sneaking disposition to separate his case from that of his friends—I hope it was not from that motive that he preferred putting the business into other hands. But in other hands I am afraid it is—*whose* I know not. I only know that the opportunity of publishing it to advantage is lost by having deferred it till after the meeting of Parlt., till the minds of people are full of other matters, and the attack itself forgotten—tho' the mischief done by it is not likely to be so soon effaced."

The person whom Pitt selected for this delicate task was a Mr. Courtenay, son of the late Bishop of Exeter, and author of an essay on finance which had met with general approval. His pamphlet was written from Long's notes, under Pitt's superintendence, and is entitled " A Plain Answer to the Misrepresentations and Calumnies contained in the Cursory Remarks of a Near Observer, by A More Accurate Observer."   There is none of Canning's sparkling wit, none of the keen lashes with which he could make his enemies writhe in impotent fury. The dignified self-restraint of its tone contrasts favourably with the violent invective of the " Near Observer " ; but the impression left on the reader's mind, whether by accident or design, is that Pitt was separating himself from Canning. There is a sharp hit at Vansittart in the suggestion that, if Mr. Pitt were supposed capable of guiding Mr. Canning, Mr. Addington might be able to influence the Secretaries of the Treasury. Further on it is distinctly stated that " Mr. Pitt disapproved highly of Mr. Canning's parliamentary conduct."

After this, reconciliation between Pitt and Addington was impossible. The Grenvilles and Windhams had now coalesced with Fox, and after vainly endeavouring to gain Pitt to their side, began a violent attack upon the Ministry in Parliament. Pitt was, according to himself, "assailed in prose and verse" by his "eager and ardent young friends" Canning and Leveson. Canning was like a hound in leash, fretting and chafing at the delay which was really occasioned more by the state of Pitt's health than by any other cause. "He pauses—and hesitates—and shirks—and shuffles to avoid going into direct open avowed parliamentary opposition—but it is all in vain. Go he must, like all Ex-ministers before him—a little sooner or a little later—and if he will not let me go before him, I must wait his time."

One is irresistibly reminded of the witches' song that Gillies Duncan chanted to King James:—

> "Cummer, go ye before,
> Cummer, go ye;
> Gif ye will not go before,
> Cummer, lat me."

But Canning was true to his chief. Among the papers at Roydon is a copy in Canning's own writing, of a letter to Lord Grenville, dated February 20th, 1804, in which he declares himself "unpledged as to any connection with any New Government (however otherwise unexceptionable), in which Mr. Pitt should not be included."

Another of the King's attacks of mania precipitated the crisis, and Addington was forced to resign in April 1804.

Canning had busied himself with the scheme of "a comprehensive administration," which should include Fox and Grenville. Pitt was willing enough, and the obstacle, as usual, came from the King, who positively declined to admit Fox. Lord Grenville refused to take office without his new ally, to Pitt's bitter indignation, and Canning at first would accept no post under the new *régime*. He gave as his reason that "he was not yet ripe for office." Perhaps he was piqued at the downfall of another of his airy castles—perhaps he was beginning to see how much harm he had done to his chief's cause in the last three years—perhaps he was honestly weary of the plotting and chicane, the petty jealousies and the "tangle and toil that none can unravel." But his moods were of short duration, and in the end he consented to become Treasurer of the Navy.

Unfortunately for us, Frere left Spain in the summer of 1804, and we have only a few triumphant lines sent by Canning to reach him at Madrid before he set out on the homeward voyage :—

"How P. at length came forward in Parlt.—how the Government was obliged to turn itself out—how the scheme of a large, comprehensive Administration had nearly succeeded, and by what means it failed—how I did all I could for it, and how I would fain have been left out of that which was formed instead of it, but how, in spite of myself, I am Treasurer of the Navy—are matters for many a long conversation, and would swell my letter beyond even the bulk of that which was lost in 1801. . . . I long to see you. Pray depart from your sworn silence for once, and give me due notice of your coming, that I may be sure to be at home to receive you, or (what if I had proper notice I would do) may endeavour to meet you on your road to London.

"My wife and children (three in number, the last a girl) are all well.   Ever yours, G. C."

In a postscript Canning adds that Leveson has been appointed Ambassador to St. Petersburg, and that Charles Ellis is going to Jamaica. "If you were not returning, I should feel very desolate at parting with Charles and Leveson. Come therefore, as quickly as you can."

With Frere In England there was no necessity for Canning to write long letters, and a few notes of the most trivial character are nearly all that can be found to illustrate Pitt's last years of office. We can gather that those years were disturbed by squabbles among Pitt's own followers. In December 1804 Lord Harrowby met with an accident which compelled him to retire from the Foreign Office, and in the shifting of places that followed, Pitt seized the opportunity of bringing in Addington under the new title of Lord Sidmouth, as President of the Council, thereby causing much ill-feeling. Canning promptly tendered his resignation, but was induced to withdraw it. Lord Hardwicke and Mr. Foster had a violent quarrel, which Canning describes Pitt as attempting to reconcile "in his usual balancing way." Canning and Pitt were returning to their old affectionate terms, as we learn from a letter of Charles Ellis's sent to Frere from Jamaica :—

"*Feb. 5th*, 1805.

"Canning will not write as much about himself as I should be anxious to know, and nobody can do it as well as yourself, if you will only write just that sort of account which you would yourself like to receive. As there is nobody in the House between him and Pitt, this Sessions, must, I conceive, be of the greatest importance to his Parliamentary Reputation, and I trust he will be able to improve so fine a Situation to the utmost. It gave me the greatest Pleasure to learn by his last Letter that they were returning to their former footing of cordiality, and that P. was weary of the vagaries which had from time to time estranged them during the Goose administration, and particularly that you had been in some measure instrumental to their Return."

Lord Sidmouth soon found his position intolerable, and resigned, as was announced to Frere in the following lines scribbled on a small sheet of notepaper :—

"Sat., *July* 6, 1805.

"The Doctor is out again,
So things may come about again."

Otherwise, there is scarcely an allusion to public events in Canning's letters to Frere during the rest of the year. There is an account of a meeting with Pitt, who was "proud and really with justice of his Continental Confederacy"; and an allusion to a visit paid by Canning and his wife to the King and Queen at Weymouth, where they "were not *over* and *above* well received."

The first indication of the blow that was to fall on England and on Canning himself occurs in a note to Frere dated from South Hill, January 9th, 1806.

"My Dear Frere,

"What has become of you? . . . I am here till next week. Pitt I hope is coming here on his way from Bath. He is very ill, and the Continent worse. But He, I hope, will get better."

Frere was apparently staying with his brother Edward at Clydach, far removed from newspapers and dispatches. This letter is followed by two hurried scrawls, from Charles Ellis, sent one after the other, in the hope that they might reach Frere somewhere and somehow. Pitt is dangerously ill—dying—and Frere must come to comfort Canning.

Last of all comes a little scrap of paper torn from the end of another sheet, on which Canning has written a few lines to Frere. He tries to discuss some paper which has been sent for his inspection, breaking off abruptly with "God bless you,"—and then his overwhelming grief finds expression in the piteous cry "But five hours dead! nay, not five, not so much! and to be mentioned already merely as a fact. Alas!"

Pitt was stricken down before his work was done; and Canning, to whom part of the task—Catholic Emancipation—had been bequeathed, was destined never to complete it, although his life was to be spent in toiling for its sake. Disinherited by his parents' follies of the wealth and position that should have been his by right of birth, disinherited by his own good qualities as well as by his own follies from the political influence that should have been his by right of surpassing talents, he was now to face the world "a masterless man."   In those few years in "the camp of observation on Bagshot Heath," as his enemies nicknamed South Hill, he had sown the winds of mockery and dissension.   He reaped the whirlwinds of envy, malice, strife, wilful misunderstandings, and incurable prejudices, that were to toss him hither and thither, just as he seemed to be nearing the goal of his hopes, until the summons came for him to follow his old chief once more.

CHAPTER V.

LOVE-LETTERS OF A HUNDRED YEARS AGO.

" AN Irishwoman born, whose family are proud indeed, and whose more Mature Years were Spent in Scotland, where that foolish pride was not lessen'd by everything I had met with there."

ELIZABETH JEMIMA, Countess of Erroll, to J. H. FRERE.

There is a tradition that John Hookham Frere was one evening at a party in a London house where he was introduced to a very beautiful woman. They went together to supper, but, on the way downstairs, he became so interested in conversation that he drank off the glass of negus (other versions make it a glass of champagne or a cup of coffee) that he had procured for her, and offered her his arm to return to the drawing-room. In after years she would tell the story with infinite zest, and add, " This convinced me that my new acquaintance was at any rate very different from most of the young men around us." This good-humoured lady was destined to exercise a strong influence in Frere's life.

Elizabeth Jemima, Countess of Erroll, was one of the daughters of Joseph Blake, Esq., of Ardfry, whose eldest son was created Lord Wallscourt in his father's lifetime. The date of her birth is uncertain.

Ardfry, in County Galway, is said by a contemporary

to have been "the real model of Castle Rackrent," and the glimpses of the Blakes incidentally afforded to us by their correspondence show them to have been very Irish. Elizabeth's portrait, painted by Sir Martin Shee and now at Roydon, represents an extremely handsome girl with large dark eyes and masses of dark hair. She wears a scarlet riding habit and broad-brimmed hat, and looks out of the picture with the masterful smile that may have won the heart of George, fifteenth Earl of Erroll and Lord High Constable of Scotland, whom she married on January 25th, 1790. Little is known of her life with her first husband, but tradition says that he left her to the care of his mother and sisters in the depths of the country— perhaps at his family seat, Slains Castle. Readers of *Corinne* will remember how Madame de Stael's heroine found the English ladies sitting solemnly round the tea-table in the absence of their husbands; but even this harmless amusement was forbidden by the Countess-Dowager. Lady Erroll's maid therefore used to brew "a pot of tea" over her mistress's fire, and the young ladies were in the habit of stealing to their sister-in-law's room after their mother had retired to bed, to enjoy themselves. One night, as they were all gathered *en déshabille*, the door was suddenly flung open and the Dowager entered, awful as Lady Macbeth, in nightdress and nightcap. She swept one indignant glance round her, and then stalked from the room, leaving the assembled ladies shaking in their slippers.

In June 1798 Lord Erroll's death took place—under melancholy circumstances, according to De Quincey, who met the young widow and her sister travelling by the canal steamer from Tullamore to Dublin, and was struck by the overwhelming grief of Lady Erroll and the radiant loveliness of Miss Blake. "Lord Erroll had been privately intrusted by Mr. Pitt with an official secret—viz., the outline and principal details of a foreign expedition ; in which, according to Mr. Pitt's original purpose, his lordship was to have held a high command. In a moment of intoxication, the Earl confided this secret to some false friend, who published the communication and its author. Upon this, the unhappy nobleman, under too keen a sense of wounded honour, and perhaps with an exaggerated notion of the evils attached to his indiscretion, destroyed himself.   Months had passed since that calamity when we met his widow ; but time appeared to have done nothing in mitigating her sorrow."*

This story is in some degree confirmed by a letter from Henry Dundas (afterwards first Viscount Melville) to J. H. Frere in December 1800.   Frere had recently been appointed Envoy to the Court of Lisbon, where Lady Erroll was ordered to spend the winter.   Lisbon was a favourite health resort in the last century.†

"My dear Sir,

"I take the opportunity of sending under your Care some Letters for Lady Erroll to recommend her to your particular Attention.   I learnt that you got acquainted with her at Falmouth.   She has great Merit, and has had a very unfortunate Life, and will be much flattered by any Civility you can shew to her."

In a foreign country, such an acquaintance would soon ripen into intimacy, and when Lady Erroll returned to England, she was on the most friendly terms with Frere and his brother Bartle, and also with their friend Mr.

* *Autobiographic Sketches :* "Premature Manhood."
† Thus Mr. Mundy takes his delicate wife to Lisbon in 1781, and Sally Shilton, George Eliot's "Caterina," is sent thither in 1792. (See *The Cheverels of Cheverel Manor.*)

(afterwards Sir Robert) Ainslie. At first Bartle seems to have been her favourite.

"If I was to wish for a lover, I should exactly wish such a being: he has all the little ways to the heart," she confessed; and she kept up a correspondence with him, sending and receiving numerous messages to and from "His Excellency." Her earliest dated letter to J. H. Frere was written in 1804, but, as some of the correspondence has been lost or destroyed, it is possible that she may have begun to write to the elder brother before that time.

From this point until the time of her marriage with him she wrote constantly and voluminously, telling him all that she saw, heard, did, or thought. After taking away all that was meant for him alone and could interest no one else, we have enough to give a vivid picture of the writer, a typical Irishwoman, careless, warm-hearted, quick-witted. At one moment she is crying herself blind over Bartle's illness, at the next she is laughing at the extraordinary behaviour of the Russian Embassy; to-day she may be sitting by her fire in "Old Cat Hall," thinking of her latter end, and hoping to make a handsome corpse; to-morrow she is making charades with a party of friends, giggling like a school-girl, until she has "a Red face," or dancing, the gayest of the gay, at a children's ball. No consideration can stay her either from cutting a joke at her friend's expense, or from hotly defending an absent foe; and while she is ready to advance a large sum to relieve an embarrassed sister-in-law, she forgets to pay her milliner £1 16s. for "a white Oldenburgh bonnet."

She had a suite of rooms at Hampton Court Palace, but, cordially detesting "Old Cat Hall" and all its inmates—who must have been considerably tried by her vagaries—she was always ready to escape to other surroundings, and there were no lack of opportunities for flight. The childless widow, said to have been one of the most beautiful women of her time, was a welcome guest, and she boasted that it was never any trouble to her to make herself agreeable in society. She might easily have consoled herself for the loss of her first husband, but, whether Frere had already made an impression on her heart, or whether she was reluctant to tempt fortune a second time, there is no whisper of any lover but himself.

After reading through the correspondence, one is left to wonder at the perversity of some modern writers, who talk of the modesty and refinement of our grandmothers and are shocked by the outspokenness of the ladies of our own day. Our grandmothers had their own code of what was correct in speech and morals, and did, or did not, act according to it; but it was a different code from ours. Lady Erroll was a woman of exemplary life, against whose character there was never a breath of scandal; but she tells stories that cannot, for very decency, be repeated in full, and enters into medical details that would only interest a physician.

The work of deciphering her letters has been a task of difficulty. Her ladyship wrote in large scrawling characters, which seem at first sight clear and bold, but which prove almost illegible. Her use of capitals is eccentric, even for those days, her spelling is arbitrary, and she never condescends to put any stops. " I wish I could write better I can't read this myself," she observes at the end of a long letter. She often forgot to put the date, and it has not always been possible to supply the omission.

The first of the dated letters was written on May 3rd, 1804, when Pitt had at last returned to office. Lady Erroll was displeased with the new administration. " In truth I like it less every day, though I know it is Right I should like it, but I can't for my life, *in my Heart* . . . . . .

I see everything in the present administration to disgust me, and nothing to please. I hear that Ld. G. Leveson does not go to Russia and that the Boy Palmerston goes, a very fit person (I *suppose* of *experience*) to be Ambassador to such a Court of so much consequence to this Country, but I can't believe it, such nonsense! It would appear almost that Mr. Canning has chozen all his Ambassadors from Ld. Malmesbury's Dinner-parties in Spring Gardens and Faggs too . . . . . . Fitzgerald met Ld. Sefton and Willm Wyndham at a Borough Brokers on Tuesday last where he went to buy a Seat for his son, there were four Seats to be Sold but no body was allowed to have the two Maidstone Seats who Voted with the present Ministers, therefore he was off, and the terms of the other two not fair he thought."

It is possible that some of Lady Erroll's aversion to the new ministry arose from the fact that Canning was one of the members. She feared and disliked him—partly, it may be, from a natural jealousy of her lover's dearest friend, but also from a woman's instinct that he was working against her. Canning, happy in a perfect wife, had views of his own about Frere's marriage, and did not think the careless, unbusinesslike Irishwoman the best helpmate for the man who was already known as "the most indolent of God's creatures." "Do not open this before that Canning man, I am afraid of him," begs a postscript scribbled on the margin of a sheet. Although she was ready to send her letters to Canning's care so as to avoid exciting comment among Frere's relations, and although, as we shall see hereafter, she turned to him when in real anxiety about Frere, she could never refrain from a disparaging remark about "your pet Mr. Canning," and whatever he did was certain to be wrong in her eyes.

There are several ways of spelling her title, and others must sometimes have made mistakes ; but when Canning unwittingly leaves out an " l " her ladyship, whose own spelling is not beyond reproach, is mortally offended. Her jealousy breaks out in such flashes as these : " I am afraid they [*i.e.* Frere's family at Roydon] will think I am the Real Cause of y^r staying in London, but I could tell them that it is Mr. Canning that you can't exist without." . . . " Y^r Mr. Canning I see has been barking at the landed property Bill." . . . " I dare not allow myself to expect you here as I shall, I know, only disappoint myself by doing so, as after Wednesday next you will be Watching the fighting of the House of Commons and never from Mr. Canning's side and adieu to poor old Woman." . . . " That Canning Man takes away my own Man from me. If he goes on so, I shall begin to believe the Naughty people who told me that *he was 'a most Selfish Man,'* you made me believe the contrary, but you have not produced the proofs."

One of the liveliest of her letters describes how her friends tricked her into meeting Canning at a dinner-party, in June 1805 :—

" Lady Georgina Eliot . . . was to have a big Dinner and which I was obliged to fix myself. I was going to Wimbledon to my Dear Melville pet and I was order'd to make him fix a day to meet Count Worenzow,* his Daughter, the Harrowbys,† and some of the Hopes, those were the people Mr. Eliot told me to name to him. . . . Lord Melville fixed upon the 29th. . . . I return'd here on Friday Evening that I might with Miss Eliot (the Nice)

---

* Count Simon Woronzow, the Russian Ambassador.

† Lady Georgiana Augusta Leveson-Gower, daughter to the Marquess of Stafford, married the Hon. William Eliot, afterwards second Earl of St. Germans. Lady Harrowby was her sister.

arrange the Rooms and see all in proper order, we both got up early and gather'd all the flowers we could and Dress'd the Drawing Room, after, I dress'd the lady of the House to great advantage, as she thinks no body does for her so well, and she did, poor thing, look very well and was in Excellent spirits and put me in High Spirits also, she desir'd me to look well and put on all my agreeables for Count Worenzow, but I had Walk'd so much in the Heat of the day and was busy till past five that I was quite in a Real Heat and my Red face bore testimony of it pretty well, lord Melville's excuse which arrived with a tender note to me, besides, did not even Cool it, nor Dressing in a Hurry and I was not able to go down before the Worenzows came in, tho' Miss Eliot told me I never look'd so well, but I was uncomfortably Hot and I had a great Hot Dinner in View. I waited for the arrival of the the Harrowbys who are always late, that I might get in to the Room with them. I heard the Sign (?) at the Door, my Windows are not front, and therefore I hustled Down Stairs as fast as possible and as I was upon the last Step close to the Drawing Room Door as you know, I found myself exactly close and opposite to whom, Do you think? No, you never can guess, the last person I expected to see or indeed wish'd to see, but there was not a possibility of a Retreat for me, when I saw a profound bow, and my Eyes met such a pair of dark penetrating Eys (*sic*), can you guess? *that* CANNING *Man*—he was announced loud and he would let me pass in before him. I thought I must have died; Lady G. was afraid to look at me, and so was Eliot too for they had play'd me a trick and injoy'd in their Hearts how Compleatly I had humour'd it by a Mistake and they guess'd my misfortune immediately. I set myself as near the Door upon the Sofa and behaved very pretty. I had taken my Determination in the instant and followed it up, I saw Charles Bentinck and glad to do something I gave him a kind nod and he return'd a fine low bow and after Whisper'd Mr. Eliot. Mr. Canning had got to the Window with Worenzow by this time but I saw Eliot ready to die with laughing to himself and presently up Bentinck came to me telling me how glad he was to see me look so beautiful and in such High Health and excused himself over and over for having taken me for Mrs. Canning yet he thought she was not so tall and he kept his Glasses stuck before his eyes the while. All this he said loud enough for all the circle of ladys to hear and Lady Georgiana look'd so funny and injoyed it so much that I could kill her and I gave her many a Reproachful look all the day, for I could not get near enough to speak to her. Miss Eliot and I had fix'd to sit on each side of Eliot at the foot of the table where 12 people were to sit and I saw the Canning man close at my elbow ready to pop into the next but I put Miss Eliot Down Close to me and he sat the other side of her which did not save me from him as she is like a thread-paper and he saw me before and behind her and talk'd to me and indeed was very Civil to me, and I was obliged to laugh at some of his fun which I had settled not to do (is that not like me?) but I could not Help it, and as I had determined to laugh the day out, I went on and did not think of anything. I saw Lady G. from the Head of the table smiling at me and watching me, and I made angry faces at her and while I was doing so she Call'd out and said ' Pray Mr. Canning, tell me have you heard from y^r friend Mr. Frere since he left Town ? ' I did not hear his answer but she was going on, a great many people were talking loud but I felt that my face was no longer *Red* and I felt very sick and that goodnatured Eliot close by me saw it in a minute and said ' Come, let us have a glass of y^r favourite red wine ' and filled it while he spoke without seeming to look at me.   I took it off without looking at him and in the instant Mr. C. turn'd Round and said 'Pray Lady E., have you been long return'd from Bath, you were very ill when you went there and I am glad to see you so perfectly well '—the letter he frank'd to me there and *how he could* have heard of my illness came across my mind immediately and his only having stop'd talking of you to Lady G.—but I answer'd very well according to the *System* I had arranged in my mind for the Day.   After Dinner he got by me and we talk'd a quantity and I kept hard at work with Lord Melville.   I was so much afraid he should name any body else and I began after the Dinner Scene to feel that I could not manage such an attack and Ld. Melville's subject * gave me plenty to keep going, one stop I was afraid of, for I was determined he should not pity me . . . I can see you laugh so Heartily at my Running down stairs to meet the Man in the World I most dreaded to meet and who I never thought of, but the Eliots thought that I would not say why but would send an excuse if I knew he was invited and I, knowing you were safely lodged in Wales, I never thought about who was invited. . . . Had you been in London you would have been asked unknown to me and I should have pop'd upon you and Canning together, which would have been only a degree Worse as I am convinced that Man's Eyes see through one, and yet I think I deceiv'd him pretty well tho' he did look me through and took opportunitys of speaking often to me and fixing his eyes upon me, and unfortunately the things I usually eat of were before him and that Wicked lady G. Eliot always said 'Pray Mr. C., Help Lady E. to that as she likes it, but Help her as if you Help'd a bird' and that obliged me to Speak to him which she wanted. . . ."

* Lord Melville's impeachment.

In spite of her dislike to her lover's friend, Lady Erroll was ready to be his champion when others attacked him. In December 1804, when Lord Sidmouth had agreed to join Pitt, and it was generally thought that the same Ministry could not include him and Canning, she writes: "Ld. Glasgow gave me a whisper when I was going out that he heard that Ld. Sidmouth was to come in and Canning go out as those two it was thought could not Stay in together. I did not believe that Canning was going out but I believe Ld. Sidmouth wants to replace the Duke of Portland * which Ld. G. said was the place named for him. I am obliged to say that I forgot entirely at that instant that I hated Mr. Canning. In short I did not feel certainly in the Humour to say *I hate that Canning man.*"

More than ten years later Canning was in evil plight. His steady refusal to take any part in the proceedings against the Princess of Wales had injured him with the Regent as much as his faithfulness to the cause of Catholic Emancipation, bequeathed to him by Pitt, was to injure him with the extreme Tories. His unpopularity had increased on all sides, and a pretext was found for attacking him in the insinuation that his special diplomatic mission to Lisbon had been created merely to enable him to take his invalid son to a warmer climate. Lady Erroll's generous, illogical soul was at once in arms for the man whom she detested. "I hear Canning is certainly coming home. I hope his appearance will do away all this odious public impression against him and which now has taken a Regular bad form, he is only named as if politically dead. It was much better when they abused him and argued upon the impropriety of

* As President of the Council.

the Mission, but now the tone is changed, and one hears *what an End Canning has Made of himself*, another says *how sorry I am for him*, then again, *how that Man with Talents to be at the head of Everything has lost himself* and *forfeited the Confidence of the Country*! Within the last four months I have been hearing all this and a great Deal more and observed progressively the abuse Change into this bad Stile. I hate to write this to you but that I think it is Right you who are one of his best friends and possesses his Confidence should be aware of it all and perhaps give him some necessary hints when he arrives, as he may do something to stop the odious progress. One can Hardly suspect Castlereagh could be bad Enough to bring him into this Scrape on purpose, with an appearance at the Same time of Serving him, to lose his popularity, and yet it is gone abroad that Ministers knew no Prince was coming to Portugal when they sent him to comp^t [compliment] one, and therefore allow Every body to see that it was merely a Job to employ and inrich Canning who had Talents to command Everything in a fair way." ,

An undated letter says: "I heard much of you at Dinner yesterday, and if you heard and saw me when I took Canning's part, who was abominably abused, you would not think that I HATED him. I do not know why but I cannot indure to hear him pulled to pieces for I know he is a man of parts and of Strict Honor."

All this has carried us far from the political appointments of 1804 that displeased Lady Erroll so severely. The fashions of that year were no more to her taste.

ST. ALBAN'S ST., *July* 3, 1804.

"I can assure you that I never saw in all my life such a terrible set of Coxcombs as the New set of London men are, their Crops are cut in the oddest Manner, some have hair Curl'd at the top of the Head all along like a Real Coxcomb and others have it all forced up behind with something or other which makes the Short Hair look like a Porcupine or [as] if they [were] frightened, and I saw one Handsome Man, as they call him, with his Coxcomb along the top of his Head, but below it His Hair divided *as Mine is* and put behind his Ears, he look'd exactly like a Woman. It was quite a treat to me to see Ld. Boringdon and Ld. Villiers come in with their Brides, Dress'd like Gentlemen, their Hair powder'd and Ty'd."

Lord Boringdon's bride was Lady Augusta Fane, daughter of John, Earl of Westmorland. Canning, in a letter to Frere written at this time, calls her " a very beautiful girl of seventeen," but every one did not admire her. Lady Erroll writes to tell Frere that "Mrs. Canning made a Compleat Conquest of Mr. Eliot yesterday and I believe he Grudged the Privy Counsellors their privilege more than ever on that account, the two Brides he did not at all like particularly Lady Boringdon [whom] he thinks Horrible not like a *Woman*, you need not tell this to anybody, he was very funny about her I assure you and made me laugh quantities and about the observations of her having grown since her Marriage, her age, etc., etc., he said they must have meant her immense Arms which she did not know what to do with."

In the autumn of 1804 Lady Erroll was staying with the Eliots, "who are the people in England I am most at my ease with and who treat me and Really love me as they would a Sister and nurse me and take care of me when I am ill and uncomfortable." On this occasion she had to play the nurse, as the children, who were all ill with measles, caught scarlet fever on their recovery. "Here I am for another Month, I suppose," writes Lady Erroll, consoling herself with the thought that she was "of great use and of great consequence to Lady G." She must have been glad of a little rest at Bath, where we find her in November drinking the waters, and as usual surrounded by friends, among whom a certain Mr. Livingston was prominent. He was an elderly *beau* who had visited nearly every court in Europe, and was on the most confidential terms with Lady Erroll, whom he considered as his charge. One of her letters begins with bantering congratulations to Frere, who had just been made a Privy Councillor.

"BATH, *Jan.* 21*st*, 1805.

"If I had been able, my Dear *Right Honble Friend* to write to you before, I should not have done it, as I thought it would make you a great deal too *pert* and *Vain* to be sworn into a seat at the Privy Council and to Receive a letter from *me* in the *same* Week, yes, *me* (I suppose you will say 'and I am not at all Vain') but I am not by any means Certain that I do not Still prefer his *old Excellency* Sitting under the Rural Canopy of Chestnuts in 'Cintra's Shades' kissing one's Hand, to the Gold-embroidered Canopy at St. James's, doing the same Homage to George the 3rd—take that, Mr. Privy Councillor, and you may be jealous of his old Excellency if you like, I confess I like him and love him. . . . I have got a most Scolding letter from my Dowr. Mother in law for coming here without a Man Servt. and a kind of Nurse Maid and not content with that she wrote a letter to old Livingston to whom she has not Written for some time, and at which he has been affronted—to beg him to speak to me and to attend to me as I ought not to be without proper attendance, so you see I have made peace between those two old Creatures without intending it—for he is delighted to get such a letter of Confidence from her and they write every day now about me. . . . I did not know you were Sworn in till after that old Livingston sitting at the foot of my bed said to amuse me 'So I see Mr Frere is made a privy Councillor.' The light was in my face and I had Courage, nervous as I was, to answer 'Oh, he is, I am glad, but I had heard at the Eliots he was to be, before I left Town'—and as I do not mean to encourage y^r Vanity I will not tell you how anxiously I made my Maid bring me all the Newspapers when he was gone and I saw it over and over in different Ways."

Mr. Livingston seems to have been privileged to walk in and out of Lady Erroll's bedroom at all times. A month later, she writes, " I have not a moment and Livingston is constantly in the Room, he sat by me yesterday while I was dressing [in] his French Stile, and as there was an English Hair Dresser we spoke french all the [time], he was delighted, it put him in mind of 'the days of his youth,' and he always admires me more in my *bed* and at my Toilette and he was pleas'd and he amused me much with his *old paris* anecdotes and he put me in humour and I look'd pretty of course when I went out and he told me to be *satisfied* and that was something you know, in my favor."

She reciprocated Livingston's attentions by calling on him when an illness confined him to his room, and another letter describes her visit to the invalid. " He looks so pretty with a flannel gown and a Stick up Night cap. Lady Nelson detected me with him yesterday, she miss'd him at the partys and she Call'd and immediately come up stairs and said she would see him in or out of bed and in she came so grieved and Concern'd that I shall like her ever again, she is a most pleasing Woman and I think his lordship has a bad taste to prefer that old beast Lady Hamilton to her."

In the July of 1805 she was back at Hampton Court, consoling herself by visits to Town where she met several of the Frere brothers.   " I am obliged to say that y^r father has much reason to be proud of his family from all I have seen . . . I am in mourning for an Uncle in law.   It is the second time I have put it on since I was married for the same Woman's *two*, old men both.   I wish I could find out a 3rd old man for her, Livingston is too Young by far for her taste ; he is now in Wales he tells me upon a frightful Coast, not a Tree—Tenby, a bathing place in South Wales.   I have really been annoy'd here by Music playing all Manner of tunes Sunday Evenings under my Windows and every body Walk like a Vauxhall, full Dress'd.   I was obliged to sit by myself all the evenings as I could not go to my Wilderness without Walking thro' this ful Dress Mob and I have not Confidence enough to tell people that they are doing wrong and to pretend that I am better than other people, and particularly as there is a Clergyman and his family in the Palace a witness of what is without Joke quite Scandalous.   I don't care if you laugh at me for this but I cannot Help feeling Shock'd at what I can't get away from, as it is Close under my Windows and I have no Retreat from it."

Among Lady Erroll's elderly admirers no one was more attentive or more favoured than Henry Dundas, Lord Melville, who first recommended her to Frere's attentions. The attachment was platonic on both sides, but the lady amused herself by teasing Frere with details of the favours bestowed on "my Old Darling Melville." " I had a visit from Ld. Melville this morning : he was in High Spirits and looks young and gay and made love as usual . . . I have had two long Mornings of lord Melville at H. Court and four kisses of course, one always coming in and one going away " . . . " I have heard by this post that my Dear Ld. Melville has given me a 50 gun Ship for a friend of mine."

After reading the last extract, one is less disposed to wonder that Lord Melville was impeached on the charge of misapplying the money voted for the Naval Estimates. In many respects he had been an active and efficient First Lord of the Admiralty, but he had allowed his subordinate, Mr. Trotter, to keep a portion of the public money at his private bankers and there were entries made of large advances for " secret service," of which he could give no account. Every other Head of a Department must have done the same, and Pitt himself was not guiltless ; unfortunately, Lord Melville was unpopular with the Opposition, and the chance of striking him a blow, and at the same time affecting superior virtue, was too good to be lost. Some of Pitt's own colleagues turned against him, amongst them Lord Sidmouth, to whom this seemed a favourable opportunity of exhibiting the narrow-minded rectitude which made him so respected by the King and the British public. By a curious coincidence Dundas had carried a bill in 1785 to prevent the Treasurer of the Navy appropriating the public money to his private use.

Lady Erroll was furious with every one, and particularly with the culprit for his lame defence, and with Frere for not having been present :—" You cannot imagine how I have felt for my unfortunate friend Lord M. altho' I had no hopes from his Speech, and when Mr. Eliot came home in Spirits and repeated the Substance of it to me assuring me at the same time that it had made a very great impression upon the house, but when he mention'd what he said about Scotland I was indeed thunderstruck, tho' that did not show that he used the money for his own private purpose, yet it allowed the opposition to believe that he apply'd the Navy Money to buy Scotch Members, which tho' serving Government is a kind of thing that should never see light, and what he has, all his life been accused of, and it is hard he should suffer for his zeal to serve his country."

In July 1805, Gillray published a caricature representing Lord Melville as the " Wounded Lion," assailed by asses, conspicuous among whom are Lord Sidmouth's brother and brother-in-law, Hiley Addington and Bragge. This paper was lying on Lady Erroll's sofa at Hampton Court at eleven o'clock on a July morning when Lord Melville walked into her sitting-room, and hearing that she was still in bed, opened her door and told her "to get up immediately and not be so lazy and Idle." " I was obliged to Scold him out of my Room," she says naively. While she dressed herself, Lord Melville enjoyed the caricature, which he had not seen, and then sat down with her to eat "a Venison Pasty."

"Our public news is very bad indeed . . . . . of every kind, and I think people really are alarm'd about the Invasion as they believe it likely independant of the good private information they have that the *Great Emperor* wishes to get it over before he engages in the war against Russia. Did you know this Russian Ambassador who is arrived here from Madrid ? he arrived three days ago at Thomas' Hotel in Grand Stile 33 of them altogether, and they have made such a Riot in the Hotel that three families have been obliged to take lodgings in the Sqr to get away from their Bustle and Noise, the Courier came up to the Sqr full gallop with a Jacket all over Gold Lace cracking his Whip as hard as he could and without getting off his Horse he calls out in bad English Ho! one pot Porter, 2 pot, and three, and he finished the 3 on Horseback as quick as he could one after another to the great amusement of all the John Bulls who had gathered around him by the Cracking of his Whip and his foreign look and laced Jacket. Can't you see it all? he then got off his Horse Drunk, with the 3 *Pots Porter* and Danced about to such a degree that the Mob laughed so much that he got into a Rage at last and with difficulty Mr. Thomas got him into the House ; he ordered every Room in the House and such a Dinner as never was heard of. You can't conceive how much it amused—and foolish as it was, I write it on purpose to amuse you. Don't be affronted, trifles sometimes have entertained the most profound philosophers."

Lady Erroll's parting present to the Eliots was her own portrait by Cosway, which is still in existence and was shown at the Guelph Exhibition. " It is a great deal too handsome for *any body* I think ; he has given it a Remarkable fine Countenance grave and thoughtful." When it was finished she considered it " very Stupid looking and solemn." Certainly the melancholy figure with the beautiful neck and bust who leans her head on one arm, and holds a half-closed book, is not what one would have expected the writer of these letters to be.

On September 15th she writes a good scolding to Frere, which, by all accounts, he richly deserved. " I have heard from Every quarter 'what can have become of Frere ? where has he hid himself?' The Princess of Wales has plagued Lady G. Eliot about it and said ' For my part]I believe Mr. Pitt has sent him to Madrid, unknown to anybody to arrange there, or elsewhere, it is so Stupid of the Man to get out of the Way of his interest so intirely when he ought to be in the Way'—then the Harrowbys when they were here said over and over 'where can Frere be?' The fact is that you have been imprudent to get *out* of the *Way* when there is nothing to do but to meet Mr. Pitt and all such people at Dinner and parties of every kind, and which is always the time for a Man who is looking forward to arrange a *good Winter* for himself. If Mr. Pitt was only to meet people in London while parliament is sitting, he could never form a friendship or like anybody, he has not time, and it is exactly those foolish summer parties which he likes so much that afford good fortunes to so many who you know have no Real Merit to Advance them otherwise. He is like a School Boy, he is in his Holidays as gay as anybody and as foolish and is Dining with everybody, looking at a Dock, going in a Boat, or something, and he is *toadied* the while and can find out easily the Talents of a Man in such Mixtures, here is a Preaching with a witness you will say but it will have no effect, as I believe like the Princess of Wales who said the other day 'Mr. Canning says very true about Mr. Frere, that where ever he goes there he sticks and never wishes to move. What a pity he is so indolent,' she added, . . . The Princess of Wales has been here always talking of you, she never ceases to talk of you and *me* to Lady G. Eliot who told me she Worried her about us, and asked so many questions that she was always obliged to be upon her guard when she spoke to her, and particularly this last day, when she (lady G.) told me she saw evidently she wanted to find out whether you and I wrote to one another and whether we quarrelled or not, she seemed to hint that we were no longer friends, in short she was very tiresome and disagreeable lady G. told me, and that she got nothing for her pains . . . She [Lady Georgiana] goes on board to-day and I am playing the fool dreadfully. . . . Mr. Pitt asked me one of the days he was here if I thought Mr. Long would do well for Ireland. I told him I did not know, as I had not the pleasure of knowing him sufficiently for me to judge, but that I believed Ease of Manners and openness of address was the only thing which could succeed in that Country ; he said 'I believe you.'"

From all these troubles and vexations Lady Erroll was glad to escape to Lord Keith's house near Ramsgate where she spent part of the autumn. A large number of her friends were in the neighbourhood and they dined by turns at each other's house "one set of us like one family." In the morning the ladies sat on the pier and watched the troops embark. " It was the fashion for the ladies to meet in the fine new pier Room from which we saw all the troops march under the Window and Step off the Pier into the transports ; 3,000 already are gone, those we have sent off were the Germans and certainly the finest-looking Men I ever saw, the Ladies lost their Hearts to the Officers who came in to us in the Pier House and each Regt. made their Respective Bands Play for us, on Tuesday the Guards embark and I suppose the mornings will be spent in the same way. . . . I can't Help laughing perhaps too much at some Quizes who Ld. Keith must ask here and as we all understand our looks we do sometimes behave naughty, yesterday it was not all my fault tho' they left most part of it at My Door, the Mansfields and a great many people Dined here. I sat next to Lord Keith who is ever saying something in my Ear to set me off, on my other side was Lady C(atherine) Harris quite as bad in her quiet way, Lady Mansfield opposite with that little fright Souza by her who would talk Constantly English Portuguese and french well mix'd up together, he always appealed to me about Portugal. I touch'd my neighbours and prais'd it beyond anything, they were Ready to Die as the Man went on an hour then with his *certamenta que sim* and my two Neighbours and the Company laugh'd so loud and so much that the little Man laugh'd with us and thought he was [a] delightful Creature."

A letter written in the following month describes a characteristic proceeding on the part of this delightful Irishwoman. It is impossible to make out what actually took place, but it seems that, having to send money to a poor widow, she mislaid some bank-notes and suspected her man-servant of taking them, However, he was proved guiltless, although " a £10 Note " was missing "which has not Cast up yet but which I am persuaded is poked into some letter which I have not as yet answer'd and will come to my hand in a seasonable time perhaps."

No wonder that her ladyship was the despair of every one who attempted to do business with her ! On another occasion she writes, " Here is a fine Bore this instant come in to me, a letter from the Grandfather of my Nephew (Lord Wallscourt) to whom my Brother sent a proper full copy of my Father's Will, and as he is in Town I was order'd by Fitzgerald to send for their Copy or a Copy of it that he might save me by seeing it, and yet this foolish old Man writes to me that I must go to his House to Read it *myself* as it is too long for him to Copy and yet he expects *me* to read this long very long thingumbob." A little later, we find "You must not look this Way tomorrow, as I am obliged to give up the early part of the day to Mr. Fitzgerald (Master of the Rolls Elect) and for what, do you know? to be scolded in the most unmerciful Way for an Hour and to hear nothing but Chancery business, Trustees powers, accumulated in trust Money, accumulation upon that interest, did you ever hear

such Words and such a bore?   He began to scold to-day
but I told him it was Sunday and it was not proper to
be angry, but that tomorrow at one o'clock he might
Scold till Night if he liked.   At the same time I assured
him that it was out of his power or of any other persons
to make me like myself first.   He says I think of no body
but my Brother.   I did not like to say he told a *Story* and
I have promised in the most Solemn Manner to attend
to all he had to say tomorrow provided I was not the
Object of the business, in short [he was] to say it was
the case of a Mr. Something and not Lady Erroll's ; he
declared I was incorrigible but that I always got the better
for all that.   Adieu, I am going to Dress for a Dutchess
of Gordon Dinner with all my old Friends."

VI.

LOVE-LETTERS OF A·HUNDRED YEARS AGO
(continued).

1804-1808.

THE winter of 1805-6 passed away monotonously for Lady Erroll at Hampton Court. She saw little of her own friends, and yet could not enjoy solitude in peace, owing to the frequent interruptions of the other inmates of the Palace. She concludes a letter with "The Cats are coming, I hear them Ring, and even hear them Squalling, is Lady Erroll at home? What would they say if they knew I was Writing to a *Beau*?"

In the spring of 1806 she was again in Town, and the following letter, dated "Fenton's Hotel, March 7th," probably describes a day of her life at this time:—

"I came to Town on Wednesday, and intended to go to the Antient Music, made a Bungle about my Ticket, it was too late to get it. The Drawing Room was the object yesterday, they made a mistake in my Dress, it was not deep enough for my Mourning and the glass of my Sedan Chair was not mended; looked at my Lodgings, found them Abominable. I walked all over the Town till I was Lord, how tired! Looked in upon the Dutchess of Gordon while she took off her Hoop to Dine with the Bedfords."

This was Jane Duchess of Gordon, who rode down the High Street of Edinburgh on a pig's back in the days of her wild girlhood, and raised recruits for the new Highland regiment, when other means had failed, by allowing each man to take the shilling from between her lips. Hoops were *de rigueur* for Court dress until the days of George the Fourth, although in private life the ladies' skirts had been growing more and more scanty since the days of the French Revolution. The Duchess insisted that Lady Erroll should return in the evening, "and because I was very tired I went. I believe it was 4 o'clock this morning when Lady Harrington set me home here. I saw last night every Creature I ever knew. Mr. Grey, my old acquaintance made his way through the Crowd to tell me how Glad he was to see my *pretty* face again, he sat by me and we had a great Deal of Chat. I felt so odd sitting beside him and Mrs. Whitbread, and then the odious Whitbread Man came and joined, though I had avoided Meeting that Man's Eye for a long time yet I was obliged to be Civil because he addressed me in such a good-humoured Manner. All the New and most of the Old Lot of Monsters were there, as the Drawing Room was particularly full this Ball was so, and all the Diamonds made a very fine House look most brilliant. . . . I hope you will be amused with my disappointments when I came to Town, there were so Many that instead of being Angry and Cross I could not Help laughing at them all. Ainslie called twice but I was out and therefore did not see him. Goodnight. I am going to bed to get all the Sleep I had lost last night. That beautiful Creature Lord Temple, and Lord Darnley Winged me Down to Supper and we made a pleasant party for ourselves at a Small Table, Lady Castlereagh made one and Really was the Naked truth as she is aptly called."

The Bishop of St. Alban's now possesses a miniature formerly belonging to Sir Robert Ainslie, which is believed to represent Lady Erroll. If she really did sit for it, she need not have animadverted upon Lady Castlereagh's undress, as it depicts a coil of dark hair, an ear, a cheek, the tip of a nose, a neck, and a back undraped to the waist. Sir Robert Ainslie is said to have been a fervent admirer of the beautiful Irishwoman, and to have refrained from proposing to her because he knew that his friend was preferred. Her Ladyship held him cheap, after the manner of a woman. Frere once sent her some partridges from Roydon to tempt her failing appetite. Ainslie came to supper, and seeing her eat nearly the whole of a bird, naturally concluded that partridges were her favourite delicacy and sent her "Constant fresh supplys." "The little fool could not guess that a few lines from a certain old wretch gave my supper a particular good flavour," is all the gratitude that the Countess expresses for his kindness.

On September 23rd Lady Erroll writes: " Fox's death seems to make no noise. I asked the Dean of Windsor and Harry Legg who I meet on Sunday at Dinner what they thought of the New Great Man, they said, alas the Change will be trifling we fear, they said T. Grenville would not fill Fox's place, positively, they seemed very low about it, particularly Henry Legg, who has an office."

Towards the end of September Lady Erroll set off for Tunbridge Wells accompanied by two of her sisters and a little niece with " A Head Red enough to set one on fire." They started at eleven o'clock on Friday morning, stopping by the way to see Lord and Lady Glasgow. " The little shy peer astonish'd me with his *Extreme* Civility to the Miss Blakes, and we were obliged to stay dinner to oblige him. . . . Lord Henley * has been to see me, but he is too Stingy to ask me to Dinner as I have two Sisters, tho' he is my only Relation here. . . ."

"TUNBRIDGE WELLS, Oct. 21.

" It is such a long time since I wrote to you that I hope you cannot think me very troublesome now. . . . I must confess we lead a most Regular life here, I get up at the same Hour, Drink Water at the same time, Read newspapers, letters, and gossip, Walk, Drive at the same Hour every day. I think I laugh also at the same time too, the only Variety I have is in the Drive and William Spencer's Jokes which are levell'd at poor Sick Cross Rogers when Souza is not here."

Souza, the little Portuguese who had been at Ramsgate in the previous year, seems to have been the recognised butt of the party. The Hon. William Spencer had a great reputation in his own day as an agreeable companion and a graceful writer of *vers de société*. He is now forgotten, unless readers of the " Rejected Addresses " may happen to recall Philander's Ode to Lady Elizabeth Mugg, beginning, " Sobriety, cease to be sober."

" . . . I cannot describe the beauty of the surrounding Country here. Every day I am Drove to some Magnificent Building, either in Ruins or kept in repair by some body living in the Dwellings of Heros one has read of ; in short, independent of their Natural beauties they all interest one from almost all having been inhabited by Characters celebrated in History. I can't Help observing that all those fine Situations have been Chozen by Bishops or Monks. We went a very large party to Somer Hill of Grammont memory. I went with Lady Susan Fincastle in her

---

* Morton, Lord Henley, younger brother of the first Lord Auckland.

Curricle, the Rest Rode, and we were much amused with Souza making most tender love to Norah,* his manner of Riding, etc., etc., and his Explanations *why* he was *obliged* to order a particular kind of Stuff'd Saddle for himself, the English ones being too hard, too Smooth and too *inconvenient*, which he took particular pains to make us understand. Mr. Spencer took good care to make him say every thing he chose, and I can assure you I was ready to Expire from laughing, as was also the whole party, with the Lord Chief Justice Ellenborough, who made his fun also, and more than anybody enjoyed Norah's Coolness when Souza was pouring out his admiration in french, English, portuguese, and Italian, and the usual gestures. She was obliged to get off her Horse to get her Saddle right, and he made twenty attempts to put her up again, to the great amusement of all the party, who got round him and would not give any Help until Norah, quite tired of laughing, and feeling the Company were sufficiently gratified, told him *to get away*, which you may believe did not compose our Risible faculties. . . . Rogers left us in a passion because we laugh'd so much; he hates to see any body laugh or look happy. Spencer wrote the most Satirical lines I ever heard upon this dislike of his. I wish I could remember them for you, as they are very Clever ; but as Rogers is *his friend*, he gave them to Lady Susan to read to Lord F. and myself, and immediately after put them in the fire, and therefore I can't recollect them Regularly, tho' I remember Enough to amuse me. . . . Let me know when you hear of Bartle. Lord Ellenborough tells me that Lord Morpeth has orders to follow the King of Prussia and he supposes him with the Army, so Bartholomew will see fine doings before he gets back. Adieu."

* Lady Erroll's youngest sister, Honoria Louisa Blake.

Bartle Frere had been sent as Lord Morpeth's secretary on the mission to the King of Prussia. They arrived at headquarters two days before the battle of Jena, in which the Prussian army suffered a crushing defeat. " The King himself escaped, or rather fled, without one hundred men assembled round him,' and the Duke of Brunswick received a mortal wound. After this Lord Morpeth thought it advisable to return home at once, as Lady Erroll records.

" Oct. 30th. 1806.

"You see I am still here, my Dear Man, and very anxious to hear from you, you Lazy Mortal. Pray take up your pen, let me know if you have heard from Bartle, you might, by the same opportunity [that] Lord Morpeth has been heard of, who seems to me to have been pretty well frighten'd. I confess I am, for your brother, who I wish back again. The last news is so very bad that it discourages every hope of success against that Horrid Villain. I have been cursing all Stars and orders on account of that fine Brave Prussian Prince, who I dare say was mark'd out by the enemy from the folly of Wearing his Stars, and the King of Prussia has lost an able Support by his Death, and I fear His Majesty Stands much in need of somebody to jog his elbow, I hope the pretty Queen will keep him in order, *we ladies all here* are in hopes that by her attendance in the Campaign [it may] end Gloriously by some *Clever management* of her's. . . Our Society is much lessen'd, many of the Birds belonging to the House of Lords we have had here, are gone to Shelter themselves in London or to Canvas Counties for their friends, and to Bargain their Boroughs away. We have been lucky I must say, not to have had one single Exceptionable person of our party ; this place is famous for keeping off those kind of Naughty Lords and ladys, they never appear here, as they know the Society only mix in a kind of way to prevent their being noticed by those Chances they find so convenient at Brighton and Ramsgate, etc., etc.

"The Lord Chief Justice was gayer than any body, attended every morning pantile Walking, before Breakfast, where we all arranged our Rides. [Here a part of the letter has been torn off.] Well then, his parting was quite tender on Monday, he said he was like a Boy going to School from his Holy days to tasks and lashes. There were three ladys who disputed his Heart, therefore no body could tell why he was so *particularly* distress'd on leaving 'the *most* pleasant party he ever met in his Holy days.' Lady Susan Fincastle look'd as if she was the favourite. The Dutchess of St. Alban's turn'd the side of her Head which is not deaf to hear if she could gather anything for her Comfort, and Lady Erroll declared that she had been long in possession of his heart, but he has escap'd us all, and is now at the Old Bailey! Horrible taste! You will. think mine worse when I tell you I like Rogers, he is so ill, poor man, and so low and uncomfortable that I pity him, and I like to talk, Walk, and prose with him. His Character is singular, and he is a better-natur'd man than people in general suppose. I can't conceive his friendship for Spencer, their Characters are so opposite, they don't think alike upon any subject, their Habits [are] not like, and often I see Rogers have a Contempt for him."

" *Nov. 6th.*

" I am very anxious to hear the fate of your Brother, believe me I am and ever shall be most truly interested about him. I grieve that his Mission has been so unsuccessful, I believe Lord Morpeth was too young in the business, and too soon frighten'd. I fell in a great Scrape upon this Subject, as we were all here naturally anxious for foreign news, therefore we contrived to get to the Reading Room at four o'clock to have the newspapers of the same day which in the Morning with our letters we can't command. I got the better of Lord Fincastle, and got the papers before he arrived, but when he did come with Lady Susan, my sister, Rogers, and a few more, I scream'd out in my indignation 'Lord Morpeth * is a fine person to send, like a Child, frighten'd and run away, burnt his papers and yet Can't tell any thing but what he heard from a few Mad Cowardly Runaways like himself, but he had a Man with him, who must have been hurt to the Soul by such Childish Conduct. I dare say the poor little peer will never get alive to England!' I had hardly done when I recollected I was speaking to his friends and near relations, and flew away as quick as I could without daring to Raise my Eyes, but I found after that I need not be alarm'd as the Whole Party not only subscribed to my opinion but had the Comfort of hearing similar exclamations from the multitude who crowded to the library to hear the news which was so bad as not to incline anybody to have mercy upon the poor little Man ; for a moment nothing was heard but laughing at him and thinking how his fears affected him. One said, ' This was all to please that puppy Lord Carlisle he was sent upon such an important mission.' When I saw Lord Fincastle after, he laugh'd amazingly at me and ask'd me how I thought Lord M.'s Health suffered from the fright, as he was sure he was in a terrible one, and so we laugh'd at him Cordially, but I thought of Bartle tho' I did not say so, and was very angry for him. Don't be angry because I laugh'd at Lord M., I could not Help it, I hate a coward, and so do you."

* George, afterwards sixth Earl of Carlisle. As he was born in 1773, he was not so very young at this time.

A few days later, Lady Erroll was alone in her rooms at Hampton Court, and as usual under the circumstances, taking the most despondent view of public and private affairs. " I am sorry to find there is such very bad news from Hamburgh. I suppose at last we must content ourselves with keeping that Emperor of the Devils out of England and let him do as he likes with all the rest of the world."

Lady Erroll was still at Hampton Court in the beginning of 1807, but she seems to have been in high society, for a letter written on January 7th is full of the sayings and doings of the Royal Family. With the Prince of Wales she was on friendly terms. He once expressed a wish that she should succeed Lady Elgin as governess to the Princess Charlotte, and Lady Erroll looked forward to his becoming "a Real friend" to Frere in the future—a prospect which would have been a fatal shock to Frere's old father had it ever occurred to him as a possibility. Lady Erroll did not approve of the Duke of Clarence. " I am sorry to tell you that the Duke of Clarence told me yesterday that they are determined to enforce the Pig Iron tax with all their power immediately—'we lost it last year, but nothing this year shall be left undone to get the better of those Walkers and a whole Set of D—d Canting Religious dishonest Rascals who are as Cheating a pack as ever existed'—so much for His Royal Highness's Elegant language, you have his own words as I heard them. His greatest ambition now is to be a Col. of Militia, he sent Col. Braddyll to Brighton to ask the Prince for the Sussex Militia vacant by the D. of Richmond's Death, the P. laugh'd, ask'd if he was Mad, and told Braddyll to say any thing to him but tell [him] that Regiment must go to the Lord Lieutenant of the County, and now he is going to have the Middlesex

Militia, and turn out old Col. Bailey who has it, give him a Consideration."

His Royal Highness's elegant language need not have been so shocking to Lady Erroll, who was herself accustomed to use strong expressions. It was only patriotic to call Buonaparte the "Emperor of all the Devils," but she pities Mr. Hammond, who "has got a Daughter, poor Devil," and implores Frere to write her an amusing letter because "this house is full of Bores, the Devil take them all."

About this time a plot was framed against the Princess of Wales, "the end of which was to destroy her fair fame, if not to take away her life."* Lord Malmesbury, who had proved himself so true a friend to the Princess on the journey from Brunswick to London, now came forward, and with the help of his advice she escaped from the toils. The charge brought against her was false, but her own foolish conduct had made it seem plausible to many sober-minded persons, and she was surrounded with spies who were eager to take advantage of every careless word or look. Lady Erroll's Irish heart naturally inclined her to take the weaker side, and she wrote to Frere on March 6th, 1807, "I hear they are hard at that poor Princess of W. now, doing all they can to plague her, it can't, I fear, end well for her, poor thing." A little later, her tone is somewhat changed. Perhaps she had been talking to the Prince of Wales, or perhaps the circumstance that Mr. Eliot was the Princess's friend had roused the spirit of opposition. "I had all the Princess of Wales's History from Eliot as I came along, he is her great friend, Dined with her the day before, and has *all* her papers, which he would Show me, if he was not, and I also, going out of Town. She sent the King her long

<hr>

* Lord Malmesbury

letter of so many pages which obliged him to call his Council and all his great people who after Reading all on both sides sent a Written opinion that they thought her *perfectly* Clear'd on *every Charge*, the King sent it to her, and she offer'd to pay her Respects some days after, and the K. wrote to her that the P. had been to Windsor to request of him not to see her till his *own* Council should look over all and give their opinion, since which time she has heard nothing, and therefore, if she is not received soon at Court, she intends to publish all and the King's letter and his Minister's opinion, in which she is quite Right. The page's Evidence is good for nothing as he has Contradicted himself several times, but he said Shocking things, and Lady D. [Lady Douglas?] said that she told her herself that she fear'd . . . ."

But the Princess's confession to " Lady D." is of too confidential a nature to be repeated, especially as there was not a word of truth in it. The page's evidence was completely disproved, but the terrible risks she had run did not make Her Royal Highness more prudent in the future.

Lady Georgiana Eliot was now dead, and although Mr. Eliot seemed anxious to continue the old warm friendship, Lady Erroll was lonely and miserable. " My dearest Man, will the coming in of the old Rogues instead of the new ones allow you to come and see me in my Solitary palace, God knows it is solitary enough. It is even more so when one knows one's friends of every kind are so near as London, and can't see them. . . . The Weather is so fine now I think I shall attempt a Walk under my Windows but I am frighten'd at the Number of Creatures who Crawl out of their Cells when the Sun Shines. It is like a Warren when all the Rabbits come out in the Sun, and then reminds me of *play* at *Ladies* when I was a Child—'How do you do, Madam? fine day, Madam, the Weather is Charming, Madam,' then a *Sliding Courtesy*, [so] that I am Ready to die to keep from laughing when all this play is perform'd under my Windows. . . . Mrs. Jordan has been . . . [dangerously ill] since last Saturday, and several Doctors with her . . . they think she can't live, poor Creature—I pity her."

There were serious political changes in March 1807, caused by the old trouble—a Catholic Relief Bill. The King, as of old, refused justice to his Catholic subjects; and there was a serious misunderstanding between him and Lord Howick over a Bill which was to give to the Catholics in every part of His Majesty's dominions " the privilege of entering into the Army or Navy, of holding any rank in either, and of being allowed to attend their own places of worship." The King insisted not only that the Bill should be withdrawn, but that the subject should not again be mooted in his reign. The Ministers declined to pledge themselves to this extent, and the King dismissed them. The Duke of Portland was commanded to form a new administration, in which Canning was given the Foreign Office.

On March 24th, Lady Erroll writes to Frere :—

" I am very sorry y^r friends have not a better parliament to meet, there are some infamous Men in that House, and some Irish, I know, who ought to have been Hang'd when so many Rebels were condemn'd, and escaped by the Contrivance of their friends, and it was not much to the Credit of the Foxites to bring in Men they knew were Real *bad Men* but [they] were obliged to keep their promises which does not prove much their *former* loyalty. There is a Mr. Coughty in parliament, a famous well-known Irish Rebel.

" Mrs. Douglas * will call upon you now to fulfil y^r promise of Carrying her to India when you are made Governor-General of Bengal, she told me you promised to carry her out [as] Housekeeper but I affronted her by saying I thought you had a better taste than to Chuse such a *House*keeper in the way *Governors Carry* them to India, and I was in hopes she could not be so *entirely devoid* of principle as to go out Governess of the Governor's Seraglio."

One cannot tell how far the correspondence between Lady Erroll and Frere was suspected by the rest of the world; it was well known to his brother George, the business man of the family, and, of course, to Bartle. She believed it to be a dead secret from all her acquaintance, and smuggled letters to Frere with a solemnity worthy of a boarding-school miss in her teens. As many of her friends belonged to the opposite political camp, she was sometimes hard pressed between her fear of betraying confidence and her anxiety to give her lover a timely warning. It was true that Frere was then taking no active part in politics on his own account, but he was always at Canning's side; and Lady Erroll, in spite of fears and scruples and her dislike to Canning, was led into a grave breach of trust for Frere's sake. In January she had petulantly declared, " I am so Jealous of that man, there never was anything like it," yet, towards the end of March, we find her writing as follows :—

" Tho' I am not quite sure that I am quite Right in what I am doing in some Respects, I feel that I am so in telling you any thing that I hear and which I must

* There are frequent allusions to Mrs. Douglas in the letters; she seems to have been a kind of humble friend, with whom the Countess quarrelled and played backgammon.

be aware is of consequence to you to know. Circumstanced as you now are with y' friend Mr. C. to Whom any information you can give him, must be useful to him and gratifying to you to procure for him, therefore I send you a Copy of a letter I read myself this day, from Lord Derby to his friend here, who sent it to me for my private information and amusement. It was only Written yesterday and tho' I cannot pretend to understand its Value, yet I think you may as well see what fears and hopes the opposite party entertain, and I pray you to burn it when you have made use of it, as I believe I should not be allow'd to look at such a letter if my friendship and intimacy with you was known, and on that Score I feel *Scruples* which I can't prevent, as I can not tell people ' I feel that I must inform Mr. F. of all you tell me.' "

It is to be hoped that Frere did burn the letter, as it is not to be found among his papers.

Two days later, her Ladyship presents an amusing picture of the helplessness of a woman—and that woman an Irishwoman—when confronted with business. " I wish, my Dearest Man, that you were near me this day, or that some Man was, but there is no such thing at this time of the year to be found here. A Man called at my Door this Morning, and pok'd in three papers which were Greek to me, one was a letter to me from the Irish Chancellor Ponsonby, sign'd by himself and in all the forms of Madam, &c., &c., to inform me that Alexr. Jeffery Esq. had Exhibitted a Bill of Complaint in his Court, and that I must appear under the penalty of 100£ on the 1st of April in the High Court of Chancery, but as my Rank excused my appearing, he instructed me to appoint a proper person to appear for me,

Sign'd ' G. PONSONBY.'

"The other paper was a Missive letter Sign'd by the Chancellor to empower me on the Score of a *peeress's privilege* to appoint a person to represent me in Court,— the 3rd paper was from a Clerk to summon me and Honoria Louisa Blake, Spinster, to appear in the High Court of Chancery on the 1st of April next (all these papers Dated March 7th) to answer such things as shall be then and there agitated against you by Alexr. Jeffery Esq. At first I was rather annoy'd and astonished and did not know where to put my Wits, this was the 31st of March, and I had not time to save it any way. I did not think so much of the penalty as I did of the delay, and as I had already suffer'd from the delay of the new appointment of Ponsonby, and on the late Changes, felt I was likely again in one year to suffer again from his Removal. I did not like it, as I fear all must be gone over again, for God('s) sake keep in this Lord Redesdale until my cause is done, and don't let me have a 3rd Chancellor to tell my Story to, in less than 18 months. In old times our good old Chancellor Lifford grew old in the Service and was only able to be lifted into his Gold Coach upon State Days."

Frere responded to this appeal with a letter of good advice, but as he omitted to prepay the postage of another letter that he wrote to Lady Erroll at the same time, her ladyship was kept waiting for half a day. "So Your Excellency thinks yrself not Worth a Shilling, which yr letter could have only Cost, and I should have had it yesterday, instead of this Morning, when both yrs arrived together. . . . . .

"I hear the Chancellor Erskine has done the most impudent indecent thing ever attempted, putting the Seal to a Grant for his own Son, during the three days he was in fact only *lent* the Seals to finish the causes he had in Hand. I hear from one of his *own* party that all the Bar are Scandalized at it, and all *his friends Shocked*—and my friend Mr. Tom Steel as Paymaster falls short in his account £20,000. The Prince of Wales was quite indignant that people should have fix'd for him his political line, not having declar'd any yet, tho' he was too well with the King not to declare that it was not his intention to give opposition to the new Ministers upon Every Subject, this was the Manner he expressed his sentiments in a letter Lord Moira Shew'd Lord Derby yesterday, when the Gentleman who told me this Dined where he also heard that the late Ministers boasted that they should divide on Wednesday 108 in the House of Lords, and should have four English Bishops with them (Prettyman one). *Those* he dined with did not believe *that*, as it was said that they Reckon'd the Bishop of Carlisle and the Eliots who had decided against them. The Duke of Cumberland [is] in a rage at not getting the ordinance, and declares openly he will oppose *Every measure* of the present Administration. Is it true that he *Stole* the Minutes of the privy Council for the Morning post? for shame, I can't believe such a thing!"

When Lady Erroll next writes, she is in despair because the dissolution of Parliament would carry Frere away into Norfolk, and she was obliged to take up her quarters with Lady Glasgow, at whose house there were no facilities for a *tête-à-tête*. "If you cannot give me a Call soon, I fear much I shall not see you—God knows when—that is *quite* quite Hard to bear. You will of course have to go to Norfolk for the Election, and at all events if you should be in Town when I am sent for, I shall be in my Sister's House where there is but one Room from Morning till

Night quite full of Women so as to Render it quite impossible for me to speak one Single word to my Dear old Man in particular before he leaves Town. Now that I have told you the produce of all my Calculations you can't be Angry with me for being in a *fuss*, in a *Rare one*, I can assure you. It began yesterday from a Visit I had from the great Lord Salsbury, he came to see his Sister and he Visited Lady Mornington and myself and he told me *pos pos* that parliament was to end this day. I am thinking this instant that you may come here this day and surprise me prettily as you did before so nicely. Is Bartle come to Town yet? I see Mr. Canning has given that Nasty Monster Paget a fine appointment and to a place he knows he will never Reach,* as Ld. Grenville did to Henry Wellesley, appointed him to Madrid when he knew perfectly he never would go—but it will put some money in Paget's Pocket and then the End will be Answer'd, I suppose. I am not at all Naughty but I am annoy'd in my Heart."

In May Lady Erroll's friends and acquaintance insisted on her coming to Town, and after a little affectation of unwillingness she consented. It was clearly her duty to attend one Drawing-Room in the year, and the fact that the Princess of Wales was to be present at the next made every one anxious to be there. Moreover there were rumours of an alliance between England, Russia and Prussia against France; Frere was appointed Envoy to Berlin, and Lady Erroll wished to procure him a medicine-chest as a parting gift. She saw one " which is made on purpose now for all people going abroad," that she thought superior to his own, and she entreated Frere to go to the shop and inspect it. A passage in one of her letters

* Sir A. Paget was sent to Turkey, but returned "re infectâ." (See Lord Malmesbury's Diary.)

looks as if the relations between Frere and herself were not as unsuspected as she fondly hoped by the outside world.

" If I should see you, I shall show you some Newspaper paragraphs some very kind friends of mine have Cut out with care because they were *against you*, and enclosed to me in a *left-Hand-Writing address*, Nasty Wretches, none but Cowards would do such a thing. I can have no guess at the Authors of such Meanness and ill-nature, at the top of one I see it is the *Star* tho' only half—and *Wednesday*." After this outburst the lady consoles Frere with " I don't mind such things, believe me," but one may be allowed to doubt the assurance.

Frere's departure for Berlin was imminent, and Lady Erroll set to work to make his " neck-cloaths," in the manner of the most devoted of wives. Mr. Eliot brought his children to see her, and could find no more agreeable topic of conversation than the state of the Continent ; this was so near a delicate subject that Lady Erroll hid her blushes by playing with the children. Ainslie had discovered the truth, and the Countess dreaded meeting him. She wept over her work for Frere, which she kept in a locked drawer, and had a mournful presentiment that she was not to see him again before he sailed.

The Peace of Tilsit put an end to Frere's Berlin mission, and dried Lady Erroll's tears. There are no more letters from her of any general interest for about a year.

In 1808 the Peninsula was in revolt against the French invaders. Sir Arthur Wellesley left Cork on July 12th, with 10,000 men to support the insurrection, and reached Corunna on the 20th. The following undated fragment, evidently scrawled in great haste, must have been written by Lady Erroll when the news of his victory at Rolica had reached her :—

"Good Gracious, how happy you must be! I give you Joy with all my heart, what a triumph for us over all other Nations! I can hardly believe that It is that same Scatter'd (?) Scarecrow Arthur Westly (*sic*) I used to play at Romps with, that has done all this. I confess I feel very proud of my Country Man and I am particularly obliged to him for even giving me a feel of Cheerfulness at this Moment which is the greatest Compliment I can pay him. I had hardly sent off yr leter (*sic*) yesterday when the news Reach'd me, and I was so sorry I was not the first to give it you."

Lady Erroll's writing was still very tremulous on September 3rd, when she wrote to congratulate Frere on the victory of Vimiero. "I cannot begin this letter, my Dearest Man, with so insignificant a Subject as myself, and therefore wish you joy of our having got possession of Junot and his Army. What a miserable Handful of Portugueses appear to serve their country, we were as well without more of them, Half Starved Soldiers and Cowardly Ignorant Fidalgos at best. I have seen but a short account of it in yesterday's Morning post, my poor idea of the Geography of that Country leads me to see Sir Arthur gathering his Laurels about 9 or 10 miles beyond *Dear* Cintra northwards by the Sea, is it so? I return'd from the Caldas to Cintra by Massa and from my observations then, I take my idea. There is no Gazette as yet, at least none late last night. . . . I confess I feel great pleasure to hear that Hero Kellerman who last Novr. 12 months was dictating strict humiliating terms to Emperors and Kings after Austerlitz, was obliged to go upon his knees to Sir Arthur W——, quite nice, I like it *loads* and *quantities*!"

CHAPTER VII.

LETTERS FROM ENGLAND.

1801—1809.

FEW of J. H. Frere's letters to his family are now in existence, and from their occasional remonstrances in the letters addressed to him, it is plain that he was irregular in his correspondence, even when allowances are made for the capture or accidental loss of a mail-bag between Spain and England. At one time, goaded by the reproaches of his mother, he took to dating his letters in the small hours of the morning, which drew from her a reminder that at such a time his head should be on the pillow but not his hand on the paper. She and old Mr. Frere wrote constantly, giving just the little touches that bring the atmosphere of home to the exile, but that have no interest for other readers.

Like old ladies at all times, Mrs. Frere found much to blame in the conduct of the rising generation, and especially in that of her own sex. While at Bath with her husband in 1803, she was much edified by a sermon from the Bishop of Meath. " He gave us an excellent discourse on the duties and importance of Women, with some serious, yet not too severe strictures on modern manners, particularly the indecorous ones derived from France. The Discourse lasted an hour and ten minutes, and was the most earnest exhortation to reformation I ever heard, and I hope it may lessen the number of Maskers at a grand Masquerade given to-night by a Mr. Champness 12 miles from Bath, which being given but once in two years, is a great event in the gay world of Bath. Three or four ladies here open their houses to see masks, and many resort to them who are not invited by Mr. Champness."

The fashionable lady of 1899 would probably not understand the expression "seeing masks," but Mrs. Frere wrote to her son at the time when Lady Delacour and Belinda Portman changed costumes, and Lady Juliana Douglas went in a domino to the ball from which her sister-in-law eloped. Another letter from Bath speaks of a state of things which we can fully realise :—

"BATH, *April 2nd*, 1803.

" The contents of your letter are such as will make us earnestly desire farther intelligence from you, of yourself ; we have so long been wishing for information that to hear that you are in a state of convalescence is a great relief to our fears ; for as this influenza has spread from France over England, we were also apprehensive that it had also visited Spain, and might be more virulent in a warmer climate. It has been more violent in its symptoms in London than at Bath ; though here it has been very general, few families escaping, though many individuals. . . .

" The London Physicians lost many patients at first ; deceived by the inflammatory symptoms with which it usually commences and Cough with oppression on the Chest, led them to bleed and Blister ; they found they had so ill success that they abandoned that Practice (except where the oppression on the chest was so great as to require immediate relief) and used a saline mixture in a state of efervesence " (*sic*).

Outside his own family, Frere's best correspondent was Canning, whose letters will be found in another chapter. Frere and Canning were among the rising young men in whom Lord Malmesbury and his wife took a kindly interest, and several letters from Lady Malmesbury (*née* Harriet Cornewall) are in the portfolios. She entrusted Frere with various commissions, which he generally omitted to execute. " Alas," she complains, " you have forgot the *vinaigrilla* and the Spanish Bran to mix with it, and the little *Earthen ware* Boxes to keep it in." Although she professed to hate wars, she owned that a Spanish war would have a good effect if it brought Frere home. In the meantime she supplied him with gossip.

"May 27th, 1803.

" The public Conversation is now divided between the War and Lady Georgiana Gordon's * marriage. She has at length secured a Duke of Bedford, and it is generally supposed the late Duke bequeathed her with his Estate to his Brother. The Dss. is returned from Paris raving about Bonaparte, and talked such real high treason that, if it would not give her too much Consequence, she ought to be sent to the Tower. She declares she wishes him success, and that she wishes he may come and give us a good lesson for being so Insolent as to go to War with him. . . . George Ellis is *buried* at Sunning Hill with his *Sposa* writing Books and I fancy trying to forget the very foolish Act he did in marrying her. Old Sir Peter † is now entirely on his hands which must make him completely blest. I hope if you do come home you will give us a great deal of your company at Park Place. With all my disposition to

* Daughter of Jane, Duchess of Gordon.
† Admiral Sir Peter Parker, Nelson's patron and George Ellis's father-in-law.

distrust Mankind, and all the Lessons I have had on that score I cannot help feeling that you will remain true to our old friendship which I assure you neither time nor absence can diminish on my side. My [word illegible, but probably Canning is meant] is *tame about the house* as usual but Entirely wrapped up in *his Country*, and *pea-green* with anxiety. I say he never can be pleased as he looks as ill since we declared War as during Peace."

Lady Malmesbury's hopes were not disappointed. After Frere's return we find him sharing a box at Drury Lane with Lady Malmesbury and Mrs. Robinson. For the trifling sum of seventeen guineas, he could go to the play three times a week from September 1805 to July 1806. Lady Malmesbury had forced herself, for old acquaintance sake, to read George Ellis's new book.*

" It is very curious," she writes, " but I think so much colour and Pains might have been better bestowed. . . . As I am not so fond of MSS. and black letter as you are, I do not understand G. Ellis's penance in composing a book which however I agree with you will *set him up* as an antiquarian to *all eternity*. I wish you would Employ all your leisure in writing something. It is a sin and a shame to hide *your talents in a Napkin* as you do—and so Everybody says. Why not write a poem and dedicate it to me as Sidney did his Arcadia to the Countess of Pembroke ? one *Countess* is as good as another, and a friend is as good as a sister for a dedication, and I should have the advantage of going down to Posterity as *somebody* without any *trouble to myself*. Pray think of this and put it in Practice."

Another letter was forwarded by William Drummond,

* "Specimens of Early English Poetry."

to whom it had been addressed. The writer was Jeffrey, of the *Edinburgh Review*, and he describes the truly enviable state of an editor in the time before every youth at college and every unfledged school-girl had taken to playing with " literature."

"DEAR DRUMMOND,—

"I have made two unsuccessful attempts to see you since my return to London, and as I set out for Scotland to-morrow afternoon, I am afraid I have no chance of an audience this season. I wanted to take your commands for Scotland and to have some spiritual conversation with you upon our immortal concerns—but I was particularly anxious to have ten minutes' talk with you about the Review—and by the bitterness of my groans and frowns to have given you a stronger impression of the extremity of my present distress than I can hope to do by writing. The next No. is to be published on the 18th of next month, and I have *not a single line of MS.* in my possession. Do think what you can do for me and what you can get done. We agreed, I think, that it would be best to get Lord Holland * done by one who understood Spanish. Harris (?) has put it into my head that you might persuade your friend John Frere to undertake it. It would be extremely gratifying to me to have something of his in our journal—and I think this is easy and tempting. If you cannot get him to do it, you must do it yourself—keeping as clear of Christianity as you can. I should like to have an article upon classical learning in modern poetry from Gifford. You promised, I think, to make overtures to P. Knight on my behalf—and if you can think of any other useful auxiliary I give you full powers to treat and

* Possibly a review of Holland's " Lope de Vega " which was published in 1806.

conclude with them. Have the charity to let me know as soon as anything is done or resolved upon for my relief, and believe me always

" Very Faithfully yours, etc.,
" F. JEFFREY."

In June 1807 Frere was again threatened with separation from his family and friends. The Portland Ministry appointed him Envoy and Minister Plenipotentiary to Berlin. But of course he was in no hurry to depart, and while he dallied away the time, heedless of repeated urgings from Canning, the Treaty of Tilsit put an end to his mission. Less than a year later, Spain rose against the detested Corsican, fulfilling Frere's prediction to Lord Malmesbury, and in the October of 1808 Frere was once more in Corunna, accredited British Minister to Ferdinand VII. and the Central Junta.

It is impossible to discuss the vexed question of the degree of his responsibility for the mismanagement, blunders, and disasters of the first Peninsular campaign that ended in the surrender of Corunna and Ferrol. Napier's history still remains the authority to which the general reader turns for information on the Peninsular War, as he turns, and will continue to turn, to Macaulay for the events of the reigns of Charles II., James II., and William III. The "indefatigable folly" of Mr. Frere has been held up to reprobation in Napier's pages with all the invective which the General was in the habit of bestowing on those who differed from him. The case for Frere has been argued at length by his nephew, and it would be idle impertinence in the present writer to attempt to say anything on the question after Sir Bartle Frere had dealt with it. Any one who wishes to know what can be said for Frere may consult the Memoir in the three-volume edition of his works.

Very few letters addressed to Frere at this period have been discovered, and none are of general interest. But there are a few little notes, beginning "My Dear," and written in a mixture of French and Spanish, that recall the story of one successful enterprise with which Frere's name was associated during Spain's revolt. The story has been told before, but it seems so forgotten that there is some excuse for repeating it here.

"DEAREST FRIEND,—

"My bosom and heart is enticed for you, and i pray you to expect me. Your in all devoted friend,

M. DE LA ROMANA."

Who would not take this for a love-letter from some Spanish señora, dropped from under the folds of her mantle as she passed the Envoy, or sent by the hand of some old duenna? But it came from one who was a hero worthy of the country of the Cid, although he looked like a Spanish barber *—the gallant Marquis de la Romana. Frere and he were devoted friends, and when at Seville the two would ramble about the neighbourhood for hours, absorbed in conversation, without hats, and forgetful of the dinner, the other guests, and the flight of time.

When in 1807 Napoleon crushed Spain, he used her army as he had used the armies of other conquered countries: the best men were sent on distant foreign service, and a whole division, about fourteen thousand strong, was marched to Hamburg and thence to Denmark, where Bernadotte was gathering an army to invade

* See Crabbe Robinson's Diary.

Sweden. They were detained in Denmark by a British fleet, that made its appearance in the Baltic in March 1808, and cut off the Emperor's forces from Sweden. But the Spanish troops were surrounded by jealous guards, and no word reached them from Spain, save through French channels. While they waited in sullen inaction, Spain burst into revolt. Every Spaniard was called to defend his native land and expel the foe. There were thousands of faithful Spanish hearts and thousands of strong Spanish arms on the storm-swept islands of the northern sea, but how could they be brought back?

Romana was then in command of the Spanish division; could he know of the crisis, nothing would stay him from cutting a way to Spain for himself and his men. But how should the news reach him? Robertson, an adventurous priest, was willing to risk his life by taking a message through the French lines; but even if he succeeded in finding Romana, would the Marquis trust him, or would he suspect a trap?

When reading the poem of "the Cid" together at Madrid, Frere had suggested to Romana that the line—

"Aun vea el hora que vos *merezca dos* tanto,"

should be read—

"Aun vea el hora que vos *merezcades* tanto."

Robertson was instructed to repeat this amended line, known only to Romana and to Frere, as a sign that he had communicated with Frere and was to be trusted.

After many hairbreadth escapes, the priest, in the character of a German schoolmaster, found his way to Romana, and rehearsed the line that was his passport. The only tongue common to both was Latin, and in that stiff medium Robertson traced the course of events in the Peninsula for Romana, whose blood took fire at once. It was true that the oath of allegiance to Jerome Bonaparte had been tendered to the Spanish division, but it was accepted in complete ignorance of what was happening in Spain. Some of the troops had taken it conditionally, and two regiments had absolutely refused it. Such an oath could not bind any free Spaniard, and Romana set to work to arrange their escape. With Robertson's aid communications were opened with the British fleet in the Baltic, which prepared to give all the help in its power. When the French commandant began to suspect a plot, Romana boldly seized Nyborg, and all the Spanish regiments that could be gathered together were embarked in the captured gunboats and other vessels, and landed on the Swedish shore. One regiment marched eighty miles in twenty-one hours, and when English transports reached Sweden in August 1808, more than nine thousand men were waiting to be carried to Spain.

It is more like some mediæval legend of chivalry than a historical narrative of the nineteenth century. Louis XI., muttering in the ear of Quentin Durward,—

> "The page slew the boar,
> The peer had the gloire,"

the disguised Abbot winning admittance to Loch Leven Castle with the burden of " the Howlet "—it is of such as these that we think, and not of the mean-looking Spaniard, or of the witty Privy Councillor sitting in Lady Malmesbury's box at Drury Lane theatre. The story might have come down to us from the time of the Cid himself, and it is the only one worth recalling at this period of Frere's life.

In the summer of 1809 he returned to England with the title of Marquez de la Union, bestowed on him by the Supreme Central Junta, and took up his old mode of life in the social and literary world. By this time most of the brothers with whom he had played in his youth had married or entered upon some career. Edward, the next to him in age, lived at Clydach, on the borders of Breconshire, where he owned some ironworks. His home was in a wild and beautiful valley, far removed from the civilised world, and haunted by a tribe of goblins known as Pwccas, whom some have taken to be the prototypes of Shakespeare's " knavish sprite." An old farmhouse not far from the works had been tenanted by one of these strange beings, who worked for a guerdon of toast and ale ; and the miners and workmen told strange stories of wayfarers who had been led astray by some mocking goblin, or decoyed into the hidden caves where the Pwccas keep their treasure, to join their never-ceasing dance. Superstition still lingers among the Welsh mountains, in spite of Board Schools and the franchise.

Edward Frere was a kind master to the four hundred men whom he employed, and although the miners and other workmen in the neighbouring valleys were continually rioting and going out " on strike," those at his furnaces were generally amenable to reason. Wages were always paid on Friday evenings, that the housewives might have the money ready for Saturday's market, and although he had a shop on the premises for the convenience of those who did not care to go all the way to Crickhowel or Abergavenny, no one was obliged to make any purchases there. Other employers of labour were not so scrupulous, and the iniquitous " truck system " had, in the end, to be abolished by Act of Parliament. His talents, like his brother's, were considerable, but unfortunately he possessed the same incapacity for business. He caused a great sensation by constructing an iron boat—the forerunner of our great ironclads—which floated on the canal between Brecon and Clydach. The whole country-side came to stare at it, and the majority opined that it must be the work of art-magic. But the iron-works were not a financial success.

George, the third brother, has already been introduced as a sufferer from the vagaries of his family. Much of his time was spent in a vain attempt to reduce their affairs— and more particularly those of his elder brother—to some state of order. From the correspondence it is easy to see that he was sometimes goaded into speaking his mind, and that his brothers resented it. Happily for all parties, he had married one who was in all ways fitted to be a general peacemaker—Elizabeth Raper Grant, the beloved " Aunt Lissy " of the Highland Lady with whom we have lately become acquainted. She was a good angel to all her husband's relations and friends, as she had been to the ill-treated, neglected little Grants—the confidant of every sorrow and the keeper of every secret, the healer of all bitterness. Old Mrs. Frere, who was not herself of a mild disposition, writes *àpropos* of some offender, " I can find no excuses for her—can Lizzy? she can find excuses for all her friends' faults and foibles, and is only unforgiving to · her own."

Of William, the next in succession, who ultimately became Master of Downing College, and of Hatley, the sixth brother, there is no occasion to say anything. Bartholomew, or Bartle, has already appeared as his brother's secretary. Temple, the seventh and youngest, became a clergyman, and being, like the rest of his brothers, unusually handsome, was nicknamed " The Beauty of Holiness." At one time (1802) he was studying at Aberdeen, and wrote to his father in dismay at the habits of the Scotch ladies :—

"I have often wished I could for one day bring Susan here to see the people eat raw fish, and a sort of seaweed called *dulse* about the streets, and be pressed by the rest of the ladies to take a dram before her cheese at dinner,— and if she wished for one before breakfast she had no need to go further north, for they will tell you it is so cold that they could not do without it."

The elder of Frere's sisters, Jane, was almost entirely separated from her family by her marriage with Sir John Orde. The few letters from her that have been preserved contain nothing of general interest.

The other sister, Susanna, is a pathetic figure to modern eyes. She never married, but remained at home with her parents. When old Mrs. Frere died she became the devoted slave of her eldest brother, and though she talked of leaving him after his marriage, her own usefulness and Lady Erroll's invalid state of health made it impossible for her to be spared. Our first glimpse of her is at Bath, where her father was drinking the waters. Lady Erroll, just returned from Lisbon, was spending the winter there, and, anxious to show politeness to her friend's sister, offered to chaperon her to balls and parties. But Susanna refused. Her parents liked her to read aloud in the evenings, and as they depended on her for their amusement, she could not fail them. In later years she suffered from deafness, which was increased by the warm climate of Malta. Patient, conscientious, and quaintly prim, she continued faithful, first to her parents and then to her brother, till her death in 1839. An uneventful life, chiefly spent in ministering to others ; but one is sometimes tempted to wonder how the work of future generations will be done without some of those self-sacrificing, old-fashioned spinsters, who are becoming fewer every day.

LOVE-LETTERS OF A HUNDRED YEARS AGO.

1815.

THERE now ensues a long gap in Lady Erroll's correspondence. The last extract left her at Hampton Court, in September 1808, rejoicing over the first of Sir Arthur Wellesley's victories. When we next have a glimpse of her it is in St. James's Place, in April 1815, when all Europe was ringing with the news of Napoleon's escape from Elba. It does not appear that she had ceased to write to Frere during the interval, but the letters are not to be found. A packet was destroyed a few years ago ; and it is probable that it contained the letters written between 1808 and 1815.

Great changes had taken place at home and abroad during these seven years. To Lady Erroll the most important event was that Frere had been sent as Envoy to Madrid in October 1808, and recalled in 1809. Public opinion, whether justly or not, chose to consider him as responsible for the disasters that had occurred in the Peninsula. From that time he renounced public life.

One would have thought that his first proceeding on retiring from active service would have been to marry the woman who had so unreservedly and repeatedly declared her love for him. She had stitched his "neck-cloaths" and wept over them: what could a wife do more? But the fact remains that he was in no haste to marry her, and the reasons assigned for his delay seem ludicrously inadequate. Her friends and relations opposed the marriage with all their might; but Frere was his own master. Although he may have been unwilling to vex the good old father whom Lady Erroll esteemed so warmly, as the elder John Frere died in 1807 there was no reason why his son should not have married any one whom he pleased on his return from Spain in 1809. It is true that his mother was a determined lady, with a sharp tongue and an impatient temper, who would not have been likely to welcome a middle-aged Irishwoman as a daughter-in-law; and it has been suggested that he waited for her death before making his proposals. If so, he allowed a very decent interval to elapse between her funeral and his own wedding, as Mrs. Frere died in 1813 and he did not marry Lady Erroll until 1816.

They may have waited some years in the hopes that the Countess's health would improve. It is possible that she shrank from chaining him to her armchair, and had forebodings of what actually came to pass when, for her sake, Frere abandoned friends, home, and duties, to become a resident in Malta. In that case, one can only suppose that the poor woman in the end found herself unable to bear the prospect of long years of loneliness at " Old Cat Hall," and yielded to her lover. It must have been a dreary life for so sociable a woman; every year swept off some friend or relative. The lively Norah Blake had become the Hon. Mrs. George Cadogan, and does not seem to have been much the happier for it. Bartle Frere, one of her truest friends, was Secretary of Legation at Constantinople. The bloom of youth and beauty was passed, and the future held nothing but sorrow in store for her. It would have taken very strong resolution to send away the man who offered her a home.

But, scattered here and there, are some slight indications that it was Frere who held back. Sir George Jackson's Diary hints at some mysterious private business that kept Frere from making proper exertions at Madrid. Among the piles of documents turned over by the compiler of these records were some little notes in a woman's writing. They were in French, but gave the impression that the writer's native tongue was in some other language, and they hinted at a pathetic story. After Frere's death, when his possessions were sent home from Malta, his heirs found among them the miniature of a beautiful woman whom no one knew—perhaps the writer of the letters. Like many another man before and after him, he may have dreamed of perfect happiness, and come back, when the dream had faded, to the woman who had waited for him, uncomplainingly, all the while.

But this is mere conjecture. All that we know for certain is that at eleven o'clock on April 1st, 1815, Lady Erroll was writing to Frere. It was an hour since she had swallowed a cup of Iceland Moss Chocolate, which was then the substitute for tea at the breakfast table of fashionable invalids. She was in very bad health, and therefore disposed to abuse the Government, and to keep away from her fellow-creatures :—

" I believe you and I have Changed Characters. You are all activity and playing the agreeable to all yr. Neighbours while I hate to do any one thing and dislike seeing people above all things unless they bring me news of the Continued bloody intentions of the allies, for now I .have not a doubt if they persevere and are quick, of Buonaparte's downfall and for *ever*. . . .

"I am allowing my pen to run on as Margaret has a Member in Town who is to give her a Frank for me. I must tell you a good thing that happened to Mon^r de la Chartres here, the Ambassador. Early in this blow up in France the Wife of the Minister for Foreign affairs at paris took fright and would Run over here, so her Husband gave her in Charge to the Courier, who being most anxious to deliver his despatch to de la Chartres here, Drove to his House, and begged Madam to go into a Room for a few Minutes and that he would return and set her at a Hotel. But one of the Ambassador's servants came and said there was a lady from Paris in the Ante Room; he flew of course to the lady like a true french man and followed up the filthy Character of his Nation by being Delighted to meet his *divorced Wife*. They were mutually delighted with the Rencontre, and she went to Dinner with her *first Husband*, the odious nasty people!"

Some cause—whether continual ill-health or hope deferred—was preying on Lady Erroll's spirits at this time. There are few of the old flashes of wit and mischief, and the whole tone of her letters is desponding and depressed. On the day after the battle of Waterloo she was, as usual, writing to Frere. No news had yet reached England of what had passed among the corn-fields of Belgium on that eventful Sunday; and although it was generally known that a battle was imminent, Lady Erroll was far more concerned with listening for the postman's knock in case he should bring a letter from Frere. It was a fortnight since the Privy Councillor had thought fit to write to her, and she was divided between grief for his indifference and fear of vexing him by her reproaches. "My Dearest Man, you must not think that I am Angry or Scolding, only you know, you must believe one did not care at all about you if one did not miss yͬ letters."

" I met Lady Malmesbury at Church, she paid me great Compliments on my Restored health, &c., &c., and what I don't believe any longer and hate people to say to me, but she was in High humour because Lord M. was so well, and her daughter was Married, and when people are pleased they say pretty things because they are in good humour with every thing and every body."

She then goes on to describe the troubles of two of her friends, Lord and Lady Glerawly, who were on the verge of an open rupture. Even her kind offices in making the husband play at backgammon with her in the evenings, whenever he was not on House of Commons duty, " to keep him in humour," were of little avail. The wife was behaving well ; " she does not go out much, nor does she ever appear the least inclined to be foolish and flirt to Worry him, but all will not do, they do not seem to amalgamate at all," writes their kindly friend.

This letter was written on Monday, June 19th. On Tuesday some news arrived from the seat of war, but, according to Lady Erroll, full details did not reach London till Thursday. Her husband's nephew, Lord Hay, had been killed in the skirmish on the 16th, and she hurried off to console his family.

" Only this moment my Dearest Man has yr letter been a Comfort to me. It came as if you yrself had appeared to console me. I had been since 11 o'clock this morning until now (past 3 o'clock) with the most afflicted family I ever saw, and therefore did not get my letter untill I came home, having left Lady Glasgow, Lady Jemima, and poor Lady Jane Hay (Ld. Hay's sister) tolerably composed.   The wretched Father is hourly expected in Town, but he was by yesterday's post in some degree prepared for the sad certainty.   The *Gazette* announces this day, Ld. Hay was killed on the 16th, but as there was a Ld. James Hay engaged also, we were kept in a dreadful State of Suspense since Tuesday morning.   One person said it was Ld. James Hay and another Lord Hay, and I really think the Suspense was quite Horrid.   I really feel quite overpowered by it all, and dread seeing the poor Father !   I have been obliged to send an Excuse to the Eliots, I was to have gone to them this day if this fatal news had not arrived.   Never was known so Brilliant a Victory, and they say what Picton has done was beyond any thing ever heard of before! for which he paid his life. The dismay of London for the last two days was quite awful.   Every mind impressed with the certainty of a great carnage, and no details, but tormenting Reports. Almost all the Families in London will be in Mourning. It is believed by Government that Ld. Uxbridge is dead, we expect yet more dreadful details as ¡the loss of the last day's business is not yet ascertained.   I beg you not to be uneasy about me, for I have Wept so much that I am entirely Relieved, and the very necessity of trying to Comfort the nearer Relations of the poor Dear Boy will support me much."

On the 28th Lady Erroll writes in better spirits, having been in real anxiety to find out some way of sending her letters to Frere without the knowledge of the rest of the world.   "I was puzzling my Brains to find out how I could write to you, because I could [have] enclosed my letters to Lord Glerawly from an M.P.'s house and if 1 enclosed them to Margaret to Town, Genl. Robinson who comes back to Town to-day would hear of it, and *I hate*

Mysterys, and yet I know I can't exist without writing to you, it is the *only* Comfort I have when you are away. So I shall send a Short Scrawl to Brompton under Mr. Eliot's Frank to Douglas who will put it into the post for you, and she, I believe, is to begin a Correspondence with you as her Niece is going to be Married and she told me she intended to beg you to be one of the Trustees with Ainslie to the Settlement. A Capt. of Dragoons with some fortune besides is the intended." *

When we recall the fact that both Lady Erroll and her lover were nearing fifty years of age, all this caution seems unnecessary. Mrs. Douglas, although she occasionally had her " feelings," and took huff, like most people in her situation, was a most faithful confidant. Lady Erroll sometimes complains that Douglas is out of humour, or that Douglas has been fishing for an invitation, or for a recommendation for a nephew, but she was always ready to make use of the good woman on occasion.

" . . . Honoria Cadon [Cadogan] writes me word that she has been kissing the Pope's hand and talking Italian to him, the only language he speaks, and . she says [he] speaks it beautifully. He has a very good Countenance, and seems Doubled more from Misfortune than Age, was delighted, and enjoy'd her telling him [that] Capt. Campbell who Convey'd Madame Murat was quite a Coarse Savage Sailor, and Could only Speak English to that fine lady. . . . I have just been told a Shocking thing about poor Whitbread † I can't believe it, that Government had found out a Correspondence between him and Buonaparte, which

* This marriage was broken off, and Ainslie considered the young lady to have had a lucky escape.

† Mr. Whitbread had just committed suicide.

was the Cause of the Rash Act he Committed. This is so like what might be suspected at this Critical Moment that I am the more inclined to believe it only a Report without any foundation. Lady Saltoun has told me that it is now very generally believed and that the Privy Council had met upon it. Mind, this [is] only an Idle Report from Lady Saltoun."

Great alarm had been caused by Napoleon's departure for Rochefort on June 29th with an immense train of carriages loaded with valuables. His intention was to escape to America.

" That Monster never travelled in a Coach and Six to any Seaport and Attended by many other Carriages as Reported, on purpose, I suppose," declares Lady Erroll. " He has been too well accustomed to escape before not to know better. They have him hid somewhere, which keeps up his Spirit in France, perhaps in a Woman's Cloaths. His little fat pudsey figure could easily be disguised, and Madame St. Leu,* I dare say, presided at his Toylett and has his Boots and Spurs Ready open. All is Ready for a Surprise. I have not Common patience with Louis, except one individual, all those he has surround[ed] himself by are, I hear, determined Jacobins. I wish they would let Blucher alone and do as he likes, he is the only person who seems to have any feeling of the Cruelty the French exercised upon foreign powers. I am spiteful enough to wish they had allow'd him to blow up their bridge † to Atoms, Nasty Horrid Creatures ! Why not tumble to bits some of their fine things as well as those at Washington ? The idea is here that there must be more Blows, how Horrible ! after the late Carnage."

* Hortense, Queen of Holland.   † The Pont de Jena.

Two days later, Lady Erroll adds a postscript :—" The Hollands are hourly expected, Lord W. Fitzgerald thought to find them arrived—a Frigate gone for Canning, so a good many of y^r friends will soon be in England. Wallscourt has this instant told me official news is arrived that Buonaparte is now on board of one of our 74 Sloops. Captain Maitland of the *Bellerophon* took him off Rocheford. My prophecy is accomplish'd."

To add to her other anxieties, " George Cadogan " (presumably Honoria's husband) had returned home from Florence in very bad health, and frightened her by looking " such an object—skin and bone, and feeble to [a] degree— a pair of Green spectacles and a green patch over one Eye, surmounted with a Green Shade did not add to the beauty of his appearance." Hopes were entertained of his recovery, and in the meantime he was to be treated by English nurses and doctors. " He is gone to Chelsea where his sister Lady Louisa has now join'd him which takes him off my hands," sighs Lady Erroll, without explaining why Honoria Cadogan could not be at home to look after her sick husband instead of amusing herself with the Pope's society. " He brought me the most beautiful alabaster figure, a Venus which Genl. Robinson broke in less than ten Minutes after it was taken out of the case, I suppose for Spite because I was so positive in my refusal of giving him my company at Denston this year. He came back to Town last week, and worried me about going to him, but I beg'd to be off that visit. He was Miserable tho' for having demolished my beautiful Venus, and, I hear, sent it to a Man who says he will put her together again."

She then enters into details about the misconduct of a servant which are unfit for publication. It seems strange that she should have thought it advisable to enter upon the subject in her correspondence, but, as has been remarked already, her letters are curiously outspoken. As usual, the most amusing piece of intelligence is in the postscript :—

" I almost forgot to tell you that G. Cadogan was stopd by a Banditti (*sic*), commanded by three officers of the Legion of Honor with their uniforms and decorations etc. They took everything out of his Carriage of any Value. He met a lady after and Stopd her to guard her against them. From her Servts. he found it was the Ex-Queen of Holland, Madame St. Leu, who was going to Switzerland. Her people told him that Madame Buonaparte and Cardinal Fesch were following her, so he wished to have a look at them, pretended not to know them, but stopd to *guard them* against *three officers* of *the Legion of Honor* who with Banditti were Robbing on the High way. I am so glad they had the mortification of hearing this from an English officer. What a mean beast Buonaparte is to *live* to be a prisoner ! I can't understand his being so fond of life, has he not a pistol ? "

From a letter written on August 7th, it appears that General Robinson, in the kindness of his heart, had invited Frere to be his guest in the country at the same time as Lady Erroll. Frere was quite ready to take the opportunity of meeting the lady whom he had not seen for six months, but she was " surprised and confounded " when the idea was suggested to her. " It would appear indelicate on my part to follow you anywhere—but still, if you wish it so, I will try and do it, but indeed I fear my nerves being unequal to meet you in that way at any body's House, and I dread the Coarse Remarks it may Create. Genl. R. said ' If you come I'll get Frere to come over to meet you.' I felt my face all over in a Glow !

and I was Ready to Expire with confusion and anserd (*sic*) ' My dear Genl., if I could go to Denston, it would be to see you and Miss Robinson, and not for any body else's sake.' Pray do not be angry with me, my Dear Man, for writing all I feel to you, in whom I place all my only Confidence for Comfort in this life."

It is hard to say why any " Coarse Remarks " should have been made on the meeting between a gentleman of forty-six and a lady of about the same age, under the surveillance of General and Miss Robinson ; but Lady Erroll's scruples on the score of propriety grew stronger with advancing years. By this time Frere seems to have made his proposals, and the parade of secrecy and the delay in celebrating the marriage were alike unnecessary. Yet Lady Erroll, although rejoicing that Temple Frere had lately exhibited quite a " Brotherly Manner " towards her makes the obliging Mrs. Douglas promise to arrange a meeting at Brompton when Frere comes to Town, as Hampton Court is " so public." " I shall hate Genl. Robinson while I live for having with his ——— * Visit made me Cry ever since I got y[r] letter, and make a fool of myself by so doing . . . I shall deliver y[r] message about the pigs to Mrs. Douglas when I see her, but if you want to get a good Breed, Genl. Robinson's are the best and I dare say [he] will be glad to give you some, tho' I shall hate his pigs and every thing belonging to him while I live. I wish I was Mr. Whiter,† tho' I am not Jealous of Etymology, as I believe it amuses and interests you, but I certainly can't Patronize it as I do Homer and other things."

Having settled her mind by abusing the luckless

---

* Lady Erroll here uses a very unladylike word.

† Mr. Whiter was a learned clergyman, and a friend and correspondent of Frere's.

General Robinson, Lady Erroll finds fault with Frere
himself :—

" It is I think a pity a Man of such talents as you have,
Genius and Brilliant imagination, should thro[w] yourself
away hammering and puzzling over such Dry Stuff. You
should do as Southey does, he always undertakes three or
four things together to divide his mind, otherwise, he says,
he feels so lost and absorbed and his head so bothered
with *one thing* that he can't do it so well as by taking it
up and putting it down awhile for some thing else."

In the course of this letter there is an illustration of
the rapidity with which an unsavoury scandal will attach
itself to the hero of the hour, although there may not
be the least foundation for it. It was said that the Duke
had been surprised by the French troops when at the
Duchess of Richmond's ball. Of course there must have
been some reason for his dallying at the ball, and of
course Society applied the infallible rule—" *Cherchez la
femme*." By the time that the story reached Lady Erroll,
the lady had been discovered, and a trial was expected,
the damages to be laid at £50,000. The only pity was
that there was not a word of truth in all this circumstantial legend, and neither of the parties chiefly concerned
knew anything about it until an English newspaper in
Paris announced it as a piece of fashionable intelligence.

This letter from her ladyship filled three octavo sheets
before it was brought to a conclusion, and she then added
two more by way of postscript.

" A Note I have had from a lawyer this instant reminds
me of telling you a thing I was guilty of, so like you,
and what I should have Scolded you for. About two
months ago, Lady Glasgow told me that her Aunt, who

died, you may recollect, while you were at Hastings, whose money was in Chancery, was to be divided (*sic*), at least, part of it, amongst all the Hay Brothers and Sisters, and that I was entitled to a Share. Now I certainly am not Rich, yet, do you know, I forgot all about it intirely untill the day before yesterday, Mr Carr called to ask my Commands for paris (he was married to a Lady Hay)—and ask'd me what Money I got out of Chancery as he had got his. I told him with Shame that I had quite forgotten, that I had heard something about it—but ask'd him what I was to do. He gave me the address of the lawyer, who has to-day written me a Note to say he will come to-morrow, to pay me £85, so I am far Richer than I expected, but it is all owing to you that I can't think of anything nor lay my mind to anything. . . . The Duke of York broke his Arm yesterday, his foot Slipped coming out of a Shower Bath, and he fell upon his Arm, but he is doing very well, he is at Oatlands."

Poor Lady Erroll was nearly worn out by cares and anxieties at this time. Besides her own private distresses, she was troubled about an unruly little niece who was to be sent to school in a French convent. Lady Erroll at first thought of taking her over to Paris, under the escort of Mr. Carr, who proposed to act cicerone to the Countess and her sisters, Honoria and Margaret. Lady Erroll was tempted by the prospect, and recollected that her doctor had prescribed a little amusement. However, she could not bear the idea of leaving Frere in England, were it only for three weeks, and had, besides, a lingering fear that he would think her " Crazy," so she endeavoured to find some other escort for the child. Then she was still trying to reconcile that unhappy couple, Lord and

Lady Glerawly ; and her sister Margaret gave her much trouble. She breathes a sigh of relief at the thought that the Glerawlys are going abroad to economise, and " I think it likely that Margaret may go with them, which will be a very convenient circumstance to me I can tell you." Her hopes were dashed to the ground by the perversity of every one else, and the story of her perplexities is so amusingly told in a letter to Frere of August 14th, that it must be given in full :—

" Genl. Robinson's arrival in Town gives me a Frank, and of course an opportunity of tormenting you with a Scrawl of mine, and if that were not the case, I must have written to you to please Lady Glerawly and vex Margaret who played us a trick on Saturday. Had she put confidence in us we would not *betray* her, but she behaved so *Cunning*, so *Artfully* by us, that we declared war against her. She and the pretty * dined with us early on Saturday to meet George Cadogan who came to me to meet his oculist and Doctor, and was to return to Hampton Court at 7 o'clock. Miss Margaret said she would walk with him to Hertford Street, where his Sister had Dined, and was to carry him back. She never returned to us untill 11 o'clock at night, and then announced that she went to Berkeley Sq. to meet Genl. Robinson from whom she had had a letter that day to say that he should see her between 7 and 8 that evening in Berkeley Sqr., and this she kept Snug from us, and she was Roasted finely and Bullied. She said she had not Courage to begin the day with us by telling us of the Genl.'s folly in coming for a few days *merely* to *see her* tho' it is only a fortnight since he left Town. I said I would write all her doings to you, and she got a

* Lady Glerawly.

delightful Red face when I asked on purpose *before her*, the Genl. to keep a Frank for you, for me. Lady Glerawly and she dined with me to day to meet this old bore fidgetting, whistling about the Rooms and asking questions he does not mean one to answer as he goes on muttering to himself 'Umph, Umph.' He was very good natured to me, and walk'd me home from Lady Glerawly's last night, and quite Scandalized little Rogers who overtook us in St. James's Street and declared he thought *he ought* to Join us for the sake of my Character, which he did, and they both saw me safe into my House. I am to be bored again with Cadogan to-morrow, who is to come here at 12 o'clock to see his Doctors, and torment the Bell and the Servants the whole day, for he is to have his Dinner.   But I bear it now with not only patience but with good Humour, as he is an Invalid, tho' getting better almost Every hour since he landed in England. He says himself that he feels quite Renovated, and the oculist says that he will Recover the Sight of his Eye, even without an operation which he first thought he should be obliged to perform.   He is the most Restless odd ill-tempered Creature possible. I would not be his Wife to be Queen of the Universe, and yet his Heart is not in fault, but the Head is quite wrong often.

"What do you think of a New kind of a club House, lately set up in St. James's St., having put up a transparency on Saturday, the Birthday, 12th, 'the *Regent*, with *Wisdom in the Cabinet, Valour in the field*,' with a grand illumination which has caused much quizzing and laughing. He is, to be sure, most unpopular, never so much so as he is now, not even the intoxication of that greatest of all Victorys, Waterloo, could extract from the Mob a single indication of applause for him on the day he closed the parliament. They seem'd to think they did a great deal by maintaining a *dead Silence* and no Hissing, but they mark'd loud and Repeated applauses when the Duke of York's Carriage appeared.

"I have also to answer a Serious and Melancholy letter from Lord Glerawly who, poor Man, is in an Ugly low State of Mind, and as I know he was once in *Willis's* * care, and a little in that Way some few years after, I can't help feeling alarm'd about him, of which I have made *good use* in my Remonstrances to his Wife, who I have with Difficulty brought to write a very nice letter to Lord Annesley, his Father, who wrote her a most affecting letter about his Son's Complaints of her. She hardly knows him, and this is the first letter he ever wrote to her, and she Storm'd and Raged when she got it on Saturday, but I never lost sight of her since, and Coax'd and Managed her so well, and alarm'd her a little about Ld. G.'s Health of mind and body, that she is now determined to shew Ld. Annesley by the letter she is sending that she is not so bad as she has been Represented to him to be, and I have also got her to avoid in her letter to lord G. any allusion to his Father's letter which was Evidently written as if unknown to Ld. G., as he [Lord Glerawly] did not Frank it, altho' he is in the same house, and I have made her follow Ld. Annesley's Example and address the letter to him at once, and not under her Husband's Cover, as her Father-in-law's application to her was Evidently without her Husband's knowledge, who, I dare say would be very Sorry if he knew his Father interfered."

After recapitulating this last argument with which she had worked upon Lady Glerawly's feelings, Lady Erroll coolly adds :—

* The celebrated clergyman who attended George III.

"This I do not believe myself, as I dare say Ld. G., his Father, and Sisters, all had Managed the letter between them, which, all things considered, is a very fair and laudable Cheat if it can bring about the desired object of inducing her to Humour this odd Man a little more than she does, and I have managed her so well about her getting up that I had her in Church with me yesterday some minutes before the Service began, which I shall poke into my letter to her Husband to-day. But I must keep her in a little fright about causing him some serious indisposition of mind. There are few Women one could Venture such a thing with, but she does not feel any thing Strongly so as to make her unhappy, so I must frighten her as I would a Child, and I tell her his family will say she has driven him *Mad. . . .*"

On the following day Lady Erroll was intending to dine with Lady Glerawly, ",but George Cadogan comes in to me from H. Court to Worry and I must give up my day to him. I think I have Constantly to manage Wrong-headed Men, I have a Collection, quite, to do with. After Lady G. wrote three letters to answer Ld. Annesley's, last night, we arranged a fourth Edition which she is to send to-day, and at last we have brought her to send a very tolerable kind one. After I put up my letter to you yesterday, I set off for Berkely Sqr., Dreading her sending some Cold proud letter to her Father in law, and I was in time to save the post, and I would not allow her to send the one she was going to seal, and with some little alterations, and making her sign herself his affecte. *Daughter* which she thought *very hard* indeed, the letter will do very well and goes to-day. . . .

"... I saw a good saying of y^r friend Mr. Warde in a letter of Mrs. Cadogan's to her Husband. They call at

Florence the Austrians the *Whisker Club*. One of them, an Ugly Conceited Coxcomb, has allow'd bits of beard to grow here and there in tufts. Warde said he put him in mind of a Man who has had a bad Estate who tries to *Plant out* the Ugly features. Good Gracious, here is George Cadogan's knock—only 11 o'clock ! pray do pity me, that's all I want this day—Cadogan is off again for an hour, he says, and so I shall put up my Frank in the mean time. . . ."

On August 18th Lady Erroll had the pleasure of telling Frere that "Lady Glerawly sent a very tolerable letter to Lord Annesley, but I fear she will yet give a compleat *set to* to the Husband for having Complain'd to her Father in law of her. She says she will never forgive him, because he does not tell also what cause he gave her for Changing her Manner to him, which *I know* because Lord Glerawly told me with Regret what he had done in a Moment of fury. But I told him not to let *her* know that he told me *that*, as her pride never allow'd her to tell it to me, and if she thought I knew it, I could not argue her into good behaviour so well, as she could always say, ' What can I expect from a Man who is Capable of locking me up in my Room for nearly a Week in the face of all my Household ?' which he told me with Regret he had done, and that he saw She never forgave him, and certainly never will. It has caused all that Coldness and Horror of him, and one can't wonder at it. He is not easily managed, and certainly he could not be worse Matched. . . .

" G. Cadogan, when first he arrived, ask'd me after you in a kind Manner, but I found by him the last day he was here, that they had been saying something at H. Court, as he said in a kind of examining way, ' Pray have you and Frere Quarel'd, as I hear he has not been in Town this

Spring ? '   I must have got a Red Face, but quickly open'd my Writing Book and Shew'd y' frank to him which I had put up, and said 'There is a *proof* we have,' in a joke, and went into my Room to leave him to write, and hide my fuss, and so very Nervous am I that I cry'd quantitys, but that I can't Help, everything makes me Cry.   I can't at all stand people's Congratulations upon my Recovery— 'Oh dear, how well you are, how happy you must be to be so well.'   I could Choak them with pleasure, for the tears in spite of me gush forth, and when they add 'You look so *handsome*,' I could then Spit in their faces for Spite, for telling me such horrid lies and thinking I could be such a fool as to believe for an instant such Stupid nonsense while I know I am a wither'd Skeleton. . . .

"Lady Mornington *Really Satisfied* the last day I saw her, as Lady Worcester promises to bring an Heir, a subject which has worried her for this last year, and also Lady Burghersh is going to make her lord a Father, these two Events cause more Joy to lady Mornington than all the Wellington Victorys ! . . ."

Towards the end of August Lady Erroll was seized with a bad nervous attack, but she recovered sufficiently to escort her little niece as far as Dover at the beginning of September.   She offered to take Lady Glerawly with her, and " you can't think how delighted and pleased *the pretty* is with my having offer'd to poke her in with me, quite like a Child, and poor Honoria is now in such Spirits at having a party with her that she forgets all about the Convent."

" The little redpole Honoria B——, being somewhat difficult to manage here, is to be entrusted forthwith to the superintendence of some Superieure of a Parisian Convent,"

writes Ainslie to Bartle Frere at this time.   " The effect
of inoculating a Nunnery with this little Rack-rent will,
I expect, be curious enough."

No more letters from Lady Erroll of a later date than
September 7th, 1815, are now forthcoming.   On September 12th of the following year she became Frere's wife.
Ainslie says that she was by this time only " the wreck
of former beauty," and she seems never to have regained
her health.   Her married life, however, lasted until
January 1831.

It may interest the readers of her correspondence to
learn the after fate of those whose names occur most
frequently in her letters.   George Cadogan was created
Baron Oakley in 1831, and a year later became Earl
Cadogan.   There is no need to say more of his wife in
this connection, as her letters to Frere in his old age will
be quoted in another chapter.

Miss Margaret Blake lived to an advanced age.   A
packet of her letters to Frere has been preserved, but, so
far as they can be deciphered, they seem to relate to her
money troubles, being either requests for new supplies or
thanks for past favours.   She was continually in difficulties.
There is a story of "an old Miss Blake " who lived at
Hampton Court Palace going to pay a morning call on
the Duke of Clarence and his wife at Kensington.   When
she took leave, the Duke attended her to the gate, and
discovered that she meant to depart in a hackney coach.
This, according to the etiquette of the period, was as
unusual a proceeding as it would be for a modern visitor
to Buckingham Palace to drive away in a costermonger's
cart ; but the Duke concealed his feelings, and opened the
coach-door for the lady.   She skipped into the coach, and
putting her head through the window, called back to His

Royal Highness, " You tell the man where to go, and pay him, Billy."   If this were Margaret Blake, she must have been a sore trial to Lady Erroll.

All Lady Erroll's efforts to reconcile Lady Glerawly to her eccentric husband were unavailing.   After seventeen years of discomfort their marriage was dissolved by Act of Parliament in 1820, by which time Lord Glerawly had succeeded his father as Earl Annesley.   " The pretty " died in April 1827, and Lord Annesley married again in July 1828.   At his death, ten years later, he left a large family by his second wife.   The only child of his first marriage died before him.

The " little redpole," Honoria Blake, survived the discipline of a French convent, to make her home with her aunt and her aunt's husband at Malta.   In 1837 she married Lord Hamilton Chichester, who left her a widow with no children.

We cannot part without regret from one who has gossipped so pleasantly to us of the days of long ago. There is a charm and a spontaneity about Lady Erroll's letters that we miss in the well-turned periods of the learned and distinguished men who corresponded with Frere in his later years.   They wrote carefully, elaborately, with, perhaps, a glance at a larger audience ; she put down, as she says, everything that came into her head, and wrote to Frere as she would have talked to him.

She had her defects ; but they were the defects of her qualities, of her birth, of her education.   We have already noticed the coarseness that disfigures occasional passages in her letters ; this was a feature of the time, and not peculiar to herself.   Some of Frere's other correspondents surpass Lady Erroll in her frankest moments ; but it is impossible to quote from them to support this assertion. A hundred years ago, a good governess discoursed to her pupils on subjects which married women would scarcely mention to each other at the present time. There lies before me a little book which was given to Mary Anne Greene (afterwards the wife of Edward Frere) by her father—"Dialogues between a Discreet Governess and Several Young Ladies of the first Rank under her Education." The subjects of the Dialogues cast a lurid light on the morals of gentlemen of the first rank in the year 1780, the year of publication, and Mary Anne Greene's descendants find it necessary to keep her book under lock and key.

It must be owned that Lady Erroll was not the best wife for Frere from a practical point of view. An active notable woman who would have kept his accounts, looked after his property, and superintended his household, might have counteracted the effects of his own indolence and aversion to business. But housewifely and businesslike qualities never came out of Castle Rackrent, and although the *ménage* at the Pietà was a standing grief to the staid soul of Frere's sister, the master of it was very happy.

Occasionally we find a trace of a common defect in generous, impetuous spirits like her own—the disposition to leave a good work to be completed by other hands, when the novelty of it had passed away. Lady Erroll could begin with eagerness, but she was impatient or careless of detail. Yet, when all these imperfections have been taken into account, a very lovable woman remains to us, who never turned against a friend in adversity, and whose heart was open to all who appealed to it. Childless herself, she was full of kindness to her friends' children, and to her husband's nephews and nieces; with no home for many years but her little rooms at Hampton Court, she was always ready to welcome a guest. And no one, after reading the story of her struggles with the Glerawlys, with George Cadogan, and with the other wrong-headed persons amongst whom her lot was cast, can doubt that upon her rested the blessing which is one of the hardest to win—the blessing of the peace-makers.

CHAPTER IX

SOCIETY IN 1809—1816

ALTHOUGH in Spain he held the rank of Marquis, in England Frere had no greater dignity than that of a Privy Councillor, bestowed on him after his first mission to the Peninsula. An English peerage was twice offered to him and declined, nor was he to be tempted into active life by an opportunity of going as Ambassador to St. Petersburg. The general impression was, that he regarded his recall from Spain as an undeserved censure, and was resolved to have no more to do with the public service. But, as very early in his diplomatic career we have seen him withheld from throwing up his appointment and coming home only by Canning's earnest remonstrances, it is fair to conclude that natural indolence had something to do with these refusals. His father's death in 1807 had left him owner of considerable property, and he had a pension from the Government: why should he exert himself more? To use Sir Henry Holland's admirable description, his life " became an indolent intellectuality with a sort of sarcastic indifference to fame and to the bustling world around him."

Meanwhile his talents were a passport into the most exclusive circles, and some of the letters addressed to him at this time give us tantalising glimpses of celebrated personages. London Society was then small and exclusive. Those who were outside the pale attempted in vain to pass within it ; those inside the magic boundary encountered each other over and over again, and were almost like members of one family. The place of meeting might be Holland House, where the noble owner, always suffering and always amiable, gathered round himself some of the brightest intellects of the time, in spite of the eccentricities and insolences of his wife—who, like many disagreeable people, could be charming when she wished to please. On a dressing-room window in the east turret of Holland House, Frere wrote with a diamond these lines :—

> " May neither Fire destroy, nor Waste impair,
>   Nor Time consume thee, till the twentieth heir ;
>   May Taste respect thee, and may Fashion spare."

All applauded the graceful wish, with the exception of Rogers, who, when the lines were repeated to him, observed in his peculiar tones, " I wonder where he got the diamond."

Another well-known resort was the house of Lydia White, an enthusiastic spinster who was never so happy as when surrounded by a party of lions, and who entertained almost to the last day of her life, when, changed, feeble, swollen by dropsy but still rouged, she was unable to leave her sofa. It was at her table that Scott avowed his impression that he had written the lines describing the death of Higinbottom in " Rejected Addresses." Frere's diary records that a bad cold once prevented him from dining with her.

All the talents were represented in those assemblies. There was a cluster of poets : Walter Scott, with his northern burr and kindly smile ; melancholy Byron, always uneasy lest some gaze should rest on his deformed foot ; Moore, prince of good fellows, rattling off song or story, as the fancy seized him, in his irresistible brogue; Rogers, cadaverous and spiteful.   There were the wits— Sidney Smith, Joseph Jekyll, and Frere himself; and the physicians, Holland and Warren, whom Canning nick- named the oil and the vinegar.   There was Canning, handsome as ever, but worn and thoughtful ; Charles Ellis, his second in that memorable duel with Castlereagh ; and Castlereagh, with his beautiful features, so cold and im- passive that, when Shelley saw Murder in his vision of Anarchy, "he had a mask like Castlereagh."   The Misses Berry dispensed hospitality and talked to willing ears of Strawberry Hill and its former owner.   The Misses Fanshawe wrote to beg Frere to drink tea with them. Here and there flitted the restless form of " Caro " Lamb, the victim of a passion for one who treated her with the consideration that a man usually reserves for the woman who throws herself at his head.   At intervals appeared the half-paralysed figure of William Stewart Rose, attended by his faithful and erratic follower, Hinves, the ex- Methodist preacher, whom all his master's friends treated as a comrade.

A short drive would bring Frere to Highgate, where Coleridge stood on the hearthrug and descanted on all things in heaven and earth.   Charles Lamb's stutter could be heard in loving banter with Crabb Robinson, and Mrs. Gillman helped the pudding which Lamb found so in- digestible.   Or if Frere were too lazy to do more than saunter along Albemarle Street, there was Gifford, busy over the new *Quarterly Review*, and old one-eyed John Murray sat in the little back-parlour to which only a few privileged persons were admitted, Frere being among the number.

It is unfortunate that our only memorials of these years

occur in detached passages in letters addressed for the most part to Bartle Frere. After his elder brother's recall, he remained for some time at Madrid as Chargé d'Affaires. In 1811 he was appointed Secretary of Legation at Constantinople, where he spent several years. His family kept up a constant correspondence with him, although under adverse circumstances. The arrival of letters every three or four weeks was regarded as "a great luxury," and these letters took from two to five months on the road. Sometimes the letters from his brothers and sisters are worth quoting, but most of the particulars interesting at the present day were supplied by his old friend and colleague, Sir Robert Ainslie, who still preserved his warm affection for Bartle and his hopeless attachment for Lady Erroll.

Sometimes a scrap of paper with a few lines in Rose's exquisitely neat writing is enclosed in the sheets which Ainslie sent out to Constantinople. It was probably "the habit of office" that made Ainslie date and number his letters like despatches. One of the first gives a story of Lord Eldon :—

"You may perhaps not have heard of the pun made by the Lord Chancellor of England, Lord Eldon, no punster either. On the night when you and many others were disappointed by Ld. Wellesley's not making a speech in the House of Lords, some person enquired whether Ld. Wellesley's speech was in the stile of Cicero or Demosthenes. 'In neither,' says the noble Lord, 'but in that of Tacitus.'"

A parallel to this may be found in the story that Lady Morgan, wishing to introduce her sister Olivia to an old gentleman, asked him if he knew her Livy? "Yes, madam," growled the gentleman, who had already suffered

in an encounter of wits with the Irish girl, "and I wish
to Heaven your Livy were your Tacitus."

"(June 1812).   Ld. Grey has been informed by the
Police that they have received a letter (not yet traced
to the author who must be mad) that the writer is determined to put Lord Grey to death, for he cannot bear
the manner in which he enters the House of Peers.   As
no Gentleman in years alters his mode of walking into
a room, this seems to be hard measure towards poor Lord
Grey. . . .

"Warm work in the House of Commons, Mr. Frere.
Last night, Mr. Sheridan was to justify his public character
against Ld. Yarmouth's attack.   He spoke for some time
and well enough, but little to the purpose, at length he
was taken unwell, and now I am coming to my story,
some unprincipled man gave him a glass of water.   Water
to Sheridan !   The consequences were as might have been
foreseen.   He was done up for the night, and till he
washes off this pollution from his gastric regions by right
Cogniac or Nants in profusion, who is bold enough to
say that he will be ever well enough to repeat his
attack ? . . . .

"(July 1813).   The papers will give you a grand account
of our *National fête* at Vauxhall, which was paid for
by 120 Gentlemen with buckles at their knees and on
their shoes.   Admission of course could only be obtained
by tickets which *if sold* were, I understand, worth ten
or fifteen Guineas, each, but every Old Soldier, or every
kinsman of a Soldier on the Continent, had full permission
to stand anywhere except at Vauxhall and see the rockets
explode in the air, which, as the night proved dark, must
have been a cheering sight to them.   The account of the
French Marshall's Bâton being exposed upon the table

during dinner between two of Mr. Gunter's finest pieces of confectionary will I hope gratify you, there was something so dignified and courageous in swallowing Turtle and even drinking three times three unappalled by such a guest. I must regret to the last hour of my existence that I was out of Town upon this occasion. My sister Anne however was there, escorted by the Mansfields, whose carriage like most others had a pole run through its pannels going there. After a journey of four hours they got within half a mile of Vauxhall, they then squeezed through the crowd and got in. But the coming back was at such imminent risk of suffocation that Anne seems to think that the Combatants at Victoria underwent less danger. . . .

"His Excellency* is in very great preservation at Blake's Hotel, as usual; his present Turn seems to be Virtu and the collecting Medals, but, as usual, he is, I have no doubt, a Hog for Greek and Classic lore. I dined with him just before quitting Town, and met amongst others Lord Byron, who meditates an immediate visit to the Greek Islands, but waits for what he finds difficulty in obtaining, a birth on board some Man of War where he may securely laugh at French Privateers, or, what is more dreaded, American Frigates. You perhaps know his Lordship who appears to me singularly clever and agreeable in conversation, but not the Man for whom Ladies should die, either in sighs, or by Stabbing. Yet if you do not in your Kiosk hear the silly gossip of London, I must impart to you what I have heard, little as I ever hear of such things, but it is the talk of the day. Lady Caroline Lamb married to Wm. Lamb whom you may remember at Cambridge, a very handsome Man and clever, has cast the eye of affection since a long time upon

* J. H. Frere.

Ld. B., but, as the course of true love never did run smooth, he has always avoided her. She is tall and thin,* and he calls her the Spectre which haunts him. Sitting next to her at supper the conversation turned on Waltzing. She said 'Could you bear to see the Woman you love waltz with another Man?' He said he should not particularly wish it, but saw no great mischief in the thing. 'Should you like to see me waltz with any man but yourself?' He said he should have no objection whatever, upon which with no more ado the fair Lady whips a knife into her own side. Venus I believe interposed in the shape of a pair of stays, so that the blow was by no means fatal, and the World jests at her scars."

"(24th Nov. 1813). We are sending to Holland every soldier this country holds, and the Prince of Orange will land with our Guards in Holland as his ancestor landed with the Dutch guards here in 1688. . . . I have been as usual in Lincolnshire since my last, and there have met with a Russian Genl. Sablokow, who married old Angerstein's daughter. He was employed in the Russian campaign. He is a pleasant Man, in many respects not distinguishable from any English Gentleman, and yet thorough Russian. He said that very little quarter was given on either side, though at last prodigious numbers of French were made prisoners; they are now employed, whether they will or no, in rebuilding Moscow. The inveteracy of the Peasantry is hardly to be described. As to the feelings of some of the Russian superior officers, take one of a man who, he says, is at present at the head of the staff with the Emperor of Russia. One of this man's officers came in to give a report of the Day's work—'I

* Other authorities describe her as small and slight, with pale golden hair and large hazel eyes. (See "Life of Edward Bulwer, Lord Lytton.")

have brought in 300 French Prisoners.' 'Well?' says the General very sulkily. 'We have recovered much plunder and Church Plate they had with them.' 'Sir,' says the General, 'if you had met so many Russians laden with Church Plate, how should you have treated them?' 'I beg pardon,' says the young officer. He went out without another word passing, and had every Frenchman bayonetted. . . .

" . . . We Londoners are now become quite valiant and can hear the report of the Tower Guns and Park Guns without flinching, indeed we almost hear them every day, certainly more extraordinary Gazettes are published than ordinary. It is like the last scene in the common run of plays where Poetical Justice is so conscientiously administered, and the persecuted Hero of the preceeding acts becomes absolutely weighed down and oppressed by fortune's favors. The Guns are now firing for what we are told is the advance of Ld Wellington after another Victory and even the occupation of Bordeaux."

The year 1814 surpassed the years of Jubilee 1887 and 1897, in the number of distinguished guests that it brought to London, and the brilliance of the festivities held in their honour. Mrs. George Frere writes on July 9th :—

" This town has been in a bustle which has turned everything topsy turvy, and the quietest of us have felt the effects of it. Our Londoners seem as if they were crazy, and pursue the foreigners with an eagerness which makes one feel ashamed of one's Countrymen, all trades have been stopped, for nobody would work, and happy those who had gowns and shoes ready made, none could be got to order. Poor Lady Laurie [a cousin] fancied she wanted to go out of Town to Susan, but first the great people went

to Ascott races and then to Oxford, and for five days the
post chaises were all engaged and horses for the first
stage out of London were charged at five guineas the
pair. Peace was proclaimed on Monday, and the crowds
were so great near Temple Bar that those who fainted
from the fatigue and heat were laid under the bodies of
the carriages to give them air."

Ainslie writes on the same subject :—

"We are illuminating for Peace, we have Emperors and
Kings as our Visitors, and yet we are not in the least more
contented or happier than when at War. The farmer
thinks the present low price of corn caused by the downfall of Bonaparte, and is wishing to have him again. The
Politicians are angry that we have not driven a harder
bargain as to the terms of Peace. We are hissing and
hooting our Prince on every Public occasion, and calling
to him 'Love your wife!' 'Where's your Wife?' At
Paris things are not better, all the Emigrants are unhappy, discontented, and disappointed, natural enough,
the Parvenus, the same thing. As in former times our
women find the French women ugly, and they return the
Compliment with interest, but what is rather odd, the
Russian Emperor is quite shocked at the indecent naked
mode of dressing of our women. Another gossip here is
that our young Princess has all manner of Capricious
movements against the *futur*, and that being asked at
dessert what her royal stomach would be pleased to take,
she answered, ' Anything but an Orange.' *

"The Cockneys, as the Papers will tell you, have been
hauling about Emperors and Kings without Mercy. The

* The marriage treaty between Princess Charlotte and the Prince of
Orange was soon afterwards broken off.

fashion of persecuting them in this manner was so inconceivably violent as, I believe, to have very much indeed taken from the pleasure these foreigners would have had in visiting this great Country. Old Blucher says it is an excellent Country to eat and drink in, but the worst he ever knew for sleep or quiet. No village within 200 miles but sent up its population to *see the Emperor.* Old Bailey was present at the annual meeting of the Charity Children in St. Paul's, which you know is really a most interesting sight. The foreigners were there, but had contrived very successfully that their intentions should be kept quite secret. It delighted them as much as anything shown to them. Genl. d'Yorlk (?) said he had lived long and seen much, but 'did never see anything that did come so near his heart.' Bailey told us of a Wiltshire farmer who had arrived that morning in Town to 'see the Emperor.' He luckily was near St. Paul's when the Emperor arrived, forced his way without any ticket into the Cathedral, and as Alexander was coming out, shook him violently by the hands. This fashion of pawing, which the Majesty of the People has adopted, is quite odious. The D. of Wellington is just returned and they are treating him in the same manner, but he will not suffer it. Our illuminations very grand, with many allusions, affected enough, to Divine Providence and our brave Allies. Bayley quoted one of an Alehouse keeper whose sign is the Cock, of a less courtly nature, 'John Bull's the Cock of the Walk.' Better sure than such as this, ' To Jehovah, to Brit. and Alexander.' You will observe that Brit. means Britain, but the space was not wide enough to insert the lamps, or the economizing a few lamps became an object. You will see in the *M Chronicle* an allusion to the motto on Ld. Hertford's house, which oddly enough was 'The Prince's Peace.' The ancient custom of getting near a Monarch's garment to touch it as a remedy against all illness is very credible to one who has seen the late eagerness of the Mob exerted in the same manner. Indeed, happy the Man who could say he had touched a Cossack or a Cossack's horse as dirty as his master. This I frequently witnessed."

Miss Frere was staying with a cousin at Dover at the time of the arrival of the Russian party. She describes the Emperor as "much like a good English country gentleman," and the Grand Duchess of Oldenburg as "pretty, like her brother, with a sweet expression."

Ainslie continues his letter :—

" I will not surfeit you much longer with this image of the Times, its form and pressure, but will just give you an instance or two of our present temper, from what is chalked on the walls, the authors being, I presume, the same gentlemen who shake foreign Potentates by the Hands, and Cossack Horses by the Tails. We poor farmers are very miserably off just now from the low sale of our produce. The Populace who have got the Corn Bill thrown out wish to finish our Misery by hanging us all. They chalk up 'No starvation! No Landlords!' But the severe Poetry against our Prince, which I must write to Rose, which some Juvenal of St. Giles's has chalked up, is as follows :—

> 'I wish for this great Nation's sake
> The Devil would our Prince Regent take ;
> And when with him to Hell he's been,
> That he'd come back and take the Queen.'

. . . His Excellency has, I believe, been to Portsmouth to see the Grand Naval Show exhibited to our illustrious Visitors."

Among the distinguished foreigners who visited London at this time was Madame de Stael, whose ungracious behaviour to her courteous entertainers did not make her popular. Ainslie, who reports that she frightened all the women and above half the men, and wearied the remainder, tells how she was received at Lord Jersey's house with all the attentions that would have been shown to a foreign princess, and how she turned away with the contemptuous remark, '*qu'il n'y manquoit que l'esprit.*' Another of her sayings is reported by Mrs. George Frere. "Madame de Stael says she is sure the English ladies are so good she shall meet many of them in Paradise, and she is very sorry for it, for they are very dull." If there were any truth in some of the scandalous stories to which Ainslie alludes, "Corinne" had little reason to disquiet herself about the inhabitants of Paradise.

Ainslie, although he declared that he was never in the way of hearing gossip, contrived to send a great deal of it to Constantinople. When he wrote in September 1814, every one had rushed to Paris, but he was inclined to think that they would soon return, " the old noblesse being too needy and starved to pay for wax candles and sour lemonade, and the new people feeling quite averse to such delights." The Duke of Wellington gave great offence by the simplicity of his dress and manners to the Parisians, who forthwith nicknamed him " Milord Vilain-Ton."* " It is believed he has been shot at, twice," Ainslie wrote in November ; "the Ladies ascribe this to the risks incurred in affairs of Gallantry."

Lady Erroll was recovering from a desperate illness. Farmers were in evil plight, and Ainslie's letters are

---

* " O Wellington ! (or Villainton—for Fame
Sounds the heroic syllables both ways)."
Byron (Don Juan).

despondent in tone, even when he had to write of Napoleon's surrender :—

"July 24th, 1815.

"We are just now in full gossip as to the disposal of Napoleon' Bonaparte whom the Telegraph of yesterday signified to have arrived in the *Bellerophon*, an event which, some three years since, the maddest calculator on the reverses of fortune would never have dared to contemplate, but such have been the rapid changes, particularly within the last two months, that it is almost matter of indifference, and I am convinced that thirty years ago the introduction of shoe strings instead of Buckles would have made as much impression. The Parisians, and indeed French in general, are just now perfectly mad—despising themselves thoroughly, hating foreigners most sincerely, and looking forward to neither glory or happiness, so that that excellent individual Louis 18th will have a most unenviable situation among them. Every principle of honour being utterly extinct, among them, they cry Vive l'Empereur, Vive le Roy, or Vive le Diable, (as one of them told an Englishman) with equal indifference. Not but that the Soldiery have shewn more consistency. The wounded men all died with Vive l'Empereur in their mouths, and at Brussels, where Louis 18th had left some of his people with money to take care of the wounded, they refused such assistance, saying they neither wanted such a *grosse bête* or his money. The Parisians are accused of wearing ribbons with white on one side and tricolor on the other, ready for all emergencies. The Prussians at Paris, having no measures to keep, must be very unpleasant visitors, one report says that their officers do not in the least check themselves, and upon entering a Coffee House for instance, will turn out the French who may happen to be in their way without the least ceremony, making use of some such terms as this, '*Faites place aux Vainqueurs T—.*'"

"(Aug. 26th 1815). My Sisters are again upon a visit to Paris. Polignac returned for his Wife last week, and the same party occupy again the same House and are hearing the same enthusiastic cries of 'Vive notre bon Roi, Vivent les Bourbons,' as they did last year. Polignac was with the Duc d'Angoulême. He is a very good fellow himself, and I am convinced, sincere in what he says, though of course he must be partial to the Duke. He represents him as having gained real popularity in the South, for, 'altho' he went to Mass regularly,' yet, as he obliged no one to go with him, and was always on horseback looking to the soldiery, shewed himself very brave under fire, and positively refused to escape himself when his little army was surrounded, he is much esteemed. Unfortunately no one that ever I heard speak has one word to say in favor of the Duc de Berri except that he is not ill-tempered—a negative sort of character ill suited to these times and his situation. There is certainly amongst the other misfortunes of the Bourbons a jealousy of the D. of Orleans. The D. was lately assuring the King that all that had been said of his ambition and evil intentions was false. The King answered he had always considered it so. The Duke persisted in not letting the matter drop, and repeating his asseverations, when the King, who, it seems, is fond of a pun, said 'Lorsqu'un *Coussin* vous a piqué, il ne faut pas trop frotter, crainte d'envenimer la blessure.' This is as certain as that in the Vicar of Wakefield, the Minister said to his Valet, ' Jerningham, bring me my garters.'"

Dining with the Mansfields, Ainslie met a certain Russian admiral with an indecipherable name which might be read "Tchitchagow."   "He was mentioning that in the Hospital of Minsk, when paying a morning visit, he not only saw French soldiers gambling upon the bodies of some comrades who were just dead, using them as a table, but they had stuck upright in the corners of the room several tall figures also just dead by way of sentinels, having first painted their faces and put them into a sort of Masquerade dress—this at a time when the survivors could hardly expect to escape for many days themselves, and in fact very few did.

"There is an anecdote related of Col. Ponsonby, who was severely wounded in many places at Waterloo, that being left for dead on a part of the field immediately afterwards occupied by French Sharpshooters, he was placed with many other bodies to form a sort of rampart to these gentlemen, one of whom observed him to shew signs of returning life and perception just as his party were in their turn obliged to retreat. This fellow made a sort of bow to him, saying, 'Adieu, mon cher, je vous quitte, nous sommes battus,' and went off. A French officer however saved his life by giving him some brandy, telling him that should the French regain what he feared they had lost, he would make a point of sending for him."

When Ainslie next wrote, in December, he had just returned from a visit to Paris to attend the wedding of his sister Mary with her cousin, Sandilands, of the Coldstream Guards. The Duke of Wellington and other general officers had given some very grand balls in the magnificent palaces assigned to them as quarters, but the English were detested in Paris, although the Parisians were obliged to own that the conduct of our troops had been exemplary. The restoration of the masterpieces of painting and sculpture stolen from other countries by Napoleon and his Marshals, had half emptied the Louvre, and although what remained was enough to delight foreign visitors, no Frenchman could bear to look upon the empty frames and vacant pedestals. Among Ainslie's new acquaintance was Jerome Bonaparte's repudiated wife, Elizabeth Patterson, of Baltimore. "She is clever and pretty. Her son, the only child she had by him, was left in America. They talk of him as the very image of Bonaparte, and he must resemble him in more ways than one, for Mansfield told me he had taken the liberty to box his ears as a punishment for having beat a lesser child than himself, after which he sent little Boney to kiss and make up. Little Boney did kiss his adversary, but availed of the opportunity to give him a severe bite on the cheek." *

"A witticism, or I don't know what to call it, perhaps a very old one, delights William Rose just now beyond measure. Here it is. The present Archbishop of Canterbury, on becoming a Bishop, consulted a Divine whether he might continue to hunt. 'You may hunt, my Lord, but you must not hollow,' was the answer of the Oracle. Rose is getting it engraved on a Seal, and swears that if the Times were not so hard he would have ordered a service from Wedgwood with the same motto. He is trying his hand again at officiating Reading Clerk to the House of Lords, where Report says, for I have not yet been to enjoy his misery, he is quite melancholy and gentlemanlike. I don't know whether I mentioned to you his ecstasy in having sent Hinves to Warren upon some Medical point. Hinves returned saying that the Doctor looked as if he wanted Physic more than his

---

* This boy was afterwards known as Jerome Bonaparte Patterson. He married and left one son, a soldier.

Master, a saying Warren was not long kept ignorant of."

In 1816 George Frere wrote to Bartle to announce J. H. Frere's marriage with Lady Erroll, in a curious strain. The man of business and the man of genius did not always agree. " I am sick of all brothers but Temple and you," George once wrote in weariness of spirit, when sending Bartle some stockings and tooth-powder. " John and William and Edward are very good sort of people to be unconnected with. You are more of a philosopher than I am, and can bear these things better, and yet I have read Jemima Placid* since you have, but you have made the best use of it." On the present occasion George was very philosophical. " It is an Event which you must long since have expected to hear, and yet the very circumstance of its not having happened before, makes it a sort of surprise that it should happen now. Aye, dear Bartle, it is very true, and whether it is a pity or no, time must demonstrate."

Evidently George Frere was at as much of a loss as we are now, to know why the wedding had been so long postponed. There was no longer a mistress at Roydon to resent the presence of an Irish bride. Mrs. Frere had died in 1813, after a life of unobtrusive charity and good works, and her end was worthy of a right-minded, conscientious gentlewoman of the old school. She summoned her eight children who were then in England round her death-bed, and after calm and cheerful talk, " bade them go to dinner, which she trusted they would enjoy, and never to let their sorrow for her make them neglect their own health." Those were the days when ladies gave

* " Jemima Placid, or The Advantage of Good-nature," by Miss Dorothy Kilner, a nursery story of the last century.

toasts at dinner, and while her children were still at table a message came down from their mother—her last toast —"Our Union and the Marquis of that name." *

Frere's wedding was as unconventional as many of his other proceedings. He gave his sister Susanna great offence by not letting her know the day on which it was to take place. Lady Erroll was very anxious for George Frere's presence at the ceremony, but no intimation of the date came from the bridegroom. George, who had gone into Devonshire, concluded from intuition that it would be Thursday, September 12th, and reached town by the mail that morning just in time to join the party. The bridegroom was "in very good humour and good spirits, took his snuff and cast his Joke like Sir Condy.† His head is full of Verses which he thinks to publish, and his plan is to live at Roydon entirely and come to London no more, which he hadn't need, to be sure, for I saw the bottom of Mr. Blake's ‡ bill since January last, near to £800."

That afternoon, Mr. Murray, sitting in the little back parlour at Albemarle Street, received a visit from Mr. Frere. Being as "much exposed to authors" as the Duke of Wellington, Murray never allowed them to read or recite in his parlour, but "His Excellency" was a privileged person, and the verses which he repeated were so interesting that the dinner hour approached before either was aware. The publisher begged the author to share his dinner and continue the discussion, but Frere excused himself. "I was married this morning, and Lady Erroll is waiting for me to take her down into the country."

* J. H. Frere, who was Marques de la Union in Spain.
† Sir Condy Rackrent. (Miss Edgeworth, "Castle Rackrent.")
‡ J. H. Frere usually stayed at Blake's Hotel during his visits to London.

" They are gone to Hastings, where they have engaged no Lodgings and will find none, so that what has become of them I don't know," wrote George Frere to Bartle. " He is one of the cleverest, best, and oddest of mortals, to be sure."

CHAPTER X.

A DELICATE SITUATION.

1820.

FOR some years after his marriage Frere continued the same busily idle life, amusing himself with occasional literary *jeux d'esprit*, and translations from Aristophanes and the " Poema del Cid." " The Monks and the Giants," a mock heroic poem which purported to be written by William and Robert Whistlecraft, harness-makers, of Stowmarket, in Suffolk, was published by John Murray in 1817 and 1818. It is difficult to understand the enthusiasm it excited in such men as Scott, Byron, and W. S. Rose, but its chief merit was the gracefulness and ease with which Frere had adapted the octave stanza of Berni to English verse. " Beppo " was written in imitation of this model.

Lady Erroll's health, never strong, was a constant source of anxiety to her husband, and a severe cold, caught when visiting " the new rooms built at the British Museum for the Elgin marbles," wrought permanent damage to her constitution. Tunbridge Wells and other health resorts had no good effects, and a serious attack of illness in the summer of 1820 obliged Frere to take her abroad. A sea voyage was recommended, but although she recovered some strength in the Mediterranean, it was evident that she would never be able to endure the rigours of the English climate. Frere inclined to Palermo as a residence, but finally decided upon Malta, because he felt that, his pension being drawn from England, it should, if possible, be spent among English subjects.

Before leaving England, which he was only to see once again for a few months, Frere had to take part in a delicate and important negotiation. Some of the details were noted down by him at the time in a locked MS. book, which has only just been discovered at Roydon. So far as is known, it was his only attempt at keeping a journal, and it did not continue for very long. On the top of the first page is written : " This Book was given me on my Birthday May 21st 1820 (Whitsunday) by my dear Lady—whom God preserve to witness many returns of it."

On January 20th, 1820, the poor old man styled by courtesy King of Great Britain and Ireland closed a life that had been clouded by many sorrows, and a reign that had been glorious in spite of himself, and was succeeded by a son of whom few have been able to say any good. His failing health and enormous debts obliged him to lead a less disreputable life than when he was the boon companion of Fox and Sheridan, but nothing could make him either liked or respected. By his elevation to the throne the once gay and laughing hoyden whom Lord Malmesbury had lectured, who had romped at Blackheath, and slept in the new chintz bed at South Hill, succeeded to the position lately held by virtuous, economical, hard-hearted Charlotte of Mecklenburg-Strelitz. She was now a middle-aged, childless woman, wandering from place to place on the Continent, and causing scandal wherever she strayed, her fresh comeliness gone with youth, her headstrong imprudence changed into reckless effrontery ; but she was Queen Consort, and she intended to take her rightful position.

George IV., who had always hated the luckless wife thrust upon him by his father and mother, was determined that she should not come to England. Great pains were taken to collect evidence against her, but although her own folly had given ample cause for the worst suspicions, the evidence was pronounced inadequate by the Cabinet on February 10th. A compromise was then suggested, by which Caroline should bind herself not to assume the title of Queen, or to set foot on English shores. But she would have nothing less than her rights, and at one o'clock on June 5th the guns at Dover fired a royal salute to the wife of their new King as she stepped on to the pier. On reaching London she took up her abode at the house of her friend Alderman Wood, in South Audley Street. On June 6th the King sent a message to the House of Lords requesting them to take the necessary steps for considering a Divorce Bill.

Canning had always been the friend of Caroline of Brunswick, and his name was among those implicated in the unsavoury fictions of Sir John and Lady Douglas in 1806. Thanks in great measure to Lord Malmesbury's advice, the Princess was cleared, and the charge against Canning was so patently absurd, even to his enemies, that no notice was taken of it. But now, when those who wished well to the unhappy Princess could scarcely believe in her innocence, Canning felt that he could not join in the proceedings against her. The first-born son, whom the once-radiant " Fairy Godmother " held in her arms at the christening, when Pitt sparred with Leigh, had been released, not three months since, from a life that had known little but suffering and helplessness borne with steadfast patience ; and the memory of those bygone

days of hope and rejoicing must have been fresh in
Canning's heart when he demanded an audience with
George IV. It is at this point that Frere's diary begins.

"June 25th.—Canning had an audience of the King,
who received him, he said, with some formality at first,
but it wore off, and he became in very good humour.
He told him that he was come as He (the King) had
said that he wished he had done before, instead of
stating his difficulties to Ld. Liverpool about 8 months
ago—that things had got to that stage in which it was
not possible for him to take a part—that he did not
come to offer his resignation, which would look, he said,
like giving himself an air as if he had something to
complain of or disapprove of, that this was not the case;
he disapproved of nothing that had been done, and had
nothing whatever to complain of, but that his task as
a minister was one which from personal feelings and
old recollections he could not perform—that there were
inconveniences every way in his remaining in office
without taking a part, or in leaving the Govt. at this
moment, that he therefore merely came to place the
decision in the King's hands. The K. said he would
take some time to consider it, and dismissed him with
great kindness and cordiality. Canning came away very
much pleased with the manners of the whole thing.
The King told him that in the year   * he had scratched
his [Canning's] name out of the informations, and rallied
him a little. . . .† 'To be sure it does seem odd that
we should be sitting together on this sofa and talking
upon this subject.'

* The date is illegible, but it is probably 1806.
† Two sentences are here omitted. Their meaning is not clear,
but they seem to allude to the matrimonial troubles of a friend of
Canning's and Frere's, with whom we have no concern.

" The only way seems to be for the whole thing to be gone through in the House of Lords (who are the only real tribunal) by a Bill grounded on facts to be proved in evidence. His [Canning's] going out would be full of difficulty and liable to infinite misconstructions of the most opposite kinds.

" Wednesday, June 28. Dined at home—Ld. Lansdowne, Granville, Morpeth, Fox, and others. Went in the evening to Lady Lansdowne's, who has opened Sumner's great Room—met my old friend, Sir Robert Wilson. We began talking of the subject of the Queen, and I lamenting the opportunity which she had lost of coming out of all her difficulties with the appearance of deference to the resolution and Address of the House of Commons, which would have been in reality a triumph, in as much as she would have forced the Govt. (contrary to their own declaration) to negociate with her here in England, and would have obtain'd a point in being treated as Queen in the Papal States which she had made her residence. I said that this opportunity having been thrown away, I for my part saw no hope but that things must go on from bad to worse—such a mediation and such a compromise were not likely to occur again, and the rejection of them had created great irritation in Parliament. He said he did not think a compromise absolutely hopeless. I said I was glad to hear him say so, that I knew other wiser heads than mine did not think the thing so absolutely impracticable, and to find that he was of the same opinion gave me some hope. He said he should see Brougham the next morning, and would then call upon me ; he understood, of course, that by ' the wiser head than my own ' I meant Canning's.

" On Thursday morning he called and said that B[rougham] and himself had thought that an immediate personal opening might be made if it were first understood that the same terms should be granted and accepted on both sides. I said I would ascertain this as far as I could, and he then said that the communication might be begun thus :—

"That the King might give orders to Sir B. Blomfield, or some other person immediately attached to his person, to write to her Banker or to Br[ougham] placing a sum of money to her credit in order to obviate any difficulty or delay in bringing witnesses. That upon this the Queen might write a Letter to the King in the character of a person overcome by such an act of generosity, and placing herself at his discretion, upon which the same terms might be offered to her and would be accepted by her. That a conclusion of this kind, and between King and Queen, might still take place after the rejection of all interference of Ministers and Parliament (mere subjects after all) who it might be said had no right (according to her feelings at least) to interpose in the family quarrels of Royal persons.

"I then went and saw Canning, who was of opinion that the same terms might be obtain'd.

"Friday (June 30th).—I saw Canning, who said that the proposed mode of beginning the thing would not do, as it was already known in the House of Commons that money was placed at the Queen's disposal for that very purpose by Ld. Liverpool—and seemed moreover suspicious of some design to lay a trap to meet the report with a clamour about an offer of money and bribery. There was moreover a paragraph in the *Times* (Brougham's, or rather her, paper) mentioning a prospect of compromise but imputing it unfairly to hesitation on the part of the Govt.

"I went to Wilson's in Ryder Street at two o'clock, but he was not return'd. I called at Davenport's in the next street, and went to the exhibition of Old Portraits, and called again, but not finding him at home, was going away to wait at the Travellers' Club, when I met him at the Corner just return'd from his meeting * very much worried, and saying that he had had great difficulty in stopping a resolution to intreat the Queen not to leave the country.

" I then told him the first inoffensive objection to the scheme, viz., that it was already known that the Queen could not be in want of money for such a purpose. He took it so quietly and readily that it disarmed me of any suspicion I might have had (of him at least) from Canning's remarks and the Article in the *Times*. I then suggested what had occurred to me since I had left Canning, viz. that she might send to desire to see Ld. Liverpool, that she had known him, and he was a person upon whose honour and secrecy she might depend, and whose mildness of manner would prevent the interview from being at all painful; that the secret would remain between themselves, and nothing more would be known than that an interview had been had with the first Minister, and that the thing was settled and at an end—that she might send for Ld. Glenbervie, her old steady acquaintance, and send him with a message desiring to see Ld. Liverpool. As I was going, he asked me whether it would not be better for her to send for Canning. I said certainly not, that Liverpool was the Minister, that Canning had wholly expended himself in her service, and as far as her affair was concerned could hardly be considered as a part of the Govt.

" I dined at Hallam's; there was Crabbe, Heber, Rose, Mansfield, R. Heber and his wife. Wilson called me out in the evening into Hallam's study, and told me if I would call upon him two hours after, at Brougham's in Hill

---

* A meeting in Southwark which Sir Robert Wilson had been obliged to attend.

Street, I should know the result of Brougham's con-
ference with the Queen. I went accordingly, and saw Sir
Robert alone in a Room below stairs. The impression
upon my mind was that nothing was advanced or likely to
advance as the urgency of the case required. He said
that she had spoken with great irritation of Castlereagh's
being appointed to negotiate in the first instance—'He
whose brother * had behaved with such disrespect to her.'
Why was not Canning employed? to which Brougham
said that it would have been as if he himself had been
employ'd, at which she laugh'd and said, 'Ah, poor Dear
Canning, he would do the best he could for me.' Finally
what was proposed to me was that Ward should call and
leave a card, that upon this she should be persuaded to
send for him. I said that this would not do, that the time
was too short; if they could not advance faster that they
would have to make their arrangements the moment before
the report came down (which was fixed for Monday or
Tuesday) as if under the impression of immediate fear.
Finally that there was only time to do the one thing which
I recommended, viz. to send for old Glenbervie, and send
him to Liverpool. But I was so satisfied that I could be
of no further use after giving that advice that I should go
out of town for five or six hours the next day. . . .

"On reporting this to Canning, he told me that the time
was much shorter, that the final Cabinet was fixed for
Saturday night or Sunday morning, after which no new
resolution would be likely to be adopted.

"When I came home it was late, for when I called upon
Canning he was already half undrest and going to bed, and
at home I found that not a bit of sealing-wax was to be

* Charles, Baron Stewart, afterwards third Marquis of Londonderry.
He was Ambassador at Vienna from 1814 to 1822, and one of his duties
was to collect information regarding the Queen's conduct.

found for my note.   So I waked Beaumont,* and told him to go early to Sir R. and to tell him that I would call upon him before ten, leaving the carriage in Arlington Street.

" (Saturday) Which I did, and merely said that the time was barely left for doing what was recommended, for that the decision would be taken that night or the next morning. . . .

" I returned to Canning, and we talked a good deal but without reference to the possibility of anything being done. I only regretted that I had not mentioned Sir W. Grant as a person to be sent for, being an old frequenter of her parties, and a man of such steadiness of character.   I returned home, and Sir Robt. W. called again, and said that different people had been talked over, that she objected to Glenbervie as too old—to Sir W. Scott and Ward for some other reason—but that upon my name being mentioned to her, she said everything of her high opinion.   I said it was (as it was) very painful to me to wish to decline such an office, but the same reasons which should prevent her from sending for Canning should induce her to send for anybody else rather than me as being in a manner belonging to him—that I could not take a step without bringing him under the imputation of having departed from the nullity and neutrality with respect to the whole question in which the King's indulgence had placed him.   I then suggested that Sir W. Grant should be sent for.   This struck him as much the best course, and I urged that not a moment should be lost.   He left me, promising that I should hear the result in the morning."

Having, as he hoped, put the Queen's business into a satisfactory train, Frere went out to dinner, and learned,

* Frere's valet, who had been with him for some years.

on his return, that the final meeting of the Council was was postponed until two o'clock on Sunday—a fact of which he at once informed Sir Robert Wilson.

"Sunday. The messenger before I was up brought me Sir R.'s letter clearly showing how little influence he possessed over her. On the evening before she had allowed herself to be dragged by a mob huzzaing in front of Carlton House. . . . The evening before (Friday) there had been a similar excursion, not so offensive to the King, but equally undignified, in going to Guildhall with the carriage dragged by the Mob in her way home."

On that fateful Sunday, after hearing prayers, which were always read to him when he was unable to attend the morning service, Canning called on Frere, and they waited together until two o'clock, the last hour at which the period of possible compromise expired. No message came, and Frere, exhausted by a violent cold, went early to bed, and sent an excuse to Lydia White with whom he was engaged to dine. On Monday he lay in bed and wrote his diary. On Tuesday (July 4th) came a note from Brougham, which has been kept between the leaves of the diary. Brougham complained that "like everything else, the Q.'s seeing Grant has got into the newspapers," and Wilson who enclosed Brougham's letter assured Frere that neither Brougham nor himself was to blame. The fact was, that the Queen was beyond the control of her advisers, and could not be stayed from ruining herself.

On Wednesday Canning came to see Frere, with an account of Sir W. Grant's interview with the Queen. She began by protesting "her innocence and resolution and so forth," to which Grant rejoined by asking why she had wished to see him. She then referred him to Canning, who said that the compromise which had at one time been possible, was rendered out of the question by the measures which had been taken by the Government and by " her cavalcades with the mob." He could only advise the Queen to throw herself upon the King's generosity, which might even now be extended to her.

The publicity of a trial was not desirable for either party, and Frere was distressed to hear that a majority of the House of Lords' Committee had overruled a moderate report drawn up by Lord Harrowby, and substituted "a most bitter one " which appeared in the papers, on that Wednesday morning.

" What a change since Saturday sennnight ! she might have left the Country in triumph, having baffled the King and braved the Govt., and received the address and thanks afterwards from Parliament—but the very spirit of infatuation seems to have possessed her—receiving the deputation of the House of Commons with the utmost haughtiness and scorn—and shaking hands with the mob out of the windows of her carriage, at Dover, at Guildhall, etc. What is most strange is that no adviser is discoverable except the absurdest of all mankind, Alderman Wood and Dr. Parr whom, this day week, Sir R. W. mentioned seriously as the adviser of her rejection of the address of the House of Commons. I of course suspected Burdett, who must have been the Dr.'s introducer—but W. said that he (Burdett) was most anxious to get her out of the scrape. The result seems to be that we are placed between conviction and revolution."

On this day (Thursday, July 5th) Lord Liverpool introduced the Divorce Bill into the House of Lords. From that time Canning ceased to advise the Government in any way.

"Friday.—Saw Canning. I found that he agreed with me in thinking the divorce a very strong measure, and full of difficulty. He told me that he had written his opinion of it to Ld. Liverpool (before the Bill was brought down), that the debate of last night confirmed him in his view of the danger attending it, that he was quite surprized at Liverpool's allowing himself to be drawn into such a resolution. He attributed it chiefly to Castlereagh and Wellington. I told him what I said to my Lady last night. 'My Dear,' I said, 'you know that as soon as Canning ceased to advise them, they would fall into blunders, and I believe they have begun already.' He told me that during the debate Sir R. Wilson passed close by him, and said to him in a whisper 'This is only the beginning.' The whole question in fact now bears a different character. It is no longer a simple question of the Queen's demerits, but of the King's merits, and the whole advantage of the former forbearance is thrown away. . . . When the ultimate conclusion (viz. divorce) appears, it becomes almost impossible to resist the inference (a perfectly true one as far as the King is concerned) that the object of divorce had been in view from the beginning, and was the real motive of the Milan Commission.

"Thus in ten days after her great blunder, another is committed by Govt. which may possibly give her the advantage again, but with infinite danger to the peace of the Country. The story of her receiving poor little Sir Tommy Tyrwhit is true: 'Tell the King that I can not meet wid him here, but I shall meet him oop there.' I wish so for both their sakes!

" Saturday July 8th.—The Coronation is put off, it was strongly debated in Council, and came (a very unusual thing) to a vote in Cabinet—Castlereagh and Wellington for persevering. Canning said truly 'we must look to things now as they furnish topics. If I was Brougham I would not wish for a finer topic than the Queen in her present situation and a Coronation going on at the same time. Wellington would have no objection to a Coronation purely military, he thinks that things must come to force at last. It may be so, perhaps, but the occasion would be a most odious and inauspicious one.'

" It is pretty well ascertained that one of the boxes which was hired to view the procession was intended to be occupied by the Queen. This would have been a fine *coup de théâtre*, and ominous too, for the last Queen that saw her husband crowned was the wife of Charles I,* and on such occasions the people look out for omens."

At this date the diary breaks off. Whether the preparations for leaving England gave Frere no time for writing, or whether his dislike of taking up a pen overcame his wish to make use of his Lady's present does not appear ; but the rest of the leaves are clean as when they were first opened, although yellowed by time. It has been no easy task to decipher this fragment, most of which was written in bed, with a bad pen, in the minutest characters. Here and there a few sentences have been left out for the sake of compression, and all irrelevant matter has been omitted. Otherwise the diary is as Frere wrote it, with the exception of the last sentence—a characteristic and untrue remark of the King's, which it was inadvisable to publish.

* Henrietta Maria refused to be crowned with her husband on the score of religious scruples.

CHAPTER XI.

COLERIDGE AND SOUTHEY.

"In such goodness as both *my* Mr. Frere (the Rt. Hon. J. H. Frere)
and his brother George (the lawyer in Brunswick Square) live,
move, and have their being in, there is Genius."
(S. T. COLERIDGE to H. CRABB ROBINSON, June 1817.)

WHEN the "Highland Lady" whose diary has recently been given to the world used to visit her aunt Mrs. George Frere in Brunswick Square, she often found there a restless figure, with wild eyes and snowy hair, who would stand on the hearthrug and pour forth incoherent rhapsodies, reminding the bystanders of the inspired singer in "Kubla Khan." This was Coleridge, who had then been placed under the care of Mr. Gillman at Highgate, in the hope of curing him of the opium habit.

There is nothing to show how Coleridge and J. H. Frere first became acquainted. It was perhaps through the medium of George Frere, as Coleridge at one time sends a request through him to be allowed to prefix four lines from the translation of Aristophanes' "Frogs" to one of his own essays. But before that date he had corresponded with Frere. The earliest of the letters was sent with a copy of "Sibylline Leaves" on July 2nd, 1816.

Frere did his best to help Coleridge in various ways—by bringing his writings under the notice of Canning and other literary men, and by solid assistance in money.

Coleridge was one of the ten Associates of the Royal Society of Literature instituted under the patronage of George IV. in 1824, and received from the King's bounty an annuity of a hundred guineas. William IV., on his accession, refused to continue these payments ; and, in consequence of representations made to the Government, Earl Grey offered Coleridge a private grant of £200 from the Treasury. This the poet declined, but, according to Sir W. Scott,* he made no objection to receiving the former annuity of a hundred guineas from Frere's own purse.

His letters to Frere are written in a minute hand, and are not easy to read. He is fond of indulging in Greek quotations, but his Greek is as destitute of accents as a lady's Greek was said to be in the early days of the higher . education of women. Some words are quite illegible, and the sentences are unmercifully long. The anxiety which he displays in the first letter to be cleared of the charge of idleness is amusing :—

"Dear Sir,—

"Should I have the good fortune to find you at home and disengaged this morning, I shall have superseded this Scrawl—the object of which is to excuse myself for the liberty, I take, in obtruding on you the accompanying Sheets—which consist of a 1st Volume, and part of a Second of my literary Life—more accurately perhaps, Sketches of my intellectual Life and Principles—in which my chief purposes were, 1. to defend myself (not indeed to my own Conscience, but—) as far as others are concerned, from the often and public denunciation of having wasted my time in idleness—in short, of having done nothing ;

* *Journal.* Mr. E. H. Coleridge says that S. T. Coleridge ultimately accepted £300 from the Treasury.

2. not merely to state my own principles of Taste, but to settle, if possible, and to put to rest with all men of sense the controversy concerning the nature and claims of poetic Diction.—There is with these a third Volume entitled Sibylline Leaves, a collection of such poems as I dare consent to be known as of my own Will as well as Authorship.

"I had hoped to have sent them during your confinement—and then I might have ventured to hope that you would have returned them enriched with a few marks of your pencil—if they were only mere symbolic signs of your disapprobation of particular passages, lines or words. With grey hairs and a subdued spirit it would be too late for me to *begin* the attempt to flatter—and be assured it will be but an act of justice to the simplicity of my character if you give full belief to my assurance, that my sole motive for entreating your friendly perusal of these pages originates in my thorough conviction that of all the men I have yet met with in public or literary life, you possess beyond comparison, the purest and manliest Taste : and I say less than I mean and feel, when I add that I have on my shelves long original poems, epic, and romantic, full of images and incidents, and *mother-and-child* sentiments and sensibilities, and these of great celebrity (*reputation* at least), the whole excellencies of which concentrated do not impress on my reason that sense of inventive and constructive power which I appeared to myself to see in the one Imitation of the Parabasis from the Knights of Aristophanes."

The next letter was written on a Thursday in December, and accompanied the first of his Lay Sermons, "The Statesman's Manual." It seems to have been intended for George Frere :—

" J. Gillman's, Esq.,
" Highgate.

" Dear Sir,—

" The inclosed ought to have reached you last week : and it was by accident that I discovered the piece of forgetfulness that occasioned the delay. The second Sermon will (*Deo volente*) appear next week, and is (comparatively, at least) popular both in matter and style. The title to the present ought to have been, and I had so directed it—addressed to the Learned and Reflecting of all Ranks and Professions, especially among the Higher Class.

" It had passed thro' many an anxious revisal, and yet you will observe on a mere Turning-over of the Pages what a Gleaning the last produced me. And I doubt not that you and your Brother would enable me to return from the same Stubble with another Sheaf under my arm.

" I should in truth be exceedingly obliged to you for any remarks of this kind that might occur to you during the Perusal. I fear that your general censure will be that I have lost my cause between Justice Nimis and Justice Parum—that I have said too much of my peculiar code of philosophic Belief, having said so little."

The next letter is also addressed to G. Frere, Esq., and is docketed by him " recd Dec: 19 1816."

The four lines from the translation of " The Frogs " of which Coleridge wishes to make use are taken from Euripides' speech to Æschylus :—

" When I received the Muse from you I found her puff'd and
    pamper'd
With pompous sentences and terms, a cumb'rous huge virago ;
My first attention was applied to make her look genteelly,
And bring her to a lighter shape by dint of lighter diet."

"Dear Sir,—

"I hear from Mr. W. Rose that your brother is in town. Will you be so good as to present my unfeigned Respects to him, and say that I should take courage to request a favor of him if I could but let him know even as I myself know it, that he may refuse it without giving me the least pain. It is to permit to place four lines of his as a free translation of the corresponding Lines in Aristophanes' Frogs ('When I received the Muse from you,' etc.), which I have prefixed to one of the essays in the rifacciamento of the Friend now printing—with or without his name as he may prescribe. I have likewise to say that I have spoken and in part quoted a passage in the kind letter with which you honored me when I was at Mudeford (*sic*) as an observation of another, which had impressed me with its importance. I hope you will not be offended by this liberty as no name is mentioned or referred to.

"I hope you received my first Sermon. But I shall have far greater pleasure in presenting the second to you, to your approbation of which I look forward with a sort of consolatory Confidence. Mr. W. Rose has written in higher terms of the Statesman's Manual than I had dared anticipate. He has paid me the same Compliment that Socrates did to Heraclitus, 'what he understood he liked very much indeed, and what he did not, he gave me credit for.'

"Pray could you inform me whether and how I could direct a copy of each of the Sermons to Mr. Canning? I thought of sending the same to Mr. Vansittart and Lord Sidmouth, but I scarce know why, I feel a *withdrawing* at the thought—and could more comfortably brave the dyspathy of a man of Genius and strong sense, than——in short the Meeting of the British and Foreign Bible Society at the

Egyptian Hall, and a few other things of the same kind have not digested well with me."

The next letter introduces the celebrated German critic Ludwig Tieck.

"*Friday* 27 *June* 1817, HIGHGATE.

"My dear Sir,—

"We have had for some weeks in England one of the most celebrated Literati who as a poet and Philosophic critic is by a large and zealous party deemed second only to Goethe. I became acquainted with him at Rome—his name Ludwig Tieck. His literary Career bears a striking resemblance to Wordsworth's. Assuredly I have both seen enough of the Man and read enough of his Works to feel no hesitation in expressing myself in the highest terms concerning his Genius and multiform Acquirements. He is intimately acquainted with the Literature of Spain, Portugal, Italy and England, in addition to that of his own country and to his classical Erudition—in truth he is well acquainted with the Writers of every European country, and reads the originals—but his intimacy with all *our* Writers, even the most obscure, from Chaucer to Dryden inclusive, above all with the contemporaries of Shakespear, is ASTONISHING. I felt myself a mere school-boy in these respects, whether I considered the width or the minute accuracy of his knowledge. Refer to a line in any of the obscurest works ever attributed to Shakespear, and he will immediately tell you the place and page in one or more Editions, and repeat the passage. I fretted myself sore with the continued Wishing that I could have had the pleasure of Lady Erroll's and your company on Tuesday and Wednesday, which days he spent with me at Highgate. He speaks English very pleasingly ; though when together we found it by far the best each to speak his own mother tongue, and in a few minutes we became wholly unconscious that we were not both speaking the same language : as the words conveyed the thoughts to each without any intermedium of mental translation. . . . I put a question to him concerning the present convictions of Scientific men in Germany respecting Animal Magnetism, and at length asked him Have you yourself ever seen any of these wonder-works ? The detail of facts in which he sub-stantiated the affirmative of this, the known estimable-ness and purity of his moral character, the *uninventable* circumstantiality of the cases, and the fineness and yet the winning simplicity with which he sympathized with the painful struggle which, he foresaw, he must excite in Gilman's mind (for my philosophy had converted me *à priori*) between the incapability of either believing the facts or disbelieving *him*, could not have but deeply interested Lady Erroll. . . .

" But these Tieckiana have seduced me from Tieck himself and the purpose of this letter. For the last 15 years or more he has devoted his Time and Thoughts to a great Work on Shakespear, in 3 large Volumes Octavo. . . . Mr. Tieck has been a daily Reader at the British Museum with persons transcribing for him ; and on Monday he goes to Oxford, and from thence to Cambridge for the same purpose.—I write to solicit you, my dear Sir ! to procure for him letters of Introduction to both Universities. It is much at my heart, that a Scholar and a Poet of such high and deservedly high reputation on the Continent (for it is not confined to his own Country) and so good a man to boot (to which I may safely add, a polished Gentleman) should receive the marks of respect due to him from the country and countrymen of Shakespear. If Mr. Heber be in Town, I doubt not, that a word from you would be sufficient. Nay, for in such a cause I dare be bold, I would say that it would not be beneath Mr. Canning's attention, would his Leisure permit it and should you see no impropriety in making the Request. . . .

"My eldest son, Hartley Coleridge, from Oxford, is now with me ; his manners are rather eccentric—otherwise he is in head and heart all I ought to wish."

The following letter is a highly characteristic production. Coleridge evidently thought himself an injured being, but, even after reading his elaborate explanations, one cannot wonder that Mr. Rogers was anxious about the fate of Mr. Rose's book. In spite of these warnings, Frere allowed Coleridge to make use of his library, as appears from an undated note in which the poet returns thanks for the loan of the books which he has not yet opened.

" HIGHGATE, Tuesday Noon,
" 16 July 1816.

"My dear Sir

"Friday is the same to me as Thursday ; and were it otherwise, the inconvenience must, I flatter myself, have stood under the rubric of Duty to have kept its ground against the pleasure of meeting Mr. Canning. Tho' I should take shame to myself, if I were torpid to the interest, which an eminent public character naturally excites, *as such*; yet the recollections of his being your friend and schoolfellow, were uppermost at the instant, that I received your kind invitation. . . .

"Your remarks on the 9th Book of the Iliad were perfectly convincing to my mind ; and have strengthened an old persuasion of mine that we shall never *feel* as Englishmen what the Iliad really is till we have it translated as a metrical Romance, with such enrichment of metre and rhythm, as he who had a right to attempt such a work, would have supplied to him by the Genius that constituted the Right. That such a thing is practicable, your Aristophanies (*sic*) have now satisfied me. . . .

"Now, my dear Sir! will you pardon me if I take the liberty of unbosoming myself to you on a circumstance, which tho' a seeming trifle has both wounded and injured me. Many years ago Mr. Sotheby lent me the old Folio Edition of Petrarch's Works. I read it thro' and communicated my remarks. Just on the eve of my leaving England for Malta, I had the book put up to be returned ; but in the depression of Disease, and amid the bustle and heart-sickness of leaving all I loved, with little confidence of ever seeing them again, this was forgotten, and the Book remained at Keswick. It was not till long after my return that I discovered this. I then had the Book sent up to London, and supposed it to have been returned—but by another piece of Ill-luck, it was sent (tho' directed to Mr. Sotheby) among Morgan's books to Bishopsgate Street, from which place it did at length arrive at its true owner. Likewise, some ten years ago, poor Charles Lamb took it into his head that he had lent me a volume of Dodsley's old plays. . . . At length, however, I was lucky enough to procure the odd volume from Southey, and gave it to Lamb. . . .

"Except these two cases, and I dare challenge all my acquaintances to mention a single instance in which I have ever furnished occasion for this Charge, I have been most grievously sinned against in this respect ; and for that very reason have been cautious not to offend myself. Yet on the strength of this slander Mr. Rogers (I write without the least resentment) prevented Mr. Rose from lending me Carl Gozzi's Works, which he was previously most ready to do, and which I had in vain endeavoured to procure from Leghorn.   From the same cause, I doubt not, Mr. Hare refused to let me have the Reading of such works of Giordano Bruno, as I had not had an opportunity of seeing (a unique collection of which he purchased for a trifle at the Roxburgh Sale) tho' I had in the *Friend* announced my intention of writing the Life of G. Bruno with a critique on his system and that of the Pantheists of the same age (Behmen, etc.). I could mention other instances ; and as I never borrow a Book but for some specific purpose, and that too of importance to me, this has been a very serious injury to me even in a pecuniary View.   For instance Murray has offered me £200 for an octavo Volume of Specimens of Rabbinical Wisdom (in the manner of those in the *Friend* and including them).   The descriptive Title of the Work would be—the modes with the advantages and disadvantages of *oral* instruction compared with the age of Books—and if it be well executed, it will be worth more than twice £200.   Yet I am much deceived if but for the aforesaid cruel Slander I should not have had the [? word illegible] procured for me, without which or some other translation of the Mischna and [? word illegible] I cannot go on with the work.   Now Sir, should you have a favourable opportunity of mentioning these circumstances to Mr. Rose, or any other proper person, you would greatly serve me.   But at all events forgive the freedom I take in making the request—for it is with most sincere respect and sense of acknowledgement that I remain

"my dear Sir

"your obliged

"S. T. COLERIDGE."

There is a gap of ten years before we come to the next letter, which is a unique specimen of an invitation to dinner, worthy of the man who turned a lecture on Shakespeare's heroines into a dissertation upon the ethics of flogging schoolboys. The friend to whom Coleridge looked with confidence for the excitement of a philosophical spirit was his disciple Joseph Henry Green, Professor of Anatomy to the College of Surgeons and the Royal Academy, and Fellow of the Royal Society.

"GROVE, HIGHGATE.

"My dear Sir,—

"Shall I be presuming on your kindness if I tell you that on Friday my excellent friend Mr. Green, and Mr. Tulk, the late Member for Sudbury (a thoroughly good and amiable man, and in many ways worth knowing) dine with us; these two with Mr. and Mrs. Gillman and myself, constituting the whole party: and if I venture to request the honor—to express the wish at least—of your joining us —should you chance not to be pre-engaged? Of Mr. Green I need only say that to him I look with confidence for the excitement of a philosophical spirit, and the introduction of Philosophy in its objective Type, among our Physiologists and Naturalists—the one side of the Isosceles Triangle, the Basis of which is the Dynamic Logic, and the Apex Religion. The Historic *Idea* is the same in Natural History (physiogony) as in the History commonly so called, but polarized, or presented in opposite and correspondent forms. The purpose of the latter is to exhibit the moral necessity of the whole in the freedom of the component parts: the resulting chain necessary, each particular link remaining free. (Our old chroniclers and Annalists satisfy the latter half of the requisition; Hume,

Robertson, Gibbon, the former half; in Herodotus and the Hebrew Records alone both are found united.) In the History of Nature the same elements exist in the reverse order. The Absolute Freedom, WILL both in the form of REASON ($\Lambda o\gamma o\varsigma$; $T\iota o\varsigma$ $\mu o\nu o\gamma\epsilon\nu\eta\varsigma$; $O\Omega N$ $\epsilon\nu$ $\tau\omega$ $\kappa o\lambda\pi\omega$ $\tau o\upsilon$ $\pi a\tau\rho o\varsigma$) and in its own right as the Ground of Reason ($\beta\upsilon\sigma\sigma o\varsigma$, $a\beta\upsilon\sigma\sigma o\varsigma$) is the principle of the Whole in the Necessity of the Component Parts. And in this spirit my Friend contemplates and is labouring to make others contemplate, the Law of Life both as a Surgeon and as a Professor of Comparative Anatomy and Physiology.

"Mr. Tulk would interest you, were it only that it is something to meet with a Scholar and a man of Taste and Talent, who is a Partizan and Admirer of the Honorable Emanuel Swedenborg; but of the genuine school."

Frere endeavoured to interest Lord Liverpool in his *protégé*, and received a vague but kindly answer, which did not commit the writer.

There are also two undated letters from Coleridge. One of them bears no date beyond—

"GROVE, HIGHGATE,
" *Wednesday night.*

" My dear Sir,—

"It is a great delight to me to be anywhere with you. And more than so—for to you I can say this, secure of the right interpretation—it is a source of Strength, and a renewal of hope, and of the hope I most need—viz. : that I am still in the region where the sympathy of sane minds can follow me, and have not been toiling after shadows. I shall have much pleasure in availing myself of Lord Hastings' condescension, and still more in the preludium.

"Dared I shape my expectations to my wishes, I would say, I expect you on Friday at an *early* hour. And if I might wish *aloud*, you would hear me craving and hoping that you might have a portion of your MSS. with you.

"With sincere respect, I am,

"My dear Sir! your obliged

"S. T. COLERIDGE."

In the same packet as the letters from Coleridge lie a number of letters from a very different character— Robert Southey, whose Dactylics and Sapphics Frere and Canning had formerly parodied in the *Anti-Jacobin*. The small, neat writing is clear to read, although he apologises for it ; and the placid, contented tone of the busy man, happy in his friendships and his proof-sheet, is as different as possible from the incoherent metaphysics of the other poet. After reading through the list of Southey's works in prose and verse, it is difficult to imagine how one hand could manage to cover so many reams of paper before the invention of typewriters. Frere helped him with the History of the Peninsular War, and several letters express gratitude for information and corrections.

"KESWICK, 30 *Dec.* 1820.

"My dear Sir,—

"I am now in the press with the history of the Peninsular War. The first chapter is merely introductory, concerning the state of the three countries which were directly involved in the contest. With this therefore, I had no occasion to trouble you, but upon coming to matters of fact, I have desired Murray to send you the proof-sheets.

" . . . At present what would be most serviceable to me would be that sort of information which you could communicate in a leisure hour concerning the leading members of the Central Junta—who they were, what were their views and characters. In the few opportunities which I have had of conversing with you on Spanish affairs, a single expression of yours has given me light where I most wanted it. . . .

" During the contest my anticipations for Spain were always hopeful. I wish they were so now. But at present my best hope is that other countries, and especially Portugal, may be warned in time, by the tremendous example which is likely to be afforded them there. Brazil I hope may escape, for if a revolution should take place there, the country will soon be divided among hordes of banditti, as is now the case with the provinces of the Plata, where the Revolutionists have been left to themselves. If Spain were under a settled government I believe it would not be long before deputies from Buenos Ayres would be sent to solicit that it would send out a Viceroy and put an end to their miserable state of anarchy."

In March 1826 Southey had nearly finished the second volume, and was anxious for more corrections from Frere.

" Are you aware that Godoy * has written some Memoirs ? " asks Southey in April 1826. " An Italian whose name I forget (an Abbate I think he was) wrote to me some five or six years ago from Milan, informing me that he possessed a copy of them, which, as he presumed it must be of the greatest importance to me, was at my service

* The " Prince of the Peace."

for 2 or 300 guineas (I forget which). As I did not answer the proposal, a son of Mr. Scarlett's wrote to ask if I had received it, and I then replied to him that the Italian appeared to me to have calculated very largely upon the credulity and wealth of an Englishman. Mr. Scarlett, however, in a second letter assured me the Abbate was a respectable man, and in reference to the price which had been asked, observed that he (himself to wit) had taken it for granted that the Government was at the expenses of any materials for my intended work. If the memoirs in question have found their way to the press, I have not heard of them. But it would be interesting to see what sort of story such a person could set forth in his own behalf. I once met a gentleman who by some accident had fallen in with him in Italy just after the conclusion of the war. Godoy spoke of Ferdinand, said that Spain would never be tranquil under him and concluded by saying ' I have known him from his childhood—he is a bigot, a tyrant, and a liar.' . . .

" That neither the nobility nor the people of this country would under a like trial display half the virtue which the Spaniards displayed, I am but too well convinced. And in spite of all ill aspects I cannot believe that a nation which has given such proofs of national worth, can be lost without hopes of redemption. The dogma that human will constitutes law never would have been taken for the foundation of such opposite systems with implicit confidence on both sides, if the lawyers had not accustomed men to such a scheme and practice of law as plainly enough have proceeded from human will—and for the most part under the Devil's direction. The Romish clergy have hardly been more active and successful in corrupting Christianity, than the lawyers of every country in supplanting by their own craft the real principles of law, and in confounding the distinctions of right and wrong in their practice.   And it is chiefly from this class of men that our constitution-makers and menders proceed."

Frere had been endeavouring to obtain leave for Southey to consult documents at the Foreign Office.   It is evident from the following letter that permission was not readily granted :—

"My dear Sir,—

        "I am very greatly obliged to you for what you have done, and tho' not without a suspicion that the same difficulty would not have been felt, if the same thing had been asked by Lord Holland for an Edinburgh Reviewer, or by Lord Lansdowne for Tom Moore, I am nevertheless very well satisfied with the result.

"It is not of the slightest importance to me whether my work is supposed to have been assisted or not by the communication of official papers.   But in point of fact, it is and will be believed, by all that great portion of the public who know nothing about statesmen and reasons of state, that I have all that assistance from Government, which they naturally suppose Government ought in such a case willingly to afford.   Of such an opinion Murray has the advantage. . . ."

There are no more letters from Southey until August 23rd, 1837, when he writes to thank Frere for sending him some verses supposed to be by Cowper.   He had been on a round of visits which carried him down to the Land's End.   Among his hosts were Sir Thomas Acland, who entertained him in three counties, and Derwent Colerid ge The literary world was then inundated with "chatter about S. T. Coleridge, no more trustworthy than the majority of such publications."   One of these, by Mr. Allsop, had irritated Southey to such a degree that he wrote in his copy of it, " The proper title of this book would be Coleridge Collops with Jackanapes Sauce." " When I think," he exclaims to Frere, " that these books, and such as these, will be resorted to hereafter as materials for biography, I am almost tempted to say as Sir Robert Walpole did of history that I *know* it must be false."

The last letter from Southey was written on January 23rd, 1839, only four years before his death. He begins by asking Frere to take some notice of a young midshipman whose ship was then stationed at Malta, and then turns to his own employments :—

" The world is greatly changed since we last met, and no part of it more woefully than those countries in which, next to our own, we once felt the liveliest interest. I have learnt to regard the course of public events with something very like indifference. But time has dealt gently with me, and I pursue my habitual course of life with as much content- ment, tho' not with as much ardour as in the days of my youth. It will not be long before I shall have the History of Portugal in the press, and I continue to collect materials for a History of the Monastic Orders, for which I have long been preparing, and which I believe to be the most useful work on which I can employ the remainder of my life."

It is now the fashion to decry Southey's writings ; but the old man himself, diligently and placidly continuing his task, although the shadows were falling around him, is no despicable figure. He had long been suffering from in- cipient softening of the brain, the real cause of the apathy which gave rise to many painful comments at the time of his first wife's death. Wordsworth pronounced him "completely dead to all but books." After his second marriage, in 1839, his faculties rapidly deserted him ; and when death released him, in March 1843, nothing was left but the shell that had contained the once active mind. Conscientious, independent, disinterested, the world was the poorer for his loss ; and though Byron parodied " The Vision of Judgement " and Macaulay derided the " Colloquies on Society," posterity will remember the writer as one of the few men of letters who had the generosity to welcome Carlyle's " French Revolution."

CHAPTER XII.

LETTERS TO AN EXILE.

1820—1845.

NEAR the head of the Quarantine harbour of Malta, separated only by a white streak of roadway from the blue tideless waters of the Mediterranean, stood (and stands to this day) a large flat-roofed house. From the entrance hall, where a bright-coloured macaw perched amongst semi-tropical plants, or on the edge of a tank of cool water, a double staircase led to the picture-gallery and principal rooms. At great labour and expense, a steep hill behind the house had been cut into terraces and crowned with a temple. Earth, brought from a distance, was carried up the flights of steps, and laid out in flower-beds.

Here it was that John Hookham Frere spent the last years of his life, surrounded with every luxury that a refined taste could create and that money could supply.

To busy men who were in the midst of the fray, his life seemed stagnation. To those who saw the crisis through which England was passing, it seemed something worse. One who had learned lessons of statesmanship under Pitt, and worked side by side with Canning, had no right to bury himself with his books among roses and vines, when there was so great a need for clear heads and cool brains. But Lady Erroll could only live in a warm climate, and Frere's chief object in life was the care of her health. When her death set him free to return to his duties at Roydon, the climate of Norfolk was unlikely to suit one who had spent ten years under a southern sky, and it was too much trouble to move. He wrote and talked of coming home, and would have no alterations made on his English property, wishing, at his return, to find everything as it used to be. The situation was appreciated by George Cornewall Lewis when he wrote, in 1836, "Hookham Frere found himself in Malta sixteen years ago, at his wife's death, and has forgotten to return to England." *

In spite of his isolation, he did not lose touch with the world which he had left. After toiling through the mass of papers sealed in packets by his executors, one is struck by the wideness of his sympathies. Any literary question, any new book, would of course excite a lively interest to the day of his death; but his friends appealed to him on every imaginable point, in the confidence that was never deceived, that he would understand their difficulties and share their enjoyments. A young man whom he had known from a boy, and for whom he had written some of the "Fables for Five Years Old," quarrelled with his father; Frere was called upon to make peace. A friend had been ransacking Venetian archives, to find proof of an obscure mediæval scandal, but without success; Frere will realise his disappointment. Lady Cadogan retails social gossip, with a conviction that Frere will like to hear of her girls' beauty, and their prospects; Lady Davy is equally certain that he must be interested in the progress of her last cold. Savants send long sheets filled with antiquarian lore; a fond mother describes the

* This of course is an error, as Lady Erroll did not die until 1830.

wedding of her only daughter. Religious enthusiasts favour him with their interpretation of the unfulfilled prophecies, and young ladies write pretty little notes to thank him for some kindness or courtesy.* Nephews and nieces write of their hopes, of their doings at home and abroad, with perfect freedom ; and one of an even younger generation appears on the scene, and dictates to an aunt affectionate inquiries after the welfare of "dear Uncle Frere's" peacocks.

It was partly this marvellous gift of sympathy that kept him from dropping out of the cognizance of younger men, and partly the tradition of former times. Those of his contemporaries who still survived remembered what he had been in the fulness of his power ; the rising generation looked with reverence on one who had talked with Walter Scott and Byron and all the great men of his day. Malta, besides being a health-resort, was a convenient halting-place for travellers to or from the East, and few visited it without bringing a letter of introduction to Mr. Frere. Once inside his door, the spell of his gracious kindliness fascinated even those who, like Sir G. C. Lewis, were inclined to think his opinions old-fashioned and behind the times. His gentleness, his dignity and courtliness, delighted all who knew him, even as, in our own day, these same qualities in one of his nephews charmed an age that, with many old-fashioned vices, has laid aside many old-fashioned virtues, including good manners.

In spite of his gentleness, he could sharply rebuke want of tact and good breeding in others. There is a story told in the Memoir, which will bear repetition here, of his sitting at a dinner party next to a lady who persisted

---

* It is worth noticing that one of these young ladies can appreciate a Greek author with far less parade than a girl of to-day exhibits when she has dipped into Browning.

in asking him his opinion on the doctrine of purgatory, regardless of all hints of his dislike to discuss such a question in such a place. At last his patience gave way, and he confessed that his only ideas on the subject were derived from some carvings in a Maltese church which represented the souls rising out of flames. "I told her that if the reality were at all like that, I was clearly of opinion that the flames were necessary for the decent clothing of the figures. After that, she managed to talk about something else."

If his style of living were luxurious, his generosity was extreme. Not only did many nephews and nieces thank "Uncle Frere" for a start in life, but there is continual mention in his correspondence of acts of kindness to those who had no claim upon him save that of common humanity. He was not always judicious, and if there is some excuse to be found for the alterations in his garden, which gave work to many hungry Maltese, there is none for his habit of daily filling his pockets with a quantity of small coins to fling to the beggars by the wayside when he drove out. But it is easy for a rich man to give money; the little kindnesses which cost thought are a more troublesome business, and in these Frere excelled. The lace bought for a niece, the key of the gardens lent to a friend that he might enjoy the shade and cool breezes whenever he chose, the schemes for the benefit of emigrants from Roydon to the New World, all show that Frere did not think his obligations to his fellow-men were satisfied by opening his purse.

Among the correspondence of his later years are some letters which are worth preserving, although, as with the Sibylline books, one can but feel that the value of that which remains is enhanced by the value of that which has disappeared. In some points these letters are not so interesting as those addressed to him in his youth. There is a modern air about the thought and phrasing, and we feel that the times and manners were not far removed from our own. Some of the more voluminous correspondents, Canning and Gabriele Rossetti, speak for themselves in separate chapters; the following extracts are taken almost at random from the portfolio which holds the letters sent to Malta, from 1820 to 1845.

The Reform Bill was the chief measure which occupied public attention in the thirties. Most of Frere's friends, as became good Tories, viewed it with abhorrence, and had some excuse for hating its supporters in the riots and disorders which it occasioned.

The social aspect of the struggle is shown in a long letter from Lady Cadogan—formerly Honoria Blake—written in November 1831. She was evidently attached to Frere, who acted the part of an affectionate uncle to her children, and frequently wrote to him after her sister's death.

"The fever of Reform being abated, we hear no more of it, and no one reads the Petitions. No flirtations or marriages are going on, because the Families of People disposed to flirt thought differently on *the Bill*, and therefore it was impossible they *could* be friends. So I have none of these to write about. There is never anything clever, anything funny, said to repeat, because People vex themselves with Politics and never think of Wit or anything else. . . . Whilst I was writing that no body thinks any more of *the bill*, the frightful accounts have come of the Riot at Bristol. . . . Lady Clanricarde * says if her Father was Minister, that bill would not have been brought in, but were he alive and not Minister he would

* *Née* Harriet Canning.

vote for it—all circumstances continued (*sic*)—and I believe she is right. . . ."

"For the 1st time I believe we are in a bad way, for I always felt that we were secure amidst the crash of other Governments, but now the breach between us and the People is so widen'd, the gauntlet thrown by the Peers is taken up, the People become more bold in their demands, and all agree they must get what they ask. This is awful —and awfully like 1792 in France—but I am transgressing my rule not to write on the subject. The truth is, the Bristol Riot has frighten'd me. The looks and manners of the lower class here are *menaçants*, they hustle one in the streets, and actually are so rude in the Farm Houses and Gardens, they dislike selling to us. All the Servants shew by their * that they think their day near at hand and ours nearly done. In short it is truly alarming, and you and all absentees ought to come and look after their own, and coax the People—that is the only chance. Old Lady Keith says, the People all think Reform means bread and meat, when they find out it does not, they will be furious."

Frere preferred to remain on his island, and watch the gathering storm from afar. His wife was now dead, and there was no real reason why he should not return to England. But most of the friends of his youth in the political world had passed away. A statue in Westminster Abbey was all that remained of Canning, and Frere may well have shrunk from stirring the Medea's caldron in which the constitution of England was now seething, without the presence of the one man who could have saved the country, if he had not fallen beneath an overwhelming load of toil and disappointment. Frere's own view of the political future was gloomy enough. "It

* A word omitted.

is the privilege as well as the duty of your age to hope,"
he said to younger men, but he foresaw little save evil
from the changed conditions of government. Even the
recently coined name of his party was offensive to him.
"Why do you talk of Conservatives? a Conservative is
only a Tory who is ashamed of himself."

He found a sympathiser in the Chevalier Bunsen, who
wrote from Rome on June 12th, 1832 :—

"I have sad forebodings of a general war becoming
unavoidable by the restless spirit of revolution in France.
May God protect England in this awful crisis ! I wish I
may be wrong, but I feel upon the subject of reform, and
have done so from the beginning, as an admirer of your
immortal friend Mr. Canning, I believe, ought to do; in
short, as Lord Haddington and Lord Harrowby do.
There is a great spirit of innovation abroad ; it might be
for good, for real improvement of human institutions, but
I am afraid it will be for utter destruction, for preparing
an aera of byzantine dullness, and despotism. It will begin
(or rather has begun) with the reign of *mediocrité* and
shallowness, and will end with that of rogues and tyrants."

Frere's correspondence at this time is not cheerful reading. Some of his friends were expecting the end of the
world from a political, others from a religious point of
view, and there was scarcely one of them who was not
aggrieved by some change in the old order of things.

The world of literature afforded brighter prospects than
the world of politics. Happy was the new author who
could win from Frere a favourable verdict on his book.
Henry Taylor was much gratified to hear that Frere could
appreciate "Philip van Artevelde," and owned that, next
to Canning's approval, he valued that of Frere. Leigh

Hunt, through Lady Holland, expressed very similar sentiments. Cobbold, the author of the once celebrated tale " Margaret Catchpole," owed to Frere an introduction to Lockhart, who interested himself strongly in the book (although the author complained that some of his best paragraphs had been sacrificed). Frere kept up his interest in literary questions to the last, reading almost incessantly. In the first violence of his grief for Lady Erroll's death, he found distraction in the study of Hebrew, and after a paralytic seizure which threatened his life, he succeeded, in spite of his doctor, in getting out of bed and possessing himself of a book.

Among those who presented letters of introduction to Frere in 1833 were three Englishmen, who, according to Miss Frere, had " a becoming simplicity and placidity of deportment." These were Archdeacon Froude, his son, and the son's friend, Mr. Newman of Oriel. After the Archdeacon's return to England, he wrote a long letter to Frere, giving an account of their travels :—

" An introduction to Mr. Bunsen, the Prussian Minister at Rome, procured for us access to every object of difficult access. . . . As Mr. B. is one of the best antiquaries of the day, he was of the greatest service to us in directing our attention to matters most deserving notice. My son's search in the Vatican for the originals of Becket's correspondence was not successful. . . . You are aware, I dare say, that a considerable body of documents connected with the early periods of English history have been selected from the papal stores and transmitted to this country. During Mr. Canning's administration, a liberal allowance, under the direction of Mr. Bunsen, was given to persons employed in the research ; but I think he considers much less has been done than he might have reasonably expected. Whatever they are, I am afraid it will not enter into the views of those now in power at home, to follow Mr. Canning's intention to give them to the public. . . . When my son and I left Rome, Mr. Newman went to Sicily, but in consequence of a very severe epidemic fever by which he was attacked in the centre of the island, he was obliged to give up his intended tour. His recovery, as he lay in a wretched hut between Leonforte and Castro Giovanni, is attributed to the accidental passage of a medical person with sufficient skill to relieve him."

Newman's name occurs a few years later in a letter from Sir C. Lewis, dated November 21st, 1838 :—

"You have probably heard of a new sect which has lately grown up at Oxford, called Newmanites, from their leader Newman. Their opinions closely resemble those of Archbishop Laud. Sydney Smith says, that if he was sending a young man to Oxford, he should give him the following advice : *Numen abest, si sit prudentia.*"

In former days Frere had chiefly relied on Lady Erroll to supply him with news of Society. This was now furnished by Lady Cadogan and Lady Davy. Lady Cadogan has already been introduced, and Lady Davy is familiar to all readers of memoirs and diaries of that time. By birth a Kerr of Bloodielaws, a distant cousin of Sir Walter Scott, she was married to a Mr. Aprecce, and found little happiness in the union. When set free by her husband's death, gay, clever, with a comfortable fortune, her ambition was to become distinguished in the literary world, and "*tenir salon*" like the French ladies of the Ancien Régime. In the course of a visit to Edinburgh she turned the heads of several distinguished professors, including Playfair, who knelt down in the street to fasten her bootlace.   But the lady's choice fell upon Dr. Davy, who was made Sir Humphrey to do away with any objections on her side to a *mésalliance.*   Davy wrote to his mother that "this charming woman" was "eminently qualified to promote" his best efforts and objects in life ; but, as frequently happens when persons of distinction come together, the marriage was not a success.   " She has a temper, and Davy has a temper," wrote Scott, who was sincerely attached to her, in spite of her want of good taste in science and letters, "and these tempers are not one temper but two tempers, and they quarrel like cat and dog, which may be good for stirring up the stagnation of domestic life, but they let the world see it, and that is not so well."

At the time of her correspondence with Frere, Lady Davy was again a widow, still lively and interested in all around her, and writing long letters in the angular pointed hand which was then thought to be ladylike.

An undated letter of Lady Cadogan's, evidently written about 1838, says :—

"Lord Holland is a terrible wreck, and poor Dudley gives great uneasiness to his well-wishers, for *friends* one can hardly say a man who has no intimates—no one who can take charge of him or govern him in any way. He commits all sorts of inconsistencies, breaches of decorum, but nothing to authorize their placing him under restriction. He gives constant dinners, invites 36 People, and provides places for 14 ; when the company arrive he never takes any notice of them, but sits in an armchair, either looking at the Fire or reading or sleeping—he does not wait for the royal Dukes or get up from Table when they come, but eats and drinks voraciously and speaks little. He is grown fat and full, and they think his disease is pressure on the Brain, and they cup him and bleed him, after which he seems more awake, but with a vacant smile on, so that I sometimes have a suspicion that he is playing tricks, but *à quoi bon*, one asks. Poor man, if he is really growing foolish, it will be sad. If he had married and surrounded himself with relatives and friends, and had legitimate uses for his £72,000 a year, he would have been a happier man and a more useful member of society. . . . For young Ladies London is in a terrible state. The opera too bad to go to, and People not giving Parties because the Reform Bill takes up all the men's time and spoils the Ladies' tempers. Many stay out of Town for fear of the Cholera, and all together we pass sometimes a week without going out at all and see very few People at Home. Luckily my girls are very well content with this—for tho' they like Balls and are danced with and admired, they have not the strength, Phisical or moral, of regular London-bred girls to bear incessant raking and crowded Rooms. They are either more rational or fonder of their health than we used to be, for I never remember staying away from anything *because I was tired*, and they stay at home frequently out of pure laziness. They are both very nice-looking girls, but less likely to marry than any girls I know, for they are very difficult, and not yet of an age when the *necessity* of pleasing themselves strikes them. I wish they were each 2 or 3 years younger that they might better suit the rising generation. You never saw anything so Handsome and comendable (*sic*) in every way as the *coming of age* are, and so much better brought up, so much more gentleman-like, than used to be the Fashion in my day, when young men were either Statesmen or blackguards—for instance, young Abercorn—you would hardly *make him* otherwise than as he is—but there are 5 or 6 others equally *valuable* in their way—but too young to think of marrying yet. . . . Lady Mary Paget is going to be married to Mr. Vivian, Sir Hussey Vivian's son—a tall Mustached long-necked, long Spur'd A.D.C.—very young and they say very good. They are to be some day very well off, so there is nothing to be said against it—but I don't like the kind of animal."

Lady Cadogan suffered from a cough, every winter. In May 1842 three physicians "were in vain," but by July she had recovered sufficiently to write an account of every symptom to Frere. In the course of this letter she tells him, " Do you know, I think Lady Holland is dying of a broken heart—in her own odd way: she eats and talks and visits, but she is a perfect Niobe—for ever in tears— and weakened evidently. Did you hear of her being so angry with Sidney Smith for saying ' How can a sensible woman like you expect the man should give up his house to you?' 'But I am not a sensible woman—I never was a sensible woman—and you know that very well'—quite angry at the false accusation. And she is right—nothing pays so ill as being reasonable or sensible when caprice and *exigeance* are at a premium."

In the autumn of the same year Frere received a visit from Lady Davy, who was on her way to Rome.

Lady Davy found the Cadogans wintering in Rome, and the description of the jealousy between the two ladies is very amusing. " Dear Mr. Frere," writes Lady Cadogan, " I am made very unhappy by the crowing of Lady Davy, who comes to me at least once a week with messages from you—thereby letting me know that you write to *her*, and not to me." There was a little consolation in the knowledge " that some mutual friends of your's and the Lady's insinuate that she does *not* hear from you *quite* as often as she says she does."

Lady Davy had established a warm friendship with Lady Grenville, to the mingled amusement and indignation of Lady Cadogan, who told Frere, "I have not seen *our Jane* to wreak my woman's vengeance by saying you had written to me, but I shall not miss the opportunity whenever it may occur—but Jane does not cultivate *us*. She is always talking (and I suppose) thinking of 'The Carlisles,' 'The Grosvenors,' 'The Sutherlands,' 'Lady Grenville and Lady Granville'—and so on. She gives Tea and Dinners but not to 'The Cadogans,' altho' she comes here whenever I ask her. She told us the other night that she had once won 21 odd tricks running at whist. Some one near me said 'I'll be bound she *play'd* a great many more.'"

Another letter informs Frere that "Lady Davy is in great force—not much improved in her Italian, nor yet in health by her own account. 'This morning I could do nothing : I read a Chapter in Livy—wouldn't do ; I tried to translate Euripides—wouldn't do ; I tried an Adagio on the Piano—in vain ; tried to write my Journal —in vain ; at last finding my Stomach out of order I took a Pill.'"

Lady Davy's blunders in foreign languages were a continual joy to her acquaintance. Hayward * tells the story of her shouting to her postilion, "*Allez avec votre ventre sur la terre*," and of her nearly destroying an Italian lady's character by a mistaken application of the word *meretrice*.

After her winter in Rome, Lady Davy was able to enjoy the return to old friends and old habits in London. In September 1843 she wrote to Frere :—

"I have found my friends generally prosperous, and

* "Essays Biographical and Critical."

the four years of separation have scarcely told on many. The Berrys, especially Miss Berry, *tale quale*, and with undiminished hospitality and spirits at the receipt of company and friends. Lady Charlotte Lindsay, always their Summer Inmate, is I conclude the Wit of Richmond. She is grown smaller, but talks and works with equal assiduity. Lady Holland I din'd with at Richmond. She is certainly looking ill; but her Dinner Circles are extended, and her own activity of paying visits and going out wonderfully augmented. I am rather provoked at the pity she demands plaintively for her 'miserable' little nutshell, when I recollect it held Lord Holland in suffering and privations. She is trying to house herself, as she *now* requires, *comfortably* . . . ."

In the course of the winter of 1843-4, Lady Davy was between life and death with influenza, "the pestilent Epidemic which is usual to our Winters, but in this extraordinary mild one has raged with extraordinary fury." Her cough was cured by "a morning draft of a *small* quantity of *old* Rum in new milk." "It is *said* to be *the* remedy which has wonderfully restored Lord Melbourne; but I am apt to believe his lordship may indulge in extra doses; it is to me very Nectarian, though I am told its right of swallowing belongs to Stage Coachmen (will there be any left to defend their right?) and Bishops."

By March Lady Davy was once more able to visit her friends. "Miss Edgeworth is like a Bird, hopping, chirping, and singing outright; it gladdens one to see Authorship and age so lively, and enjoying life so thoroughly."

In May Lady Davy was again very ill, but comforted by her doctor, who pronounced medicine useless, and prescribed "Curaço in Hock." Lord Melbourne was declining, in spite of the rum and milk. "On literary subjects I think him very clear, and his memory gracefully various ; yet I fear many days are listless, and his past life has made the Table and the talk indispensably necessary, though each are said to do him harm." Lady Holland was still weeping all the morning, and receiving company all the evening.

On New Year's Day, 1845, Lady Davy wrote from Bowood to wish Frere the compliments of the season. She had made acquaintance with Archdeacon Wilberforce, and found him "a most taking person, his voice that of his father, eminently. sweet, clear and touching. His conversation too, has the playfulness and entertaining *gentle* Wit he had a right to inherit. I conclude Royal favour will be-mitre his brows ; and probably he may in time be written to with *Arch*; his Countenance and air will be no disparagement."

"Did you know Mr. Kin(g)lake in his passage to the East some years ago? He has recently given us a very amusing Book, lively, spirited, perhaps free, written then, but read eagerly now, 'Eothen.' A work has appeared lately full certainly of ability, but of peculiar views, not I think likely to do as much evil as it is the fashion to believe ; because the common Reader will not, I should conceive, understand or be entertained. Its tendency is however unsafe to established Belief. You may choose between Lord Francis Egerton, who would burn it in open Day, and Miss Berry who is in the seventh Heavens by its grand view of the Creator and *his* Creation. The Vestiges of Creation and Surplices and Charges are alone discussed, so I have nothing to tell you of, save that Little Moore still, who is here, warbles with touching Pathos."

Frere was not likely to sympathise with controversies about surplices. Sound Churchman as he was, his religion was tempered by common sense. On one occasion, when an appeal was made in his presence to the oft-quoted " Ornaments Rubric " to justify some innovations in ritual, he rejoined, " But if I were to appear at church in the costume of Queen Elizabeth's time, would the clergyman consider it a sufficient justification for my disturbing the gravity of the congregation that I could prove the dress to be in strict accordance with the usages and sumptuary laws of three hundred years back ? "

Several of the sealed packets are entirely filled with letters from men whom Frere had known in former days, and who on that account considered that they had a right to ask his help. These letters are not amusing as a rule ; they bear too strong a resemblance to the communications that many of us receive continually from poor relations and undesirable acquaintances.

There is more variety and far more originality in some of the " petitions " with which the lower class of Maltese were always attacking the generous Englishman. What, for instance, can surpass the businesslike terseness of the following ?—

" To His Honourable, etc., etc., etc.

" The humble Petition of Vittoria Tabain of la Vittoriosa

" Sheweth,

" That your Petitioner being a poor Woman (as per annexed Certificate) and having no means to maintain her large family,

" Therefore humbly begs your Honour to be pleased to grant her any Charity, and as in duty bound will pray."

But for perfect *naïveté*, it would be hard to match the

request of one who signs himself "Publio Dorgmaina, *hand Coachman.*"

"To the Honourable Lady Frere,* etc., etc., etc.

"Lady most Hono^{ble}

"I take the liberty to submit in your ladyship's gracious Consideration that Costanzo Fenioli (very good man) a particular Friend of mine, has been condemned at the Public Works, with Chain in Foot, and he prayed me with tiers to beseech to Your Ladyship so that may be graciously pleased to pray your Ladyship's Friend, Colonel Balmains on behalf of the said Costanzo Fenioli, to be exent from the Public Works in the Streets and admitted in all kind of Works in the same Prison. And with the greatest Respect as my duty requires, and most partial Esteem, I am, most honourable Lady," etc., etc.

* Lady Erroll.

CHAPTER XIII.

THE LAST OF CANNING.

"Noch vor zwei Jahren bekleideten wir mit diesem Amte
(Gonfaloniere der Freiheit) einen englischen Minister, das Geheul des
hochtoryschen Hasses gegen George Canning leitete damals unsere
Wahl; in den adlig unedlen Krankungen, die er erlitt, sahen wir die
Garantieen seiner Treue, und als er des Martyrertodes starb, da legten
wir Trauer an, und der achte August wurde ein heiliger Tag im
Kalender der Freiheit."

H. HEINE.

THIS is not a biography of Canning. The events of
his life are only given in detail when they are
described in his letters to Frere. This source of information fails us almost entirely between the years 1806
and 1823.

It is true that more than seventy of the letters at
Roydon were written by Canning during the seventeen
years that followed Pitt's death. But for the most part
they are the merest scraps, of no interest to any one.

During the greater part of the time Frere was in
England, and seeing Canning so often as to do away with
any necessity for correspondence. During his second
mission to Spain, in 1808-9, Canning had occasion to send
him a long letter with a full account of the duel with Lord
Castlereagh, and the causes that led up to it. But the
letter was as unfortunate as everything else connected
with Frere's second mission; it never reached the hands

252

for which it was destined, and is therefore not to be found among the Frere MSS.

Those seventeen years, if they brought honours and distinction to Canning, brought also disappointments and sorrows. His faithfulness to Pitt's memory kept him from accepting the brilliant offers made by Lord Grenville in November 1806; the memory of an old friendship occasioned his retirement from office in 1820. His steady devotion to the Roman Catholic cause—Pitt's legacy—lost him the honour that he had coveted most of all, save the Premiership—that of representing Oxford University in Parliament. With talents surpassing those of any English statesman of his day, he was "just as far as ever from the end"—that seat on the Treasury bench with Lord Lansdowne had prophesied for him as long ago as 1790, and which he had ever set before him as the goal of his ambition.

The fiscal and financial reforms which Pitt had never been able to effect, and which he had bequeathed to Canning, were still visions, not realities. Frere once asked Canning what had become of those schemes which they had discussed so eagerly in their youth. Canning ran over the names of the men with whom he was obliged to act. "What can I churn out of such skimmed milk as *that*?" he asked bitterly.

He had his private griefs also. Joan was still at his side, and the little "Toddles," who once interrupted an important letter to Frere by insisting that her father should come and play with her, had now grown into a woman, capable of sharing his thoughts and his troubles. But "little George," very early in his short life, developed an incurable lameness. There are frequent references, in the letters to Frere, to the treatment which the boy was undergoing at the hands of various doctors, who, one after another, flattered the parents with hopes of a recovery. But all, whether eminent physicians, or mere quacks consulted when other means had failed, could do nothing for the son who had been such "a fine healthy boy" at the time of his birth. He became a helpless invalid, unable to move from his chair. For his sake, Canning accepted the Extraordinary Mission to Lisbon in 1814, which drew down upon himself such disinterested indignation from Mr. Whitbread. Frere spent the whole summer and autumn of 1814 between Lady Erroll, who was seriously ill, and Canning, who was preparing for his departure from England. His sympathy and companionship must have been an unspeakable comfort to the poor father. Among the letters is a half-sheet of paper on which Canning has written :—

" My Dear Frere,
      " The wind is fair, and we are setting off.
            " God bless you.
                        " Ever yours,
                                 "G. C."

It was sent from Portsmouth on Sunday, November 6th, 1814.

The mild climate of Portugal could not arrest the progress of the disease, and the gentle, amiable boy died in the spring of 1820, to his father's bitter sorrow. How sharp a trial Canning had to face on his return to England has been shown in another chapter.

Queen Caroline's friends were her husband's enemies, and when Canning would have returned to office after her death, in 1821, George declined to receive him. In 1822 he was appointed Governor-General of India, and was on the point of leaving England with wife and daughter, when

Lord Londonderry's suicide left the Foreign Office without a chief. The post was offered to Canning, and, sorely against his will, he came back into harness.

Everything was against him. It was a time of trouble, both at home and abroad. In March 1820 the revolutionists in Spain won a new constitution for themselves. Their success encouraged the Neapolitans to rise in arms against their King, Ferdinand of the Two Sicilies. The spirit of revolt spread to Portugal, where John VI. was ready to grant a new constitution. Both he and his chief adviser, the Marquis Palmella, felt that the old despotism was dead. But the King was almost torn in pieces by rival factions. On the one side were the Absolutists, headed by his own wife and son, who would tolerate no change in the existing order ; on the other, the violent Revolutionaries, who would be satisfied with nothing less than "the Constitution of 1812."

Ferdinand's tottering throne was supported by Austrian bayonets, and in 1823 Louis XVIII. sent the Duc d'Angoulême with a French army to crush the rebels in the Peninsula. Fain would Canning have played the game of Pitt's day, and sent an English army once more to sweep the eagles back across the Pyrenees. But he saw that it could not be.

At that time England was of small account in international politics. The days were forgotten when alone she had faced the great Emperor, and hurled back the tide of war from her very gates. One man swayed the councils of Europe, and that man was Metternich. We talk with just shame of the years in which English statesmen suffered the dictation of Louis XIV., and some say that such a thing could only be possible in the reign of the worst of the Stuarts. Few of us realise that at the beginning of this century our Foreign Office was under the control of Austria. Dispatches from one of our representatives abroad were carried to Metternich and opened before they were forwarded to England.*   Lord Londonderry, while affecting publicly to disapprove of the Continental system of the Holy Alliance, in secret gave Metternich every assurance of his good-will and favour. It was not until long after Canning's appointment to the Foreign Office that Metternich could or would realise that the new Secretary was not playing a part to delude the House of Commons, like his predecessor.

It was under these circumstances that the following letter was written to Frere. Canning was recovering from a sharp attack of gout in his hand, which had obliged him to dictate all his correspondence—no great difficulty to the man who could dictate two dispatches on two totally different subjects at the same time. The characters are straggling and hard to read, but the opening sentences show that the old mischievous spirit was not yet quenched :—

"Gloucester Lodge,

"Aug. 7th, 1823.

"My Dear Frere,—

"In good truth I have used you scandalously ; and I know not how to atone for such usage, unless the stopping the Malta Mail of this week, till I have finished a Letter, may, from the inconvenience which it will occasion to the general correspondence of the Island, be accepted by you as an atonement.

"Positively this Mail shall not go without a letter from me to you ; but while I am writing, here comes the French Mail, which I must open—and then I will resume the thread of my discourse.

* "Greville Memoirs."

"I found not a moment to resume this letter yesterday. So I have stopped the Mail another day—and now I will write on without interruption.

"First. Let me thank you for your communications, verse as well as prose. I do not laugh at your solution of prophecies. I do verily feel sometimes as if the 'ends of the world were come upon us.' It is clear that the present state of things cannot last. It is one of heaving and struggling between conflicting principles. Which will get the better, Heaven knows; but that the struggle cannot be eternal, is plain. Àpropos to this topick—singularly àpropos—here comes Mr. Owen of Lanark, for a second audience (one of two hours I have already given him to my infinite cost and suffering); his purpose being to show that nothing but the Establishment of his parallelograms can cure the Evils of the world, and specially of Ireland. I won't see him. I won't. I am writing to Mr. Frere by the Malta Mail, and Mr. Owen may set off for Lanark if he will; but see him now I will not. So to proceed.

" Coming down to mere earthly things, I was delighted to find your notions of what was the best line in politicks tally with my own. I do not deny that I had an itch for war with France, and that a little provocation might have scratched it into an eruption; but fortunately the better reason prevailed, and I look back upon the decision with entire and perfect self-congratulation. Never was the Country so completely satisfied with the course taken by the Government—or I might say so grateful for it. For they saw, and felt in their own hearts, and judged by their own feelings, that there was a great temptation the other way. The considerations which really dictated the decision, are they not written in my Speech of the 30th of

April, of which I inclose you a Copy, and to which I refer you for all that I could say?

(Here read the Speech.) "So far then, so good. But what is the conclusion? I protest I know not. This only I know, that, if the Spaniards have little to boast of in the War, France has little to show, for all the exertions which she has made and is making. The difficulties increase every hour, and if six weeks do not put her in possession of Cadiz and of the King, she is no forwarder than when she crossed the Bidassoa.

"The truth is that the French Government never seriously resolved upon the war, and upon the plan and object of it, but suffered themselves to be driven on from position to position (*political* position I here intend) by the Ultrageous party of their followers—their pokers and goaders—and have been lured on from one military position to another in Spain, by the unexpected facilities of their advance; till they are now at the extremity of the peninsula with all the fortresses unreduced behind them. A failure before Cadiz would rouse the population against them, and make their retreat as murderous as their advance has been bloodless. The capture of Cadiz would involve them in difficulties of another sort—the Allies with Russia at their head being all for the *Re Absoluto*, and the French being pledged to something liberal and representative, and the Spaniards agreeing upon nothing but to hate and persecute each other. We are not of all this— and have no disposition to get into it. Neither Spain nor France cares much for our interference, unless we would interfere as partizans, but the Allies lament themselves heavily at our separation from them; and cannot, for their lives, imagine how it has happened that in disclaiming their principles, we should have said what we really mean, and should thereafter continue pertinaciously to act as we have said. A little prudery—a little dust for the eyes of the H[ouse] of C[ommons] they could understand, and some prepared for it—but this real *bonâ-fide* disapprobation astounds them; and the sturdy adherence to it, when nobody is by—when we might just lift the mask and show our real countenance to them, without the world's seeing it—this is really carrying the jest too far—and they can tell us plainly that they wish we would have done and 'cease our funning.' The history of all this I could' tell them in two words—or rather in the substitution of one word for another—for 'Alliance' read 'England'; and you have the clue of my policy.

"The most perplexing part of the affairs of Spain is the influence that the good or ill turn of them (be good or ill which it may) is likely to have upon Portugal. Palmella is there in a most critical situation. If the French are baffled in Spain, a new Jacobin Revolution may break out in Portugal. If they succeed, that evil may be avoided; but another of an opposite sort may spring up, in an Ultrageous fashion, hostile to all modification, and trundling Palmella and his moderate Reforms out of doors. The best thing for all the world would be a compromise in Spain; but that is the one thing not to be had. Long years of havoc must precede it.

"Connected with the questions of Spain and Portugal are those of their respective Americas; which are severed beyond all doubt from their respective mother-countries for ever. What a world does this consideration open!

"Yet, with Europe and America thus pressing upon my attention—and Africa too—for we have Slave Trade matters in abundance—(and Malta too was in Africa till Van * moved it by act of Parlt.)—shall I own to you— I often turn with longing eyes to the Quarter of the

* Vansittart ?

World which I have abandoned, and wish myself governing some eighty or a hundred millions, in the shades
of Barrackpore. Nothing but the Event of this time
twelvemonth * could have changed my destination ; and
whatever might be the dictate of publick duty (and I
believe I estimate that aright) I am far from sure that
publick duty alone would have induced me to acquiesce
in the change.

"But poor Joan could never abide the thought of India
—nor Harriet either. They had made up their minds to
go with me ; but when the opportunity so unexpectedly
arose of my staying here with them, and in a situation and
under circumstances to all outward appearance so full of
all that just ambition required—why, it was impossible to
resist ; and most reluctantly I gave up the solid for the
shining, Ease, wealth, and a second publick life in the
House of Peers, for toil, inconvenience, and total retreat
after a few—a very few years of splendid trouble.

" The sacrifice was enormous—but it is made. You can
have no conception of the labour which I undergo. The
two functions of For. Sec. and Leader of the H. of
C. are too much for any man—and ought not to be
united ; though I of course would rather die under them
than separate them, or consent to have separation in my
person.

" I have no reason to be personally dissatisfied with the
Session. Opportunities of personal display there were but
few. That of which I inclose the fruit, was the Waterloo
of the campaign. For the rest my business has been
rather to defeat prophecies and to disappoint calculations
of evil, than to seek occasions for what I do not want—
additional κύδος in debate. I have been very forbearing
in combat—using the scalping-knife never above once or

* Lord Londonderry's suicide.

twice, and almost disusing keener and brighter weapons, till I am in danger of being thought exceedingly dull. This—because it was prophesied I should 'lay about' me. And as to the conduct of business, I have studiously and anxiously put Peel and Robinson as forward as possible, never taking their concerns out of their hands (as Carlisle used to do Van's) and only supporting them *en second ligne* where necessary. This, because it was foretold that I should engross and forestal everything. In short, I doubt whether Mr. Pelham himself, in the days of Whig stagnation, would have been a quieter Minister.

"But oh that we had such days and nights of Gods—such *superûm labor*—as Mr. Pelham's was! The exhaustion of strength is really terrible. What do you think of 10 hours pr. day as the average of our sitting for four days in the week, and for seven weeks from Whitsuntide to the end of the Session! The average from Easter to Whitsuntide was only nine. That of the Session before Easter only six. But the latter two-thirds were overwhelming; and not the less so from the utter uninterestingness of greater part of the discussions. Ten hours of the four-and-twenty in the H. of C. (for *I* am always there) leave you exactly fourteen for the necessary occupations of food and rest, and for the whole business of my Office —not to mention the details of all other business that is to come before Parlt. . . Society, you may suppose, is out of the question. Exercise and air wholly so. Nevertheless, during these periods of the Session, that is since Easter, I have been well. A rigid abstinence, including total abjuration of wine, during the five working days of the week, has, I have no doubt, greatly contributed to this effect. Before Easter, however, I had a swingeing fit of the Gout—the fruits (I have as little doubt) of the labours and confinement and anxiety of the autumn and winter;

by which fit, and in part by the bad treatment of it, I feel myself (between ourselves) sensibly impaired.

"I do not think that I have many years' work in me; and when I retire, my retirement will be like Bertram's 'tropick night,' sudden and total.* A new reign, a new Parlt.—and some other Epoch, I could anticipate as likely to produce this result.' I sometimes feel as if might say to 'afford this opportunity'; for although the world supposes that I have arrived exactly where I wished to be, I am arrived ten years too late for enjoyment, and perhaps for advantage to the Country. However, end when it may, my political life shall end with my present station. I will not engage again in contentious politicks—nor will I live in the world, after I have taken leave of politicks altogether. How little does the world believe how little I *personally* care about the time when all this may happen!

"But it is time to close this prospect, which has opened further into futurity than I intended. My present views are bounded by the hopes of getting out of Town for a fortnight or three weeks, ten days hence—my first Excursion since I came into Office. And I shall go the lighter for having discharged a debt of so long standing to you.

"I ought not, however, to conclude without saying (as part of what is most essential to my comfort)—that Liverpool is as cordial, and our opinions in all important points as much the same, as I could desire—the latter more than I could have promised myself.

---

* "Mine be the eve of tropic sun.
No pale gradations quench his ray,
No twilight dews his wrath allay;
With disk like battle-target red,
He rushes to his burning bed,
Dyes the wide wave with bloody light,
Then sinks at once, and all is night."
Rokeby, canto vi. 21.

" And so with Joan's and Harriet's kind remembrances and mine to Lady E.—farewell.

" Ever yours,

" G. C.

" Poor Charles, you perhaps know, has hurt himself grievously (now a twelvemonth ago) by a fall from his horse—but I hope he is getting better, though slowly. I believe indeed he writes to you by this Mail."

To restore the balance of power, Canning now decided to acknowledge the independence of the South American Republics. It was a step on which he had been determined ever since his coming into office, but all his colleagues were against him, with the exception of Lord Liverpool. The King would not hear of the measure, and was strengthened in his opposition by the Duke of Wellington. Canning had been Wellington's greatest support in and out of Parliament during the Peninsular War; but this consideration had no weight with the Duke. Canning held to his point, and having succeeded in winning Peel to his side, determined to conquer or resign. For three hours the battle raged in the Cabinet, until Canning emerged, flushed, wrathful, worn-out, to write a formal resignation of his office to the King. Lord Liverpool followed his example, and their colleagues, realising the seriousness of the position, yielded to the overmastering will of Pitt's heir. The measure was carried in the teeth of all opposition, and Canning, to use his own words, " called into existence the New World to redress the balance of the Old."

After the triumphant conclusion of this struggle, Canning went down to Bath, where Lord Liverpool was taking the waters. In their youth these two had been nicknamed " the Inseparables," and Liverpool was ever Canning's staunch ally, although the King did his best to sow dissension between them.

Mrs. and Miss Canning were in Paris, paying that visit to the British Embassy which Lady Granville's charming letters to Lady Morpeth have described for us. After more than a year's silence, Canning again took up his pen to write to Frere :—

"BATH, *January 8th*, 1825.

"My Dear Frere,—

"Is it possible that the year 1824 should have passed away, without my having once written to you? I fear so, and yet I can assure you that it is not from want of having had you frequently in my thoughts— for I can call to mind abundance of occasions on which I have caught myself saying to myself, 'Would that Frere were here that I might know what he would think of this matter.' Still less has it been for want of a due sense of acknowledgement of your kind letters, (one included which Charles Ellis showed me) or for your verses, which—both Psalms and Cid—pleased me prodigiously. But it has been truly and literally for want of time.

"My occupations are overwhelming. The same office in 1808-9 was nothing in point of work, compared with what it is now—and the House of Commons was nothing, when taken (as I then took it) arbitrarily and occasionally, compared with the eternal Sitting to which I am now doomed, whether there be anything worth sitting for or no.

"The Session, to be sure, was anything but arduous, and anything but long. But while it lasted, my day closed at five—and if the House lasted till past twelve, my next morning was shut up within a space of six hours, for all the business of the Office—Cabinets, audiences, interviews, and reading of H. of C. papers. I say nothing of eating and drinking, and nothing of exercise, for during the Session—except on Saturdays and Sundays—such joys are not for me.

"And yet I have the Gout. I am just now recovering from a severish fit, which has left me weak but I hope, well, and safe for the Session. I came hither, rather to be out of the way, and to lead a quiet life for a week or ten days, with Liverpool, than because *my* Gout needs Bath ; for my Gout has all come favourably out, and therefore I do not drink the waters. Liverpool does (not for Gout), and they agree with him surprisingly. He and his new Mylady (an excellent helpmeet for him) are settled in a house in Gay Street—there—that house with the red door just opposite the end of this street in which I lodge ; my lodgings are here (within sight as you perceive and) within a sixpenny chair's fare. I have two younkers of Secretaries with me (one of them a FitzMorley—a very superior and excellent young man ; the other a Son of Ld. Bristol's whom I have taken to make his father happy) whom I work very hard all the morning till about ½ p. one, when Liverpool presents himself at the door on a grey mare, and with a pair of huge jackboots, of the size and consistency of firebuckets (only not lettered). I mount a grey horse to join him on his ride, (with one or other of my aide-de-camps) and with boots not quite so large and stiff as his ; but in revenge with a pair of large gouty woollen shoes over them. In this fashion, we parade through the Town, to one of the outlets towards the Downs ; gallop for an hour and a half, and then return to finish our respective posts and dress for dinner. We dine regularly at Liverpool's. In the Evening I send my younkers to the play or Ball—and I go and drink tea with my Mother, and then about ½ p. ten home to bed.

"Ten days of this regular life ought to set me up for the year—and I trust will do so. To be sure, a dinner with the Mayor and Corporation of Bristol impends over us, for next week ; but it is not Turtle Season, and I trust therefore that the Bristolian feast will not undo the effects of Bath temperance.

"But where are Joan and Harriet all this time? you will say. Why am I at Bath without them to nurse me? Why, they are at Paris, on a visit to the Granvilles ; and most fortunately they had set off for Paris before my attack of Gout came on. Otherwise I should not have got them away ; for which I should have been very sorry. Their excursion to Paris is precisely the point, in which *they* benefit by my station. Their reception has been attentive and flattering beyond measure—by King, Court, Ministers, Ultras, and Liberaux —for there is certainly this peculiarity about me, that while Kings and Courts, etc., are civil *as to a Minister*, the Liberals are still more forward on account of what Prince Metternich considers as my Revolutionary principles.

"This is not, however, true of *all* Kings and Courts. I am afraid that there is one who, if he knew *how*, would send me to any Court or Country so that he could get me out of his own. And yet, I take my oath, I serve him honestly—and have saved him, in spite of himself, from a world of embarrassments In which a much longer entanglement with Prince Metternich and his Congresses would have involved him. It is not generally known, but the truth I really take to be that my fall was determined upon not many weeks ago. The S. American question was the step that was to trip me up ; and there

were those deep in the secret Cabals of   *, who warned
their friends that the Ides of December would see a
change.   The Ides of December, however, came, and
they are gone ; and here am I still with the S. American
Question carried, *non sine pulvere*, but carried.   As you,
no doubt, receive the English Newspapers, I need only
say that what you read in them upon this subject is
nearly correct.   I did, while I lay in bed at the Foreign
Office, with the Gout gnawing my great toe, draw the
Instructions for our Agents in Mexico and Columbia
which are to raise those States into the rank of Nations.
I did, the day after I rose from my bed, communicate
to the Foreign Ministers here (and first in order, as
beseemeth, to those of the Holy Alliance) the purport
of those Instructions.   The thing is done.   They may
turn me out if they will and if they can :

> ' *Non tamen irritum*
> *Diffinget infectumque reddet,*'

an act which will make a change in the face of the World
almost as great as that of the discovery of the Continent
now set free.   The Allies will fret ; but they will venture
no serious remonstrance.   France will fidget ; but it will
be with a view of hastening after our example.   The
Yankees will shout in triumph ; but it is they who lose
most by our decision.

   " The great danger of the time—a danger which the
policy of the European System would have fostered, was
a division of the World into European and American,
Republican and Monarchical ; a league of worn-out Govts.
on the one hand, and of youthful and strring Nations, with

---

* An illegible character has been written here, which looks like W ;
perhaps Wellington is intended.

the U. States at their head, on the other. *We* slip in between; and plant ourselves in Mexico. The Un. States have gotten the start of us in vain; and we link once more America to Europe. Six months more—and the mischief would have been done.

"Had they turned me out upon this question (and I would have gone out if I had not carried it) it would have been only to bring me in again with all the Commerce and Manufactures of England at my heels. They therefore (whoever may be comprised in that *they*) thought better of it; but no doubt they will be on the watch to revenge themselves, when they may; and I must walk with caution and good heed, knowing that there are mines and trapfalls all around me. Liverpool and I have agreed throughout; and he has acted with me most firmly and strenuously. Could they have separated him from me I think they would have ventured the trial.

"I think I have pretty nearly exhausted all that I had to tell you of myself. Of publick concerns, Ireland only gives us any uneasiness. And that not so much from apprehending any immediate danger of an explosion there (for there is *none*, I verily believe) as from the apparent and utter hopelessness of ever bringing that unhappy Country to a settlement.

"It never was in such a state of prosperity—never. Land pays its rent; Commerce increases rapidly; Manufactures are planted in parts of the kingdom where never before capital ventured to trust itself; Justice is administered with a more even hand than ever before, and is acknowledged by the people to be so; and even the sore Evil of tythes has, by an Act of last year (one of the wisest ever passed by a legislature) been in all instances lessened, and in many entirely removed.

"But in the midst of all these blessings (for such they

are) the demon of religious discord rages with fury hitherto unknown. The Catholick Demagogues fear that the equitableness of Ld. Wellesley's administration should put Catholick emancipation out of sight ; and the old Protestant faction take advantage of the indiscretions and violences of the demagogues, to spread an alarm of rebellion ; to decry Ld. Wellesley's system of leniency and impartiality, and to call for the return of the ' iron times.' Such is the real history of the factions which now agitate Ireland, but I hope—I believe—the storm will pass away without bursting. As to any practical good to be done in respect to the Catholicks, they have made that hopeless for years to come. This Country is once more united, as one man, against them !

" The new feature in the case of Ireland at present is the interest which Foreign Powers take in it. France, and more especially the Jesuit and propagandist party in France, certainly have their eyes fixed on the struggle —and, if the Foreign Ministers thought (as they most undoubtedly did) and wrote to their Courts in 1818 and 1821 that England was about to be swallowed up by a Revolution—it is not wonderful that they should be inspiring fears (or in some instances, perhaps, hopes) of the like Catastrophe in Ireland.

"But they will be disappointed. A few unpleasant nights in Parlt. we shall have ; but six months hence Mr. O'Connell and the Catholick Association will be with Spa-fields and Manchester; and the Protestant fanaticks and polemicks will, I hope, have shrunk back into their shell.

" And now, my dear Frere, here is a long Letter ; not long enough to atone for so long a silence—but enough to show that that silence has not been the silence of neglect or of oblivion.

"Make my homage to your Lady. Continue to let me hear from you ; and be assured that I am, as ever, My Dear Frere,

"Sincerely, affectionately, and unalterably yours,

"G. C."

In September 1825 Frere returned to England for a year, and once more visited his old haunts and his old friends. Canning and he must have had much to say to each other, and much to lament. If the one was breaking down under the feverish stress of political life, with old hopes unrealised, old visions faded, the other had been stranded on the little island in the Mediterranean Sea, to waste his life in a sort of busy idleness. Frere's health had caused some uneasiness to his friends, and occasioned the following letter written by Canning shortly before the friend of his boyhood left England for ever. It was probably the last that he sent to Frere :—

"FOREIGN OFFICE, *Aug.* 31 1826.

"My dear Frere,—

"What is become of you? and when shall I see you? and how do you do?

"I am here, with the exception of to-morrow, Friday, (when I go to Windsor to a Council) till Monday sennight —on which day, the Gods consenting, we shall set off for Paris.

"I had forgotten, I go to Coombe on Sunday to dine and sleep—which is another exception.

"Do you know—I have been thinking, and so has Joan, that you were not well when last we saw you—and I earnestly wish you would take some good sound advice before you set out on a long journey.

"Send for Holland, or for Warren, the one oil, the

other vinegar—perhaps both together would be better—
and do not mind cupping and blistering and calomelling if
they tell you that you want it—as my mind misgives me
that they will.

"I have been unwell at Brighton—with bile, and *viscera*
—but Sir H. Tierney set me right, and assures me that the
attack (and it was a sharp one) has saved me a fit of the
Gout.

"The truth is I am overworked. But I am wonderfully
well, considering.

"Let us take care of ourselves.

"Ever affectionately Yours,

"G. C."

We are all familiar with the scenes that passed in rapid
succession during the last year of Canning's life : the death
of Lord Liverpool ; the Premiership accepted under very
altered conditions, to the sorrow of such men as Walter
Scott, who thought that a sacrifice of principle was involved;
the four short months of supreme power ; the sudden
collapse ; the terrible sufferings of the last few days ; and
the end coming in the room at Chiswick in which Fox had
closed his eyes upon the world.

At the time of the burial of a celebrated Englishman
in Westminster Abbey, *Le Temps* observed, "Happy
England ! she can give her children truly national
funerals !" It is an honour which it costs her comparatively little to bestow, but few attain to it. A cenotaph
with an appropriate text is deemed fitting guerdon for
some of the noblest of her sons. Canning's funeral was
private, at his own request ; but the corpse was followed
to its grave in the Abbey by thousands who had loved
and honoured him in life—a better tribute than the
presence of the crowds who flock to gape at an idle

pageant. His son and his kinsman, the Great Eltchi, were afterwards to be laid with him.

Frere wrote three epitaphs for Canning, of varying lengths. The shortest is the best :—

> "I was destroyed by Wellington and Grey.
> They both succeeded. Each has had his day.
> Both tried to govern, each in his own way,
> And both repent of it—as well they may."

Some of the letters given in a previous chapter show how, when it was too late, the thoughts of many turned to Canning as the man who might have guided England through the storm. With him died the last of the statesmen who led and governed, instead of following the popular outcry. The Reform Bill has changed everything, and the modern politician takes his tone from the mob instead of giving the tone to them. It is as though Prospero should have given his wand and book into the hands of Caliban.

With his aspirations to redress grievances and to right the wrong, Canning was regarded with disfavour by the old Tories, and the opposite party disliked and feared him. He whom Heine saw as the *Gonfaloniere der Freiheit* was fated to win little but mistrust even from those whom he tried to serve. After tracing the story of his life from the bright promise of youth to the stormy close, it seems at first as if it were a mournful record of unfulfilled ambitions and disappointed hopes—his whole labour only the writing on the sand which the tide washes away. Yet it was not so. Although another took the honour which should have been his, it was his unceasing efforts that cleared the way for deliverance. The negro slave—the English Roman Catholic—the Greek patriot—all had reason to bless his name.

For the rest, was it, after all, so hard that his own wish should be fulfilled—that he should be cut down with his marvellous gifts unimpaired, his unconquerable will firm within him? Defeated, he may seem to be, but " out of the day and the dust and the ecstasy, there goes another Faithful Failure."

CHAPTER XIV.

AN APOSTLE OF THE JEWS.

1830—1845.

FRERE'S brother Hatley had early developed peculiar religious views, to the distress of his parents, who were most orthodox. A theory that war was contrary to Scripture induced him to resign his commission in the Guards. In later life he employed himself in inventing a new system for teaching the blind to read, and a new interpretation of the unfulfilled prophecies. "Frere's method" is now superseded in blind schools by the more modern systems of Moon and Braille; and the millennium —of which he twice fixed the date—seems no nearer than it was.

His other brothers deplored the kindness of heart which led him to extend hospitality to religious enthusiasts who were not always as clean as might be desirable; but J. H. Frere, out in Malta, and not brought into personal contact with Hatley's friends, was disposed to listen to his direful prophecies, and look for the end of the world.

One of those most firmly persuaded that the Day of the Lord was at hand was Joseph Wolff, traveller and missionary; but this belief, instead of taking away the motive for exertion, spurred him through incredible toils and dangers that he might win a few more souls before it was too late. There is some uncertainty about the date of his first meeting with Frere. In a letter to Wolff's wife, Frere declares that he never met Wolff until 1830; but Wolff, in a letter to Sir Thomas Baring, speaks of making Frere's acquaintance on his way to Jerusalem in 1827. It is probable that Frere's memory deceived him, as the tone of Wolff's letters from Quarantine in 1830 shows them to have been written to a valued friend, not to an illustrious stranger known only by report.

Joseph Wolff, the son of a rabbi of the synagogue, was born in Bavaria in 1796. He was sent to the gymnasium at Bamberg, where he showed signs of great promise. He was received into the Church of Rome in 1812, and continued his studies at Vienna, Tübingen, and finally in Rome itself, at the Collegio Romano and the College of the Propaganda. An awkward habit of speaking his mind without respect of persons, which he retained throughout his life, soon occasioned his banishment to a religious house in Switzerland. Even the heads of the College can hardly have expected him to stay there, and Wolff soon escaped to England, where the London Society for the Conversion of the Jews sent him to study Oriental languages at Cambridge. In 1819 he became a member of the Church of England, and shortly afterwards made the acquaintance of Hatley Frere, of whom he speaks with much affection in one of his letters. In 1821 he started on the first of his missionary journeys to the Jews of the dispersion. In 1826 he was back in London, and there won the heart of the Lady Georgiana Walpole, daughter to the Earl of Orford. It was a pure love-match on both sides. She gave up home, kindred, and civilisation to wander over the world with him, while he refused to touch a penny of her fortune, and made a formal renunciation of all claims upon it at the time of his marriage. Their honeymoon was spent at Jerusalem—then unvisited by Western potentates under the guidance of Cook—and on the way they stopped at Malta. Wolff and Frere were soon on friendly terms. Frere, having studied Hebrew in his old age, could appreciate Wolff's profound knowledge of rabbinic lore, and no one could be with the missionary without being struck by his fervent zeal and unusual simplicity joined to unusual shrewdness.

In 1830 the Wolffs were again at Malta, and Wolff wrote to Frere on September 17th from the Lazaretto, where they were undergoing quarantine.

"DEAR SIR,

"I send to you the Copy of the Resolution of the Committee of the London Society for promoting Christianity among the Jews, with my reply to it—of which I wish to send several Copies to England. . . . If you therefore could be so kind to correct the English and give it a more Gentlemanly style I should be exceedingly obliged to you—and then procure to me a *confidential* person to copy it. In confidence be it told you that my views on Prophecies have brought me in collision with the Missionaries here. . . . We shall have much to converse together on my leaving the quarantine. . . .

"I am with great regard, dear Sir, yours truly,

"JOSEPH WOLFF, Missionary."

Their quarantine lasted for some time, and before it was over Wolff developed an idea which struck Frere with dismay. He intended to leave Lady Georgiana and her little boy in Malta, and journey to Timbuctoo in search of the Lost Tribes, with no other equipment than the second-hand robe of a dervish.

"As I intend to leave Malta next January," he wrote

to Frere on December 9th, " I don't know at Malta or anywhere else a gentleman to whose kind protection I would have such confidence to recommend Lady Georgiana than to yours. I am sure that you will act as a father to her. Now having done my duty as a tender husband to my wife by recommending her to your fatherly protection during my absence in Africa, I take the liberty to suggest to you the following request " :—

The request was that Frere should recommend some furnished lodgings in Valetta for Lady Georgiana to occupy during her husband's absence.

The projected journey was too wild a scheme for any sane man's approval, and Frere wrote an earnest letter of remonstrance, pointing out the dangers of the way, and the certainty that Wolff would never return to his family. Wolff's reply is very characteristic :—

" Dear Sir.

" Does it not seem to you that at *Teman*, Jeremiah xlix. 7, a celebrated School existed where *wisdom* was taught, and that Jeremiah alluded to that school ? "

He discusses this point for some time, and then suddenly remembers the business in hand :—

" Now about my departure. Your *counsel* is certainly most valuable to me—but do you not think that as I am determined now to make my Missionary errands according to Mark vi. 7, 8, 9, I cannot be in great danger in Africa—and am better able to make it according to that method than to *Bokhara*, where I would be obliged to make the expense of 2 Sea voyages—to Alexandria first and then either to Caramania or to *Mocca*. Our journey to Jerusalem did cost Lady Georgiana a great deal—and lately she was obliged to pay for me £100*st.*—so that if I go first to Africa and then to *Bokhara*, I give her time to recover from the heavy expence—and if I go from Timboktoo to the Cape of Good Hope, I shall be assisted at the Cape from the Governor for whom I have letters—with which assistance then I can go to *Bokhara*—and thus Lady Georgiana can during that time educate honourably my child. Lord Orford can make me *no reproaches* of having obliged Lady Georgiana to live in a low manner—and then returning from *Timboktoo* and *Bokhara* I hope to embrace you whom I have learnt to love and esteem as *a father*, and in whose counsel Lady Georgiana has such great confidence."

To this period must be assigned an undated note, which Wolff concludes with "I think Saturday next I will leave this Island either to *Timboktoo* or *Bokhara*; wherever I go your kindness will always be to me unforgetful."

Frere exerted himself to the utmost to prevent the expedition to Timbuctoo. To attempt to prevail on Wolff to remain in Europe was, as Frere himself said, "merely a waste of words"; but it might be possible to turn his energies in a less hazardous direction. Among Wolff's most cherished dreams was that of discovering in the heart of Africa some remnants of the Jewish nation. In the course of a long conversation with him, Frere repeated some particulars—learned from Lord Hastings —respecting the traditions of the Afghans, and the names of some of the tribes of Cabul indicative of a Jewish origin. Wolff caught at the bait, and consulted a large map of Afghanistan, and—again to quote Frere—"seemed to have convinced himself that the object which he had in view was, at least, as likely to be obtained, in the

East." So far, so good ; but Wolff now proclaimed his intention of travelling in the garb of a religious mendicant, and taking with him neither money nor any equipment. Most people will agree with Frere that " this was not, certainly, a mode of travelling which any sober adviser would have recommended."

Shortly afterwards, Frere learned from General Ponsonby the particulars of Wolff's conduct at the time of his marriage, and could not help respecting the independent spirit that refused to touch a penny of Lady Georgiana's fortune. The result, in brief, was that Frere prevailed upon Wolff to accept a sum which, although trifling in itself, was sufficient to defray the expenses of the sea voyage that had been the chief obstacle to the journey to Asia. Wolff sat up at one o'clock in the morning to write the following letter of thanks :—

" Dear Patron,—

" Tho' it is late in the night I can not but express to you my most cordial and affectionate thanks to you for your kind and christian offer by which I shall now be enabled by God's grace to carry the tidings of Salvation to my benighted brethren in Persia, Afghan (*sic*), Samarcand, and Bokhara—that I shall never cease, dear Benefactor, to pray for you . . . and not only for you but likewise for Lady Errol, Miss Frere, Miss Jane Frere, and Miss Blake, you will easily believe me."

In a letter written a few days later, he says :—

" I hope that I shall be able to realise the apostolical manner of going without *scrip* and without *purse*. I have already bought myself from an Armenian an old oriental habit of a *Dervish*, which I will shew to you tomorrow."

Whether this exhibition took place or not is uncertain,

as Frere was particular in his ways, and may not have
relished contact with the garment.   Various traditions
of Wolff's brief stay in Malta have been handed down
by former residents to the present day.   One story tells
how Lady Erroll, sitting by her window, was astonished
by the irruption of a figure in the garden, leaping over
her flower-beds, and shouting as he ran "Oh, Lady Erroll,
Lady Erroll, have you any calomel?   Little Drummond
is very ill, and the doctor says that calomel will kill
him, but I think it will do him good, so please give me
some of it."

On another occasion, he was returning to Malta after
an absence, and of course had to undergo quarantine.
He was anxious that Lady Georgiana, who had remained
on the island, should come into the Lazaretto with him;
but she, knowing the discomforts of that abode, declined
to do so.   However she came to see him, and as he
talked to her from behind the grille, he rolled up his
handkerchief into a .ball, and flung it at her.   The indignant attendants at once declared that Lady Georgiana
was infected, and must go into quarantine with her
husband: and go she did, without any of the numerous
things indispensable to the comfort of a lady in the
Lazaretto.   Wolff was devoted to his "lovely Georgiana,"
as he always called her, but he could not resist the delight
of teasing her by telling in company the story of their
journey across the desert, when they were slung in baskets
on either side of a camel, and a large stone had to be
placed in his basket to make the balance true.

On December 29th, 1830, Wolff left Malta in the
Triumphante.   He did not lose any time in beginning
his labours ; on the 30th he preached to the crew, and
distributed six French Bibles amongst them, "which they
began immediately to read," he tells Frere.

" 1 Jan. 1831. I was delighted by observing the sailors reading the Bible I gave to them. . . . I observed the mate make the sign of the cross ; it is delightful to observe some religious feeling, let it be expressed in whatever a shape it may. The sign of the cross made by an old Roman Catholic woman is more consoling than to hear the blasphemy of a *polished, well-educated* and *poetical Infidel!* And it is sorrowful to observe that Duglas in Edinburgh does not blush to write that Progress of *Infidelity* was the first step to true Christianity! Sadducees never came to the Lord, but a Pharisee. . . .

" 2 Jan. The Captain asked me why I submit to so much sufferings and privations? I replied, 'You have shed your blood for temporal liberty, how much more have I to give my blood for the nations in order that they may obtain liberty in Jesus Christ! The glorious liberty of the children of God! The time will come (I continued) that the Three coloured flag of the Father, Son, and Holy Ghost shall be hoisted everywhere—and this will be a day of eternal memory, and there shall be not only at Paris but from the rising of the Sun to the going down thereof a cry of Glory!

" 5 Jan. I was surprised that the French ascribe to themselves the Victory at Trafalgar. They say that if the Government would employ Captains of Merchant ships they would certainly beat the English fleet. And the French permitted the Allies to come to Paris in 1814—so the Persians say after the Russians take a country of them that the Shah permitted them to take it."

On January 8th Wolff reached Alexandria, where he was kindly received by Mr. Bartholomew, a Wesleyan missionary.

In February the news of Lady Erroll's death reached Wolff, and he wrote to condole with Frere. He was still at Alexandria, where he had busied himself with "taking *Bibles* out of Magazines and Customhouses which were sent 12 years ago by the Bible Society to be distributed to Jaffa and Cyprus, and which were almost eaten by the rats."

A letter to his wife at this time was evidently sent for Frere's perusal. It begins with an explanation that Gog and Magog are identical with Russia, followed by a paragraph headed " History of my present servant."

" Philipp Joseph Diock, born at *Juluk* beyond Darfoor, walked about when a boy eight years of age in the fields of his native country, in company of other boys, to eat the wild fruits growing upon the trees, when suddenly Bedouins, the enemies of his country, came, and took prisoners the whole troop of boys. They brought poor *Diock* with the rest to the tents of their camp, consigned the weeping boys over to their wives, who tried to silence them by caresses. A few days after, they were brought to Egypt, where an Italian, Filippo Nardi by name, bought him and gave to him his Liberty after 14 years' service. He came after this into the service of Mr. Gliddon, where I instructed and baptized him, and gave to him the name Philipp Joseph Diock—but alas, he is something addicted to drinking, but I hope to cure him *by God's grace*—for I never take either spirits or wine with me on my journies through the Deserts. He has a great desire to see again, as he says, ' *his Savage country.*' On my asking him why, he replied ' To see there the ashes of my father if he should be dead—to see there the ashes of my mother if she should be dead.' On my return to Rosetta he came *to Europeans*, who

made him drunk—he spoke to me in the following manner :
' You have saved my Soul, and therefore I am affectionately attached to you, and I would cut one's throat if
he was to do you harm.'"

This outburst only drew from his master the rejoinder
that Diock's soul was not yet saved if he got drunk. Wolff
was busy preparing for his departure, but found time to
preach " for two hours less five minutes," at Mr. Gliddon's
house on Sunday evening.

The next letter is full of Rabbinical and Talmudic lore,
interesting perhaps to Frere, but not to the general reader.
Wolff's letters resemble a commonplace book in which he
jotted down anything that struck him at the moment.
The following extract is entitled " Affecting Story of a
Greek Slave related to me by John Barker, Esq., H.B.M.
Consul-General."

" During the Massacre upon the Island of Scio in the
year 1822, a boy of an Ionian Greek was made slave. In
the year 1830 the master of that Greek boy came to
Alexandria with the boy, where he went to the Turkish
bath, and where he met by chance an Armenian Christian.
The Turk addressed himself to the Armenian Christian,
and said ' Buy this slave of me, for I don't know what to
do with him. I wanted to make a Turk of him, but he
is obstinately attached to the Greek religion.' "

"*Armenian* : ' I don't want him.'

" In the night the Armenian dreamed that the Greek
Servant with his wife in the house of Signor Dusiza, a
Merchant at Alexandria, were the parents of that Greek
slave. The dream had made such an impression on him
that he went to the Greek servant of Dusiza. The wife of
that Greek servant went immediately to the Harem of
the Turk. The Greek slave suddenly recognised his

mother, and exclaimed 'My Mother!'   The Greek servant of Dusiza went to Mr. Barker, who claimed the boy as an Ionian Subject from Ibrahim Pasha.   Ibrahim Pasha cited both the Turk with his slave, and the parents of the slave who came with their little girl.   The resemblance of the slave with the girl was so striking that all were convinced that they were children of the same parents.

"*Ibrahim Pasha to the boy*: 'Go over to thy parents.'

"The boy joyfully obeyed.

"*Ibrahim Pasha to the Turk*: 'You go your way.'"

The civilisation of the West was even then exerting a baneful influence on the East.   Wolff mentions a certain Hurshid Bey, one of Muhammed Ali's generals, who in a large company of Europeans and Mussulmans, took a slice of ham in one hand and a bottle of wine in the other, with a shout of "Huzza!"

From Alexandria Wolff went on to Damietta, in the hope of finding there a ship to take him to Lattachia, the first stage on the journey to Aleppo.   At Damietta he was the guest of the British Vice-Consul, Signor Michaele Surrur, an Arab Catholic.   Wolff and he were great friends, in spite of the pomp and state affected by the Vice-Consul, who always spoke in a loud voice because "a great man ought to speak louder than a little man."   They enjoyed a long discussion on the Second Advent, none of those present venturing to dissent from Wolff's views, with the exception of a Greek Christian, "who had not more light on this subject than many of the Protestants have opposed," and who was peremptorily silenced by the Vice-Consul.

With Mahommedans Wolff was always on friendly terms, and his character of a religious devotee gained him their respect wherever he went.   "Jews and Mohammedans," he writes, "are not such infidels as the Evangelical

Party in England are. Jews and Mohammedans have never limited so much the power of God as the Protestants and especially the Missionary Societies do. I foresee great, very great judgements coming over the Protestant Churches—they may succeed in converting some among the savages who have no books, but certainly they will never be the Instruments of the Conversion of the Jews. There is no such godless nation in the world than the Protestants—they have more confidence in their steam-boats than in the power of God. The Turk, when he perceives an Earthquake, he exclaims 'This is of the Lord.' The Protestants ascribe it to some cause in the Atmosphere. The Arab, on seeing a Comet, concludes that the decrees of the Lord are issued upon his creatures; the Protestant laughs at it! The Syrian Christian lays the hands upon the sick persons; the Protestant, smiling, declares it to be Superstition."

Being unable to find a ship at Damietta, Wolff returned to Alexandria, and thence set out for Aleppo in February. There is a gap in the letters, his next diary being dated from Tabreez, where he arrived in July. From this we gather that he left Erzeroom on the 14th of June, suffering severely from an internal complaint, "which obliged me to stay in places and lose my Tartar tho' I had paid him." He was so ill at one stage that he was obliged to take a priest from an Armenian Convent with him, because "I wished to have a Christian with me in case that I should die." Overtaken by a shower of rain, two hours' journey from Bayazid, Wolff took refuge in a Kurdish tent, where he met an aged Dervish from Bokhara. Wolff and he talked long together on religious subjects, and Wolff at last asked, "What will become of the world?" The Dervish answered, "The world will become thus good that *the lamb and the wolf shall feed together*, and there shall be a general *peace* and fear of God upon earth—and no controversy on religion—and all shall know God truly—no hatred."

"Who shall then govern this world?" asked Wolff, to which the Dervish replied that "Jesus should be King of the whole world for thirty-six years."

"Whence do you know this?" was Wolff's not unnatural question. The Dervish answered, "From the Book" [the Koran]. Wolf then asked, "What do you think of Christians?" to which the Dervish's answer was, "If you wish me to tell you according to the Book, I consider them as Infidels—but if you wish to know my thoughts I tell you that *we are all images of God*—more I cannot tell you."

Well might Wolff consider this man "the most superior Dervish" he had ever encountered. After a few more questions and answers, they parted, and Wolff was left with the conviction that "a missionary often finds more *light* and confirmation about the truth of the word of God by conversing with Dervishes and Jews than one can find in the lectures of cold, even orthodox Professors in the Universities of Germany, or among members of committees of Missionary Societies."

Wolff called on the Prince of Khoy, who received him graciously ; and was visited by two Moollahs and about fifty Persians. On the 3rd of July he started again on his travels, this time in a "Tukhtruan" or moving chair, so that he reached Tabreez in a better condition of health. The English residents at Tabreez—Captain Campbell, the Chargé d'Affaires, Mr. McNeill, and others—showed him every kindness, and procured him letters of introduction to officials at Khorassan and Bokhara. Interspersed with an outline of his plans is an affectionate entreaty to "dear little Drummond" not to write so quickly, as a little more time bestowed on the letters would make them more easy to read. The traveller's health was rapidly improving under the care of an English doctor; and he wrote, "I eat now with the appetite of a *Wolf*, not of *Wolff*. Dr. and Mrs. McNeill treat me like their brother; tell this to Lady Georgiana, in order that her mind may be easy."

The next letter of any importance is written on a large sheet of coarse grey-green paper, such as might be used to wrap up a parcel, and is dated from "Sarakhs in Turkestan," February 12th, 1832. It is addressed to "Mirza Baba Hakeem Basha," and is annotated by Campbell, by whom it was probably sent on to Malta. Wolff's mission was prospering. "Mullah Tatsh, the Cadi of the Turcomans, has declared me to be the fore-runner of Mehde, and that I was predicted in the Hadees—viz., that an Apostle of Jews shall appear before the arrival of Mehde the Great. This noise is gone abroad to Organtsh and Bokhara, and the Turcomans bring to me their families to pray over them, and more than 50 promised not to make slaves again."

In a letter addressed to the same person, a few days later, Wolff adds, "The report of my Mission has spread to Khiva."

On February 18th Wolff was in the Desert of Mowr. All the Jews of the territory had come on horseback to meet him, and they took him to their tents, where he was treated with the greatest hospitality. Thence he proceeded on his way to Bokhara, then no place of resort for tourists under the protection of the Russian flag, but the very mouth of hell.

The King or Ameer (Wolff gives him either title indifferently) was a monster of cruelty. Horrible stories were told of his dungeons into which men were thrown at the caprice of the tyrant or his favourites, that insects might devour their living flesh from their bones. Sometimes the knife brought a release ; sometimes they were left to sink under torture and starvation ; or suddenly brought back to the daylight, after long years had passed, and restored to their friends, who had mourned them as dead. Bokhara was of great importance as the chief slave market of Central Asia, and the horrible wickedness that prevailed within its walls could only be compared to the abominations of the old Canaanitish cities.

Here, as everywhere, Wolff's indomitable resolution carried him through dangers from which a regiment of soldiers could not have protected him. He was allowed to visit the Jews of the town, although conversation with Mussulmans on religious subjects was forbidden. The Goosh Beekee (lit. "King's Ear") or Prime Minister, at first suspicious, became his friend and patron, and invited him to tea. So much, and no more, was he allowed to write to Captain Campbell, when drawing on him for more money before setting off for Balkh and Cabul. Little did Wolff think, as he rode away from the city, that twelve years later he should come back, at far greater risk, in search of two of the Ameer's victims.

In the meantime things were not going smoothly with Lady Georgiana in Malta. At the conclusion of his letter to Campbell Wolff had written, " Be so kind as to accept the bills of Mirza Baba for the money I have drawn on you, and you will be reimbursed by Mr. Frere at Malta." Campbell apparently forwarded this letter to Frere, who was dismayed at the thought of being made answerable for Wolff's expenses. He wrote a long letter of remonstrance to Lady Georgiana, pointing out how willing he had been to assist Wolff in his mission, but expressing his annoyance at finding himself " converted into a kind of Grand Seigneur who is sending out Missionaries at his own expense." He particularly objected to the general misconception that he was responsible for the route taken by Wolff, and for Wolff's manner of travelling. Anxious to prevent Wolff from "adding another name to the list of the victims of African discovery," he had indeed suggested that Afghanistan was less dangerous than Timbuctoo, and supplied Wolff with the means for a sea voyage. But, as Frere acidly observes, "to have suggested such a mode of travelling would have been a degree of absurdity to which, I hope, I am not yet arrived."

Lady Georgiana's answer was judicious and admirable. As a good wife she defended her husband, while she apologised for his want of business habits. "I am assured he feels for you the most sincere respect as well as affection, but you know he is not attentive to forms." Wolff's unceremoniousness had in no way lessened Frere's esteem for his character, and the affair was soon adjusted to the satisfaction of all parties. Lady Georgiana must have let Wolff know how matters stood, for his next letter to Frere, written from Delhi on December 20th, overflows with gratitude. "That great kindness" he thought himself unable to repay, but he sent remittances both to Frere and to Lady Georgiana, so that his debt might be settled.

The meeting with his family was to be deferred longer than he expected. When writing from Delhi, he expected he reach Malta in four months; but the August of 1833 found him no farther on the way than Madras. His progress had been somewhat delayed by a violent attack of cholera morbus, which had seized him on his way from Hyderabad, and brought him to the brink of the grave. He was reported dead in several newspapers, but struggled back to life with the aid of strong remedies—forty grains of calomel and a cautery.

It was during his travels in India that he learned to

know and love Arthur Conolly, with whose name his own was afterwards to be so tragically associated. But for all other details the reader must consult Wolff's published diaries. After a hurried note from "Connamore in Malabar," October 17th, 1833, giving the names of forty-seven stations in India at which he had lectured and preached, Wolff apparently wrote no more letters to Frere until the summer of 1835. By that time he had reached a comparatively civilised place, but he was still yearning after Timbuctoo.

"BLACKHEATH, 1 *July* 1835.

" My dear Mr. Frere,—

" All the books of my first Edition is gone, every one of *them*—and a *second Edition* is now printed, to which I have got again several hundred *Subscribers*. That despicable faction of Nonsubscribers dwindles away rapidly. I have been lately at *Norwich* and lectured there—the Mayor took the chair, and I saw visible blessing, for a Jew has since applied for *baptism*. Worldly-minded people will call this boasting, but really would to God that I could mention that a thousand Jews have since applied for baptism ! I would have no hesitation to mention it to my dear patron and dear Miss Frere. Last night I expounded at Mr. Hatley Frere's. . . .

" A warm correspondence was carried on between me and D—— ; he abused me like a *pickpocket*, and still signs himself your affectionate H—— D——. . . . I am every day somewhere else, and then leave always behind me a *shirt*, and take one of my host's, so that I promote the circulation of *shirts*."

A printed syllabus of one of Wolff's lectures is still preserved. There are no less than thirty-nine heads, and one fears that he must have exceeded the " two hours less five minutes" which the audience at Mr. Gliddon's house in Alexandria had endured. The lecture dealt principally with his mission to Jerusalem, in which Lady Georgiana was of great assistance, to judge from some of the headings :—

" 5. Lady Georgiana preaches to the Jews with the child in her arms.

" 14. Lady Georgiana preaches in the Harem of the Mufti of Damiat.

" 15. Lady Georgiana's preaching to the Jews and Jewesses at Cairo.

" 20. Comparison of Lady Georgiana's Pianoforte with the Songs of Orpheus.

" 34. Lady Georgiana's School at Jerusalem."

On this occasion no collection was made, and the tickets were given away. This lecture was probably delivered at Malta, whither Lady Georgiana and Wolff again betook themselves in November 1835.

After this visit Frere heard no more from Wolff until the August of 1838, when a letter in the well-known irregular handwriting reached Malta :—

" PARK SHOT, RICHMOND, SURREY.

" My dear Mr. Frere,—

" I know that you will be glad to learn again some tidings of your old *friend Joseph Wolff*. For my part I have not forgotten the kindness I have received by you, and therefore now take the liberty to mention to you that on the 25th of May the Dublin University has kindly conferred ·upon me the Honorary Degree of LL.D. On the 25th of June I was admitted to the Holy Order of Priesthood by the Right Revd. the Lord Bishop of Dromore, and last July I was appointed Chaplain to the Lord

Viscount Lorton—and ten days ago I delivered two lectures in the Vice-Regal Lodge before the Lord Lieutenant, his Houschold, and the Archbishop of Dublin. Lady Georgiana travelled with me through Ireland, and so did my boy, for his vacations had just been. He goes on exceedingly well at School, and knows already the Latin Grammar—his talents are generally admired by all. He speaks French as well as he does English, and reads also the Hebrew."

Wolff and Frere were to meet once more. On his way to Bokhara to rescue Stoddart and Conolly in 1843, Wolff stopped at Malta, and was supplied by Frere with a letter of introduction to Sir Stratford Canning, which proved of the utmost service. On his return, nearly two years later, he apparently spent no time in Malta. There is a letter from him written on board the *Duke of Cornwall* steamer, thanking Frere for a proffered loan of money which the arrival of remittances from England made it unnecessary for him to accept; and then Wolff vanishes for ever from among Frere's correspondents.

The most interesting portion of his life has necessarily been omitted here. It is impossible to give a full biography of all the notable personages whose letters have been reproduced. So far as can be ascertained, Wolff never wrote to Frere during his second journey to Bokhara. The sending of a letter was such a danger in itself, owing to the Ameer's suspicions, that Wolff never wrote, even to his wife and son, except in case of urgent need. The story of his going single-handed to rescue the men for whose protection the English Government had refused to stir a finger must be read in his published diaries.

Anything from his pen is too interesting to be left in oblivion—for he wrote as he talked and as he thought— but it is feared that, to those for whom he is but a name, the foregoing chapter will give an inadequate idea of his personality. He might be visionary, hasty, disposed to take offence, and tenacious of his opinion. But his earnest conviction that the end of the world was at hand was never made the excuse for neglecting any task ; if he were quick to resent a slight, he was slow to forget a kindness ; and his indomitable will enabled him to surmount difficulties which to other men seemed impossibilities. To the people of Bokhara he was simply " Khoob Ademee" ("the good man"); the wild races of the desert recognised what manner of spirit was in him when they called him by the name of " Baba Elias."

CHAPTER XV.

LITERARY FRIENDSHIPS.

Gabriele Rossetti.

> "Yea, thou shalt learn how salt his food who fares
> Upon another's bread—how steep his path
> Who treadeth up and down another's stairs."
>
> *(Div. Com. Parad.* xvii.)

ON July 13th, 1820, Ferdinand, King of the Two Sicilies, stood before the altar of his royal chapel in Naples. His right hand was on an open Bible, his eyes were raised to the cross, as he swore to defend and maintain the Constitution which he had just granted to his people, and called the vengeance of Heaven down upon himself should he break the oath.

In the March of the following year Ferdinand abolished the Constitution, and suppressed it with the aid of an Austrian army. All who had taken part in the late disturbances were marked out for punishment. A court-martial was established to examine into the conduct of all ecclesiastics, soldiers, and public officials for the last thirty years. Some were hanged, others scourged; those who escaped by flight were condemned in their absence.

One of the worst offenders in the eyes of King Ferdinand was a certain Gabriele Rossetti, who had held the appointment of Curator of Ancient Marbles and Bronzes in the

Naples Museum. A skilful draughtsman, and possessed of a beautiful tenor voice, he was a well-known character in literary circles. There was a popular catch which linked his name with that of a great composer :—

> "Rossini, Rossetti,
> Divini, imperfetti."

But he had drawn upon himself the unfavourable notice of the Government by becoming a member of the secret society of the Carbonari, to whose influence the revolution was due, and by writing verses. Every one had sung his "Ode to the Dawn of the Constitution Day," beginning "*Sei pur bella cogli astri sul crine*"; and a verse of another poem, even more objectionable to Bourbon ears, was notorious :—

> "I vindici coltelli
> Sapran passarvi il cor;
> I Sandi ed i Luvelli
> Non son finiti ancor."*

The reference to the assassination of Kotzebue by Sandt, and of the Duc de Berri by Louvel, was not likely to be taken in good part by the King, and the poet spent the spring of 1821 in close concealment. But he was not fated to join the eight hundred victims who are said to have perished under the Bourbon's vengeance in one year. The wife of Sir Graham Moore, the British admiral, knew and liked Rossetti, and persuaded her husband to an act of mercy which was not strictly in accordance with international etiquette. One day Sir Graham's carriage drove down to the harbour, and from it stepped a gentleman in a British uniform who embarked for Malta. Once under the English flag, Rossetti's

* "Vengeful blades will pierce your heart; Sandts and Louvels are not yet extinct."

life was safe from King Ferdinand. It is curious to note the occasions, during the Italian struggle for independence, when the unofficial interference of one of our admirals has been of service to the cause, or to individuals.

Rossetti's sufferings in the cause of freedom, his hair-breadth escape, his reputation as an improvisatore, created a general desire to see him among the leaders of society in Malta. In a versified account of his life, the poet speaks of the report which flew through the island

> "that Italy's Tyrtaeus had arrived,"

and of the invitation to him to improvise " in some noted house." He recited six times in the course of the evening, and his spirited declamation aroused general enthusiasm. Next day he received congratulatory visits from all the *élite* of Malta :—

> "But one beneficent and reverend mien *
> In which I read exalted characters,
> A diction which, arising from the soul,
> Goes to the heart, and fixes what it says—
> This 'mid the throng I noted. . . .
>
>   *   *   *   *
>
> Nor did his presence lessen his repute.
> Unconscious of his fame he singly seemed,
> To hear it named was what he could not brook;
> Courtesy generous, and without display.
> Learning immense, and greater modesty,
> Ah, who could paint that noble-natured man ?
>
>   *   *   *   *
>
> One day, when he accorded praise anew
> To chants of mine which wakened his surprise,
> I answered him, ' In you I seem to see
> The imperial eagle by a sparrow charmed.
> I know my verse has earned me banishment,
> But I, excelling some, bend low to you.'

* I owe the translation of these verses, as well as other materials for this chapter, to the kindness of Mr. W. M. Rossetti [see Preface].

> And later, when I saw how plenteously
> He dealt his succours to the sick and poor,
> I in John Hookham Frere discerned the type
> Of the sublime Christian philosopher.
> None but an angel could portray him true;
> I feel my eyes grow moist to speak of him.
> He called me friend, and that has been my pride.
> I felt myself grow better by so great
> A pattern. Nevermore he left my thoughts,
> And even in death within my heart he lives."

In a note the author adds, " What I indicate regarding the Right Honourable J. Hookham Frere is far less than the truth. All Malta was full of his munificences, and still resounds his praise; and when in the sequel I quitted that Island for England, I found widespread confirmation of his repute as a most erudite man and a genuine Christian."

It is strange to find Frere, the sound Tory, the disciple of Pitt, becoming the warm friend and patron of the hot-headed revolutionist who had been obliged to fly for his life from an incensed king. But, as a rule, when a man attempts to foment disorders, his fellow-subjects style him a rebel; it is only in other countries that he becomes a patriot and a martyr. Frere could not have sympathised with the Irish victims of 1798, any more than, a few years after his death, his countrymen could appreciate the grievances which the People's Charter was expected to redress. But Frere could, and did assist Rossetti, just as our fathers were quite pleased to shout themselves hoarse for Garibaldi. History is for ever repeating herself, and many of those who reject the notion of Home Rule for Ireland as a monstrous absurdity were honestly ready to upset the balance of Europe by championing Crete against Turkey.

Frere endeavoured to persuade the authorities at Naples to overlook Rossetti's poetical sins, or to regard them as the irresponsible utterances of a visionary. But King Ferdinand's nerves had received a severe shock, and every Carbonaro was a deadly enemy. Frere wrote to his friend Mr. Hamilton, at Naples, asking his good offices on Rossetti's behalf, and received the following reply, dated September 9th, 1822 :—

"Dear Frere,

"I have been most unsuccessful in the Enquiries I have made respecting the merits of Rossetti—and am very sorry to say that even his best friends and admirers are the loudest in condemning him for the pains he took during the Revolution to preach up Carbonaro Doctrines ; and only yesterday or the day before one of his dicta was quoted to me, as descriptive of his usual language—'I giorni dei *Santi* e dei *Lovelli* non son finiti ancora.' I cannot therefore have the face to ask the Government here to say a word in his favor, or to go out of their way to exempt him from the operation of any general Regulation, and I fear he must submit to his lot, if the orders under which our people are acting at Malta are to be rigorously enforced."

On September 28th King Ferdinand granted an amnesty to persons concerned in the revolutionary or constitutional movement. Thirteen men are excepted from it, and the last name on the list is that of Rossetti.

The first letter yet discovered from Frere to the unlucky poet must have been written at this time. It is written in French ; but after Rossetti had settled in England, Frere used his own language for correspondence, while the exile's replies were always in Italian. To the last day of his life Frere never learned how to spell Rossetti's name.

" Mon cher Rosetti,

"Je sçavais il y a long tems que quelques uns de vos vers avaient produit une impression extrêmement defavorable dans l'esprit du Roi ; je ne vous ai jamais cependant rien dit, ne voulant pas vous chagriner gratuitement ; maintenant je vous l'avoue, afin que vous ne croyiez pas que le malheur qui vous est arrivé me fasse changer d'opinion sur votre compte, je sçais tout ce que vous valez, et le peu que peuvent signifier des vers populaires écrites au milieu d'une phrenesie populaire.

" Je trouve que c'est un malheur (puisque la manie de vos auditeurs vous demandait des sentimens de cette force là), qu'au lieu de citer des petits coquins modernes vous n'ayez pas compulsé les exemples des grands scélerats classiques, les Brutus, les Timoléons, et les Scaevola, vous auriez eu alors l'exemple des Alfieri, et de tous les pedans qui idolatrent les crimes commis en Grec et Latin au nom de la liberté.

" Mais pourquoi citer Louvel ? celui-là a assassiné le prince qui devait un jour regner sur la France, et il m'a toujours paru que vous aviez beaucoup de reconnaissance et de respect pour votre Prince héreditaire * et que vous aviez cru même que ce Prince était un peu interessé en votre faveur—

" 'Multa quidem nobis facimus mala saepe poetae.'

" Nous sommes convaincus que les paroles ne sont faites que pour être rhimée et chantées, pendant que la partie anti-poétique des hommes se persuade que les paroles doivent toujours signifier quelque chose, ainsi ils ne sentiront jamais la nécessité de mettre Louvello pour rhimer avec coltello.

* Francis, son of Ferdinand, who succeeded to the throne in January 1825.

" Pour l'exemple de Sandt c'est encore pire, car ce pauvre Kotzebue était un poete comme vous—c'etait à ce qu'on m'a dit, un homme de génie, dont le coeur était excellent, et l'estomac encore meilleur, et qui à force de vivre avec des gens raisonnables, avait renoncé à des idées romanesques sur la liberté et le bonheur des hommes. Cette idée me fait trembler, car je craindrai tous les jours de voir arriver quelque nouveau Sandt expédie par les Carbonari pour plonger un couteau dans le ventre de cet excellent Rosetti qui ne voudroit jamais que les couteaux fussent employés que contre les pâtés de pigêon. Pardonnez ce badinage sur un sujet qui n'est pas *badinable*, et croyez moi.

" Votre très-sincere ami et serviteur, etc."

Frere, perhaps with a recollection of certain passages in the *Anti-Jacobin*, which had once caused reverend elders to shake their heads, could treat the matter lightly, but the Neapolitan Government had no sense of humour, and remained blind to the difficulties of finding a rhyme for " coltello." Knowing how extravagantly some of the Carbonari had talked and acted, and how insecure was the existing order of things at that time, one must acquit Ferdinand and his advisers of any extraordinary severity in this case. In Malta Rossetti's life was safe, but " spies or other emissaries of the Bourbon Government " made his position so intolerable that he resolved upon settling in England. Early in 1824 he bade farewell for ever to southern skies, and London gave him the refuge she has afforded to so many great men who have learned in time to love her grey skies and stony pavements as much as the fairer lands that have rejected them and their message.

When the long series of letters to Frere begins, May 2nd, 1824, Rossetti was earning a precarious livelihood by teaching. He had made acquaintance with two of Frere's brothers, "who resemble you in visage, and I think also in mind and heart," and had been permitted to enter Lord Holland's library, where he beheld Frere's likeness, which he thought "so life-like that I could almost hear your words." He had called on a large circle of distinguished men to present Frere's letters of introduction. "Lord Holland, with whom I am to dine to-day, received me most cordially, and introduced me to his son. . . . Mr. Gurney . . . also asked me many questions with the interest of one who loves you. Mr. Davenport . . . showed the same warmth." Of Dr. Young and Mr. Heber Rossetti had as yet seen nothing, and Mr. Rose was out of town.

" In the dilemma of seeming to you a flatterer if I speak, or of keeping silence so as not to seem that I prefer to report the truth and take the risk, I will tell you then that every one who spoke to me about you, whether as a man of virtue or as a literary personage, has shown admiration and veneration. Of the first matter I will say no more, but must add that as to the second every one is of the same opinion as myself. All have enlarged to me on the admirable harmony and great propriety of your verse ; and Mr. John Murray said that, through you, Aristophanes is better in English than in Greek, adding that no one as yet had entered into the spirit of his author more than you, or rendered him into finer verse ; and I was pleased to reflect that he, though unacquainted with Greek, was echoing the voice of the learned. . . . By my distinguished Admiral I was introduced to the poet Campbell, who has a high opinion of you ; and how can you, my friend, remain afar from a country where you are so much known and appreciated ? . . ."

" Now I will speak to you of myself. Being resolved to

avail myself of improvising as a means of introduction and not of profit, I contemplate relying upon my other two resources as instructor and author. Your and my friends agree in saying that I ought as soon as possible to publish my poem, so that the Author may accredit the instructor. But all (to keep back nothing from you) have impressed upon me the two great difficulties—the scantiness of readers of Italian, and the great plethora of professing instructors. Italian, they say, is known by few, and the political vicissitudes of the Continent have cast upon this solitary refuge a swarm of unfortunates who have undertaken teaching. Arduous truths for me. But my hopes are not very soaring, and hence my disappointment will not be very painful. I also will enter the ball, and we shall see who has the best legs. Good conduct, love of work, few needs, many acquaintanceships, abundant assiduity, talent not deficient, must surely produce *some* result. . . . I went round to the Duke of Sussex, but at a moment when he had much company. I delivered my letter ; and a gentleman of his suite got me to leave my address, saying that the Duke would send for me. . . . To-morrow I propose to call on Lord and Lady Wallscourt. The houses are so far apart, and my feet are so weak, that the two things don't coincide. But patience is the remedy for all evils. . . .

" P.S. Last evening a very unpleasant mishap occurred to me. In coming home from a distance my pocket was picked of the letter-case in which was a note addressed to a gentleman in St. James's Square. What thieves there are in this country ! What can they do with that note, which to me might have been serviceable ? If the thieves had a conscience, they should at least restore me the note, for along with that were some visiting-cards with my address."

A few days later Frere received a letter from Mr. Davenport, whose acquaintance Rossetti had made through his means :—

"My Dear Sir,

"I have had great pleasure in serving Signor Rossetti both for his own sake and for yours, and have, as I trust, given him a pretty fair start in society here by recommending him to everybody I know whose patronage is likely to serve him, or whose Italian wants mending. The man appears to me to be good and clever, and possessed of uncommon powers of writing, tho' not without the national fault of redundancy, of which I have been endeavouring to cure him. I fear, however, that a certain parson Adams-like simplicity (of which the pickpockets have already *twice* availed themselves) will prevent his keeping his money, should he make any, by a work executed in a metre so ill-chosen for a long poem. . . .

"You doubtless know (tho' perhaps you may still lack the authority of a Reformer) that the country has completely altered its complexion in the course of last year, The weavers work, the squires sell their produce, the Jews are propitious, and the nation manifestly increasing in wealth, power, and general contentment. Subjects of political collision are scarce and at a premium; and the liberal views of the Government satisfactory to all save those who do not comprehend them. With regard to literary fun, I believe it is almost extinct, at least of the admissible sort, for of such you will hardly rank Don Juan, tho' by far in my mind the cleverest poem of the sort in any language, far surpassing both in variety and interest his Italian models. Captain Rock's adventures are certainly very clever, and unhappily too well founded on truth. There is nothing else *absolutely*. Nor is there much of news in other respects, if you except the novelty of the successful establishment of Christian schools attended by native children at Calcutta ; a liberal spirit of which Heber (the new Bishop) will avail himself. This, with Perkins' substitution of hot water for gunpowder in gunnery, and the infidelity of old moneylenders' wives, constitutes nearly the extent of my knowledge."

Mr. Davenport took much trouble to gain subscribers for the first volume of Rossetti's edition of the "Divina Commedia." In a letter to Frere, dated December 4th, 1827, which was sent with a copy of the second volume, Rossetti says : " I have dedicated it [the book] to a friend of yours . . . I owed him a pledge of gratitude for the warmth with which he promoted the printing of the first volume, he having procured me some eighty and more subscribers—all of them persons of distinction." This was Mr. Davenport. Rossetti then discusses the chances of his being elected professor of Italian literature at University College. Rose, Davenport, and Cary were among his supporters, but he had little hope of success, and the event proved him right. " There were too many dogs about this bone," to quote his own words. He concludes :—

" Of political news I cannot give you a syllable, because I know not and care not ; and to tell the truth, I understand these matters not at all. Truly it is a strange thing that I, who don't at all understand what politics are, should for politics be persecuted and exiled. Such is Fate ! If the King of Naples knew me, he would indeed have something to laugh over. But this is not the first absurdity which people make him commit, and probably it will not be the last."

Mr. William Rossetti's note on this passage is as follows :—"Certain it is that, as far back as I recollect my father, say from 1835, he took a great deal of interest and engaged a great deal in conversation concerning Continental politics. Yet it may well be that this was not the original bent of his mind and feelings, and that, even in those Neapolitan transactions which had led to his exile, he felt much more as a Neapolitan and Italian nationalist than as a politician, strictly so called."

If Frere were the most irregular of correspondents, he could be most voluminous when the fancy seized him to write. The next in order among the MSS. is a letter of three pages in which he discusses at length Rossetti's peculiar views on the interpretation of poetry. Rossetti, who was then at work on his " Spirito Antipapale," prided himself on having discovered some occult meaning, some mystical allegory, in the works of the great mediæval poets, and Frere was not disposed to accept all his conclusions :—

" MALTA, June 8, 1830.

" . . . There are I think two things to be considered. First—How much the world will bear to be told ? as, for instance, supposing you were able to show a continued Allegory running through the whole of Petrarch's amatory sonnets, would it be prudent to venture on the promulgation of such a discovery ? Would not all the admirers of Laura and all the host of sonneteers be up in arms against you—like the Madman in Horace, who was angry at his cure, and reproached his physician for having deprived him of an agreeable illusion ? "

Herein Frere showed his wisdom: an allegory appeals to few readers. Commentators—including Rossetti himself —have written for many years in all civilised languages,

20

but none of them has been able to convince more than his own little circle of disciples that she who stood on the other side of Lethe's stream and called to the wayworn pilgrim

"*Guarda mi ben ; ben son, ben son, Beatrice,*"

was Philosophy, or any other abstract virtue.

Frere then observes that "poets are of all artists the most servilely imitative ; they borrow from one another (or adopt from one language into another) the same forms of speech, the same combinations of images, the same trains of consecutive thought, or at least, what appears to be *thought*, but which is in fact nothing more than mere mechanical association. Hence we see that the old rubbish of Heathen Mythology still holds its place in poetry, and the Gods and Goddesses flourish in verse, as handsomely as ever they did 2000 years ago.

"Now there was at the time of the Revival of Learning, a little pedantic fanatical Coterie who chose to occupy themselves with projects for the revival of Heathenism, and this is a fact attested by the correspondence of Erasmus, who speaks of himself as exposed to their enmity and antipathy.

"But, I would ask, is it allowable to put these things together, and to infer from the existence of a heathenish Sect in later times (some of whom were poets, and employed of course heathen imagery) that therefore all modern poets who have made use of heathen imagery are to be set down and catalogued as belonging to the Sect which Erasmus denounces?

" . . . . With respect to secret societies, my belief is that they are the natural growth of the human mind which delights in mysterious confidences and pledges of mutual secrecy and reciprocal support : the operation of this principle may be traced even among boys at school, and I could give you an instance of it, from my own recollection.

"Historically speaking, I believe that one secret association at least may be found derived by successive changes and affiliations from the most remote times; but as to their efficacy in governing, or in any way materially influencing the affairs of the world, I am a great sceptic. They are the natural refuge of a defeated faction—of an antient form of worship when abolished—of a Reform when suppressed and crushed. And it follows of course that whenever the faction regains its ascendency, or the Reform is effected—their triumph will be accompanied with some exhibition of the symbols, and some display of the jargon with which they had before consoled their seclusion and depression.

"It is a very common error in natural Philosophy to conclude that an agent which is discovered wherever an effect is produced, must of course effect everything. . . . . I think that the very extraordinary success with which you have developed this obscure and unobserved portion of the social organization of Europe in the middle ages exposes you in a more than ordinary degree to similar errors in your estimate of the efficacy and importance of those secret associations whose existence you have detected and traced with so much acuteness, that you may be induced to overlook or underrate the efficacy of all the other mighty agents which, in those changefull and extraordinary times, were effecting alterations almost as rapid as those which we now witness. . . .

"I find that I have been writing in a very magisterial and authoritative style, but you who have seen something of the modern tone of Criticism must be aware that whenever a man devotes his time and talents to a particular pursuit, be becomes liable to be lectured and corrected by those whose total ignorance of the subject enables them in their own opinion (and sometimes in that of the world) to take a more enlarged view of it. . . . . . I shall be very glad to see what you have written, if you can find any safe way of sending it—but I think best to write this my Review of it beforehand. Nothing flattens the spirit of a Review so much as the previous perusal of the work ! ! "

A few months later, Frere lost his wife, and Rossetti's letter of condolence is touching and affectionate. It closes with an entreaty to Frere to come home—an entreaty echoed by all Frere's family and acquaintance, but which was never granted. In 1832 the " Spirito Antipapale " was published, and Rossetti sent a copy to Frere, as his answer to the objections which have just been quoted. He was now Professor of Italian at King's College. On receiving the book, Frere sent a gift of money, which Rossetti thus acknowledges :—

"8 May, 1832.

" My generous Benefactor,

   " . . . If you knew how many anxieties you have soothed in my mind by your unexpected gift, if you knew how timely and appositely it has come to relieve me from a state such '*che poco è più morte,*' you would feel all the value of your generosity, and would allow me to express in part how I regard it. . . ."

He then discusses his favourite theory " that the works of Dante, Petrarca, and Boccaccio—not to speak of very many others who wrote from age to age up to our time— are all pertaining to a sect, and in especial to the secret society of Freemasons. You will see the whole occult doctrine of the sect disclosed for the first time and applied to the works which I have been examining. . . . But above all you will perceive that the so-called 'Platonic Love' (the spirit of which passed from Spain to Provence, and from Provence to Italy) is no other than a fiction of the Sect I speak of."

After all the sage cautions which Frere had previously uttered, it is amusing to find him entirely thrown off his balance by Rossetti's "discoveries," and going beyond him in the new scheme of interpretation :—

"MALTA, *July* 27, 1832.

". . . Taking the Key which you have given us, I have applied it to Chaucer, and find that it serves to show him to have been a partizan of the Sect, and an adept in the secret language. I had before imagined it possible, that (as Dryden did afterwards) he might have translated Palamon and Arcite, merely for the sake of the Poetry without any knowledge of its secret meaning. I now am convinced that this is impossible. I find in him moreover other things most extraordinary and unexpected : namely, the point upon which you have been most reserved, and upon which you may probably think it right to continue so—in short, the doctrine of the Paulicians.* I see their main tenet distinctly asserted in two passages, and in each of them, the real intention disguised by the same artifice of a pretended parenthesis which serves to cover the blasphemy! It seems to me a subject for serious consideration how far it may be right in itself or prudent in other

---

* The Paulicians were a sect founded by one Constantine, an Armenian, who died towards 684 ; he relied greatly on the writings of St. Paul interpreted in a peculiar sense. He held the Manichæan doctrine of a good and an evil Principle, and especially that the Creator and Governor of the present world is diverse from the ruler of the world to come.—W. M. R.

respects, to give greater publicity to these prodigies! and I would give a good deal to have the opportunity of conversing with you upon the subject of your unpublished manuscripts, and to consider how far you may venture to proceed in your vindication against the blockheads who have attempted to run you down without incurring the danger of hostility from other quarters."

After thanking Rossetti for his proposal of dedicating a book to him, and suggesting that it might be wiser to inscribe it to some new friend whose good will was not "already secured as a permanent acquisition," Frere discusses the indications of the existence of a pagan sect which he had found in Erasmus's letters. He imagines a connection "between the allegorical narratives of the Celts, and those of the Poets whose enigmas you decypher." He points out that "Blanche Flour, who appears in the latter allegorical narratives, is to be found in Celtic Romance as the mother of Tristram, Tristram being an impersonification of the schismatic system of the Druids of Cornwall— the whole Allegory being satisfactorily decyphered by Davies in his Book called Druidical Remains."

If the curious reader cares to pursue the question, and has access to an old library, he will find that Dr. Davies interprets the well-known story of Tristram and Iseult in the most proper manner. "Tristram," according to him, means "proclaimer," and "Iseult" is "something covered" or "secret." Hence, the fair wife of King Mark was, of course, a new religion of which the gallant knight was the first high-priest.

Frere was unable to find in Milton anything "which appeared to exhibit the traces of a secret doctrine." Presumably, he did not extend his researches to Shakespeare, or we might have had another variety of the Great

Cryptogram.   He begs Rossetti to set aside twenty copies of his book, and to send two of them to Southey and one to Coleridge.   " In this Island, upon so delicate a subject, I do not even venture, nor indeed do I think it fair, to bring such subjects into discussion—the few copies of your Dante which are to be found in Italy are borrowed and pass from hand to hand till they are almost worn to pieces with constant reading."

This letter drew an answer from Rossetti, which, as his son observes, " contains matter adapted to surprise British readers."   The book on which he was engaged was at first intended as a second volume or sequel of " Lo Spirito Antipapale."   It ultimately became " Il Mistero dell' Amor Platonico del Medio Evo derivato da' Misteri Antichi."   As we shall see, it was never published, although it was printed, and thus we have no opportunity of judging of the contents for ourselves.   Mr. William Rossetti is of opinion that " the innermost arcanum indicated (but not manifestly set forth) in that book is that the writers of whom it treats did not believe in any Supreme Deity at all, but regarded Man as his own sole Deity."

5th September, 1832.

" My very dear Sir and Friend,

" . . . As to what my discovery really consists in, you will find it in a private MS. which I will send you under precaution.   If it were lost on the way, I should be little concerned ; if you were to put it in the fire, I should mind still less.   Born as I was and brought up in a most pious family, religion is to me a cherished senti- ment ; and I was distressed when the sight of my mind, without connivance of the will, led me on to that which I should have wished never to see."

One is reminded of the neophyte who raised the devil

and was unable to dismiss him. Rossetti then shows that his patron was mistaken in thinking that Milton was not one of " the sect."

" You, who know the *Paradise Lost* as I do the *Divina Commedia*, you with the eagle eye, can turn it to those male and female angels who eat and marry, to that mysterious Limbo, and other (of) the like. What is the name given in the Sect to him who conducts the neophyte in the grade *Ne plus ultra*, to discover the 'Lost Word' or 'Lost Parable'? And what is that word? You know it— it is the Verbum—it is I.N.R.I., which is explained in two ways. And by means of whom is the Verbum discovered? By means of Raphael, the 'illuminator of the blind.' And who indicates to Adam the future Verbum? All the doctrine of Milton, and the disposal of his canvas—all is in the catechisms of the sect; and I can prove even to indisputable evidence, that Cromwell was the head and regulator of it in his period— that he was the Christ who was to found the New Jerusalem, announced to be so near at hand; wherefrom arose all that hypocrisy both in England and on the Continent, all the mystic language controlled by that man of craft. And was not Milton the Protector's private secretary? . . . I am here writing to a man of whom one can say '*Sapienti pauca.*' If he cautions me ' Don't touch Milton, because, if you prove badly, you will be derided, and if well, you will be persecuted, and in whatever case you will be blameable,' I bow my head to the sage, and say that I myself was meaning to adopt that course."

All this was too much for Frere's credulity, and he replied on October 11th :—

" . . . I am sorry to think that your researches should have led you to conclusions which I do not think can be fairly founded upon them. You may find secret science interwoven with everything ; older almost than everything. What then ? I am afraid that you think me more learned upon these points than I really am. . . . The existence of the Antipodes—the Copernican system—were truths which at their first promulgation unhinged and disturbed many minds, and perhaps those of the discoverers among the rest. If this is the case with you, I trust the effect will be transient."

Nevertheless, in his next letter, dated January 11th 1833, Frere is again hankering after occult matters. He quotes a passage from Erasmus to the effect that " in *that Tragedy* [the Reformation] he was aware of the influence of a secret agency distinct and separate from that of the well-known authors and leaders of the Reform," and begs Rossetti to favour him with his interpretation of the characters of Theseus and Creon and the King of Thrace in the story of " Palamon and Arcite."

By some means Rossetti possessed himself of " some most interesting books of Masonry, and others of the 16th and 15th centuries, which reveal the secrets of the Sect of Love." " I frankly confess," he writes to Frere, " that I repent of having plunged into water so deep and dangerous ; my conscience has sustained a severe shock. To recover it from the trial, I have had to revert to matters of religion, which shall not cease to be my guide for the rest of my life. And so I resolved to suspend for a while the previous discussions, and to publish my *Psalmody*."

This was a poem, " Iddio e l'Uomo," which Rossetti published in 1883, and dedicated to Frere. He naïvely assures his patron that he need not scruple to accept the dedication, since "some English men of letters" had advised that the poem should be inscribed either to the Archbishop of Canterbury or to the Bishop of London.

But he could not leave the forbidden subject. "Were I to tell you all that I have lately discovered, so as to impose silence on the wordy disbelievers of my discoveries, I should astound you. I have in my hands petitions from Inquisitors to the Pope, begging him to extend their powers, as they had found out that the poets, in their fiction of love-affairs, concealed a different meaning. I have historical facts of persons imprisoned by the Holy Office in the 16th century for having revealed the keys of the conventional diction in which many books were written. And other and yet other things which I leave unsaid. But, as you have remarked, whatever may be the efforts I make and the force of documents and reasonings, it will always be impossible to convert the bigwigs of Dantism and Petrarchism."

Even the composition of religious poetry did not succeed in calming Rossetti's mind. He writes again on April 3rd, 1883 :—

". . . I will tell you candidly, my dear Sir, that that subject-matter is of incalculable peril; and this has troubled my mind, and has made less hard to me the inveterate and unjust objections which were made against me. The explanation of the mysteries, made according to the doctrines of the Sect, is of such dangerous beguilement that it may be termed the greatest blow which can ever be dealt at religion. The trying dilemma in which I find myself is this : if I choose to make the full demonstration of my theory, so as to impose silence on my gainsayers, I shall *appear* impious, and shall *be* harmful;

if I choose to state the matter with prudence and by halves, I shall always give an opportunity to the ill-offices of adversaries. In this hard case, it is better to abide the assault and be silent. Even in your eyes I shall perhaps be a bad man, or at least an anti-religious one, if I impart to you some of my interpretations: what then is to be done? Consign so much labour to the fire! At times I have been tempted to this, but as yet have not had the courage to do it."

Favourable notices of his "Spirito Antipapale," and encouragements to proceed with his work, poured on Rossetti from his own countrymen. Count Ugoni prophesied that he would, one day, "be cited as a phenomenon in literary history." But the sale of the work did not progress rapidly, only two hundred copies being sold out of five hundred.

Frere wrote on June 8th, thoroughly sympathising with Rossetti's difficulties, and affirming the strength of his own religious convictions. "In an infinite system, it is impossible for a finite understanding to affirm of any two points that they are opposite and contradictory. This I conceive is as true in Metaphysics as any Theorem in Mathematics, and this is the true answer to good people whose faith is shaken because they are unable to trace Kangaroos from Noah's Ark to New South Wales."

Three weeks later he wrote a letter of good advice, which, as it extends over four large sheets, is too long to be given in full. It is certainly among the most charming that he ever wrote.

" PIETA, June 29, 1833.

"MY DEAR ROSETTI,—

"I ought before this time to have acknowledged the receipt and perusal of your enlarged Edition, but the fact is that the microscopic beauty of your writing and the weakness of my own eyes at the time made me defer it, till I found them strong enough to go through the whole at a single effort. . . . The perusal of this proposed Edition, and the information which you give me of the exhortations received from your literary correspondents, suggest to me many more serious and anxious reflections. They are telling you ' Your work is making a great noise—you will be attacked and confound your opponents—and when you are dead, in some Biographical Dictionary under the Letter R there will be a long Article vindicating your memory. Don't trouble yourself with the prospect of persecution and opposition. Was there ever a man more opposed and persecuted than Tasso was? And what do we see now ? Has he not got a great staring Bust in an ugly Temple in the public Garden, which is the daily resort of all the Dandies and Elegantes in Naples?' This is the glorious prospect which your literary friends and advisers exhort you to entertain.

" It reminds me of a story which was told me at Lisbon. A Jew was going to be burnt, and the Rabble of boys were very anxious to see him burnt alive, and proportionably apprehensive lest he should disappoint them by recanting. They therefore followed and encouraged him with shouts of ' Sta fermo, Mose !   Sta fermo, Mose !' You can reckon at least half a dozen voices all unanimously shouting out to you ' *Sta fermo, Mose !* '

" But all these speculations are foreign to your actual situation. If you were in Italy indeed, I have no doubt that the Duke of Modena would be willing to accommodate you with a Dungeon ; which, after you had consecrated it by making it, for twenty years, the abode of persecuted Genius, would in future Ages be visited by sympathetic Tourists ; and an Album would be kept there, in which they would each deposit their extempore effusions, composed beforehand at the Inn—moreover, independent of this glorious posthumous prospect, your period of captivity would in the mean while be soothed by hearing the known voices of literary friends occasionally shouting ' Sta fermo ! ' under your window. Or you might have a tomb like that of Dante at Ravenna, the resort of poetical and literary pilgrims—observe how magnificently I treat you ! For my own part, I should not care to have a tomb, where people should come to evacuate their bad verses—any other pollution would be more tolerable. But this a matter of taste— to return to the subject.

"If such are your aspirations, in conformity with the exhortations of your Sta-fermo friends, the proper scene for them is in Italy; there you may excite a ferment, attract persecution, and acquire celebrity. In England people are too busy to trouble their heads about speculative matters, and when it is once understood that these speculations are of a kind likely to prove dangerous to Society, Society, having other things to think of, contents herself with avoiding all notice of the Work or of the Author. . . .

"If I had known you at Naples, my dear Rosetti, and had conceived for you at that time, the same esteem and regard that I have since entertained, I should have warned you against being hurried away by the applauses and acclamations by which you were then surrounded, which the zealots of party, indifferent to your future safety and happiness, and anxious to add to their political Martyrology a name already eminent in literature, urged you on to the sacrifice of all your early hopes and prospects. But then, at least, you might have been actuated by patriotic hopes and illusions. . . . But now—in the name of Heaven— for what are you called upon to sacrifice yourself finally and irretrievably?

"When you were going to England I warned you by the example of Foscolo. But, believe me, the abandonment in which Foscolo found himself would be nothing, compared to that which you would experience ; if it could be said of you that you were the Author of a "*dangerous work.*" What could your friends do for you ? I cannot easily believe that you have many friends more warmly interested for you than I am. But, how could I deny that work was dangerous, when the perusal of it would convict me of a Falsehood? or would it be in my power to persuade any man that the Author of a dangerous Work might nevertheless be a safe instructor for his family ? . . . .

"I do not know what course you may have taken, and if you should have determined to bring these matters into discussion, I might find myself indirectly contributing to the service of infidelity, if you should in the mean time have become irrecoverably bound to it,—the publication of your enlarged Edition would have so bound you,—and in that case, the dedication prefixed to the Salterio * would have marked me to all the World, either as a hypocrite, who encouraged opinions which he had not the spirit to avow openly; or as an imbecile old dupe blinded by cajolery, and unable to detect an intention which was now manifest to all the World. Others might think perhaps that a great honour was done me in having my name illuminated by a conflagration of which a man of your genius was the Incendiary—but it is an honour which I am happy to have escaped, at least for the present.

"There are many things, my dear Rosetti, which induce me to fear the worst for you. Your openness to adulation such as that of Count Segovi—(which my sister when

* *Iddio ed l'Uomo.*

she saw it, said it (*sic*) was an affront to your under-standing) and which is just a repetition of the same sort of encouragement which induced you to put yourself forward at Naples. 'They are persuading him,' she said, 'to go forward and set fire to a Mine.' The influence of your brother Exiles—I judge them whether justly or no from a sample or two I have seen here; a young man came as a refugee, he had been obliged to leave Naples, he said, having renounced the Cath? Religion. 'What religion then do you now profess?' '*Sono del Methodo.*' As he did not look at all like one of our Methodists, I enquired what the Methodo meant? When I was told in a confidential tone '*Sono Carbonari.*' About six weeks before I had seen another, precisely of the same description. That you should associate with your brothers in Exile is natural—even the satisfaction of hearing your native language spoken is an inducement—and though they may not be so far advanced in their philosophic views as the young gentlemen of the Methodo, yet it is not to be imagined that they will advise you to maintain a self-denying silence upon subjects *sacro digno silentio*, they would rather encourage you to go forward and set fire to the Mine. . . . . .

"The Gentile dispensation is essentially exoteric, and the exception proves the Rule; the Apocalypse is appointed to remain sealed to the time of the end. At this time of the end, many of the harmonies of the antient and primitive world, now prohibited to profane and impious curiosity, will be developed and revealed, but in the mean time it is an inexpiable crime to attempt to break open the sanctuary in which they are concealed, with Engines borrowed from the Magazines of profane learning. That you may avoid this guilt, and live to behold this consummation which (according to the opinions of the best and most learned Christians) is not far distant is the sincere wish of

> "Your very sincere friend,
>
> "J. H. FRERE."

Thus ends a letter, the writing of which must have been a great labour to Frere, who confesses that "the posture of writing (at least of writing legibly) is so intolerable to me." Rossetti cannot have received it when he wrote again, at great length, on July 1, 1833, to prove that "Petrarca was a sectary and not a lover." "There is his averment that his *Bucolics* contain the same matter (expressed in metaphors) as his *Literæ sine Titulo* which set forth manifestly his indignation against the papal court; and his *Bucolics* speak of his love for Laura, just as the *Canzoniere* does. Whence it can be gathered that the *Canzoniere* itself contains anti-papal philippics expressed in the conventional diction. The first solemn canzone 'Nel dolce tempo della prima etate' depicts in fact the seven sectarian grades in Petrarca's seven transformations; and his first transformation is that in which he changes into a laurel."

The uninstructed reader can but echo Rossetti's own exclamation at the close of his letter—"A most curious thing!" He condescends to the level of middle earth in the last sentences : " In this favoured island, peace is partly restored, for the vertigo of Reform seems to be dissipated from many minds. Pray Heaven it may cease altogether! The fear of influenza has made many persons flee the city."

On July 30th he writes :—"Would to God that the admirable political system of this country, which I pro-pound as the sole exemplar of the best, could become the system of my country and of all Europe! This is, in sub-stance, the supreme desire which the *Salterio* expresses ;

nor will as much, certainly, be contradicted by you. This is not an impulse excited in me by anarchical instigators, with whom I have no relations, but the spontaneous impulse of a heart which mourns over the fate of my unhappy country."

The length of his previous letter to Rossetti had prevented Frere from writing to any other correspondent by the same mail, and on July 31st he had time to say little more than : " Pray think well and consult with conscientious men and with your own conscience before you venture on the irretrievable step of revealing one of the two great antagonist mysteries. My firm conviction and apprehension is that it will be ruinous to your fortune and future peace of mind. You shall suffer no pecuniary loss by what you suppress. I have not time to say more, but may God guide you and preserve you from becoming the instrument of evil."

Frere's next letter to Rossetti is dated October 4th, when he once more filled four sheets with his fine, tremulous writing. His chief object was to dissuade Rossetti from preparing a corrected and enlarged edition of his " Spirito Antipapale," on the grounds that those readers who were not already convinced would not be influenced by additional proofs and illustrations, and that subscribers to the first edition would have a right to be aggrieved.

" But perhaps . . . it may be your intention to make a similar alteration in the character of your prose work, overlooking all the literary and bibliopolic calculations with a view to those higher duties which the Author of the ' Giovane Italia ' so strongly inculcates as peculiarly incumbent upon all the Italian Literati at the present moment.

If this is the case, the very passages to which I should object must be the same for the sake of which the enlarged Edition is to be printed. I say 'is to be printed,' for that it will be printed I feel quite sure. I am not able to engage you to forbearance by outbidding the golden dreams of an anticipated party triumph, nor eloquent enough to persuade you. But the Truth may speak for itself; and it is a truth which all history attests, that Poets engaging in politics are commonly treated with levity (you to be sure are an exception) by their opponents, but at the same time (and in this you are not likely to be an exception, nor can I find any instance of an exception) they are uniformly and invariably the dupes of their own associates. Milton was the only man of equal political demerit who escaped unhanged at the Restoration. He was the only man of equal zeal and eminence who was unrewarded during the Commonwealth and under Cromwell. Dryden was miserably rewarded by his own party while they were in power, but upon their downfall was kindly treated by their enemies and by his own. To explain why this should be, and always must be the case, would require a discussion as long as a Chapter in Montaigne—the Reason of it lies at the very root of our social nature. And if you can solve the Problem for yourself, the result may perhaps (as I should wish it to do) remain more deeply impressed upon your mind. . . ."

"Since writing the above I have read for the 10th time your Letter of the 30 of July which by-the-by came by the last Packet. And I observe in it that you say that you have no connection *relazione nessuna* with the present Frantic political sectaries. This declaration of yours, if it had struck me before, might have saved me the trouble of writing, and you of reading, the greater part of my 2nd sheet. . . ."

He then urges Rossetti to write a new book, instead of wasting time over "enlarged editions."

"The Precept so frequently repeated in the French Cookery Books is applicable to Literature — 'Servez Chaud!' An *Artiste* who aspires to fame and popularity will never allow his omelette to grow cold upon the table. He never thinks of 2nd Editions of the same dish; but serves up fresh ones 'Hot and Hot' as our own Cooks say. . . .

"By-the-by, what strange work some of your country-men are making: I do not mean politically, but poetically; I have just seen Signor Pellico's Tragedies. He seems to think that the language of tragedy ought to be something quite different from natural speech, and that all vernacular phrases must be subjected to an artificial transformation before they are fit for an heroic Character. So that his sentences look like King Joseph's Mules, when the Muleteers out of spite, harnessed them each in the wrong place. All his words seem to be out of their place, restive and fighting, Yet I am told that he is popular, popular in the Country of Berni! Cannot you do anything to set them right, either by precept or example?

"Adieu my dear Rosetti! I have not said a 10th part of what I had to say; but writing is so irksome to me, that I would rather have gone 50 miles for the sake of seeing you for ten minutes than have gone through the fatigue of this scrawl."

Poor Rossetti wrote back in great distress, on October 31st, to disclaim any connection with Mazzini's celebrated journal:—

"I don't know why you speak to me of the *Giovane Italia*, which I never read; that political tinge which appears in my poem is derived from the British Constitution, and not from the *Giovane Italia*.   I introduced almost all of it when I was doing the work in Malta, long before the *Giovane Italia* existed; I could show you the old MS. What Englishman could reject those sentiments, whatever be the party he belongs to? . . . I repeat to you, and I confirm it by solemn oath, that I am not in political relations with any one, whether on the Continent or in England. What I have written is the outcome of my investigations on Dante; and it is the result of chance that I have lapsed into these blessed politics which now infect the world."

The conclusion of this letter refers to Frere's offer to pay over to Rossetti the sum of £50 at Christmas time. Rossetti points out that he has some work, and the prospect of more, and that "in the decent mediocrity in which I and family live there still remains to me a residue of your liberality and of my industry. . . . Let me respectfully ask you not to incur further expense for me."

The eagerness of Rossetti and Frere to detect allusions to "the Sect" in everything they read, reminds the modern reader of the spirit in which a certain class of mythologists will trace 'Dawn myths' in Malory's Morte Arthur or the nursery rhyme of Jack and Jill.   Frere writes on February 14th, 1834 :—

"Did I ever tell you an odd coincidence? Ld. Herbert of Cherbury, the earliest of our Deistical writers, is represented *asleep in a Wood* in a picture, from which a print is prefixed to his Memoirs published by Walpole."

On March 31st Rossetti replies: "Very curious what you tell me about Lord Herbert, known as a free-thought writer, who is represented sleeping in a wood, the customary fiction of Dante, Francesco, Colonna and others.

One of the most singular books I have read in this line is the *Pilgrim's Progress*, which is here accounted a production of an eminently christian spirit. It is a true duplicate of Dante's *Commedia*, and is confessed as such by the author himself in his preface to Parts 1 and 2. Dante begins the course of his grades with the Eagle (*i.e.* St. John) which introduces him to the Mysteries. And thus does that Pilgrim—he begins with St. John. Dante had recourse to that shift to avoid persecution, and the author of the *Pilgrim* did the like. But his book, like Dante's, is almost sanctified by common opinion, and one should not speak about it at all. How many masked sphinxes in the literary world! I have come upon so many that it is a true marvel."

It would be difficult to conceive the feelings of the Bedfordshire tinker and the Florentine noble, had they been aware that such parallels would be drawn between them. But how is one to understand the following passage in a letter from Rossetti dated June 1st? Did Victor Hugo actually possess a sense of humour, in spite of all that has been said to the contrary? or was his a similar case to that of Monsieur Jourdain?

"Even in our own days similar works are produced, *mirabile dictu*! Besides *The Epicurean* of Thomas Moore, published in London in 1826, there came out in Paris in 1831 *Notre Dame de Paris* by Victor Hugo, which is one of the most ingenious and interesting that I have ever read of the same class. All people are plunging most eagerly into the reading of it, and how few there are who understand it! I knew here in London a friend of Victor Hugo; I told him that I comprehended the inner spirit of that romance, and could likewise make others comprehend it, and that this I could do, not by knowledge communicated to me, but by my own sole cogitation—but that I should carefully avoid doing that. When he returned to Paris, he related to Hugo what I had said, and gave him my *Spirito Antipapale* to read. And the French author, in returning the book, asked him to congratulate me upon it, adding that he was not surprised at my understanding the inner sense of his romance. . . ."

". . . My friend Charles Lyell * has translated into English verse the Lyrical Poems of Dante. . . . It is all founded on my system of interpretation, as stated in the Preface and the Notes. He has requested me to conclude his volume with a dissertation on Platonic Love, some hundred pages long ; and I could not refuse so noble and generous a friend, to whom I have many obligations. The voice of gratitude is to me a sort of irresistible command. Have no fear that I should say *much*—I will be most prudent. At every line I write, I will fancy that you are at my shoulder ; and when I seem to feel a tap of yours on my pate, I shall at once cancel or modify. . . . I will at last unmask the old fox Petrarca ; and when the mask falls, you will perceive the Platonic lover disappearing, and the Patarin sectary coming out."

By the time of Rossetti's next letter (Feb. 1st, 1836) the "hundred pages" have swelled into "two volumes, quite long." "I owe so much to that Scotch gentleman, in whom I know not whether prudence or learning or generosity is uppermost, that I could not resist his desire, although I had laid aside the idea of any such publication."

At the close of this letter, he gives us a glimpse of his domestic troubles. Some years previously he had been married to the daughter of Gaetano Polidori, with whose calm regular features, framed in the widow's cap, her son's

* Of Kinnordy, Forfarshire.

drawing has made us familiar. She was now reduced to a skeleton by a long illness. Hopes were entertained of her ultimate recovery, but in the meantime she was obliged to remain with her mother in the country, and the care of four infant children was added to Rossetti's other labours and anxieties. A timely gift of £50 from Frere enabled him to defray the expenses of her illness, and he toiled doggedly at his work. On the last day of February 1836 he sent "the first printed sheets, going on to the middle of Volume I." for Frere's approval.

Mr. William Rossetti thus explains "the sectarian omen" to which Frere alludes in his next letter. "Many of the writers classed by Rossetti as members of a secret sect (Dante, Petrarca, etc.), date some of their most important transactions as occurring on Good Friday"—as, for instance, Dante's vision of the three beasts in the wood. Frere confuses Mr. Lyell with his famous son and namesake whose "Principles of Geology" had recently been published.

"MALTA, *April 6th*, 1836.

"Your work by a singular coincidence reached me on Good Friday : shall I confess that I felt annoyed at the sectarian Omen ? I was so, and posponed the reading of it till the day before yesterday. What, in the midst of many interuptions, I have been able to read hitherto (about 140 Pages) has filled me with alarm and astonishment ; I feel convinced that of those who read what I have been reading, those who draw any conclusion at all (or at least 99 out of 100 of them) will be led to this short inference, that all religions are alike, all equally the result of human policy and contrivance, according to the words of the vulgar old infidel song—

> "Religion's a politic trick
> Devised to keep Blockheads in Awe."

"What I have read hitherto appears to be an illustrative comment upon this noble and elegant text.

"Admire, my dear Rosetti, the majestic energy and brevity of the English character and language, which comprises in a couple of Lines the enunciation of a proposition which your Petrarchs and Dantes are obliged to develop bit by bit in hundreds of Cantos and Cartloads of Commentaries.

"But seriously, my dear Rosetti, for never in my life, when feeling for another, did I feel more seriously and deeply than at this moment,—consider in what times we are living; upon the very verge of the first Christian dispensation, on the eve of those times in which it has been predicted that faith should not be found upon earth. . . .

"For myself I must say that sixteen years ago events were predicted to me by a student of prophecy (my own brother *) which at that time appeared to me, humanly speaking, impossible; and which at the present day appear, humanly speaking, inevitable. You, my dear Rosetti, according to [the] course of nature, may live, and probably will live to witness some stupendous development demonstrating that those systems which your readers had been taught by you to consider as branches of the same, were essentially the forms of two Antagonist principles. Figure to yourself what will be your feelings of horror, if the events which you may live to witness should enforce that conviction upon your mind.

"My dear Rosetti, I am afraid of appearing to act towards you with a tone of harsh and ungracious generosity. But you tell me you are writing more for the sake of your family than from any other inducement.

* Hatley Frere.

If this is the only temptation which besets you, it is one from which I should consider it an act of the strictest conscientious duty to deliver you. You have fame enough, and you are not very greedy of it, and from considerations of utility and interest, it is possible for a man to have too much Fame as well as too little. There remains therefore the simple question of profit; and if after a strict and conscientious examination you should think it better to forbear from publishing, let me know your estimate of the profit which you anticipate, and I will take care that you shall be no great loser by your forbearance. . . .

" Mr. Lyell's name brings back to my mind that stunning discovery of his. The only conclusion which it admits is one which singular as it may seem I feel compelled to adopt—that in the two opposite hemispheres of the *spiritual* world there are vast undiscovered tracts. . . ."

Rossetti replied to this letter by pointing out that Cudworth, a clergyman of the Church of England, had anticipated some of his conclusions in a work entitled "The Intellectual System," published in 1678. He also pleaded that his MS. had been read " by my aged Father-in-law, an extremely prudent man, no less than well read and of high character," and by " an English churchman, Mr. Keightley, a religious and erudite man, author of various accredited books," who both gave it their approval.

Three months later (August 1st, 1836) he gives us a glimpse of the poet whose fame was to eclipse his own, and of that poet's future biographer :

" During this past season I have had a sufficiency of employment, and I thank God for giving me the means of maintaining my family, and educating my two boys, who are now biggish—one of them eight years old, the other nearly seven. They have a decided inclination for study; they recite Shakespear with an energy to astonish the hearer, and they have that author constantly in their hands. The elder is already studying Latin and (a rare thing) with pleasure."

There is a gap in the correspondence at this date. Rossetti's reputation was gradually increasing both abroad and at home, and his talents and industry won him respect even among those who could not agree with his theories. In this class was Bunsen, who wrote to Frere from Rome :—

" Rossetti's book [which] I received from your kindness, is ingenious but not true. He has overshoot (*sic*) the mark. Dante was a precursor of the Reformers, but in another way."

Literary reputation is not enough of itself to support a family, and the struggle for existence was still hard to the little household in Charlotte Street. When Rossetti wrote again to Frere, on March 1st, 1839, he was obliged to confess :

" In health we are not lacking ; but it is now two years (and I can't conjecture the cause) that I have had little to do. Public regard for me has increased, and I have gratifying proofs of it ; but the work and the profit have diminished, and of this I have very sad evidence. Also there was a robbery in my house, by a carpenter, about £40, as you may have seen in the newspapers ; and by three insolvencies of schools I have lost upwards of £100."

It is evident from another letter that Frere assisted

Rossetti at this crisis, and there soon appeared a hope of better days. "Amore Platonico" was still growing, in spite of Frere's dissuasions. By this time it had expanded into "three solid volumes." Rossetti was uncertain whether it should be published, or whether it should go into the keeping of some men of learning alone, without ever being on the counter of any bookseller." He was less desirous than of old to avoid giving scandal, since Rome had placed his sacred poem "in which there is nothing that does not breathe the love of God and man" in the Index of Prohibited Books. Frere evidently wished to know something of Charles Lyell, who had been originally responsible for the undertaking, as one of Rossetti's letters gives a long account of the Scotchman, with whom he had corresponded for more than two years before they met in London. "He held at the baptismal font my first son, named Gabriel Dante Charles ; the last name comes from his godfather. . . . He is cited by all who know him as a true model of the Scottish gentleman ; such, in short, that I count him worthy of your friendship. . . . He knows a great variety of things, but in Italian literature he is really deep."

In the October of 1839, Rossetti wrote with mingled pride and indignation that "the Jesuits in Rome have undertaken to confute my *Spirito Antipapale* in a series of academical discourses which they read in public, with a concourse of prelates and other people, and even of Cardinals to the number of five or six at a time." Readers of our own day will at once recall several books which attained phenomenal popularity through the assistance of eminent and well-meaning divines, who solemnly warned the public against such objectionable literature. Of course the result of these Roman lectures was to determine nearly every one of the hearers to procure a copy of the "Spirito Antipapale," and of every other book by the same author. Rossetti bewailed his fate. "Whose the fault? I was expelled from Italy without solid reason, and merely because I wrote constitutional poems *after* the King of Naples had conceded liberty of the press—liberty which I never transgressed or exceeded. Had they allowed me to remain out there, this present indignation would not have arisen, for I should never have written the books which I have published here." His doom was to please neither side. Frere wrote back on November 29th, "I am amused with what you told me of Jesuit Lectures at Rome. On the other hand here is an impudent *giovane-Italia*-sort-of-a-fellow, one Zaccheroni, who is abusing you in a preface for degrading Dante as he says."

By the beginning of 1840, matters came to a crisis with the "Amore Platonico." Frere entreated Rossetti to let him buy the whole edition, that it might do no harm to public morals. Rossetti in his reply pointed out that he had been goaded into writing this objectionable work through the unjustifiable attacks made upon him by critics at home and abroad. Charles Lyell, who had been put to great expense over it, was naturally anxious that it should not be destroyed. Rossetti pleaded that he might be allowed to finish printing the whole, and then, after consigning a hundred copies to Lyell, he proposed to send the remainder to Frere. "I have not the courage (according to a phrase of Petrarca's) to burn with my own hands a beloved offspring that costs me so much pain; and, if *you* would lend yourself to this necessary office (excuse my boldness) I would despatch to you the remaining edition. Whether Neptune or Vulcan be the devourer of my vigils, I shall not see it, but I will endure it. However this may be, I will never put on sale, either here or elsewhere, a writing of such a quality." *

A modern writer has lately told us how he suffered, when condemned by his publisher either to expurgate or to suppress his greatest work, because of the respect that is supposed to be due to the morals of the Young Person. He alone could adequately sympathise with Rossetti, whose succeeding letters are full of the proposed sacrifice. In the mean time, the German men of letters were beginning to awake to the merits of the *Spirito Antipapale*. Dr. Joseph Mendelssohn explained the new system of interpreting Dante to select audiences at Berlin, and, not content with this, published his lectures and sent a copy to Rossetti. As Frere said, " between the Jesuits on the one hand, and the Germans on the other," the book was " fairly afloat."

The expenses of printing " Amore Platonico," according to Rossetti, would amount to £130. Frere, who knew by experience how expenses of this sort accumulate, sent a draft on Messrs. Hoare for £150, and must have sincerely hoped that he should hear no more of the book. However, on August 16th, 1841, Rossetti was forced to own that there was still £35 owing to the printer ; and a few weeks later, came a letter from Charles Lyell, who had generously agreed to retain only fifty copies of the " Amore Platonico " for private distribution among his friends. Frere showed his sense of this kindness by sending him, through Rossetti, a copy of the translations from Aristophanes, which, being unpublished until after Frere's death, were not easily to be obtained. Lyell evidently thought that the highest praise he could bestow upon the book was to describe how it had delighted " my son the geologist," " who

---

* The great mass of copies of the " Amore Platonico " remained in Rossetti's possession and were burnt at his death.

feasted upon it here, last Christmas, with the Greek text beside him."

He confessed that he was sorely exercised about " Amore Platonico," "a work which seemed as if it never would end, and which I heartily wish had never been begun. In a mere literary view it is most ingenious, learned, and valuable, but in the conclusion that *must* be drawn from it, in spite of all Rossetti's disguise, is hateful. I am convinced, however, that it cannot be mischievous to the world at large, as it will not only be very little read, but never by those who are of an age to have fixt religious opinions. As regards himself it is most injudicious, and might be ruinous; for (as I long since told him) an enemy could make it a bolt to shut the door of every ladies-school against him, as a teacher, and thus deprive him of bread. The work however is printed, and owing to me, and gives me much to answer for; but I esteem Rossetti, and should grieve that after eight years' labour it were not of some profit to him. What then is to be done? He is half distracted, and implores me to write to you, and entreat you to revoke the order which condemns his book to the flames. I most cordially do so. He pledges himself not to sell a copy in England, and with that I am satisfied; and as he has already sent nine copies to La giovane Italia, I give consent to his dividing the remainder between her and La jeune France. Where should we stop if we sentenced all that is *bad* to fire and faggot? Would the ' Divine Legation of Moses,' * Middleton's ' Inquiry,' or Milman's ' Hist. of Xty.' (all noble works) escape? Then pray spare poor Rossetti:

> ' E s'ella per mio prego gli perdona,
>   Fa che gli annunzj in bel sembiante pace.' "

* By Bishop Warburton.

Frere's answer to this is not forthcoming, but by the October of the same year, Rossetti had sent twenty copies of his work to Italy, and two to Germany. To divert his mind from this painful subject, he was composing " a little poem on the cholera morbus," and his children were already a great solace to him. The eldest had for some time shown his talent for painting, and, at the age of thirteen, he did " nothing but invent groups and designs." " Not wanting to thwart his inclination," wrote the proud father, " I have started him on pursuing the profession he covets. If he succeeds, he will aid my old age. A hundred times do I thank God that my four children are all studious and all good. If I can leave them a good education, leading them on to an honourable path in life, I shall die contented in the fogs of England, without regretting the sun of Italy."

There is now an interval of nearly three years in the correspondence. Frere was growing very old, and was more averse than ever to holding a pen, and Rossetti was seized with a dangerous illness. Charles Lyell writes to Frere on August 29th, 1843 :—

" Poor Rossetti has been in imminent danger since February last from a pulmonary affection. He has put himself into the hands of a Paris physician, and boards with him. On Aug. 7th he was well enough to write cheerily, and said that the fever was subdued, the pain diminished and there were other symptoms of amendment. He even hoped he might not be obliged to winter at Marseilles. His excellent wife (a daughter of G. Polidori) is with him. The London physicians thought his case very desperate."

Perhaps it was this description of Rossetti's plight that induced Frere to send him the help acknowledged in the following letter. To judge from the opening sentences, the poet had thought or imagined some coolness between himself and his patron :—

3 *July,* 1844.

" Dear and revered Sir,

"I should not have waited so long without writing to you, and would not have taken as the opportunity a new beneficence of your's, if I had not been apprehensive that my letters were no longer acceptable to you, as at one time they were. . . .

"If you are not conscious how much I owe to you, I will tell you with a greatly touched heart. I owe you my life, for God ordained you to be the means of preserving it, for the good of my family, whose education I hope to complete. If I had not had in reserve £100 and upwards which I owed to your liberality, I should certainly have died. Without such a sum I could not have quitted my business affairs for more than eight months, could not have got change of air, first at Hastings, and afterwards in France, could not in short have done what was prescribed by Doctors for endeavouring to re-establish my decayed health. . . . God grant that the £42 which you have so opportunely sent me may count for 42 years added to those which Providence had allotted to your life of generosity ! . . .

"You should know, my very dear Sir, that, barely re-covered from a long and obstinate diabetes which wore me down during about four years, I was in the best of spirits, and with doubled ardour was again working in my laborious profession. . . . Thus opened for me the year 1843, with favourable prospects, as I had a great deal to do ; when on the 17th of February (a day truly inauspicious) I was attacked by an influenza of no little severity. I did not choose to relinquish my work, and continued going about and teaching, reading and writing, without an interval ;

and soon the illness continually increasing assumed a horrid character of consumptive bronchitis."

Rossetti then describes his sufferings, and dwells fondly upon the devotion of his wife, who never left him for a single instant.

"Many a time was I tempted to write to you, but was always restrained by the fear which I have above expressed to you, and also by the idea that a narrative of my misfortunes might be taken by you as an importunate request. Pardon me, Sir. . . . .

"I was advancing towards a cure with a favourable con-valescence, when (most grievous disaster) in mid October one of my eyes was totally darkened ; a fatal consequence of the long and painful illness from which no one had believed I should ever recover. In the evening I had excellent eyes, and in the morning I found myself with one eye absolutely blind! Without external or internal pain, without the slightest visible sign of decay, my right eye was in an instant eclipsed. For three or four months I remained in a tremor for the other ; but then, thanks to God, it regained strength, and I now read, write, walk, teach, do anything—and if it continues thus, I shall resign myself to the will of Him who gives and withdraws the light. . . .

"I may render thanks to the Giver of all good for having bestowed on me four excellent children, full of health and talent, educated by their mother in the principles of religion and honour. They all four know four languages, and speak them with facility, and write them correctly—their own native language, Italian, French, and German ; the two boys know also Latin and Greek. My elder daughter *

* Maria Francesca Rossetti, author of "A Shadow of Dante."

too knows a little Greek: and possesses so much information—historical, geographical, and of all sorts—that I view her with envy and shame. My elder son, who studies painting as his own choice, in which he progresses well so as to give promise of a good artist, has uncommon poetic genius. At the age of only 13 he composed an English poem in various parts, which his Grandfather, Signor Polidori, has thought fit to print. . . ."

Mr. William Rossetti explains this poem to have been "Sir Hugh the Heron," and is of opinion that fatherly partiality has exaggerated the four children's knowledge of German.   The mention of English as "their own native language" is curious, and shows how entirely Rossetti felt himself to be cut off from that country for whom he had dreamed and sung and toiled in his youth.

In spite of his illness, Rossetti had found time to bring out a second edition of his *Salterio*, the first edition having long been exhausted. His unlucky "Amore Platonico" was still a source of trouble. "A gratuitous enemy who by the manoeuvring of Lord Brougham poses here as a man of learning and has been made Librarian of the British Library," had attacked Rossetti on the subject in "an insulting article in a Review."   Rossetti had made no reply, and refused to sell a single copy of the book to any applicant. Mr. Lyell had been guilty of publishing an Analysis of Dante's "Vita Nuova" and "Convito."   "He has aimed at confuting my system of interpreting the works of Dante—which, truth to tell, seems to me a little odd." Rossetti pours out to Frere his grievances against Mr. Lyell, who had urged him to write the "Amore Platonico," and then drawn back when two-thirds of ıthe printing was completed, who had disturbed him in the midst of collecting his Lyrical Poems to write a monograph on *La Beatrice di Dante*, and when the printing had begun left him to finish it at his own cost. Those who have seen how the "Amore Platonico," which was originally intended to fill a hundred pages, finally stretched into five volumes, will scarcely be surprised at Mr. Lyell's behaviour. But the bitterest cut of all was yet to come. "A little while afterwards he wrote to me again, asking me to draw up for him a programme of arguments and materials and authorities to uphold the literal sense of the *Divina Commedia*; and I, steadily working, made it for him. And he (a strange thing to say, and incredible to hear) made use of my work to confute my system! Who could ever have imagined and foreseen it? And why has he done this? Because a sister of his suggested to him to do it."

Frere returned a sympathetic answer, and seems to have wished for more information, which Rossetti gave on August 3rd :—

"My gratuitous enemy, patronized and put forward by Lord Brougham . . . is named Antonio Panizzi, and he succeeded in getting himself chosen Librarian of the British Museum by his Lordship's help ; and poor Mr. Cary, a man of such high merit, was set aside, so that in indignation he quitted the British Library, to avoid being subject to Panizzi."

Lord Brougham was only true to the principle which has nearly always been followed by the heads of public departments—that of exalting an alien at the expense of those who have conscientiously done the work for many years ; but Rossetti, to whom Cary had shown much civility on his first arrival in England, did not appreciate the situation.

"When, on account of my illness, I gave up teaching,

I had forty-five lessons a week—I was compelled to break off at the moment when the profits were coming in ; this year I have had only twenty-six,—what a difference!" However, Rossetti's left eye was steadily regaining strength, and he hoped to be able to go on with his work. He sent a copy of "Sir Hugh the Heron" to Frere, and from the last letter he wrote to his patron, it is evident that the young author had not desired such fame. It seems as if Frere had been renewing his old warnings, from the eagerness with which Rossetti disclaims the charge of turbulence.

" 2 September 1844.

"... No, I am not a turbulent and restless spirit. I desire the amelioration, by rightful and holy means, of unhappy Italy ; I desire a reasonable and just government, akin to this of highly favoured England ; a constitution excluding arbitrary power ; a liberty not amounting to license ; and in chief a purity of dogma, closing the path to blind superstition and violent fanaticism. Such is my profession of faith, political and religious. A republic is a dream of maniacs, impossible and perilous in the present conditions of Europe, with which it appears to me incompatible. Never was a more absurd injustice committed than that which expelled me from my native land. But, if here I find peace, and shall continue to find bread, I shall thank Providence, which for my bettering, permitted that injustice. Italy will always be a field of thistles and thorns, unless her lot be changed ; and for the present it seems to me impossible that this should be changed. Her recent agitations, the whirlwind which tosses so many minds, and the blood which smokes in more than one region, the rigours of Rome, of Naples, of Piedmont, the tenacity of the governments in their absolutism, so much upheld by the Papal Church, and so antagonistic to the spirit of the age, make me feel that my exile is not a disaster. . . .

" That dear firstborn son of mine is distressed at the idea that I took it upon me to send you those verses of his, written at a boyish age ; whereas those which he has lately composed are far superior—for he is now sixteen years old, and he himself jeers at his earliest attempts. . . .

" Your much attached,
" GABRIELE ROSSETTI."

There are no more letters to him whom Rossetti affectionately styled his " Maecenas." Frere's health was failing, and he died in little more than a year after receiving the letter which has just been quoted. We all know how bravely Rossetti struggled with his difficulties, and how fully his children realised their early promise. To his latest day, he preserved a grateful memory of his English friend. Mr. William Rossetti has described how, when the news of Frere's death reached England, Rossetti fell on his knees, tears streaming from his dim eyes, and exclaimed, with passionate fervour, " *Anima bella, benedetta sii tu, dovunque sei !* "

.Rossetti's own life ended in 1854. The last twelve years had been clouded by bodily suffering, but the mind, though weakened, was still active. The struggle for existence had been severe, especially during the seasons in which he was completely prevented from earning anything towards the support of his family, but even in its worst straits the little household never owed a halfpenny .to a tradesman. Before his death Rossetti saw the early promise of his son fulfilling itself on the one side in " The Girlhood of Mary Virgin," and " Ecce Ancilla Domini," and on the other, in " The Blessed Damozel " and " Sister Helen."

The dream of a free Italy which had filled Rossetti's young thoughts, and which had caused him to know the bitter taste of alien bread and the ruggedness of " another's stairs," was not to be realised in his lifetime. A delusive vision of help from France in 1831 had called forth his passionate cry to Italy :—

> " Sorgi, sorgi, dal sonno profondo,
> Io son l'alba del nuovo tuo di."

But this was as false a dawn as that which he had seen, star-crowned in his trance at Naples. Not until many years after his death was Italy free, from the Alps to the Adriatic, and her deliverance was to come, in the first place, from the Piedmont that had seemed to him hopelessly crushed beneath the heel of absolutism. It is pleasant to think that in the hour of her triumph Italy did not forget the man who had endured life-long exile for her sake. A proposal was made to transfer his remains to his native land, but his widow could not bear to be separated from them. Frere's prophecy was fulfilled, and an inscription in Santa Croce now records the honoured name of Gabriele Rossetti.

CHAPTER XVI.

EXEUNT OMNES.

THE epochs of our youth are marked by the gain of new friends or new interests, and those of our declining years by the loss of old ones. Frere had to pay the penalty of a long life in the death of nearly all who had been young with him. Less than a year after his return to Malta, he heard of the sudden death of Canning. The next loss was that of Lady Erroll, whose long sufferings came to an end in January 1831. For some time she had been a helpless invalid, unable to walk, and, as her family discovered when too late, terribly bullied by her maid. To the once gay and lovely Irishwoman, death could only have been a merciful release, but her husband's grief was overwhelming.

A mournful diversion came in the following November in the shape of a visit from the dying Walter Scott. Times were changed since the days of their first meeting in London, when Canning and Frere had been pronounced by him to be " far too good for politics." A certain amount of intercourse had been kept up between them, as is shown by an almost illegible letter among Frere's papers. The bearer was a son of Scott's old friend Hector Macdonald Buchanan, whose children were " ex officio " nephews to

Scott.   The removal to a warmer climate came too late to save him, and he died at Malta in 1828.*

"MY DEAR SIR,—

"Will you allow me so much interest in your recollection as to permit me to introduce to your acquaintance Mr. James Macdonald Buchanan, a young gentleman of good family and fortune whom the apprehension of a disease fatal to four elder brothers who have been cut off as fast as they grew up, obliges to remain abroad.   He is now the last male of an ancient family and his father and mother, proprietors of one of the most beautiful places on Loch Lomond, are obliged to deny themselves the pleasure of keeping their only remaining son at home, lest the severity of his native climate should prove as prejudicial to his health as it has to his unfortunate brothers.   I am the more interested in this young gentleman that from the time of early childhood my children and the young Macdonalds were always so intimate that the houses of both seemed to be the same, so that I feel particularly the distress of our good friend the father of Mr. Macdonald Buchanan.

"I have little news to send you from this quarter.   Poor Gifford, 'the Scourge of Impostors, the Curse of Quacks,' is, you see, retired to rest.   Rose I have not lately seen, but he had when I last heard of him got a new mode of treatment which always amuses his complaints for some time with the assistance of Hinvaes.   He has not been in Scotland this season, where by contriving that he shall shoot black-cock and catch salmon we generally contrive to make him happy for a few weeks.   Last time I had the pleasure of his company, I had infinite difficulty in preventing his converting Hinvaes into a sort of Minotaur by

* *Vide* Scott's Diary.

dint of cutting a bullock's hide and horns into a masque and surcoat for the more of [word illegible]. But I resisted this as not having too good a character among my neighbours to stand the various reports to which such a transformation might give rise, as one half of Teviotdale would believe I had raised the devil, and the other half that I had lost the moderate proportion of sound mind which they are disposed to give me credit for. So you may conclude and I am sure will be glad to learn that Will Rose is still the old humourist he always was.

"But you, my dear [Sir] the dweller of the classical Parthenope,* what are you doing for the Muses, Grecian or Gothick? Does Aristophanes proceed, and wherefore is Whistlecraft silent? Has the trade of collar-making flourished so much more than any other in Britain that that ingenious person has no leisure vacare musis? Let it not be and do [not] let Indolence like a second Jack the Giantkiller cut short the records of our British Titans. I know nothing which so delighted all who could enjoy fun for fun's sake without demanding some hidden satire, which I believe was caviar to those [who] cannot relish a jest unless it is (as some men prefer their dinner) at their neighbours' expense.

"Write all this nonsense down to its right cause and forgive this intrusion on the part of your old friend and Dear Sir,

- "Most respectful and humble Servant,

"WALTER SCOTT.

"EDINBURGH, JANUARY 27TH, 1827."

Frere prepared in a characteristic manner for Scott's reception at Malta, in 1831, by setting various young men to write Latin verses in honour of the occasion. One of

* Frere was then staying at Naples.

these effusions still remains, written in a thin copybook with marbled covers, and adorned with a design on the first page representing Scott's arrival. Arrayed in Highland costume, according to the artist's notions—a tunic, mantle, and Wellington boots—he stands on the deck of a vessel surrounded by Tritons, and preceded by Fame blowing a trumpet.

Sir Walter was so completely the wreck of his former self that only a melancholy pleasure could be derived from the meeting by those who had known him in his prime. The bitterness of death was passed, and those who loved him felt little beside relief when the end came, a few months later.

Year after year carried away Frere's relations and acquaintance. A bad attack of influenza ruined the health of the faithful sister who alone of all his family and generation remained near him, and in January 1839 she was laid in the cemetery beside his wife. His helplessness without her to write letters, distribute charity, and minister to his comfort in a thousand ways, was very pathetic. Lord and Lady Hamilton Chichester devoted themselves to the man who had supplied a father's place to Honoria Blake before her marriage ; but their dutiful care could not fill the void left by the removal of his contemporaries. Before his own death he was called upon to mourn the loss of Edward Frere, always a favourite brother, whose children he regarded "almost as his own." If the earlier years of his life had been spent in writing political and literary satires, towards the end of his life his chief poetical compositions were epitaphs.

His gift of sympathy enabled him to take a deep interest in the rising generation, and in the promise of at least two of Edward Frere's children he found some consolation for the thought that his own day was past and gone. Their letters were joyfully welcomed and treasured until his death. The younger, Richard, was in the 13th Light Infantry, thanks to his uncle who deplored his choice of a profession, but gave him a commission. In 1837 he went to India with his regiment, and passed through various exciting experiences.

The 13th formed part of " Sale's Brigade," which was working towards Afghanistan. In 1839 one of Richard's letters, written in the Bolan Pass, March 18th, 1839, describes the dismal march of six-and-twenty miles through the desert, after crossing the Indus.

After seizing upon Candahar, our forces attacked Ghuznee, and Richard Frere's regiment took a prominent part in the fray. On August 17th he writes from Cabul :—

" . . . On the morning of the 23rd of August we fell in at one o'clock, and marched down to within a few hundred yards of the town behind a hill where we should be in some measure screened from the enemy's fire, and here we met the rest of the party told off for the storming party, viz., H.M.'s 2nd and 17th, and the Company's European Regt. A few minutes after, the 13th moved down, and extended in skirmishing order—the R. wing to the R. of the road, and the L. wing to the L., for the purpose of covering the advanced storming party, consisting of the Light Companies of H.M.'s 2nd and 17th, and Company's European Regt., and a company of the 13th, under Col. Dennie of the 13th. You know that it is the custom to send the colours to another Regt. when your own goes out skirmishing, and as I was with our colours, I was sent to the 17th. . . . . .

" As soon as the chief engineer went forward with a bag of powder which they fastened to the Gate and blew it open, Col. Dennie's party rushed forward, before the enemy had time to recover from their panic, and got into the town. They kept up all the time a very heavy fire from the ramparts on our troops. Immediately after the 4 companies got in, Brigadier Sale who commanded the whole, led the column consisting of the Queen's 2nd, Company's European Regt., followed by the 13th (who closed in their centre directly the gate was burst open), and the Queen's 17th. Brigr. Sale was wounded in the cheek whilst leading, by a party who rushed between the head of the column and rear of Col. Dennie's party—the two rear sections of which they cut to pieces, and caring nothing for the row of bayonets opposed to them, attacked our men sword in hand, and cut several of them down, and in fact for a moment checked them; however they soon recovered themselves, and made good their entry. All this time we had been standing in column on the road exposed to the fire from the bastions, but luckily it was dark with the exception of the flashes of light from the Guns, and a few blue lights which they had burnt to try and get a sight of us, but which had much more effect in making themselves visible. In addition to this, they almost all aimed too high so that altho' their fire was heavy, our loss was very trifling considering all things, and that the balls were whistling about us in all directions. We found the entrance strewed with the ruins of the roof of the gateway, beams, planks, etc., etc., and over all this we had to make our way. Here the opposition had been considerable, as was proved by the number of killed and wounded lying about. When we got thro' into the body of the place, we formed up on an esplanade under a wall on the right which screened us from the fort. The enemy still kept up a fire from the houses, and detached parties on the ramparts. We remained here a little time, and then the

17th were ordered to attack the fort which is built on the top of the mound at one end of the town ; the road up to it winds along the face of the mound, and so the first gate is at right angles to the wall. The men leading rapped at it with the butts of their musquets, and somewhat I confess to my surprise, the gate was opened without opposition. . . . From hence we ran up a sloping road to the centre building, a square one with a tower at each angle ; the door of this was opened, and we got into the courtyard of the palace ; from hence there were stairs leading up to the roof, and from thence to the towers, and I was fortunate enough to be the first to gain the top of one of them, and the 13th regimental colours were the first displayed on the Fort.

"The rooms were soon broken open and plunder of all kinds thrown out into the court. One man of the 13th got nearly £200 in gold coins, etc. The harem of Dost Mahommed's son (who commanded the garrison) were brought out and placed under the charge of sentries, as it was supposed he was concealed among his wives. They were a collection of the ugliest women I ever saw : fair, but fat, with broad flat faces, and small eyes. I only saw one with good features among them.

"The firing had by this time pretty well ceased in the town, the inhabitants having concealed themselves. . . . There were immense numbers of horses, many of which being wounded, and many more frightened by the firing, were galloping and fighting through the streets, and trampling on the soldiers. . . . We got back to camp at ½ past 7. I must say I did not see the slightest excesses committed by the men, nor was a single man that I saw, shot or cut down after he threw down his arms."

Two years later Sale, fighting his way down from

Afghanistan, was obliged to throw himself into Jellalabad, and Richard Frere was among the " Illustrious Garrison." While the siege lasted, and for some time afterwards, there were few opportunities of sending letters.   A few lines written in the minutest characters on a sheet of thin paper rolled inside a quill, which the bearer might conceal in his ear or his turban, occasionally reached their destination.

There is one letter of considerable length to J. H. Frere dated " Jellalabad, April 29th, 1842," when communication was again open, in which Richard describes the course of the siege :—

"You will have learned from the newspapers that in October last Sir Wm. MacNaghten sent a force under General Sale to put down what at the time was supposed to be a partial insurrection among the Ghilgie tribes between Cabul and Jellalabad ; this however turned out to be merely a part of a most extensive insurrection extending from Candahar to the Khyber Pass.   We arrived at Gundamuck the end of October, having had to fight our way the whole way from Cabul through a most difficult country.   Whilst we were at Gundamuck we heard of the murder of Sir A. Burnes (which was the commencement of the insurrection at Cabul), and that the troops at Cabul, about 6000 in number, were closely besieged.   The whole country was now in a dreadful disturbed state, and Sir R. Sale determined to throw himself into Jellalabad.   At Gundamuck, there were some Khyber and Afghan levies who had been left as a garrison ; no sooner were our backs turned than these people rose against their officers, burnt the magazine and Cantonment, and it was with some difficulty that the Officers and a few men who remained faithful made their way into our camp that night.   The following day we reached Jellalabad,

which we found to be a large town surrounded by a wall
sadly dilapidated, so much so as, in many places, to have
had a pathway made over it for donkeys and bullocks
to go up and down on their way into and out of the
fort. We had heard that there were plenty of supplies in
the commissariat stores, but on our arrival found just one
half-day's supply of flour, and some barley and Indian
corn. We got into the town late in the evening, and
held the gates with small parties of our own people; the
enemy surrounded the fort in great numbers and burnt
the Cantonments, which lay about $\frac{1}{2}$ a mile from the walls.
The next morning we were able to look about us, and
occupied the walls, but as there were no parapets, we
were obliged to lie down flat on the ramparts and bastions
in order to screen ourselves from the fire of the enemy,
who in consequence of the thick cover afforded by gardens
and orchards which came close to the wall, were rather
too close for us to be safe. The next day we all sallied
and beat off the enemy with very great loss to them, and
next to none on our side. One or two of the neighbouring
chiefs came in, and we got supplies from all quarters. We
set to work to repair the walls and destroy the cover near
the town, which we were enabled to do, as we very
fortunately had with us a party of 300 Sappers and Miners,
whose tools we took and made such good use of our time
that we very soon had built a parapet all round the fort
and repaired all the breaches. On the 1st Decr. the enemy
who had been for some days gathering from all directions,
came down again in great force, and annoyed our working
parties. We again sallied, and again drove them away
with great loss. The rest of the month was passed without our being further annoyed. The beginning of January,
we heard of Sir W. MacNaghten's murder, and soon after
of a treaty having been entered into with the Cabul

insurgents for the evacuation of Affghanistan. Orders were sent down to Genl. Sale to proceed to Peshawur, but he suspecting treachery, refused to move until joined by the Cabul force. On the 12th a solitary officer arrived, wounded and half dead of fatigue, from whom we heard of the total destruction of that ill-fated army."

Richard then briefly tells the story that we know too well, of incredible folly and tragic disaster. The last that his informant, Dr. Brydon, had seen was a crowd of the enemy surrounding the party of Europeans, "who were laying about them in all directions with the butts of their musquets."

A large piece has been torn from the last sheet of this letter, but it is possible to fill in some of the details from a journal kept by Richard Frere during the siege, and sent to his brother. "On the morning of the 14th [the day after Brydon's arrival] the Cavalry patrolled some miles in the Cabul road to look for stragglers. They brought in the bodies of three officers who had been cut down within four or five miles of Jellalabad.

"On the 12th Feb. we heard of the Birth of the Prince of Wales, and a salute was fired, but powder being rather scarce, the guns were loaded with very small charges.

"On the 15th we were not a little surprised at seeing Mahommed Ukbar's camp pitched on the opposite side the river. Several of the Tents were evidently English, spoils of the ill-fated Cabul army.

"About 11 o'clock a.m. on the 19th, while we were all at work digging the ditch round the town, the fruits of two months' labour * were destroyed in a minute by a

* R. Frere writes to his brother on Nov. 30th, 1841 : "We are becoming finished builders, having had so much practice, and are at it from 7 a.m. to 10, aud again from 11 to 2, every day, Sundays included."

dreadful shock of an Earthquake. The earth undulated to such a degree that it was difficult for us to keep on our legs, the ground cracked in several places, and the noise (resembling a very high gale) was so loud that the crash of falling walls was unheard. The parapets were completely ruined, the ramparts in some places cracked, five bastions thrown down, three breaches made in the walls, and one of the gates almost thrown down. The loss of life among the Troops was very small, the whole of them being at work or on guard. . . . Such was the activity with which the Troops worked to repair their defences that before night a parapet of dry clods was thrown up all round the Town, and the breaches made impracticable. In a week the whole was in almost as good a state of repair as before. For two months afterwards we seldom passed 24 hours without one or more shocks, but none to be compared to the first.

"On the 22nd about 8 p.m. news was brought from the Cabul Gate that the Enemy were moving down to the attack ; the Troops were all immediately under arms, but our supposed Enemy proved to be two old walls, which in the moonlight had exactly the appearance of compact bodies of men."

And so the Journal goes on, with its bald record of the struggle against the forces of man and of nature. There were occasional sorties, in which the besiegers suffered more than the besieged. On March 9th, news came that Ghuznee had capitulated, but a spark of hope may have cheered the garrison on March 15th, when they heard that " Ukbar was wounded." It proved to be a trifling injury in the arm, caused by the accidental discharge of a gun by one of the Sirdar's servants. The wretched man was in consequence burned alive with his brother. Then a Moollah in the camp prophesied that an earthquake would throw down the city walls, and the enemy turned out to wait for it. The shock came in the course of the afternoon, but it was too slight to affect the garrison. On April 1st the cavalry made a sortie, and captured four hundred and eighty sheep. "Some of the sheep were given to the 35th N.I., but they (although on half rations) desired that their share might be given to the men of the 13th who required it more than they did. Genl. Sale, hearing this, ordered that 2 lbs. of flour should be issued to each Sepoy of that Regt. instead of the sheep, and the men of the 13th begged their commanding officer to express their gratitude to their fellow-soldiers of the 35th."

On April 5th and 6th spies brought word that General Pollock had been defeated in the Khyber Pass. A royal salute thundering from the enemy's camp convinced the garrison of the truth of these reports, and all the senior officers of the garrison represented to General Sale that their only hope of escape lay in attacking Ukbar while his force was weakened by the absence of the troops whom he had sent to the Khyber. The General yielded to their representations, and a sally was made on the morning of the 7th, in which the garrison, although they suffered heavy loss, gained the advantage. The enemy "broke and fled in all directions, leaving guns, tents, etc., behind them, we set fire to the camp, and brought in the guns. . . . The next morning supplies poured in, and Jellalabad was relieved. Letters were received from General Pollock announcing his safe arrival on this side the Pass. The salute, we afterwards found, was in consequence of news of the Shah's murder having been received."

In reading the diary of any siege, one is generally impressed with its baldness. All events seem reduced to the same dead level, and the writer chronicles a hailstorm and a sally with an equal degree of interest. There is no fine writing, no seeking for effect, in Richard Frere's business-like record. The account sent to his uncle, so far as it can be read, is even more dry and brief than the entries in the diary, and at the conclusion he apologises for having said so much about his own adventures, "but at this end of the world I have little else to talk about."

In September 1842 Richard was at Cabul, whither the hostages had just been escorted in triumph after a narrow escape at Bameean. "Their Keeper received a letter directing him to take those that could move across the frontier to Khooloom, and to kill those that could not stir. Fortunately Major Pottinger, who was with them, was equal to the emergency; he represented the certain reward they would get by not obeying this order, and proceeded to issue summonses to the chiefs round them to come in to him, and actually appointed a new Governor of Bameean, from whom he got a present of 1000 Rupees; those Chiefs that came in he rewarded with presents [? permission] to levy the taxes of different districts, and a Kafila fortunately passing through the valley, he levied a contribution from it, which gave him the means of distributing presents among the chiefs. They reached Kulloo on their way back; and the very day after they left it, they heard that a party of Ukbar's Horse had passed through after they quitted the place. By that time their party had been reinforced by the Kuzzilbashes who went out to meet them; and a few days after, they met General Sale. . . . They are all looking well, I think, except Ladies Macnaghten and Sale and Mrs. Sturt,* who are looking worn."

* Mrs. Sturt, whose first husband had been killed at Cabul, married again and returned to India, to be one of the first victims of the Mutiny

At the conclusion of this letter, Richard Frere apologises for haste, as his messenger is anxious to start, and looks forward to a meeting with his brother, when he will have so much to tell him.   That meeting was never to take place. On his way down to Ferozepore, Richard Frere died of fever at Rawul Pindi, in November 1842, regretted and missed by all who knew him, but most of all by the brother in Bombay who had been counting the days till his coming.

This brother, afterwards to be famous as Sir Bartle Frere, was very dear to the uncle in Malta, at whose house he had spent a month on the way out to India, taking advantage of the opportunity to learn Arabic from Joseph Wolff.   Sir Bartle Frere's biographer says of J. H. Frere : "From him Bartle in some measure derived his early political ideas, and learnt the veneration for Pitt and Canning which he always retained."   The uncle and nephew had much in common (besides a warm admiration for Mountstuart Elphinstone)—and especially that marvellous wideness of sympathy which gave them the power of entering into the thoughts and feelings of others.   Their letters touch upon every imaginable subject. At one time Bartle is diligently writing of Sanskrit to his uncle, who wished to know something about that language ; at another he has been patiently enduring, with the kindness and courtesy for which he was after- wards a proverb, a two-hours' lecture on the mulberry from a luckless cultivator "who thinks, talks, and dreams of nothing but mulberry trees."   The ancient Maharatta legends interested him at a time when few Englishmen took any note of the superstitions of the conquered race ; and so did some "red and small perfumed plantains" which he succeeded in procuring for the Pietà.   The love of a garden was born in all the Freres.

It is clear, from a passage in one of the letters, that he and his uncle were accustomed to exchange their views on the political affairs of India. At this time he was a young man under thirty years of age, but his estimate of the situation has proved singularly just and accurate.

"*Feb. 23rd*, 1840.

"Things have much changed at Lahore since this time last year; the Prince Kurruck Singh * is all but a prisoner in the hands of his Father's Minister, and all parties seem looking to us as the power who is to decide which party shall have the ascendency, instead of, as in Runjeet Singh's time, the only one in India whom it was worth their while to conciliate—so that the Punjab must probably before long become, whether we wish it or not, as much a part of the British Empire as the Nizam's dominions.

"The court of directors has approved of all that was done relative to the Rajah of Sattara. . . . No reasonable doubt could be entertained of his having held correspondence with foreign powers, which he had been warned, when first seated on the throne, would, if ever discovered, entail the loss of his kingdom; and it was perhaps a stretch of clemency, though undoubtedly a well-judged one, to offer him any choice but that of his place of confinement. It is therefore the more extraordinary that he refused the terms offered, which were simply that he should return to the old *régime* by which everything he did was under the eye of the Resident. On his growing up this rule had been relaxed by Mr. Elphinstone in consequence of the Rajah's great aptitude for public business; but its relaxation was a pure matter of sufferance, and not of right. I should not have mentioned all this, but

* The half-imbecile son whom Runjeet Singh had appointed his heir.

for a circumstance which the Governor mentioned as his explanation of the extraordinary obstinacy of the Rajah, and which struck me as very curious. Sir James says that the impression left on his mind was that the Rajah thought this Governor had no power to depose him, and that whatever the Governor and Court of Directors might do, his case would be taken up in Parliament, and his kingdom restored to him. This delusion he (Sir James) attributes chiefly to the license of the Press, which without knowing anything of the rights of the case, took up the Rajah's cause as that of an injured man, and raised in him all these extravagant hopes. He quotes an opinion of Sir J. Malcolm, that all the difficulties which attended his (Sir J. M.'s) negociations at Baroda were traceable to the liberty of the Press—then much less free than now—and concludes by a prediction that the liberty of the Press will be found to create difficulties immeasurable in our intercourse with native states, and that by operating in the same way as it has done at Sattara, lead gradually to the absorption of every one of them. Does not this sound strange from a somewhat ultra Whig writing to a Govr. Genl. and President of the Board of Control of similar politics?"

A few years later Bartle Frere was appointed Resident of Sattara, then governed by Appa Sahib, brother of the obstinate Rajah who had been removed to Benares. At the death of Appa Sahib, Sattara was "annexed" by Lord Dalhousie, in spite of the indignant protests of Mountstuart Elphinstone, Sir George Arthur, Frere himself, and many others who held to the old traditions of English faith and honour.

When the disasters in Afghanistan began to follow each other, thick and fast, Bartle Frere sent to his uncle the reports that came to Bombay from the North-west, with comments of his own. On October 16th, 1842, he writes :—

" I got a small note from Richard written on the 15th September from the Race course at Cabool. He was in excellent health and great spirits, and had the honor to command the leading company of his Regiment in forcing the pass of Jugdulluck, where Sir Robert Sale was wounded. I have only however received one of the daily letters which he says he had written since leaving Gundamuck, and the force had been several days without receiving any post. This, after all their brilliant and very decisive success, is a bad commentary on Lord Palmerston's arguments as to the soundness of the Whig Affgan policy, and his assertions that we might and ought to take permanent possession of the country."

It was not long after this that Bartle received the news of his brother's death. The blow was stunning, but he struggled bravely to continue his old work and keep up former interests. In February 1843 he sat down to write to his uncle, and after nearly filling a sheet was interrupted " by the arrival of the most unexpected news from Scinde : there had for some time past been every prospect of a rupture with the Ameers—the post had been stopped, and numerous marauders had made their appearance on the Cutch frontier—but no one was prepared for the news with which, on the 27th, Major Outram made his appearance in Bombay. He had been sent to Hyderabad to induce the Ameers to sign a fresh Treaty which has been imposed on them. After much persuasion they were induced to sign it, but immediately afterwards the Residence where he was living was attacked. He defended it with 100 men for four hours against 4000 Beloochees with 6 guns, and when his ammunition ran short made an orderly retreat to the river and joined Sir Chas. Napier, who on the 17th, the next day, with 2800 men of all arms, attacked the Enemy 22,000 strong and very well posted, and after a desperate Engagement completely routed them ; the principal Ameers immediately surrendered, and Hyderabad was given up to us on the 20th. . . . I only wish our cause of quarrel had been more just."

Napier's victory was "the hardest bought and most sanguinary battle that has occurred for years past," and our difficulties were by no means ended with the defeat of the Ameers. Bartle Frere foresaw the troubles that were to come upon us in India, when others in a higher official position were blind and deaf to the threatenings of the storm. Writing to his uncle on New Year's Day, 1844, he says : " The peace of Scinde seems threatened by combinations precisely of the kind you describe, originating in Affganistan at Candahar, and having for their object the union of all true believers in a religious war. The time for this to succeed is hardly, I think, yet arrived ; but unless means are taken to consolidate our Empire more effectually than has hitherto been attempted, such combinations will be formed every 15 or 20 years, and must at last effect their object. Unless, indeed, the direction in which the danger is to come be changed by a decay in religious spirit among the Mahometans all over the world, of which there are many symptoms."

There are other letters from Bartle Frere to his uncle, but they are not likely to interest readers beyond the circle of his own family. In one of them he announces his engagement to Miss Arthur, whom he married in the October of 1844. The husband and wife then left Bombay, and spent part of their honeymoon in Malta at the Pietà, where J. H. Frere was rejoiced to welcome the nephew after his own heart.   It was then that uncle and nephew held the long conversations on past days that Sir Bartle afterwards recorded in his " Memoir of J. H. Frere."   The newly married pair then went on to England, having, as it proved, taken leave for ever of the old uncle, who died at the beginning of 1846—in January, the month which had been fatal to his wife and to his sister.

Old John Murray, no bad judge of talent, put J. H. Frere on a par with such men as Scott and Byron, saying that he might have done anything that he chose.   Had he chosen—that was the sting of it.   With everything in his favour—talents, position, friends, health, and means—he accomplished almost nothing.   A translation of some of Aristophanes' comedies that still holds the field against newer versions—some fragmentary renderings from the Greek and Spanish, and some burlesques—these were his chief contributions to literature.   In politics his name will be for ever associated with disaster and blunders.   He held all the winning cards, but he left the game to others who were less well equipped at the outset.

Yet there is another side to the picture.   The desire for finished achievement is natural, and we would fain have something to show at the end of life.   But to those who are in the midst of the struggle, it is oftentimes a blessing to find a listener who is detached from it without having lost interest in it, who is clever enough to understand the hopes, fears, schemes, and difficulties of others, without having any personal stake in the game.   That Frere on his enchanted island could enter into other interests, however various, these extracts from his letter-bag must have shown, and if he would strike no blow for any one of his old standards, he was always ready to help others to buckle on their armour.

The fate of most of his correspondents has already been

told.   Lady Cadogan died a little while before him ; Lady Davy, in spite of her having "no stomach left," as she wrote to Frere, survived until May 1855. . In 1850 Mrs. George Frere was laid in her grave, having sought peace and ensued it, throughout her life; and exactly twelve months later, the elder Bartle Frere died.   Charles Ellis (Lord Seaford) died in the same year as Lady Cadogan. William Stewart Rose, deaf, rheumatic and imbecile, had been mourned as lost by all who loved him, for some time before death put an end to his sufferings in 1843.

The letters given in the first chapter carried us far back into a past that we only know by history and tradition ; the letters in this last chapter tell of events which, if not within the memory of many of us, belong to our own age. The Reform Bill has effected a complete revolution in politics, similar to that caused in other spheres of action by the introduction of railways and cheap literature, machine-guns and ironclads.   When John Hookham Frere opened his eyes upon the world, a naval commander put on white silk stockings and all his medals and orders before taking his ship into battle ; members of the House of Commons taunted each other in Latin quotations, and settled their differences with pistols.   Publishers and editors begged for contributions, and would pay a handsome fee in advance to a promising young author.   Tickets for the opera were not to be purchased by every *nouveau riche*, but could only be obtained from one of the Lady Patronesses.   It was a different world—more courtly, more leisurely ; now gone beyond recall.